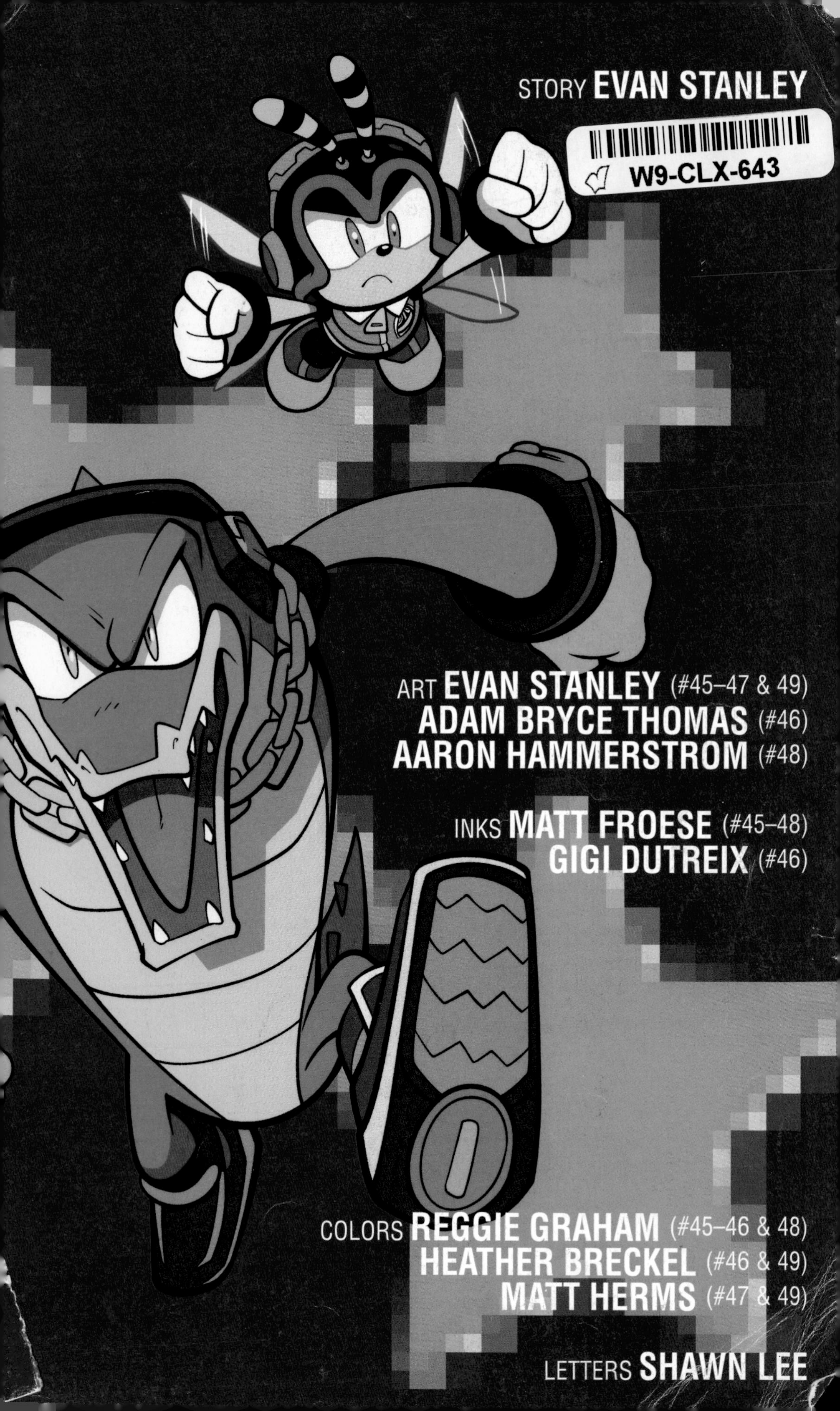

STORY **EVAN STANLEY**

ART **EVAN STANLEY** (#45–47 & 49)
ADAM BRYCE THOMAS (#46)
AARON HAMMERSTROM (#48)

INKS **MATT FROESE** (#45–48)
GIGI DUTREIX (#46)

COLORS **REGGIE GRAHAM** (#45–46 & 48)
HEATHER BRECKEL (#46 & 49)
MATT HERMS (#47 & 49)

LETTERS **SHAWN LEE**

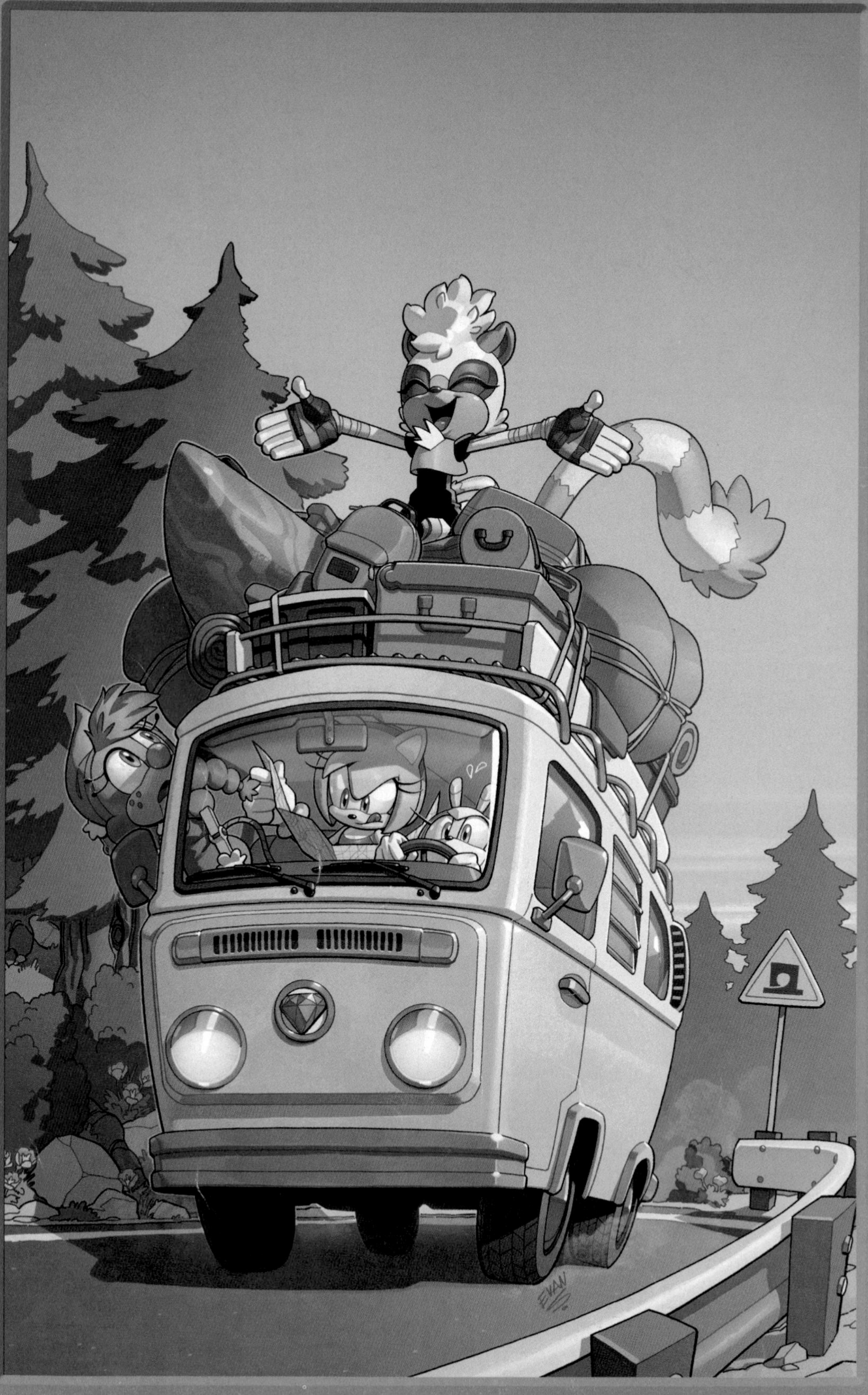

ART BY **EVAN STANLEY**

SONIC™
THE HEDGEHOG

TRIAL BY FIRE

SEGA®

@IDWpublishing
IDWpublishing.com

Cover Art by
Evan Stanley

Series Assistant Edits by
Riley Farmer

Series Edits by
David Mariotte

Collection Edits by
Alonzo Simon
and Zac Boone

Collection Design by
Shawn Lee

ISBN: 978-1-68405-930-0
25 24 23 22   1 2 3 4

Originally published as SONIC THE HEDGEHOG issues #45–49.

Nachie Marsham, Publisher
Blake Kobashigawa, SVP Sales, Marketing & Strategy
Mark Doyle, VP Creative & Editorial Strategy
Tara McCrillis, VP Publishing Operations
Anna Morrow, VP Marketing & Publicity
Alex Hargett, VP Sales
Lauren LePera, Sr. Managing Editor
Greg Gustin, Sr. Director, Content Strategy
Kevin Schwoer, Sr. Director of Talent Relations
Keith Davidsen, Director, Marketing & PR
Topher Alford, Sr. Digital Marketing Manager
Patrick O'Connell, Sr. Manager, Direct Market Sales
Shauna Monteforte, Sr. Director of Manufacturing Operations
Greg Foreman, Director DTC Sales & Operations
Nathan Widick, Director of Design
Neil Uyetake, Sr. Art Director, Design & Production
Shawn Lee, Art Director, Design & Production
Jack Rivera, Art Director, Marketing

Ted Adams and Robbie Robbins, IDW Founders

Special thanks to Mai Kiyotaki, Michael Cisneros, Sandra Jo, Sonic Team, and everyone at Sega for their invaluable assistance.

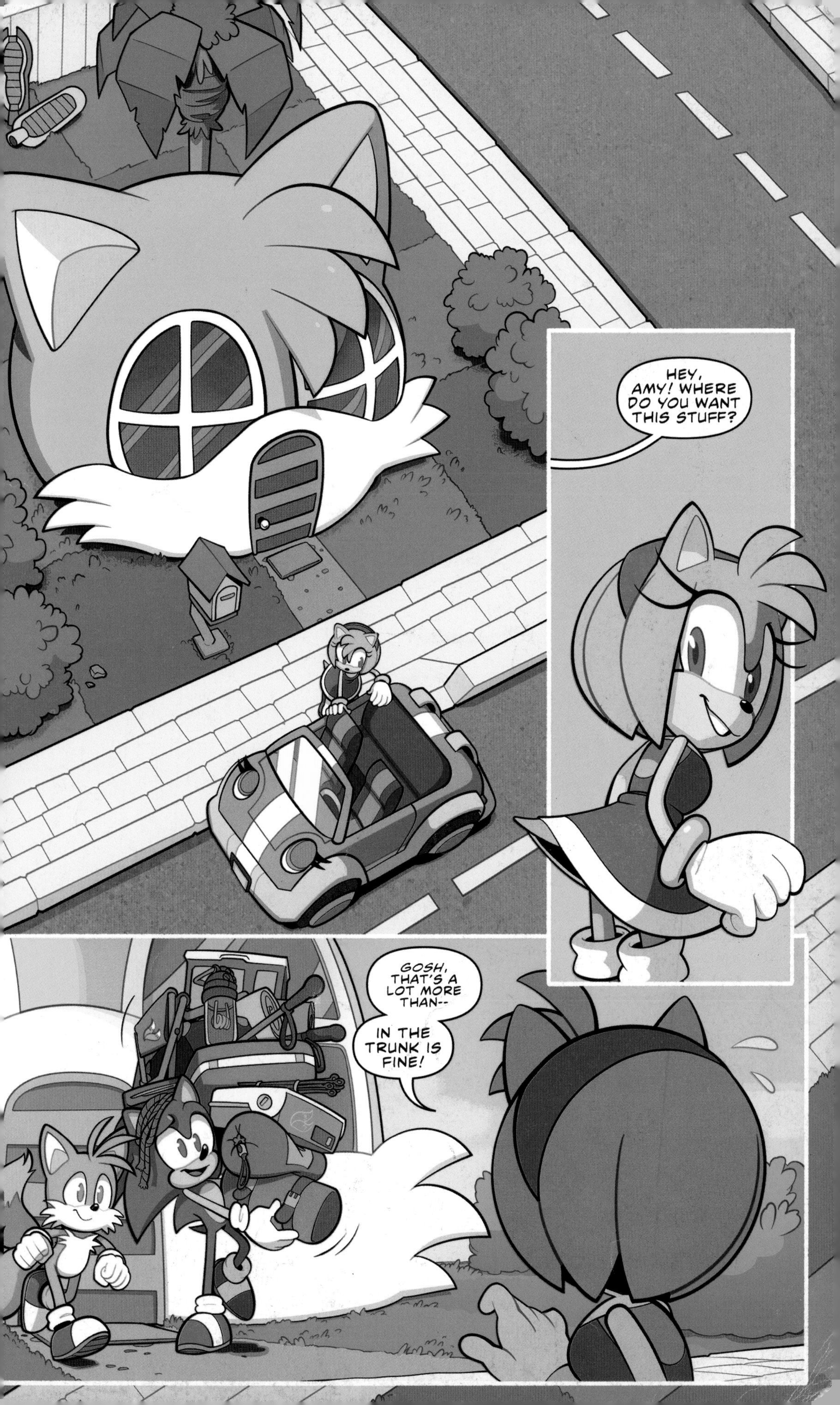
HEY, AMY! WHERE DO YOU WANT THIS STUFF?
GOSH, THAT'S A LOT MORE THAN--
IN THE TRUNK IS FINE!

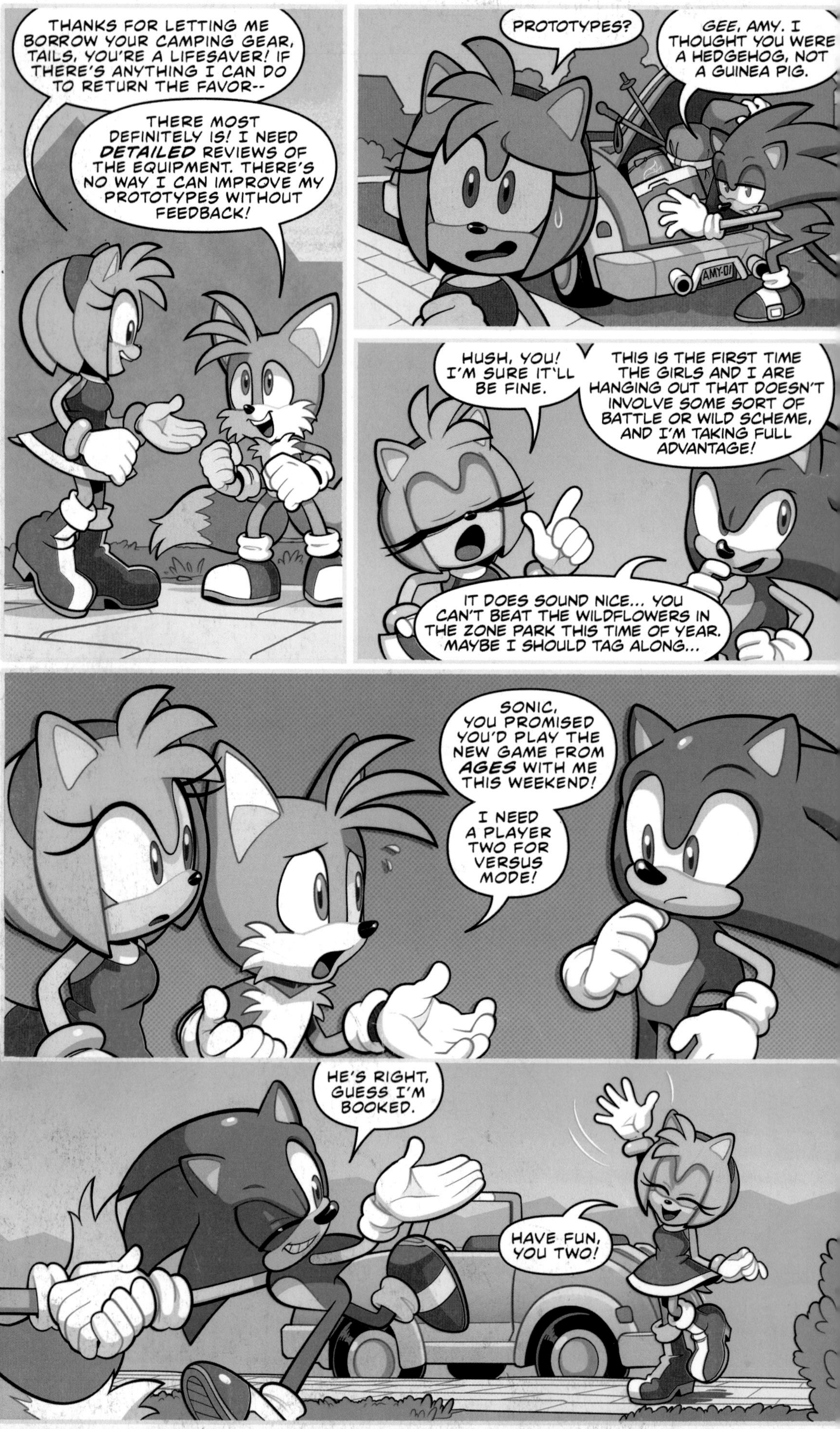
THANKS FOR LETTING ME BORROW YOUR CAMPING GEAR, TAILS, YOU'RE A LIFESAVER! IF THERE'S ANYTHING I CAN DO TO RETURN THE FAVOR--
THERE MOST DEFINITELY IS! I NEED DETAILED REVIEWS OF THE EQUIPMENT. THERE'S NO WAY I CAN IMPROVE MY PROTOTYPES WITHOUT FEEDBACK!
PROTOTYPES?
GEE, AMY. I THOUGHT YOU WERE A HEDGEHOG, NOT A GUINEA PIG.
AMY-01
HUSH, YOU! I'M SURE IT'LL BE FINE.
THIS IS THE FIRST TIME THE GIRLS AND I ARE HANGING OUT THAT DOESN'T INVOLVE SOME SORT OF BATTLE OR WILD SCHEME, AND I'M TAKING FULL ADVANTAGE!
IT DOES SOUND NICE... YOU CAN'T BEAT THE WILDFLOWERS IN THE ZONE PARK THIS TIME OF YEAR. MAYBE I SHOULD TAG ALONG...
SONIC, YOU PROMISED YOU'D PLAY THE NEW GAME FROM AGES WITH ME THIS WEEKEND!
I NEED A PLAYER TWO FOR VERSUS MODE!
HE'S RIGHT, GUESS I'M BOOKED.
HAVE FUN, YOU TWO!

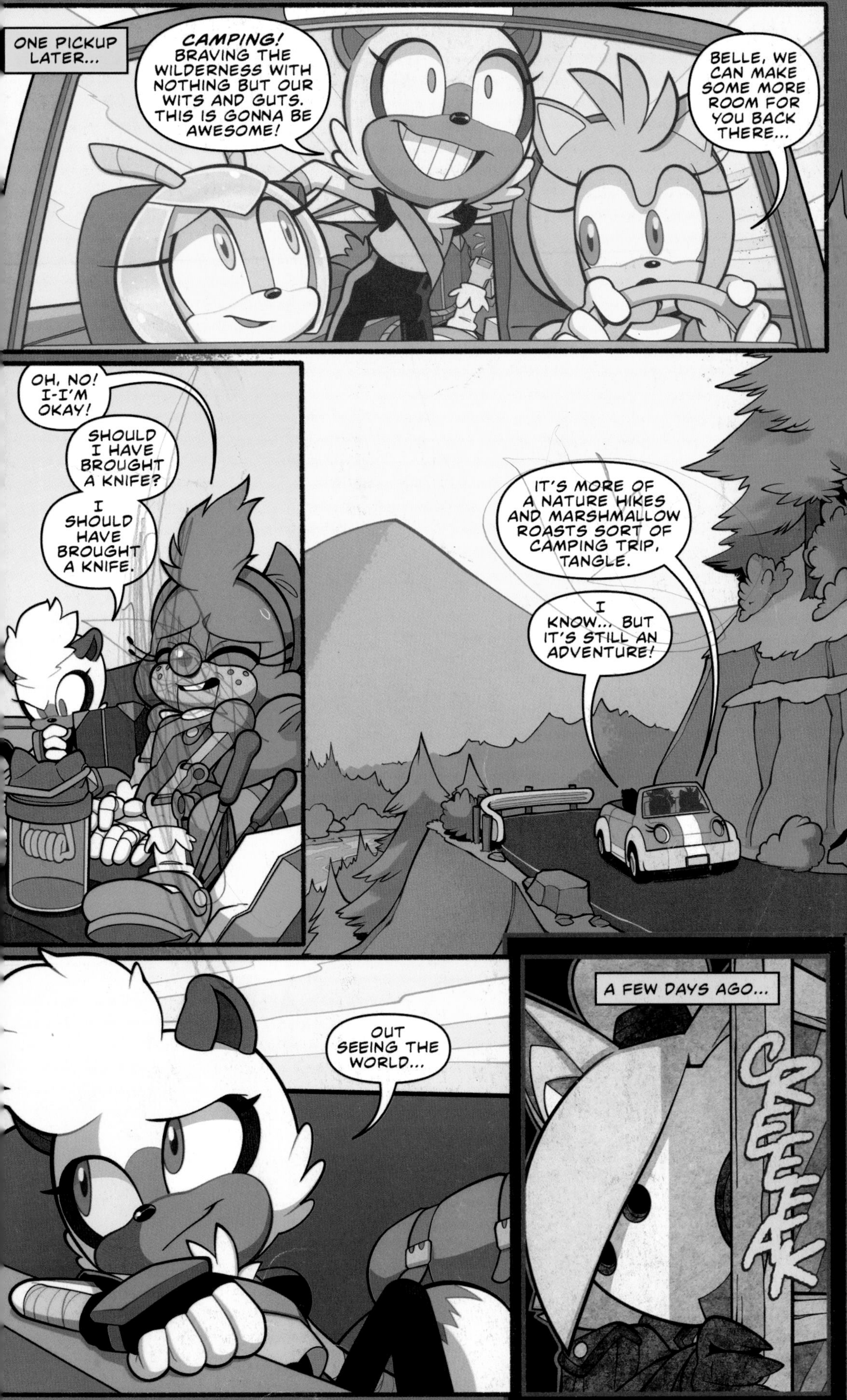

ONE PICKUP LATER...
CAMPING! BRAVING THE WILDERNESS WITH NOTHING BUT OUR WITS AND GUTS. THIS IS GONNA BE AWESOME!
BELLE, WE CAN MAKE SOME MORE ROOM FOR YOU BACK THERE...
OH, NO! I-I'M OKAY!
SHOULD I HAVE BROUGHT A KNIFE?
I SHOULD HAVE BROUGHT A KNIFE.
IT'S MORE OF A NATURE HIKES AND MARSHMALLOW ROASTS SORT OF CAMPING TRIP, TANGLE.
I KNOW... BUT IT'S STILL AN ADVENTURE!
OUT SEEING THE WORLD...
A FEW DAYS AGO...
CREEEAK

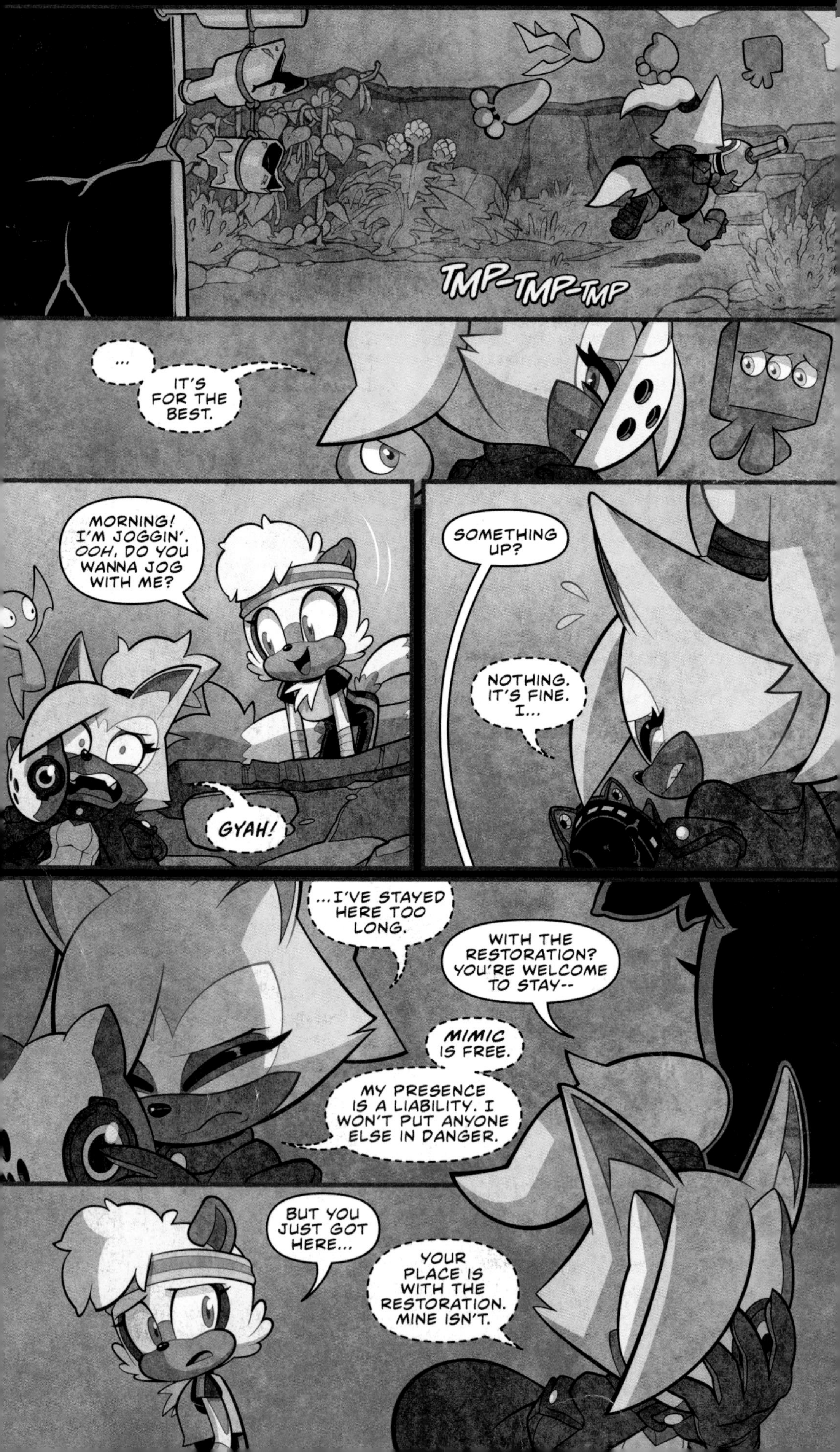

TMP-TMP-TMP
...
IT'S FOR THE BEST.
MORNING! I'M JOGGIN'. OOH, DO YOU WANNA JOG WITH ME?
GYAH!
SOMETHING UP?
NOTHING. IT'S FINE. I...
...I'VE STAYED HERE TOO LONG.
WITH THE RESTORATION? YOU'RE WELCOME TO STAY--
MIMIC IS FREE.
MY PRESENCE IS A LIABILITY. I WON'T PUT ANYONE ELSE IN DANGER.
BUT YOU JUST GOT HERE...
YOUR PLACE IS WITH THE RESTORATION. MINE ISN'T.

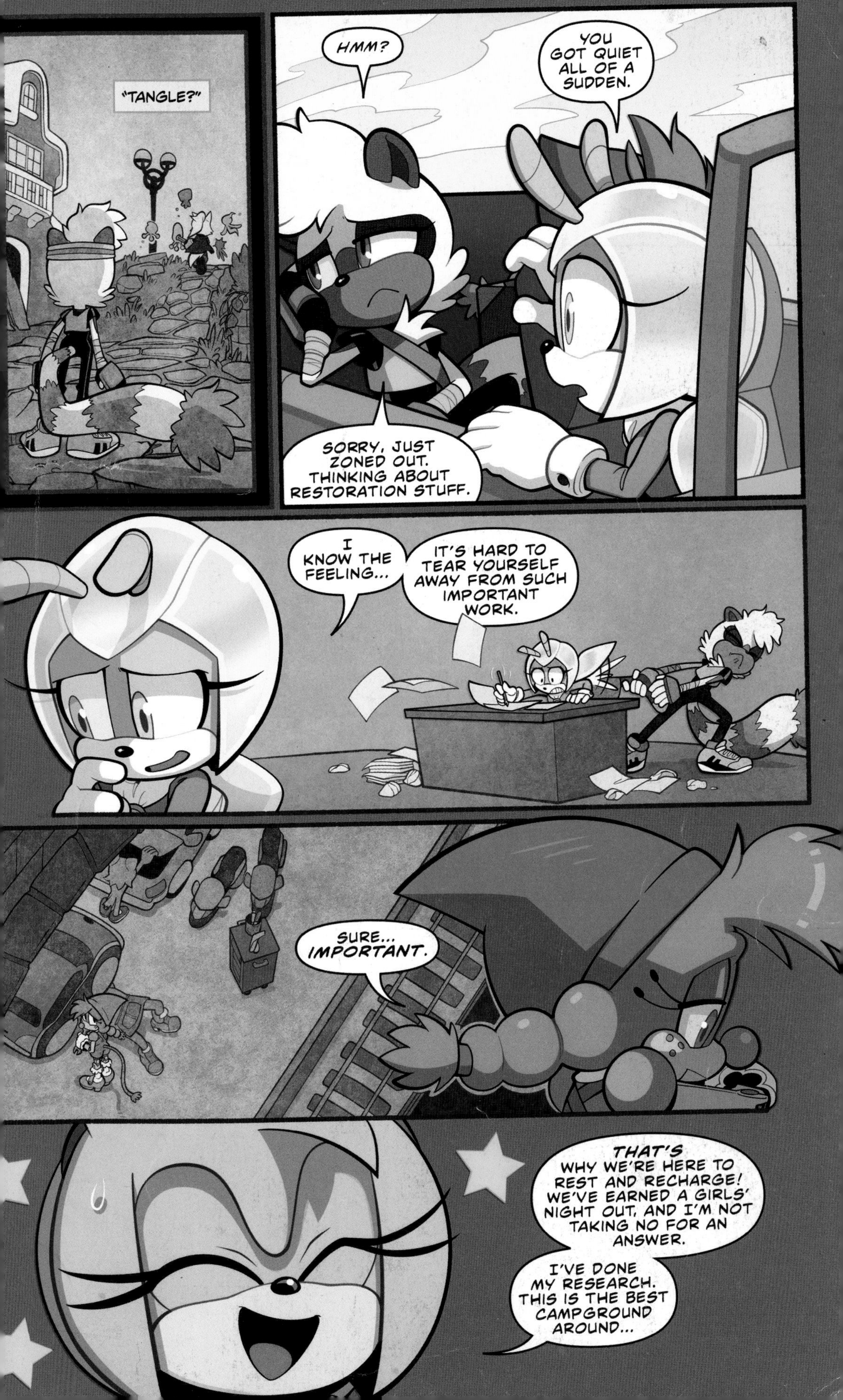
"TANGLE?"
HMM?
YOU GOT QUIET ALL OF A SUDDEN.
SORRY, JUST ZONED OUT. THINKING ABOUT RESTORATION STUFF.
I KNOW THE FEELING...
IT'S HARD TO TEAR YOURSELF AWAY FROM SUCH IMPORTANT WORK.
SURE... IMPORTANT.
THAT'S WHY WE'RE HERE TO REST AND RECHARGE! WE'VE EARNED A GIRLS' NIGHT OUT, AND I'M NOT TAKING NO FOR AN ANSWER.
I'VE DONE MY RESEARCH. THIS IS THE BEST CAMPGROUND AROUND...

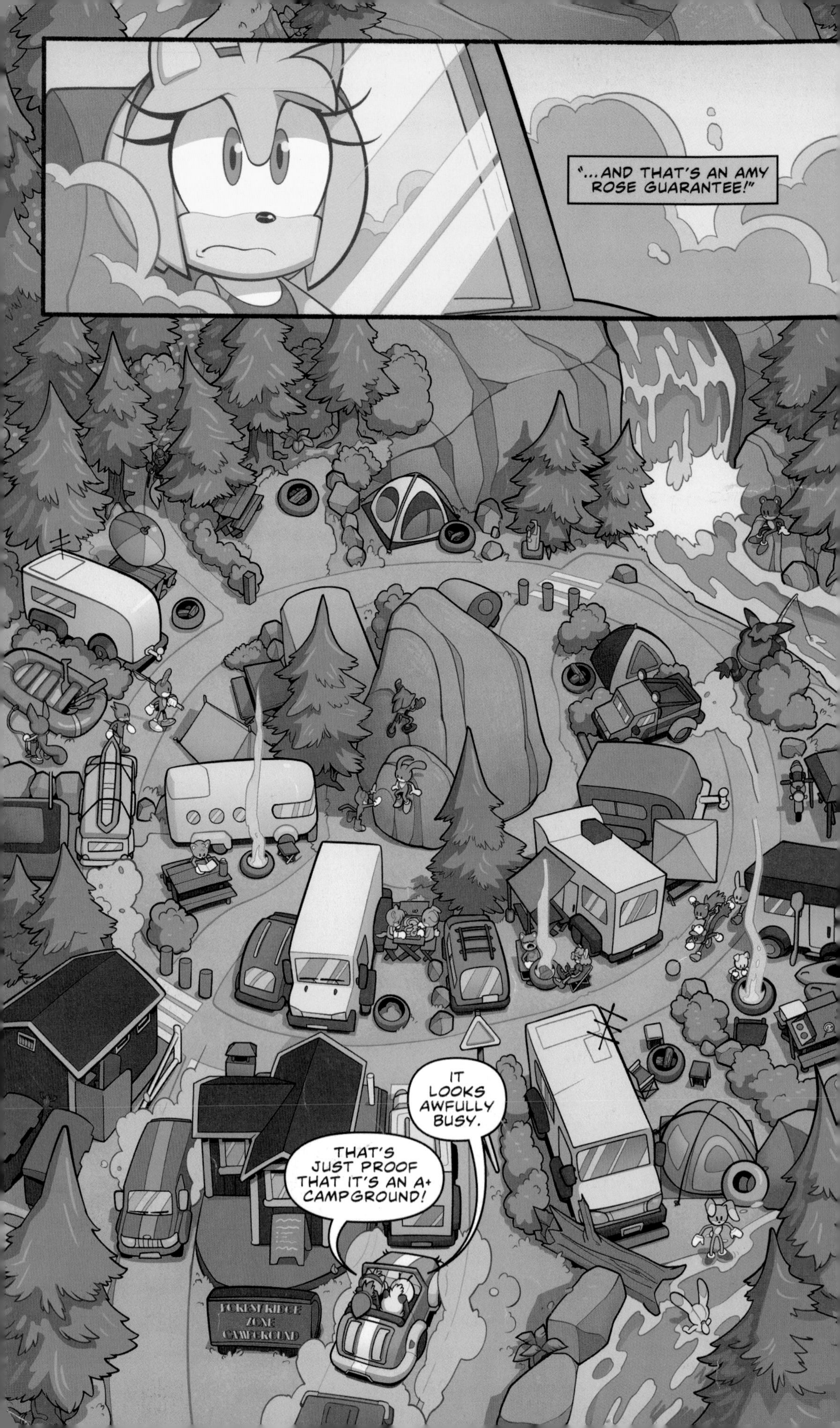
"...AND THAT'S AN AMY ROSE GUARANTEE!"
IT LOOKS AWFULLY BUSY.
THAT'S JUST PROOF THAT IT'S AN A+ CAMPGROUND!
FOREST RIDGE ZONE CAMPGROUND

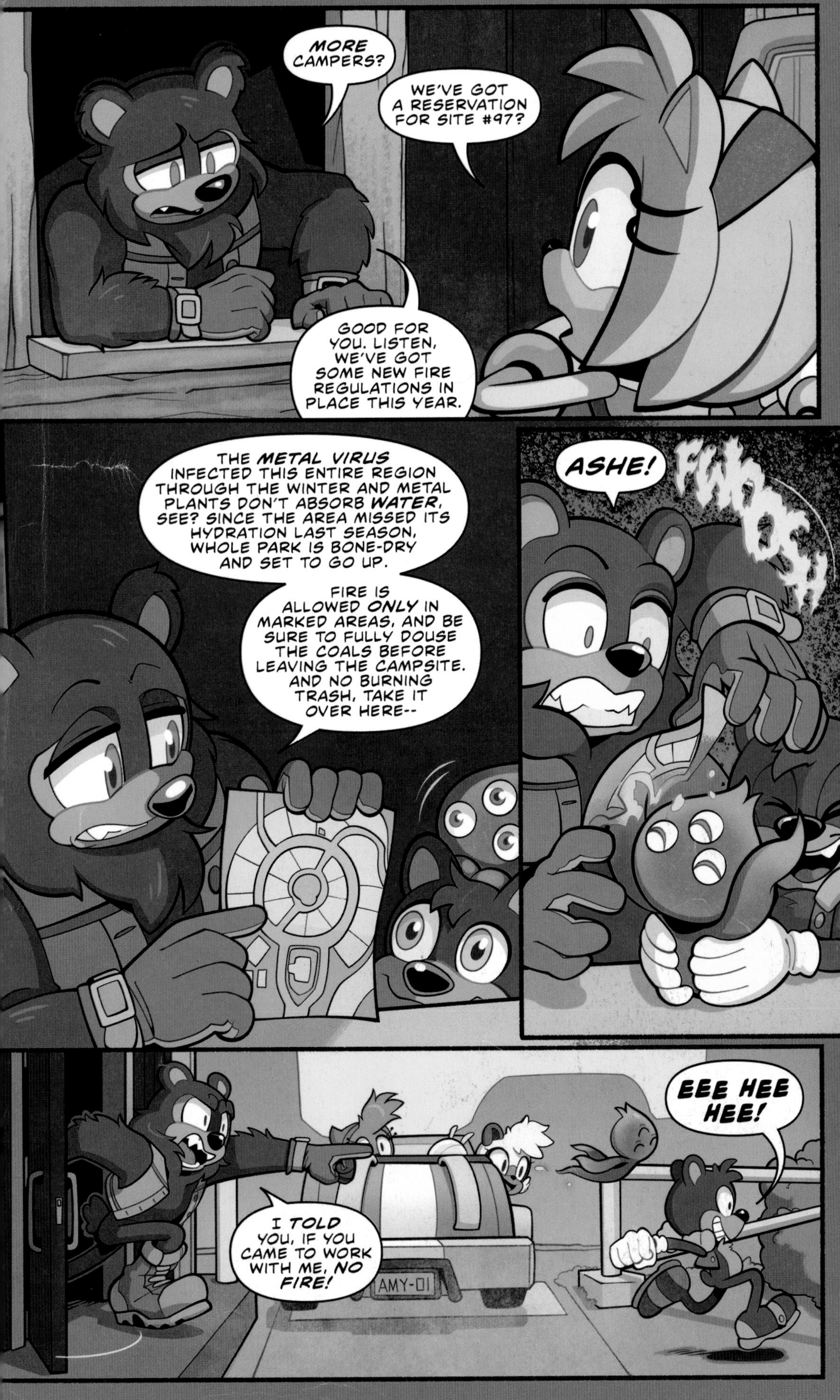

MORE CAMPERS?
WE'VE GOT A RESERVATION FOR SITE #97?
GOOD FOR YOU. LISTEN, WE'VE GOT SOME NEW FIRE REGULATIONS IN PLACE THIS YEAR.
THE METAL VIRUS INFECTED THIS ENTIRE REGION THROUGH THE WINTER AND METAL PLANTS DON'T ABSORB WATER, SEE? SINCE THE AREA MISSED ITS HYDRATION LAST SEASON, WHOLE PARK IS BONE-DRY AND SET TO GO UP.
FIRE IS ALLOWED ONLY IN MARKED AREAS, AND BE SURE TO FULLY DOUSE THE COALS BEFORE LEAVING THE CAMPSITE. AND NO BURNING TRASH, TAKE IT OVER HERE--
ASHE!
FWOOSH
EEE HEE HEE!
I TOLD YOU, IF YOU CAME TO WORK WITH ME, NO FIRE!
AMY-01

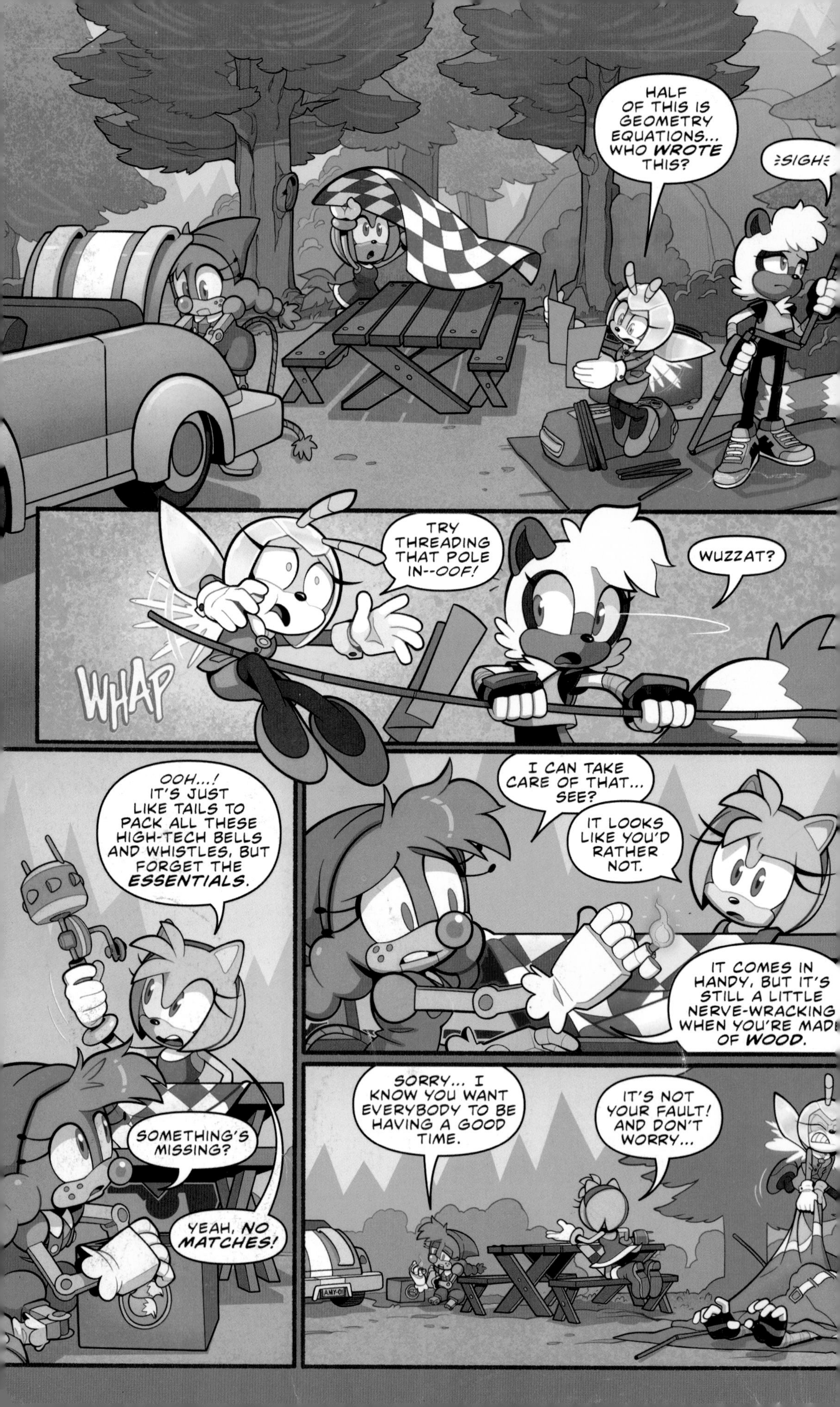
HALF OF THIS IS GEOMETRY EQUATIONS... WHO WROTE THIS?
SIGH
TRY THREADING THAT POLE IN--OOF!
WUZZAT?
WHAP
OOH...! IT'S JUST LIKE TAILS TO PACK ALL THESE HIGH-TECH BELLS AND WHISTLES, BUT FORGET THE ESSENTIALS.
SOMETHING'S MISSING?
YEAH, NO MATCHES!
I CAN TAKE CARE OF THAT... SEE?
IT LOOKS LIKE YOU'D RATHER NOT.
IT COMES IN HANDY, BUT IT'S STILL A LITTLE NERVE-WRACKING WHEN YOU'RE MADE OF WOOD.
SORRY... I KNOW YOU WANT EVERYBODY TO BE HAVING A GOOD TIME.
IT'S NOT YOUR FAULT! AND DON'T WORRY...
AMY-01

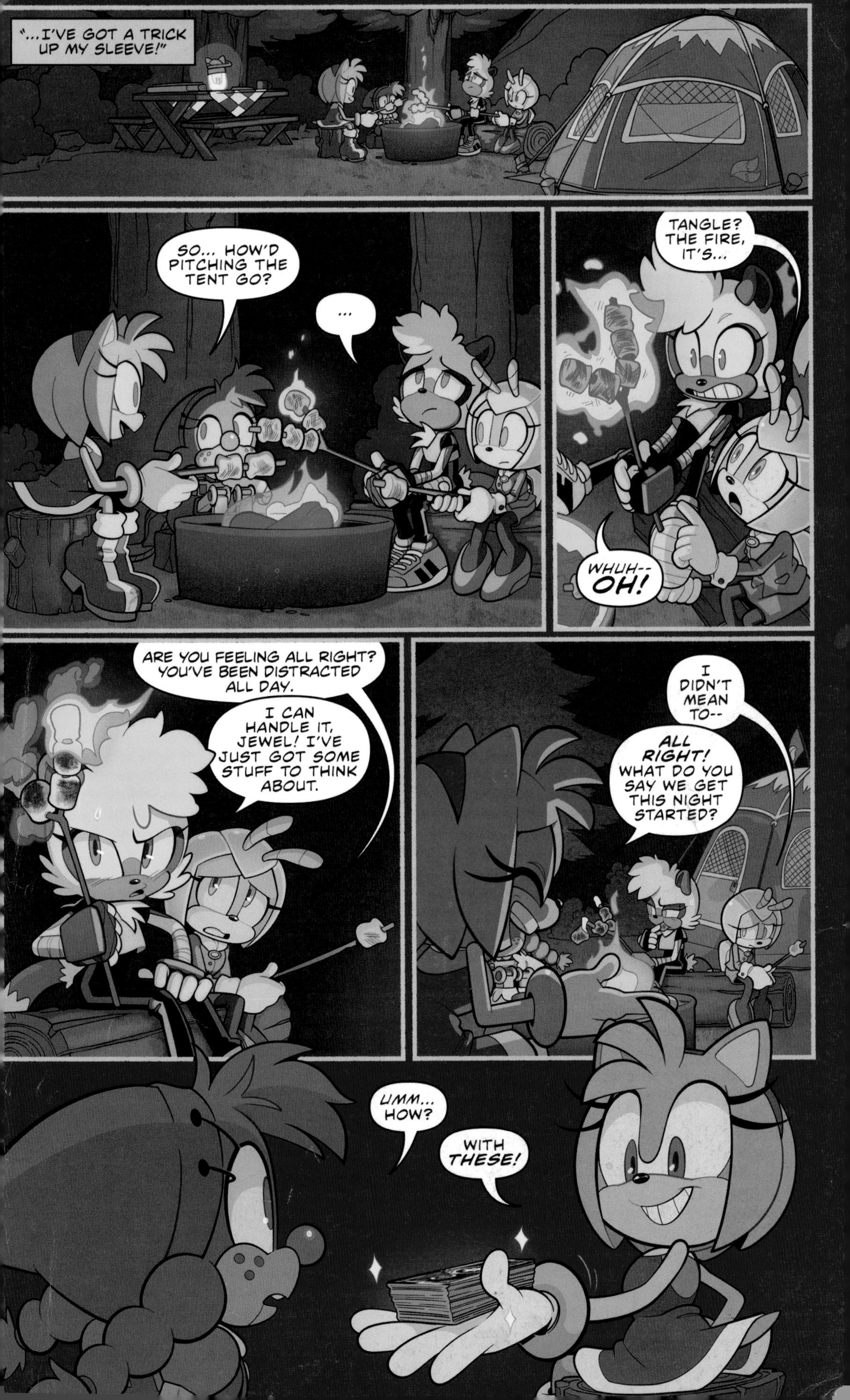
"...I'VE GOT A TRICK UP MY SLEEVE!"
SO... HOW'D PITCHING THE TENT GO?
...
TANGLE? THE FIRE, IT'S...
WHUH-- OH!
ARE YOU FEELING ALL RIGHT? YOU'VE BEEN DISTRACTED ALL DAY.
I CAN HANDLE IT, JEWEL! I'VE JUST GOT SOME STUFF TO THINK ABOUT.
I DIDN'T MEAN TO--
ALL RIGHT! WHAT DO YOU SAY WE GET THIS NIGHT STARTED?
UMM... HOW?
WITH THESE!

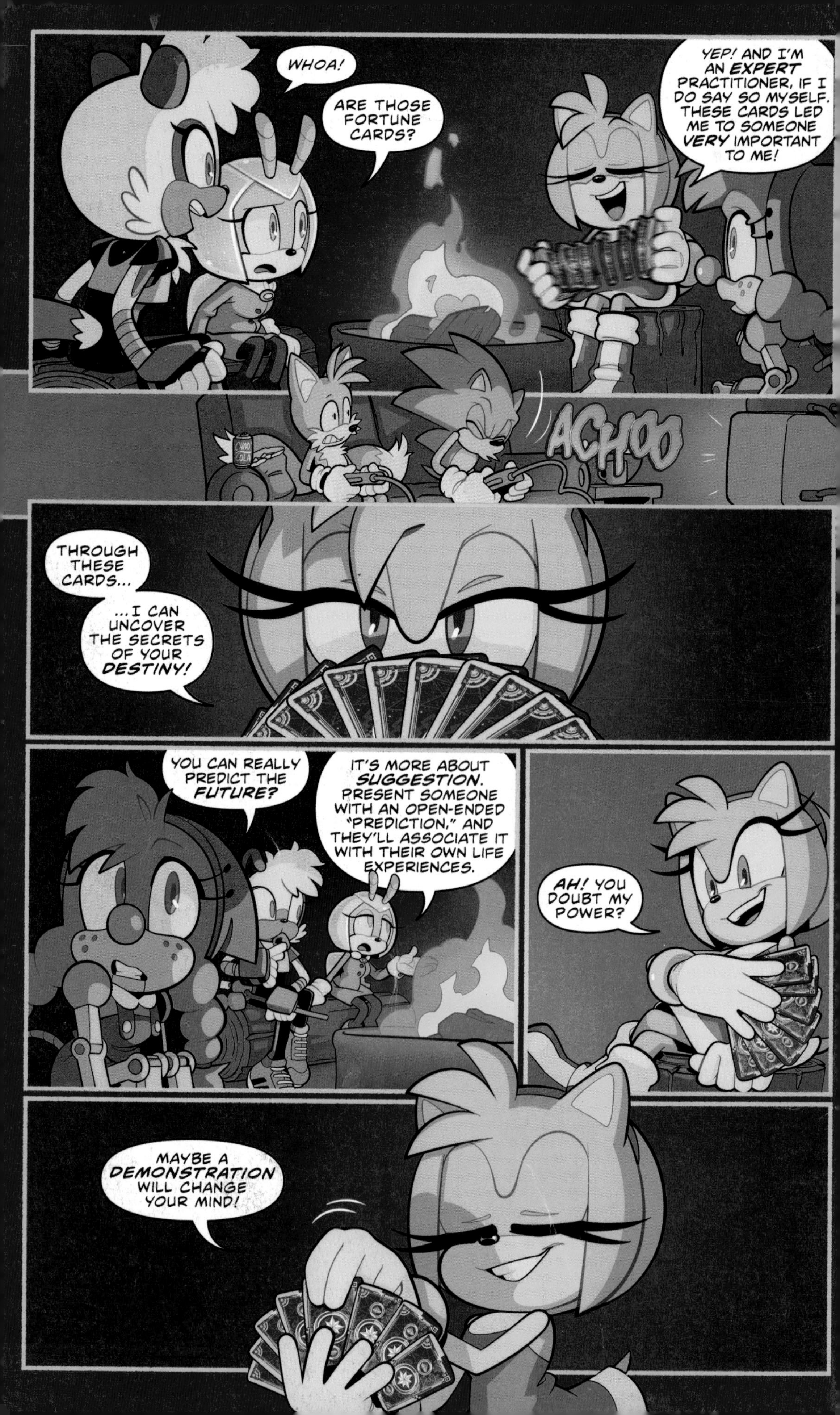
WHOA!
ARE THOSE FORTUNE CARDS?
YEP! AND I'M AN EXPERT PRACTITIONER, IF I DO SAY SO MYSELF. THESE CARDS LED ME TO SOMEONE VERY IMPORTANT TO ME!
CHAO COLA
ACHOO
THROUGH THESE CARDS...
...I CAN UNCOVER THE SECRETS OF YOUR DESTINY!
YOU CAN REALLY PREDICT THE FUTURE?
IT'S MORE ABOUT SUGGESTION. PRESENT SOMEONE WITH AN OPEN-ENDED "PREDICTION," AND THEY'LL ASSOCIATE IT WITH THEIR OWN LIFE EXPERIENCES.
AH! YOU DOUBT MY POWER?
MAYBE A DEMONSTRATION WILL CHANGE YOUR MIND!

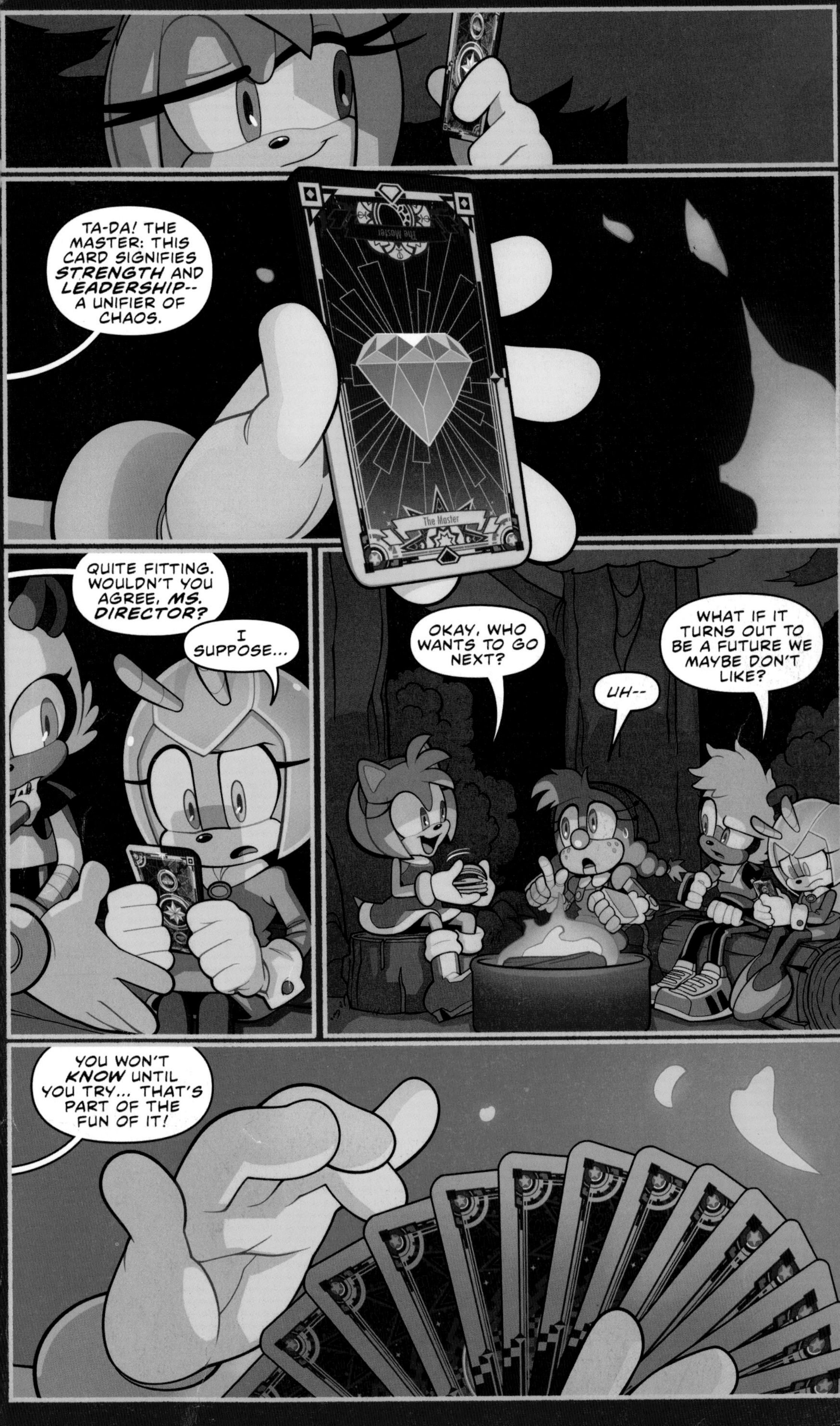
TA-DA! THE MASTER: THIS CARD SIGNIFIES STRENGTH AND LEADERSHIP-- A UNIFIER OF CHAOS.
The Master
The Master
QUITE FITTING. WOULDN'T YOU AGREE, MS. DIRECTOR?
I SUPPOSE...
OKAY, WHO WANTS TO GO NEXT?
UH--
WHAT IF IT TURNS OUT TO BE A FUTURE WE MAYBE DON'T LIKE?
YOU WON'T KNOW UNTIL YOU TRY... THAT'S PART OF THE FUN OF IT!

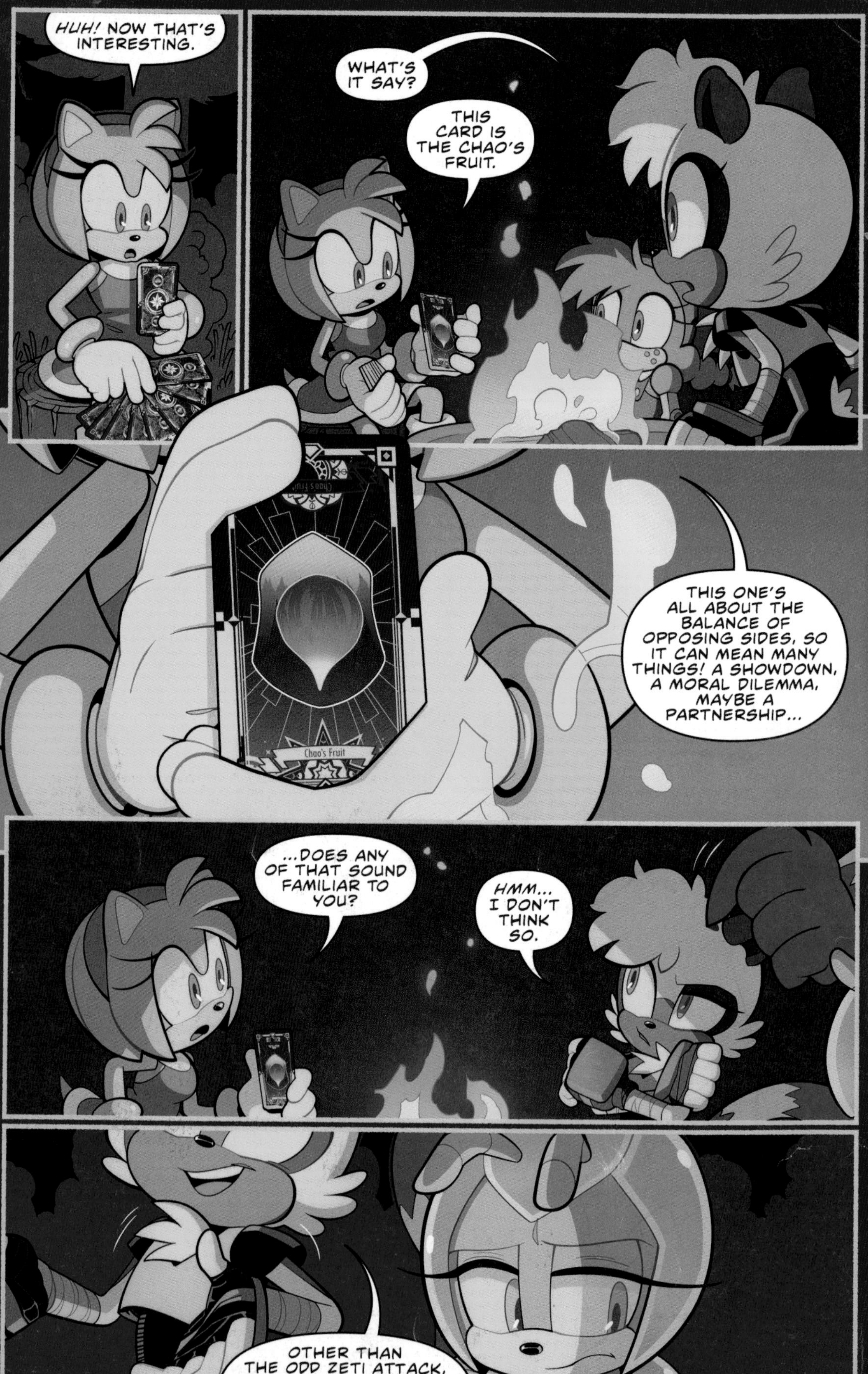
HUH! NOW THAT'S INTERESTING.
WHAT'S IT SAY?
THIS CARD IS THE CHAO'S FRUIT.
Chao's Fruit
THIS ONE'S ALL ABOUT THE BALANCE OF OPPOSING SIDES, SO IT CAN MEAN MANY THINGS! A SHOWDOWN, A MORAL DILEMMA, MAYBE A PARTNERSHIP...
...DOES ANY OF THAT SOUND FAMILIAR TO YOU?
HMM... I DON'T THINK SO.
OTHER THAN THE ODD ZETI ATTACK, WE DON'T GET A WHOLE LOT OF ***EXCITEMENT*** AROUND RESTORATION HQ.

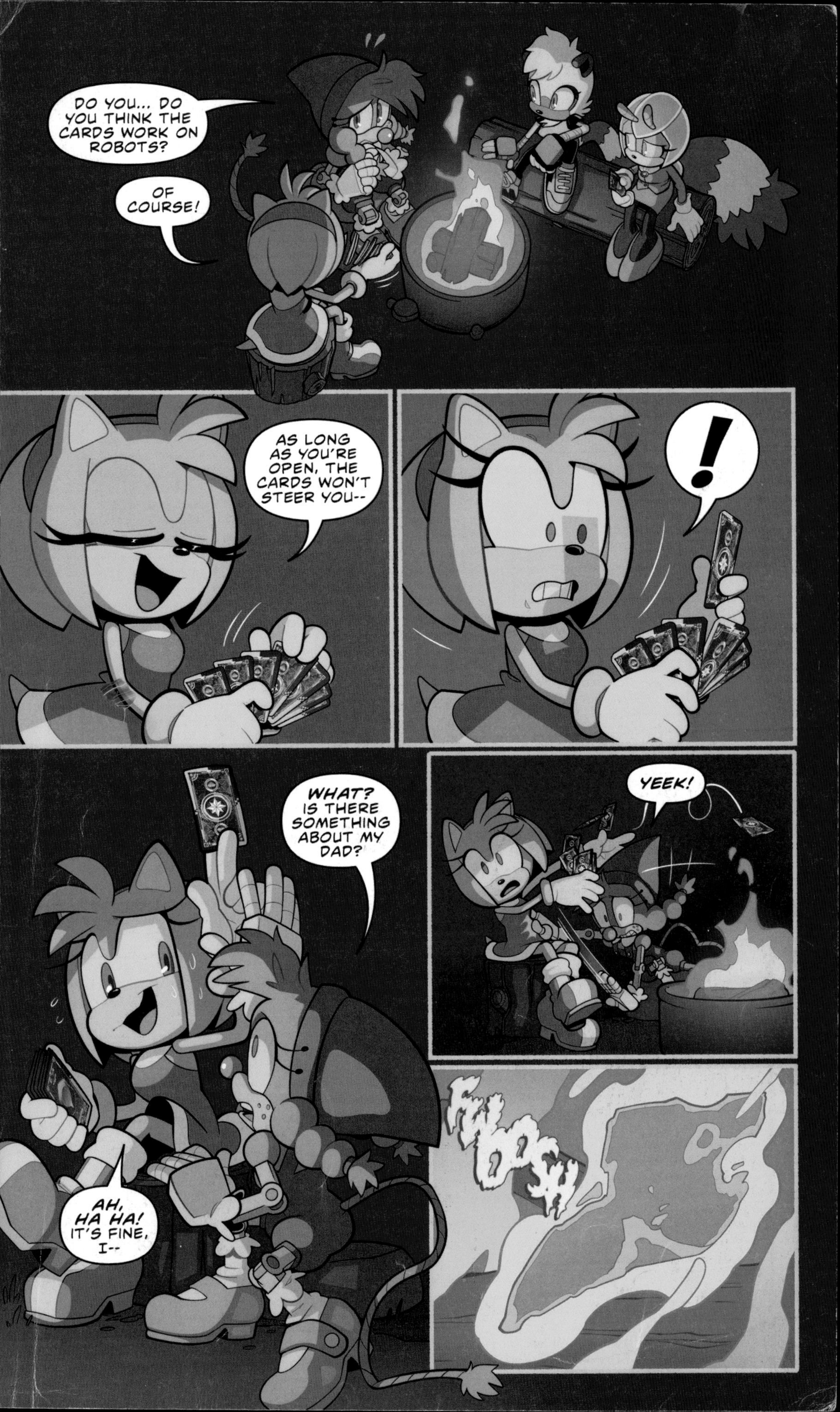
DO YOU... DO YOU THINK THE CARDS WORK ON ROBOTS?
OF COURSE!
AS LONG AS YOU'RE OPEN, THE CARDS WON'T STEER YOU--
!
WHAT? IS THERE SOMETHING ABOUT MY DAD?
AH, HA HA! IT'S FINE, I--
YEEK!
FWOOSH

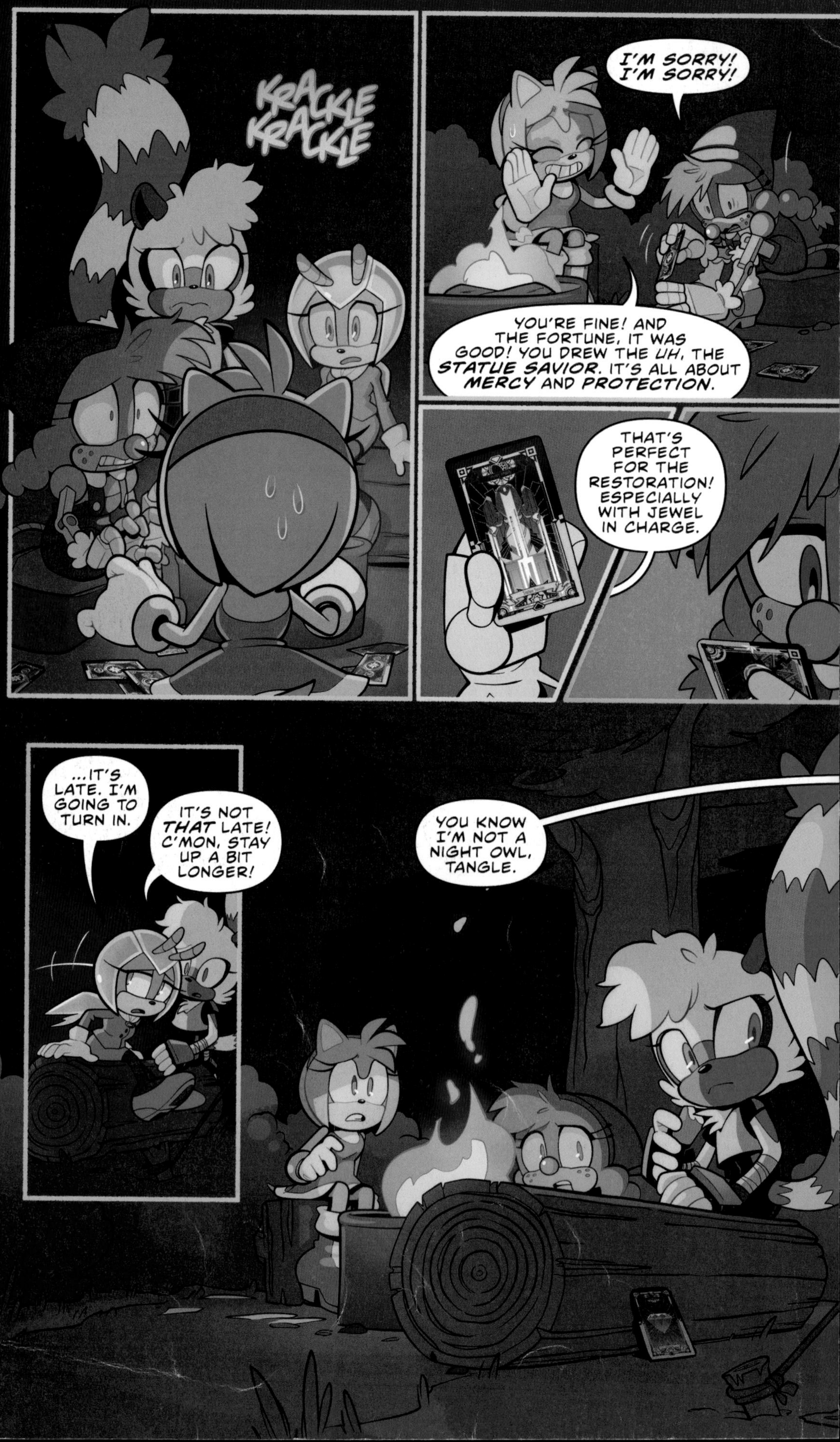
KRACKLE KRACKLE
I'M SORRY! I'M SORRY!
YOU'RE FINE! AND THE FORTUNE, IT WAS GOOD! YOU DREW THE *UH*, THE ***STATUE SAVIOR***. IT'S ALL ABOUT ***MERCY*** AND ***PROTECTION***.
THAT'S PERFECT FOR THE RESTORATION! ESPECIALLY WITH JEWEL IN CHARGE.
...IT'S LATE. I'M GOING TO TURN IN.
IT'S NOT ***THAT*** LATE! C'MON, STAY UP A BIT LONGER!
YOU KNOW I'M NOT A NIGHT OWL, TANGLE.

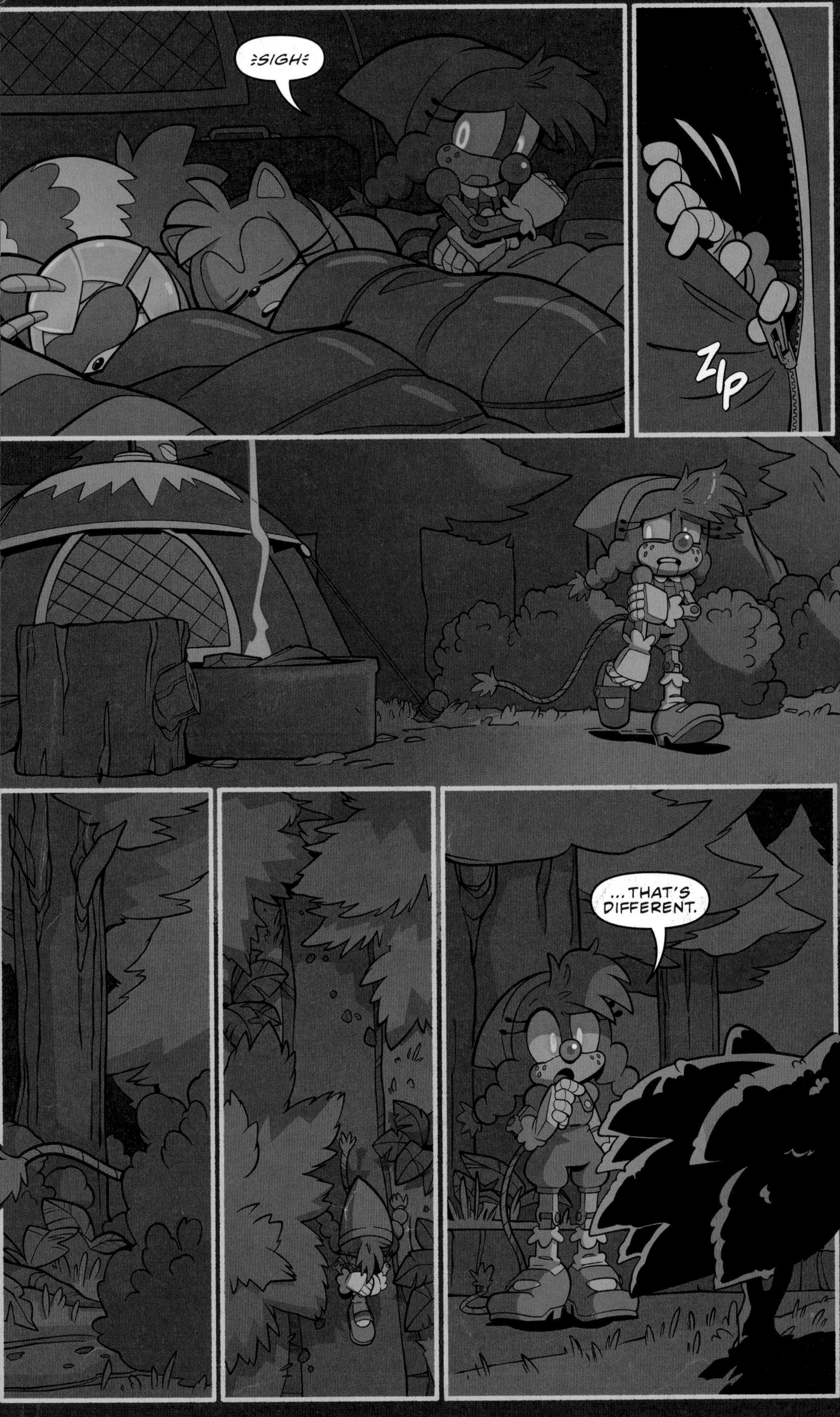

SIGH
ZIP
...THAT'S DIFFERENT.

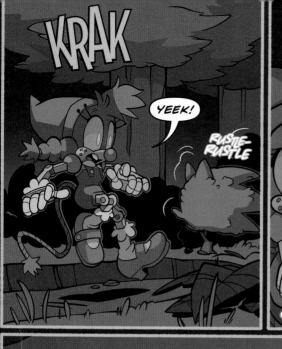

KRAK

YEEK!

RUSTLE-RUSTLE

C'MON, FLASHLIGHT, FLASHLIGHT!

CHK-CHK-CHK-CHK

SAWDUST.

KA-CHAK

PLEASE, PLEASE, *PLEASE* BE NICE...

RRRRRRRR...

...RRRROM

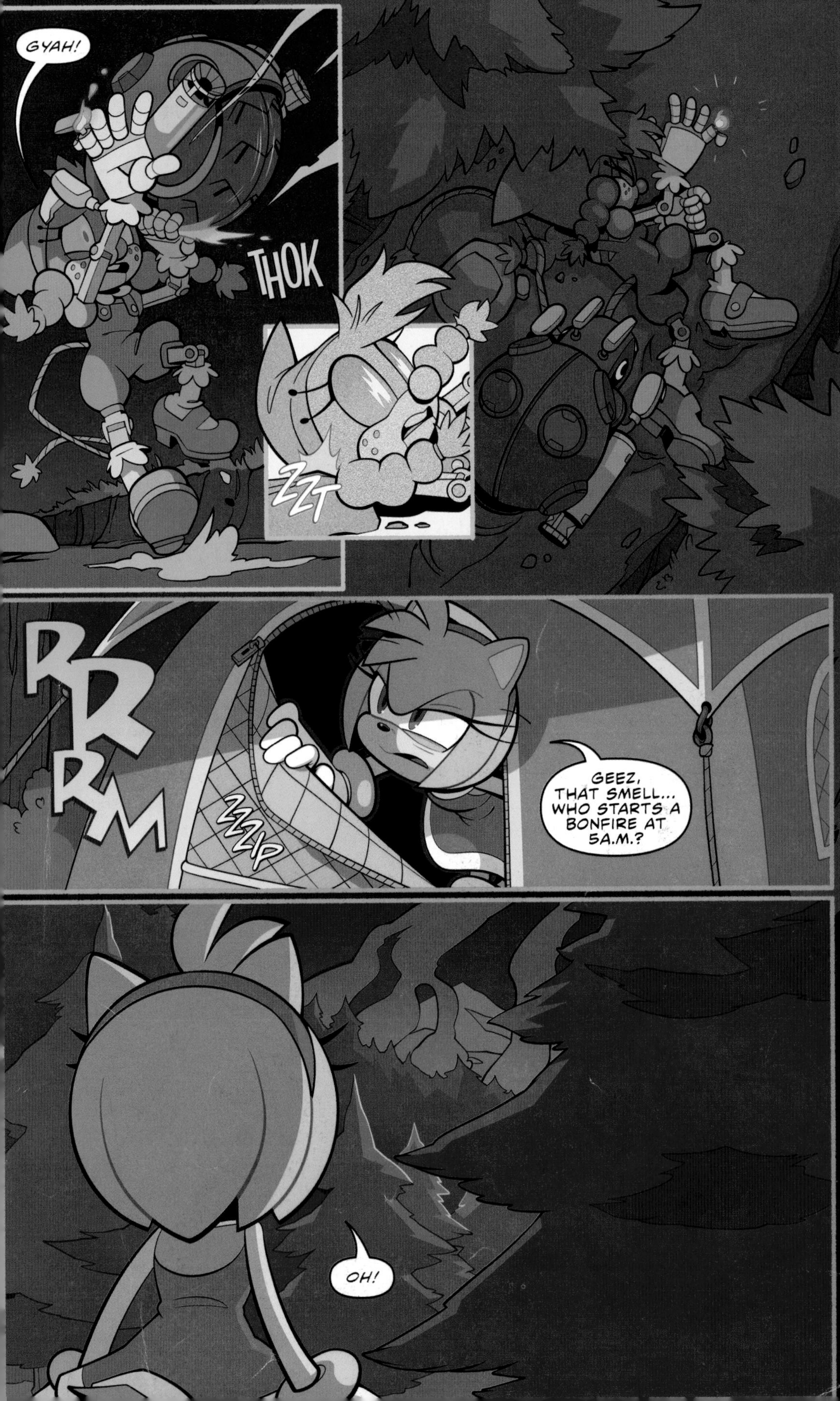
GYAH!
THOK
ZZZT
RRRM
ZZZIP
GEEZ, THAT SMELL... WHO STARTS A BONFIRE AT 5A.M.?
OH!

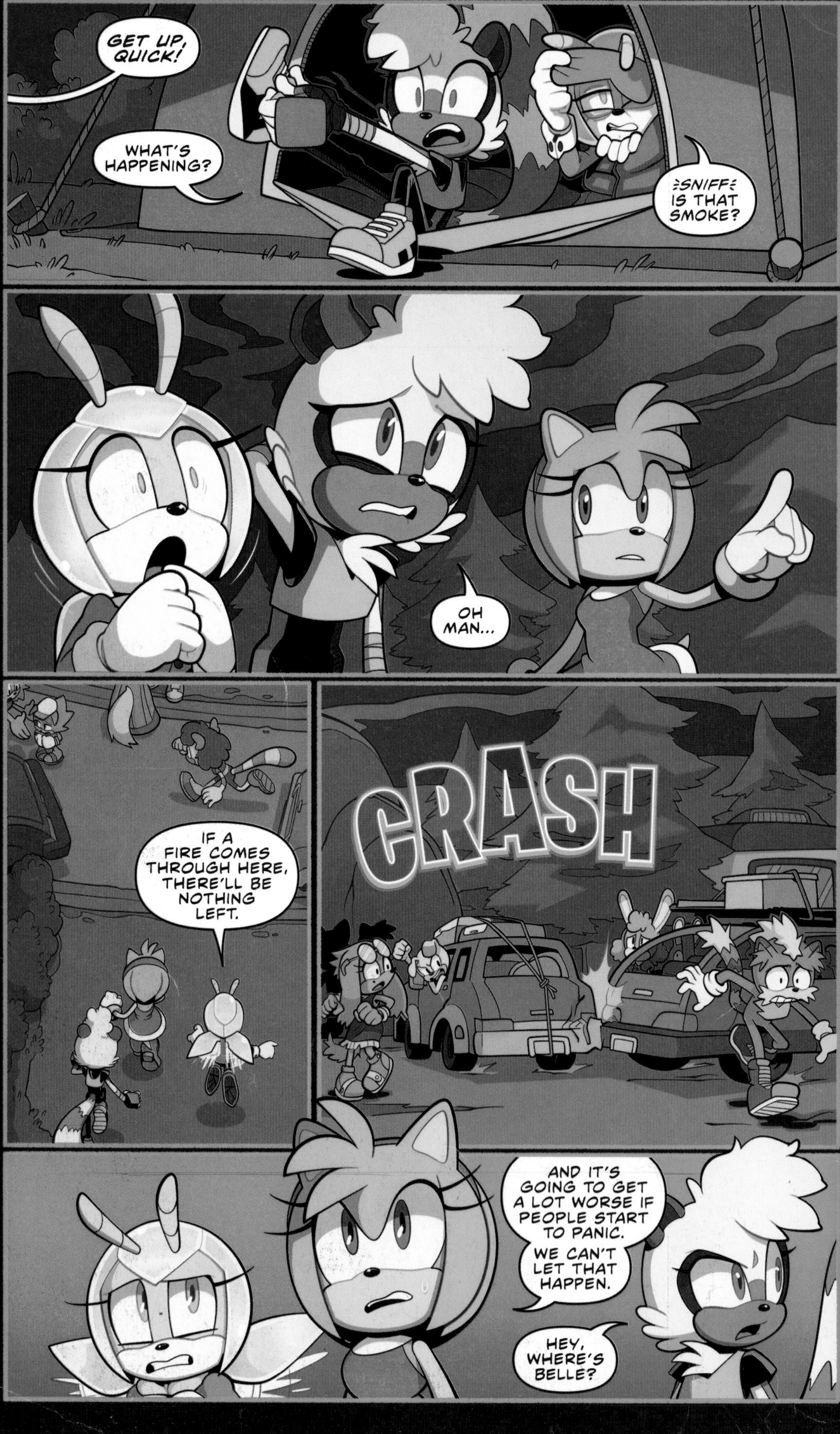

GET UP, QUICK!
WHAT'S HAPPENING?
SNIFF IS THAT SMOKE?
OH MAN...
IF A FIRE COMES THROUGH HERE, THERE'LL BE NOTHING LEFT.
CRASH
AND IT'S GOING TO GET A LOT WORSE IF PEOPLE START TO PANIC.
WE CAN'T LET THAT HAPPEN.
HEY, WHERE'S BELLE?

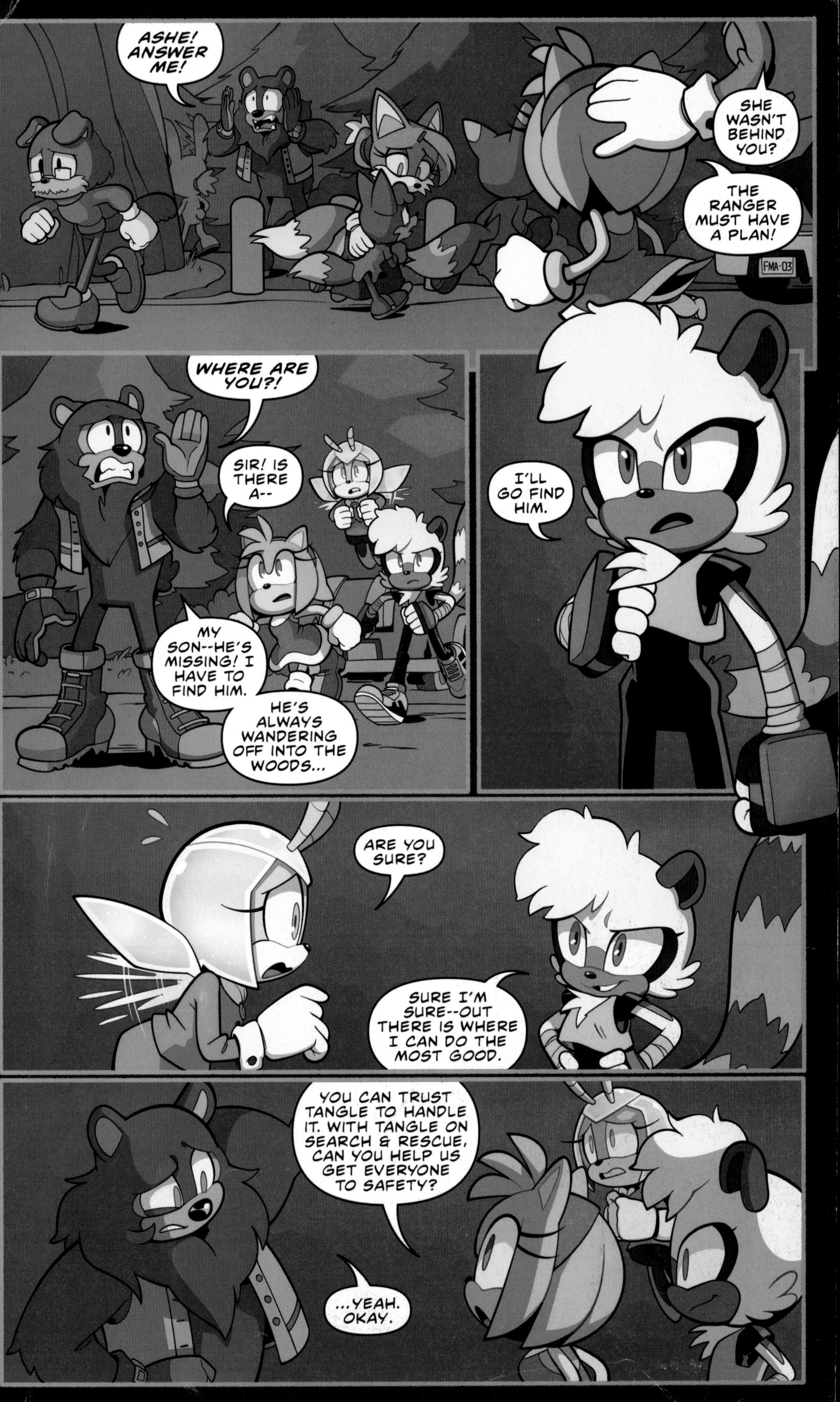

ASHE! ANSWER ME!
SHE WASN'T BEHIND YOU?
THE RANGER MUST HAVE A PLAN!
FMA-03
WHERE ARE YOU?!
SIR! IS THERE A--
MY SON--HE'S MISSING! I HAVE TO FIND HIM.
HE'S ALWAYS WANDERING OFF INTO THE WOODS...
I'LL GO FIND HIM.
ARE YOU SURE?
SURE I'M SURE--OUT THERE IS WHERE I CAN DO THE MOST GOOD.
YOU CAN TRUST TANGLE TO HANDLE IT. WITH TANGLE ON SEARCH & RESCUE, CAN YOU HELP US GET EVERYONE TO SAFETY?
...YEAH. OKAY.

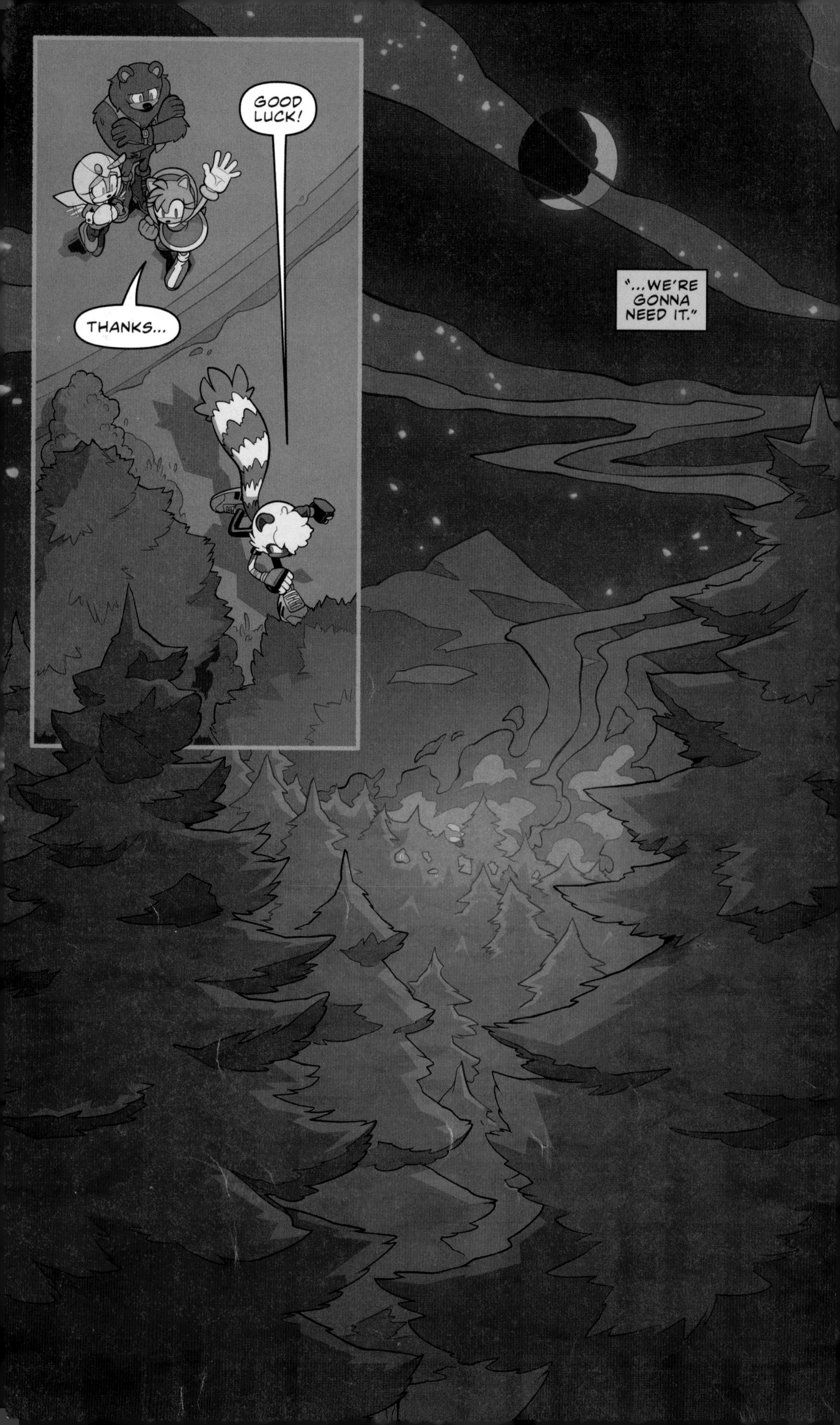

GOOD LUCK!
THANKS...
"...WE'RE GONNA NEED IT."

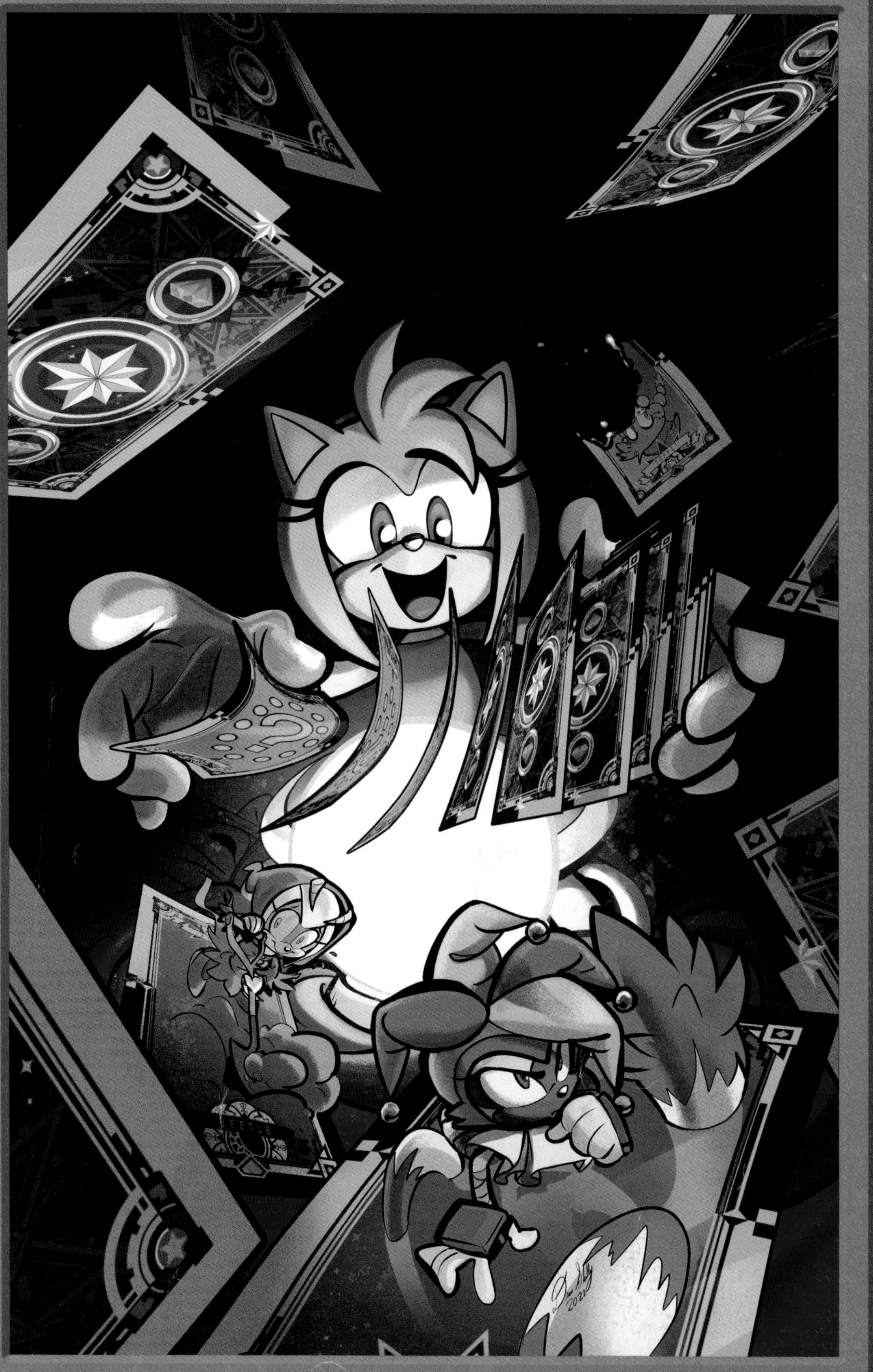

ART BY **DIANA SKELLY**

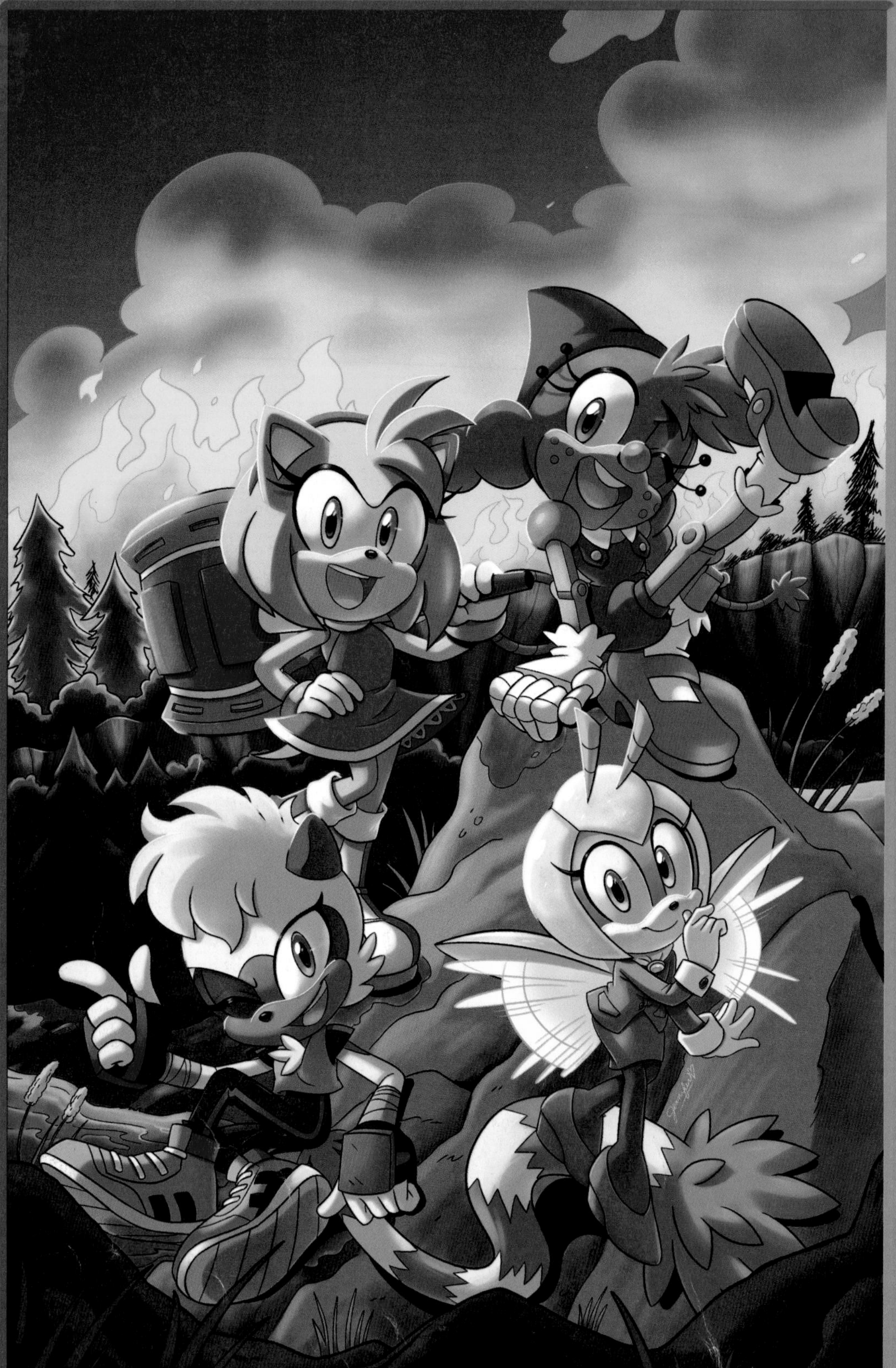

ART BY JENNIFER HERNANDEZ

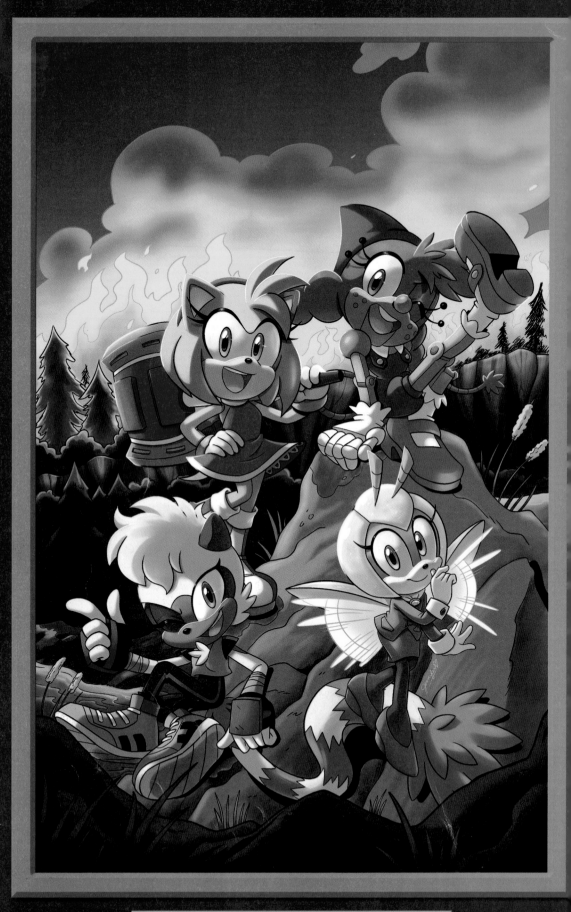

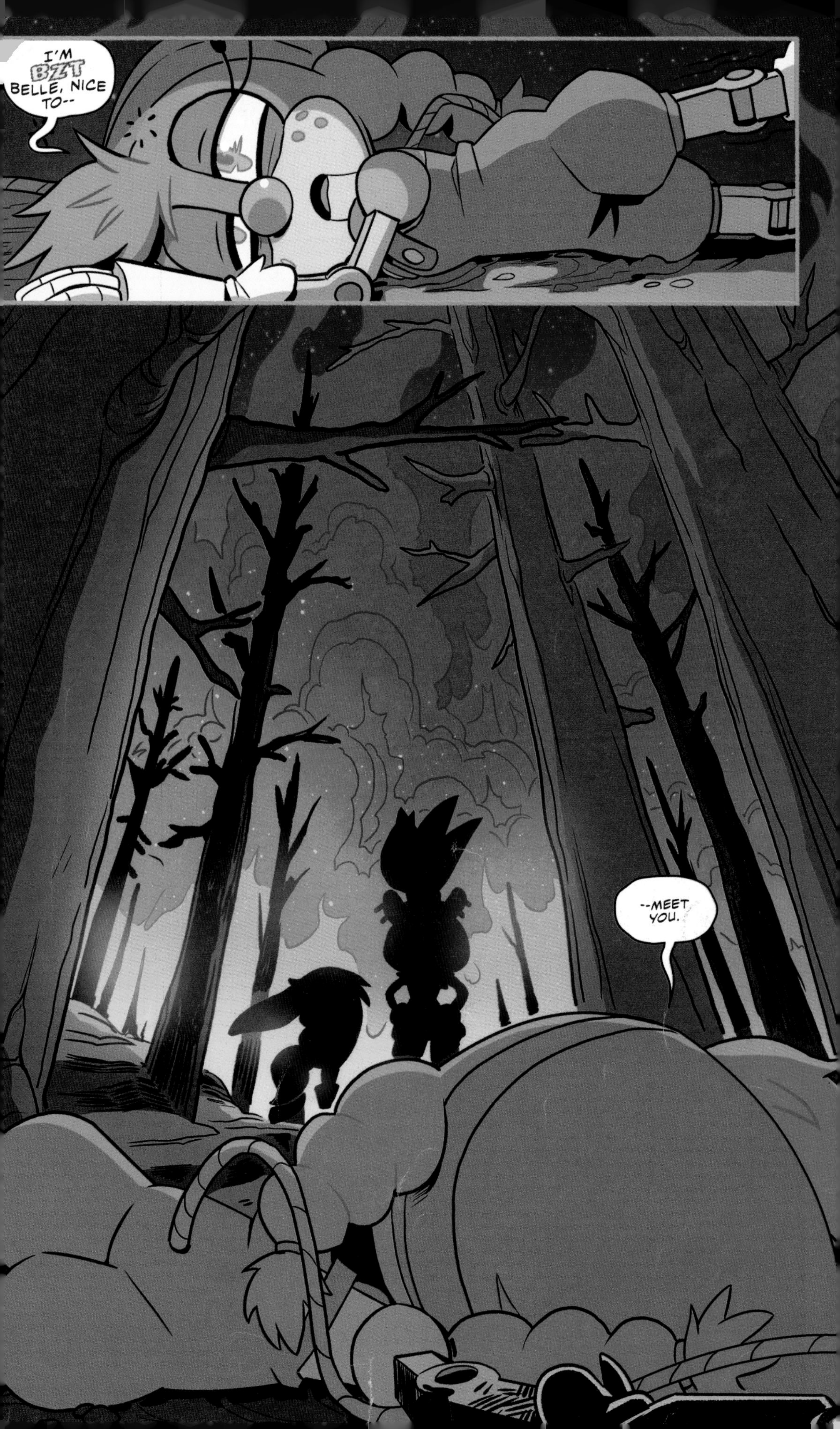
I'M BZT BELLE, NICE TO--
--MEET YOU.

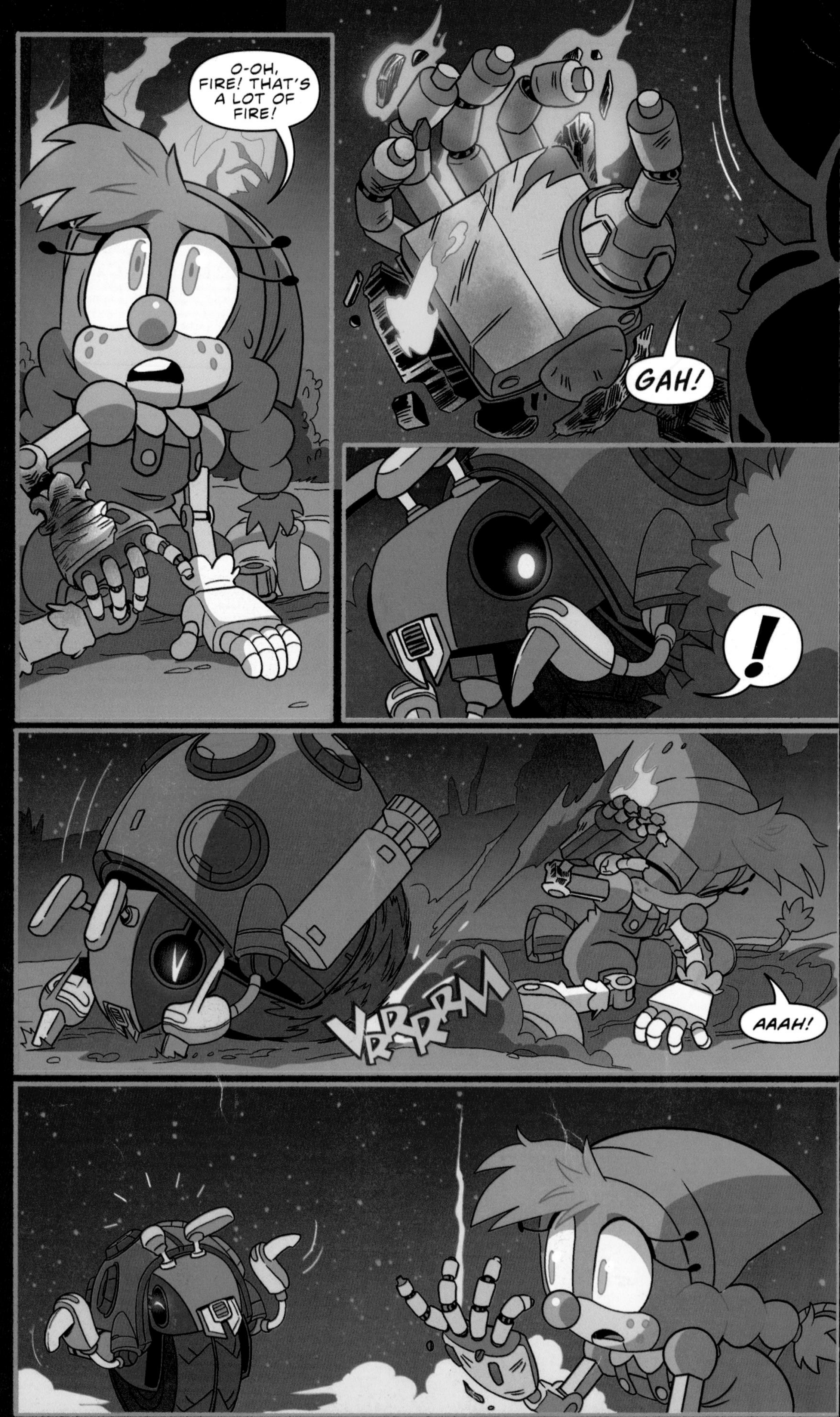
O-OH, FIRE! THAT'S A LOT OF FIRE!
GAH!
!
VRRRRM
AAAH!

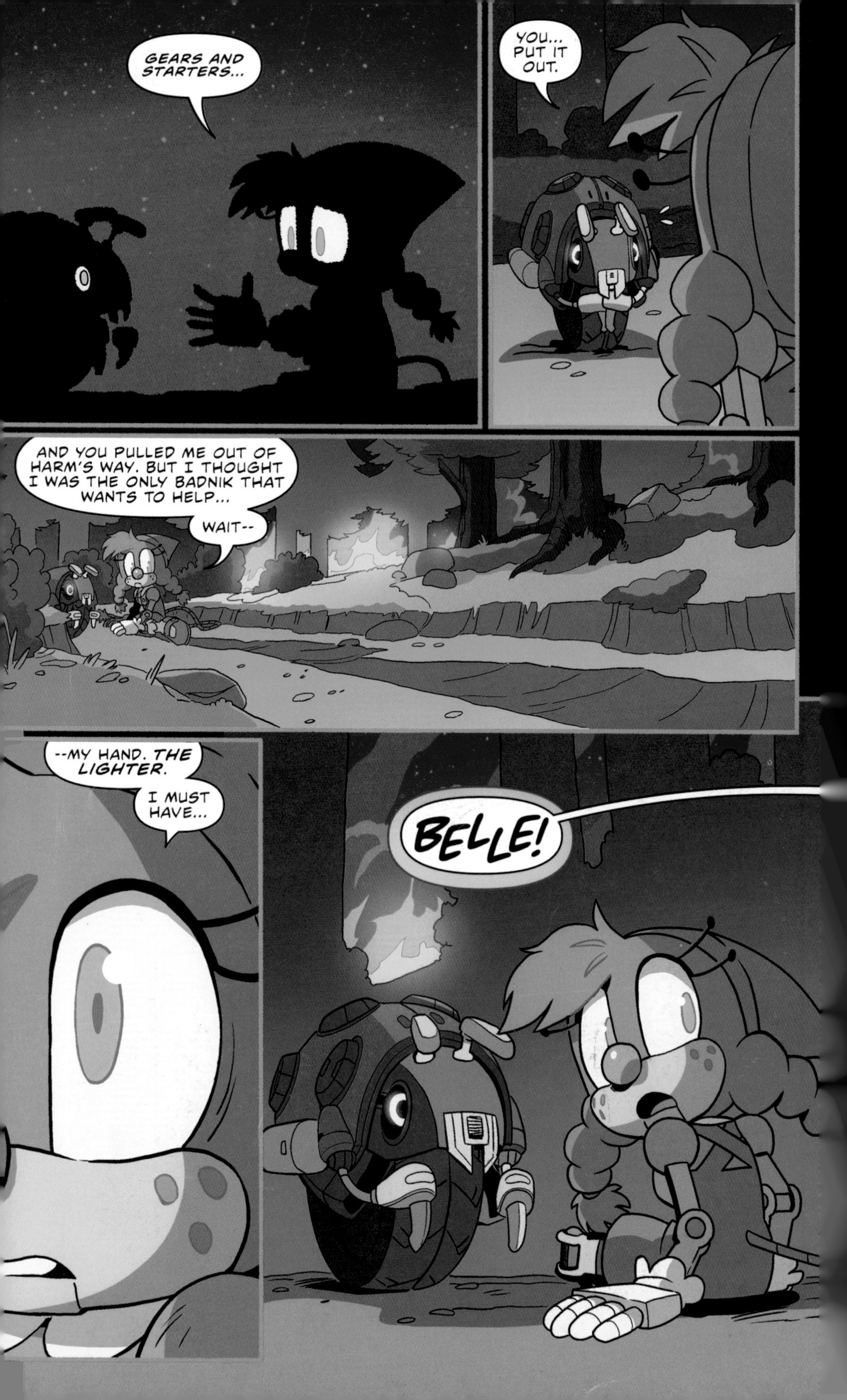

GEARS AND STARTERS...
YOU... PUT IT OUT.
AND YOU PULLED ME OUT OF HARM'S WAY. BUT I THOUGHT I WAS THE ONLY BADNIK THAT WANTS TO HELP...
WAIT--
--MY HAND. *THE LIGHTER*.
I MUST HAVE...
BELLE!

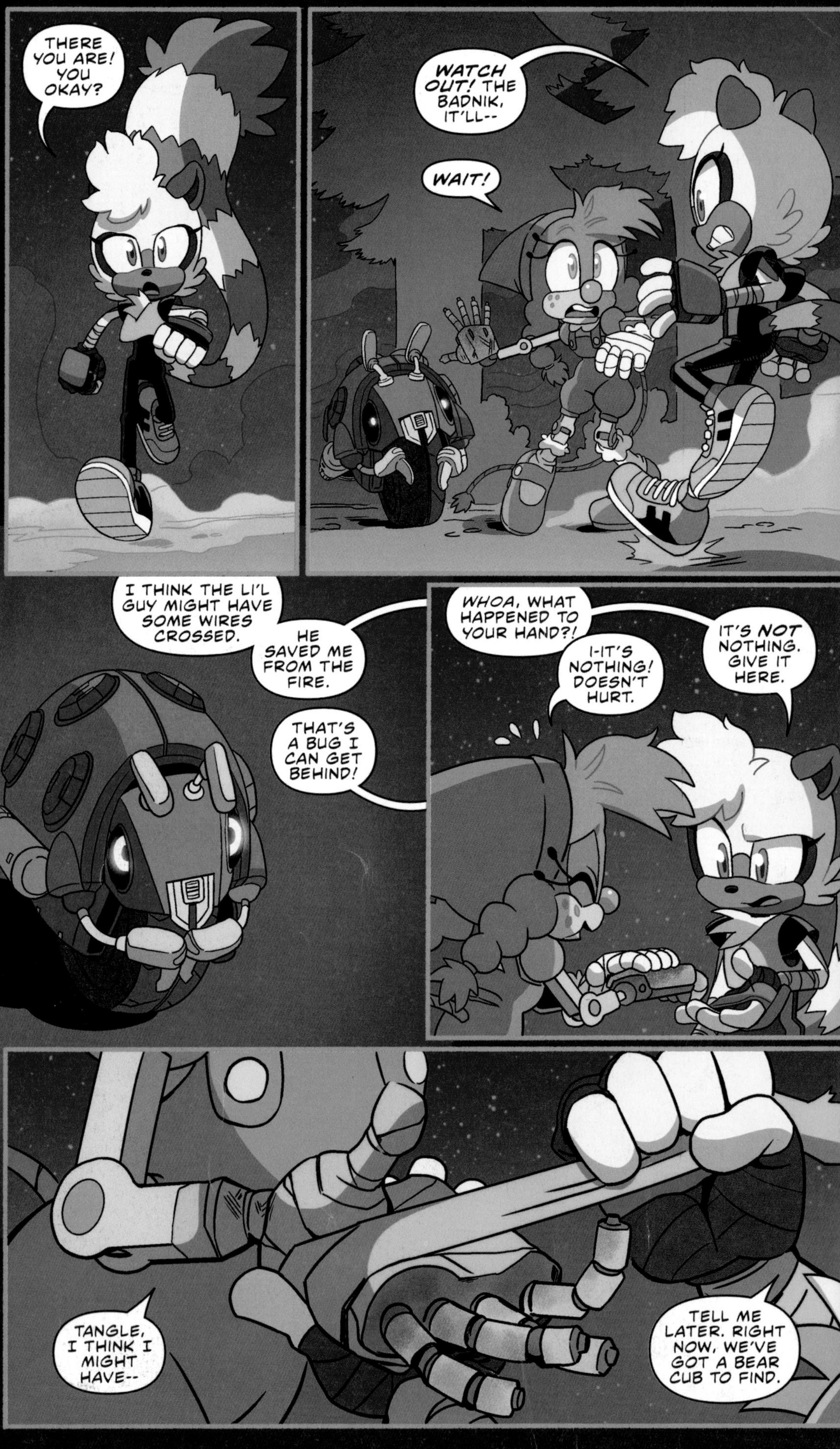
THERE YOU ARE! YOU OKAY?
WATCH OUT! THE BADNIK, IT'LL--
WAIT!
I THINK THE LI'L GUY MIGHT HAVE SOME WIRES CROSSED.
HE SAVED ME FROM THE FIRE.
THAT'S A BUG I CAN GET BEHIND!
WHOA, WHAT HAPPENED TO YOUR HAND?!
I-IT'S NOTHING! DOESN'T HURT.
IT'S NOT NOTHING. GIVE IT HERE.
TANGLE, I THINK I MIGHT HAVE--
TELL ME LATER. RIGHT NOW, WE'VE GOT A BEAR CUB TO FIND.

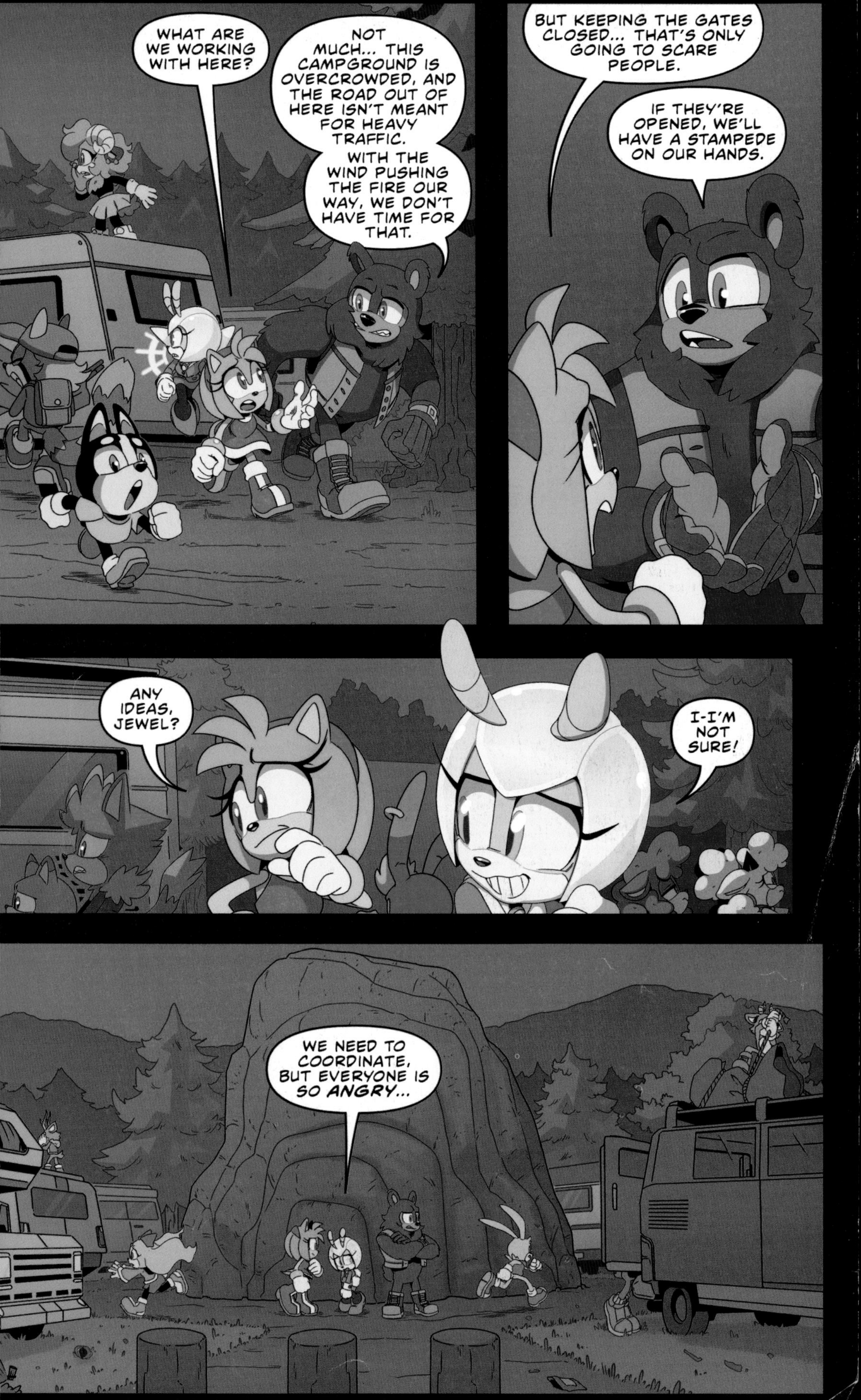
WHAT ARE WE WORKING WITH HERE?
NOT MUCH... THIS CAMPGROUND IS OVERCROWDED, AND THE ROAD OUT OF HERE ISN'T MEANT FOR HEAVY TRAFFIC.
WITH THE WIND PUSHING THE FIRE OUR WAY, WE DON'T HAVE TIME FOR THAT.
BUT KEEPING THE GATES CLOSED... THAT'S ONLY GOING TO SCARE PEOPLE.
IF THEY'RE OPENED, WE'LL HAVE A STAMPEDE ON OUR HANDS.
ANY IDEAS, JEWEL?
I-I'M NOT SURE!
WE NEED TO COORDINATE, BUT EVERYONE IS SO ANGRY...

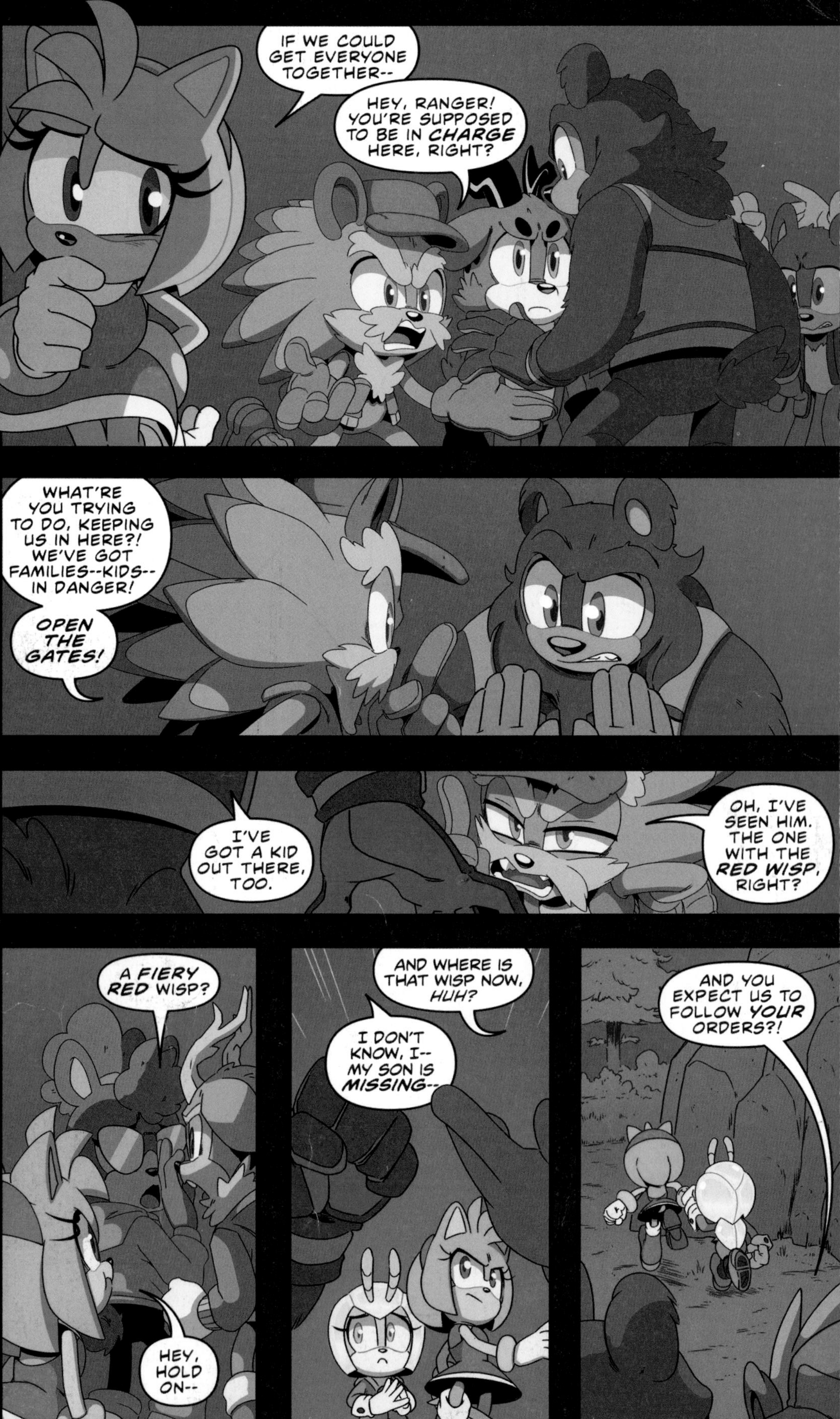
IF WE COULD GET EVERYONE TOGETHER--
HEY, RANGER! YOU'RE SUPPOSED TO BE IN CHARGE HERE, RIGHT?
WHAT'RE YOU TRYING TO DO, KEEPING US IN HERE?! WE'VE GOT FAMILIES--KIDS--IN DANGER!
OPEN THE GATES!
I'VE GOT A KID OUT THERE, TOO.
OH, I'VE SEEN HIM. THE ONE WITH THE RED WISP, RIGHT?
A FIERY RED WISP?
HEY, HOLD ON--
AND WHERE IS THAT WISP NOW, HUH?
I DON'T KNOW, I-- MY SON IS MISSING--
AND YOU EXPECT US TO FOLLOW YOUR ORDERS?!

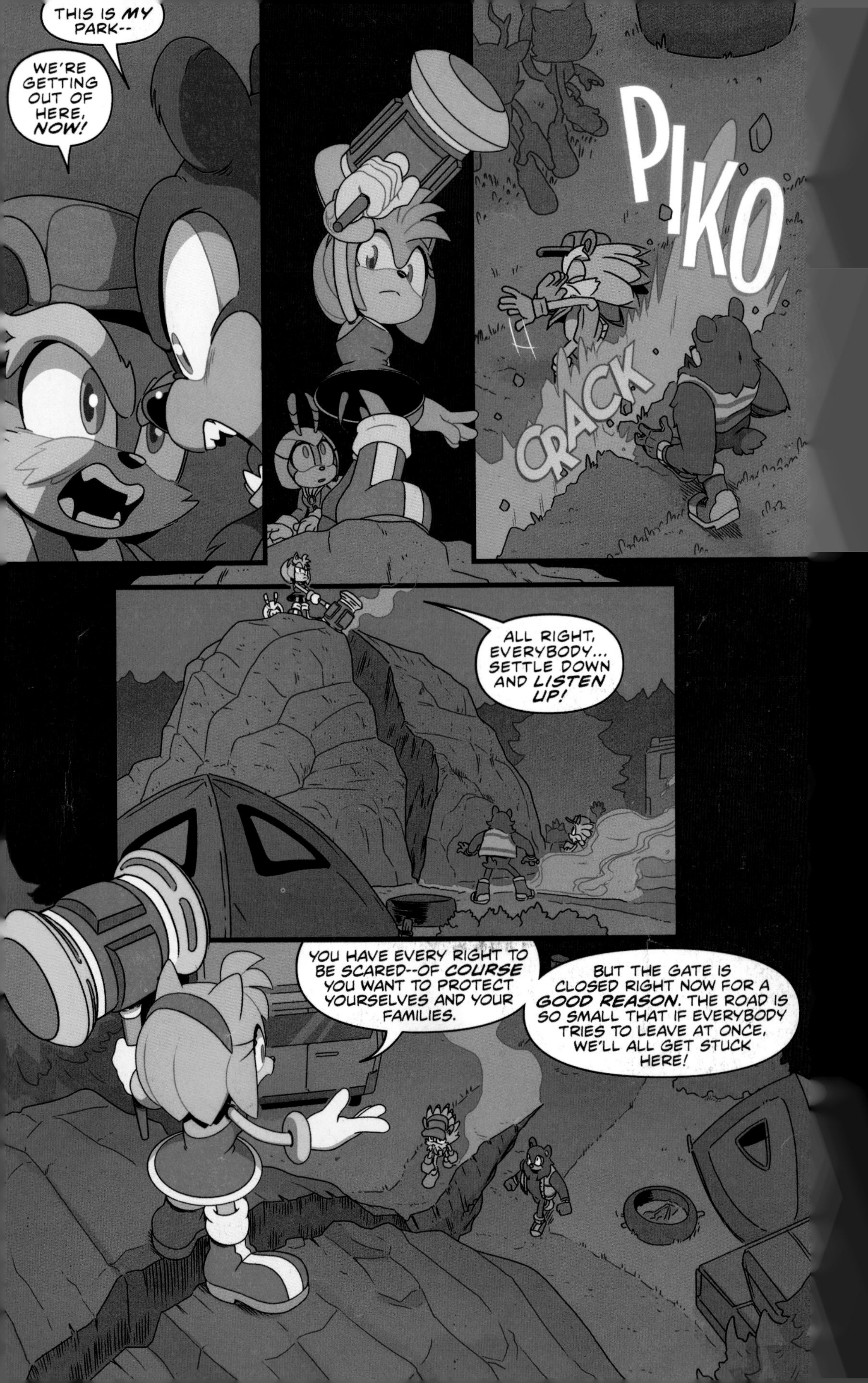
THIS IS MY PARK--
WE'RE GETTING OUT OF HERE, NOW!
PIKO
CRACK
ALL RIGHT, EVERYBODY... SETTLE DOWN AND LISTEN UP!
YOU HAVE EVERY RIGHT TO BE SCARED--OF COURSE YOU WANT TO PROTECT YOURSELVES AND YOUR FAMILIES.
BUT THE GATE IS CLOSED RIGHT NOW FOR A GOOD REASON. THE ROAD IS SO SMALL THAT IF EVERYBODY TRIES TO LEAVE AT ONCE, WE'LL ALL GET STUCK HERE!

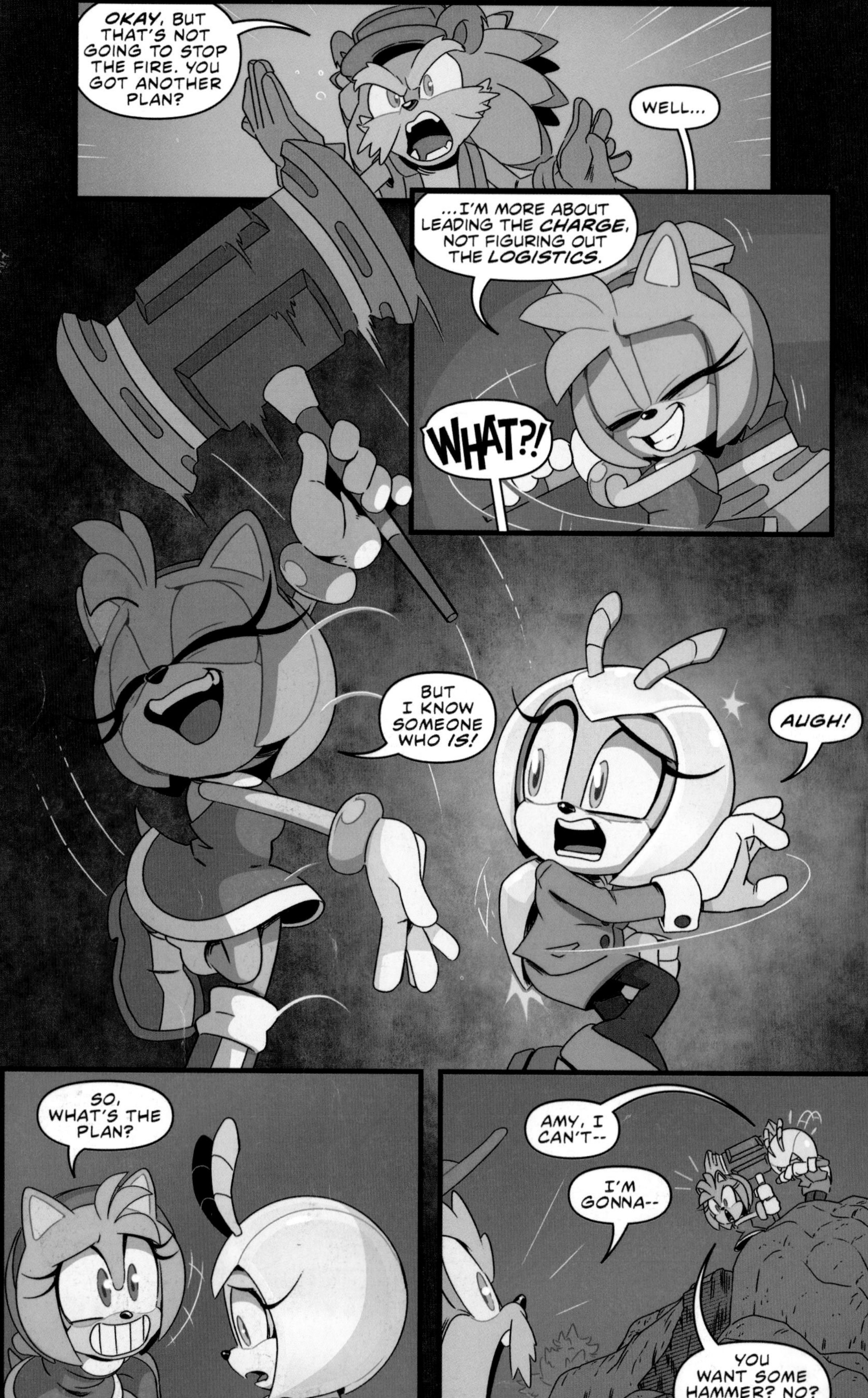

OKAY, BUT THAT'S NOT GOING TO STOP THE FIRE. YOU GOT ANOTHER PLAN?
WELL...
...I'M MORE ABOUT LEADING THE CHARGE, NOT FIGURING OUT THE LOGISTICS.
WHAT?!
BUT I KNOW SOMEONE WHO IS!
AUGH!
SO, WHAT'S THE PLAN?
AMY, I CAN'T--
I'M GONNA--
YOU WANT SOME HAMMER? NO? GIVE HER A MINUTE.

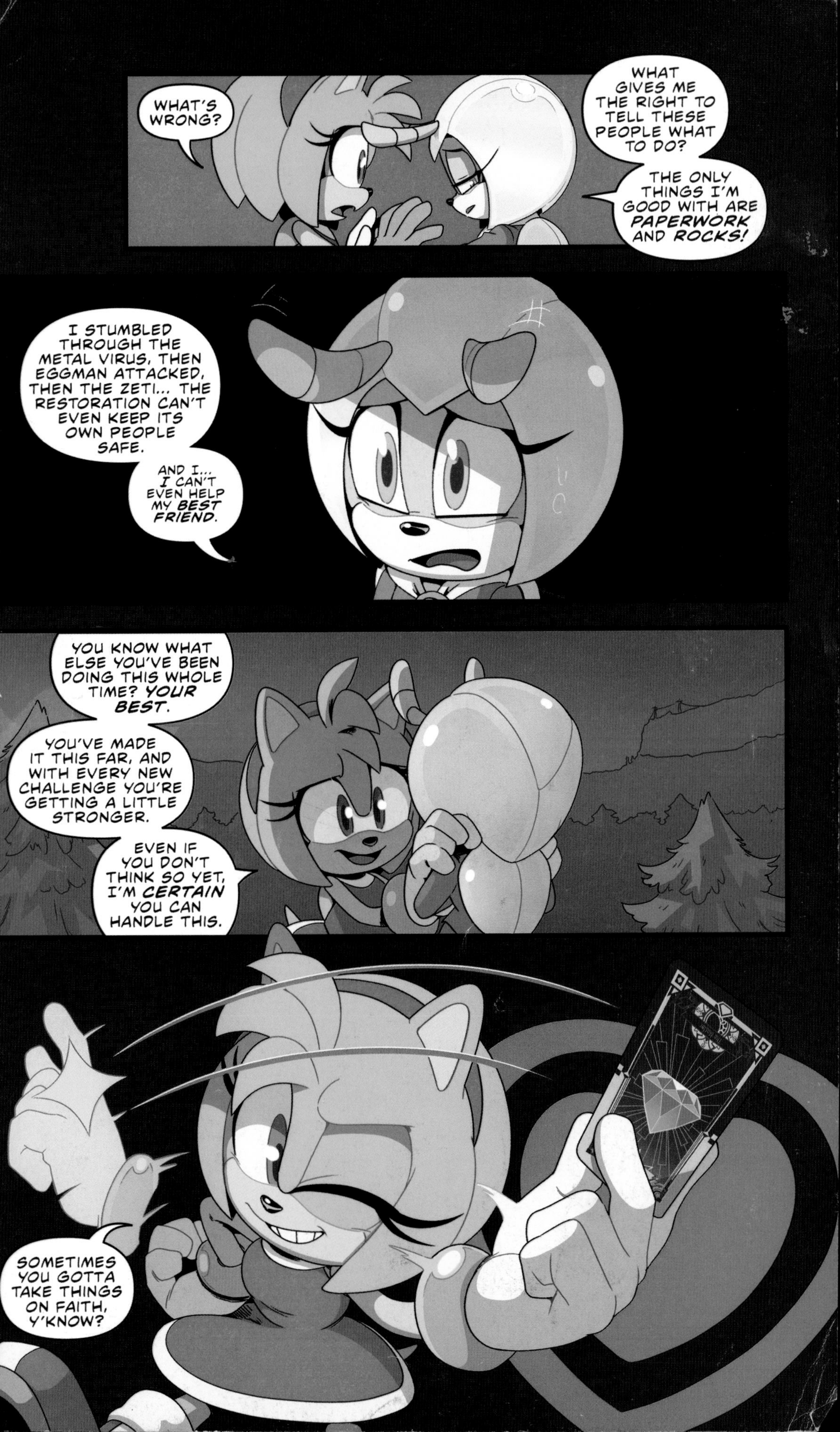
WHAT'S WRONG?
WHAT GIVES ME THE RIGHT TO TELL THESE PEOPLE WHAT TO DO?
THE ONLY THINGS I'M GOOD WITH ARE *PAPERWORK* AND *ROCKS!*
I STUMBLED THROUGH THE METAL VIRUS, THEN EGGMAN ATTACKED, THEN THE ZETI... THE RESTORATION CAN'T EVEN KEEP ITS OWN PEOPLE SAFE.
AND I... *I* CAN'T EVEN HELP MY *BEST FRIEND*.
YOU KNOW WHAT ELSE YOU'VE BEEN DOING THIS WHOLE TIME? *YOUR BEST*.
YOU'VE MADE IT THIS FAR, AND WITH EVERY NEW CHALLENGE YOU'RE GETTING A LITTLE STRONGER.
EVEN IF YOU DON'T THINK SO YET, I'M *CERTAIN* YOU CAN HANDLE THIS.
SOMETIMES YOU GOTTA TAKE THINGS ON FAITH, Y'KNOW?

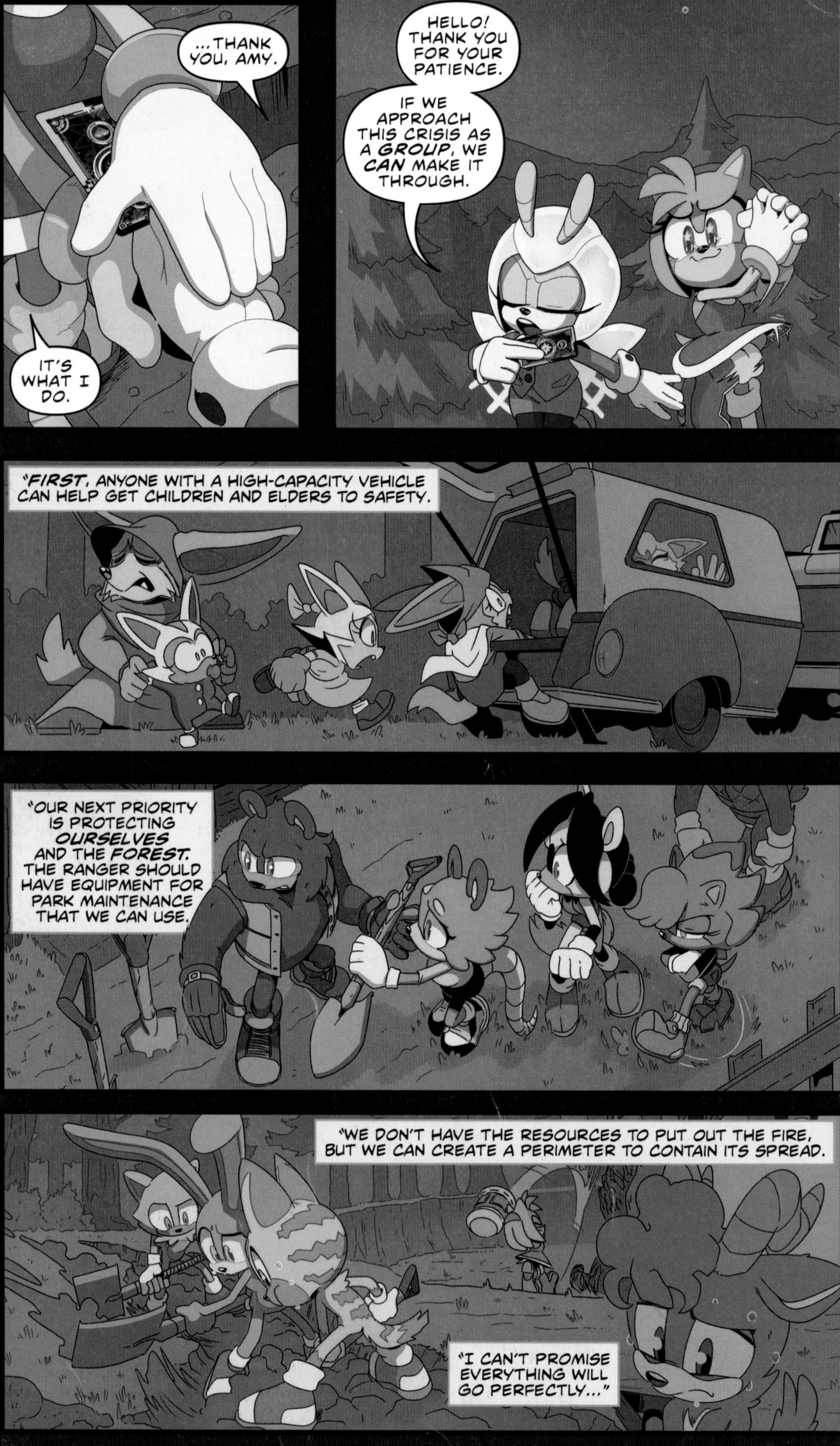
...THANK YOU, AMY.
IT'S WHAT I DO.
HELLO! THANK YOU FOR YOUR PATIENCE.
IF WE APPROACH THIS CRISIS AS A GROUP, WE CAN MAKE IT THROUGH.
"FIRST, ANYONE WITH A HIGH-CAPACITY VEHICLE CAN HELP GET CHILDREN AND ELDERS TO SAFETY.
"OUR NEXT PRIORITY IS PROTECTING OURSELVES AND THE FOREST. THE RANGER SHOULD HAVE EQUIPMENT FOR PARK MAINTENANCE THAT WE CAN USE.
"WE DON'T HAVE THE RESOURCES TO PUT OUT THE FIRE, BUT WE CAN CREATE A PERIMETER TO CONTAIN ITS SPREAD.
"I CAN'T PROMISE EVERYTHING WILL GO PERFECTLY..."

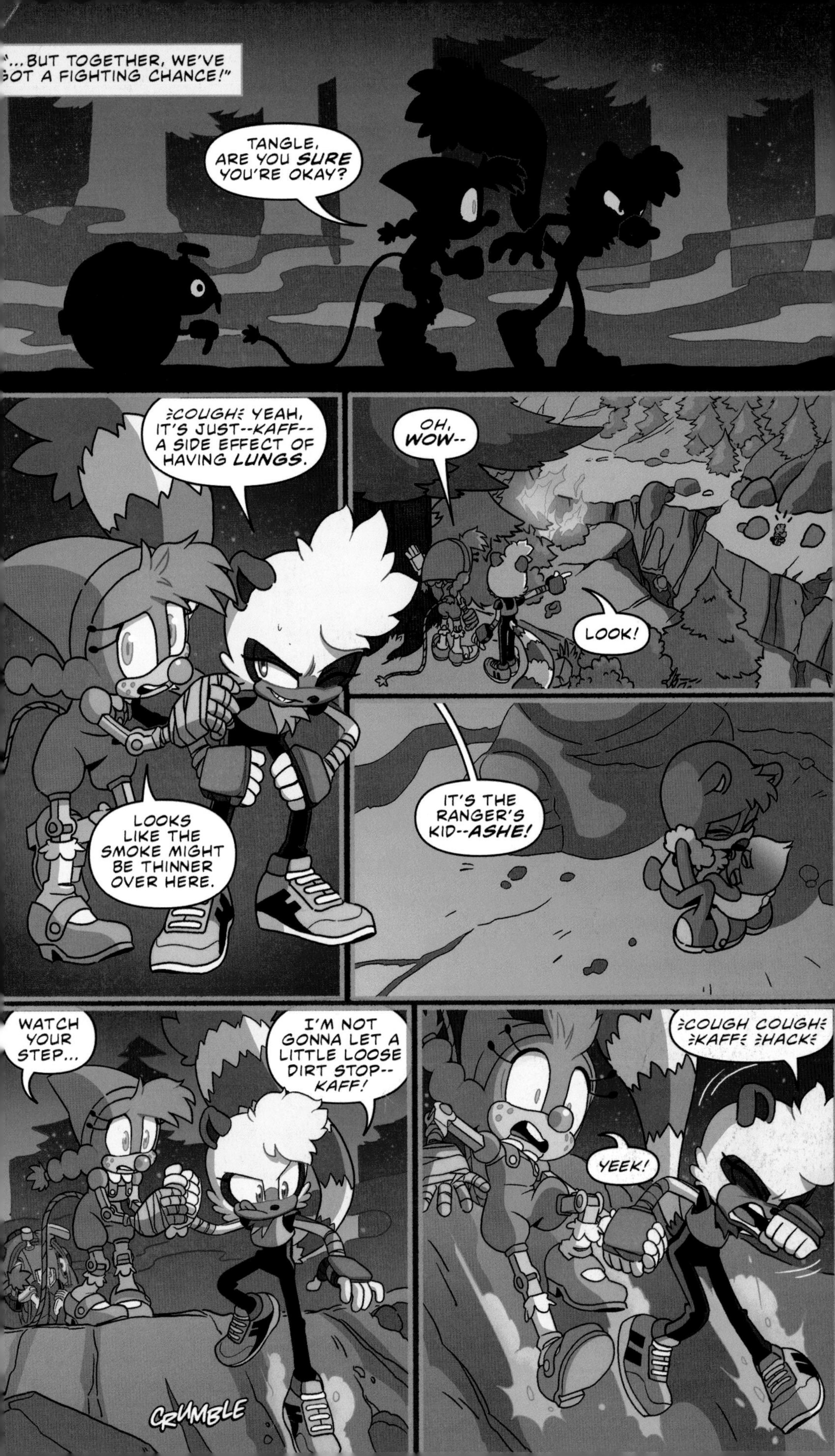
"...BUT TOGETHER, WE'VE GOT A FIGHTING CHANCE!"
TANGLE, ARE YOU SURE YOU'RE OKAY?
COUGH YEAH, IT'S JUST--KAFF--A SIDE EFFECT OF HAVING LUNGS.
LOOKS LIKE THE SMOKE MIGHT BE THINNER OVER HERE.
OH, WOW--
LOOK!
IT'S THE RANGER'S KID--ASHE!
WATCH YOUR STEP...
I'M NOT GONNA LET A LITTLE LOOSE DIRT STOP--KAFF!
CRUMBLE
COUGH COUGH KAFF HACK
YEEK!

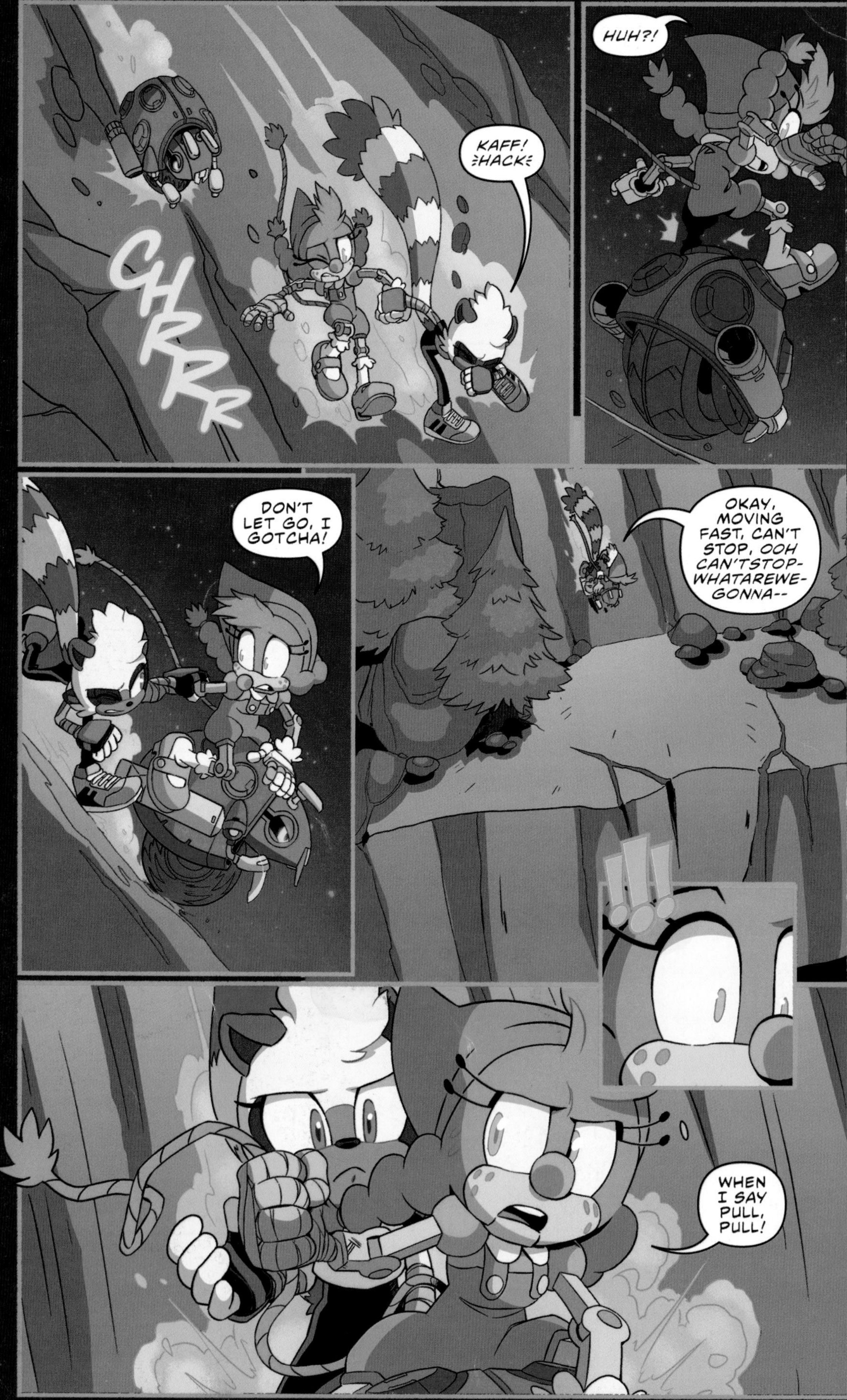
CHRRR
KAFF! HACK
HUH?!
DON'T LET GO, I GOTCHA!
OKAY, MOVING FAST, CAN'T STOP, OOH CAN'TSTOP-WHATAREWE-GONNA--
!!!
WHEN I SAY PULL, PULL!

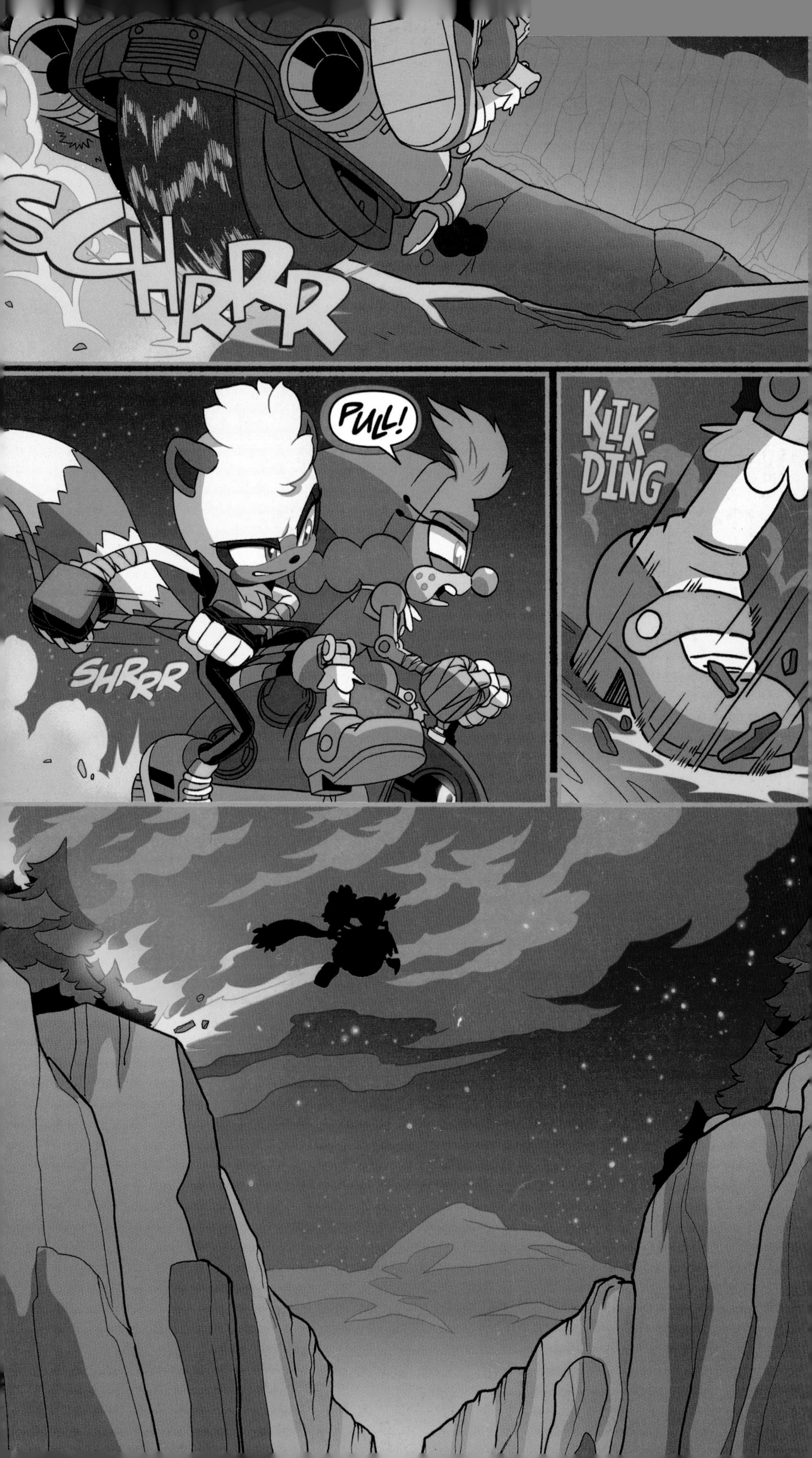
SCHRRR
PULL!
SHRRR
KLIK-DING

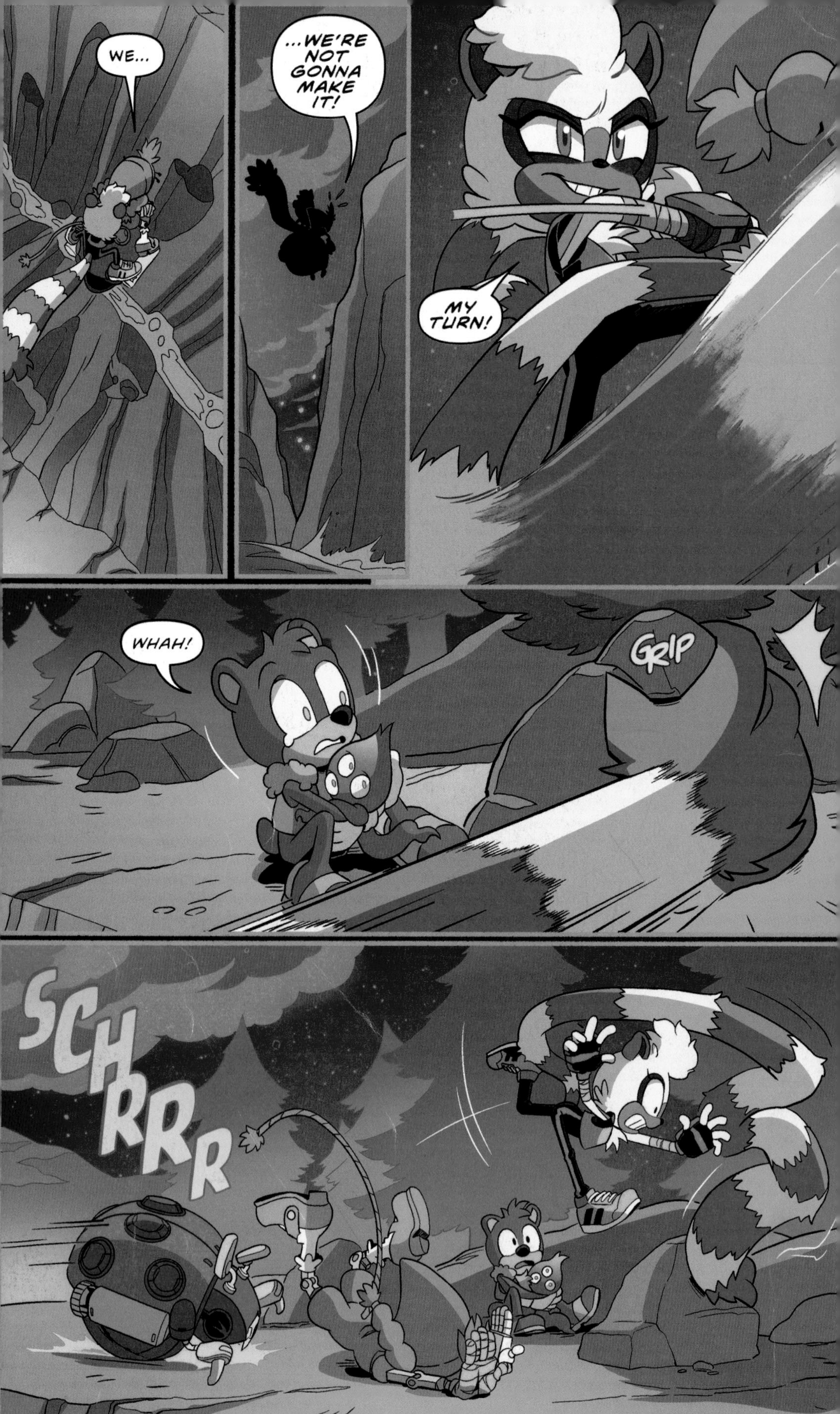
WE...
...WE'RE NOT GONNA MAKE IT!
MY TURN!
WHAH!
GRIP
SCHRRRR

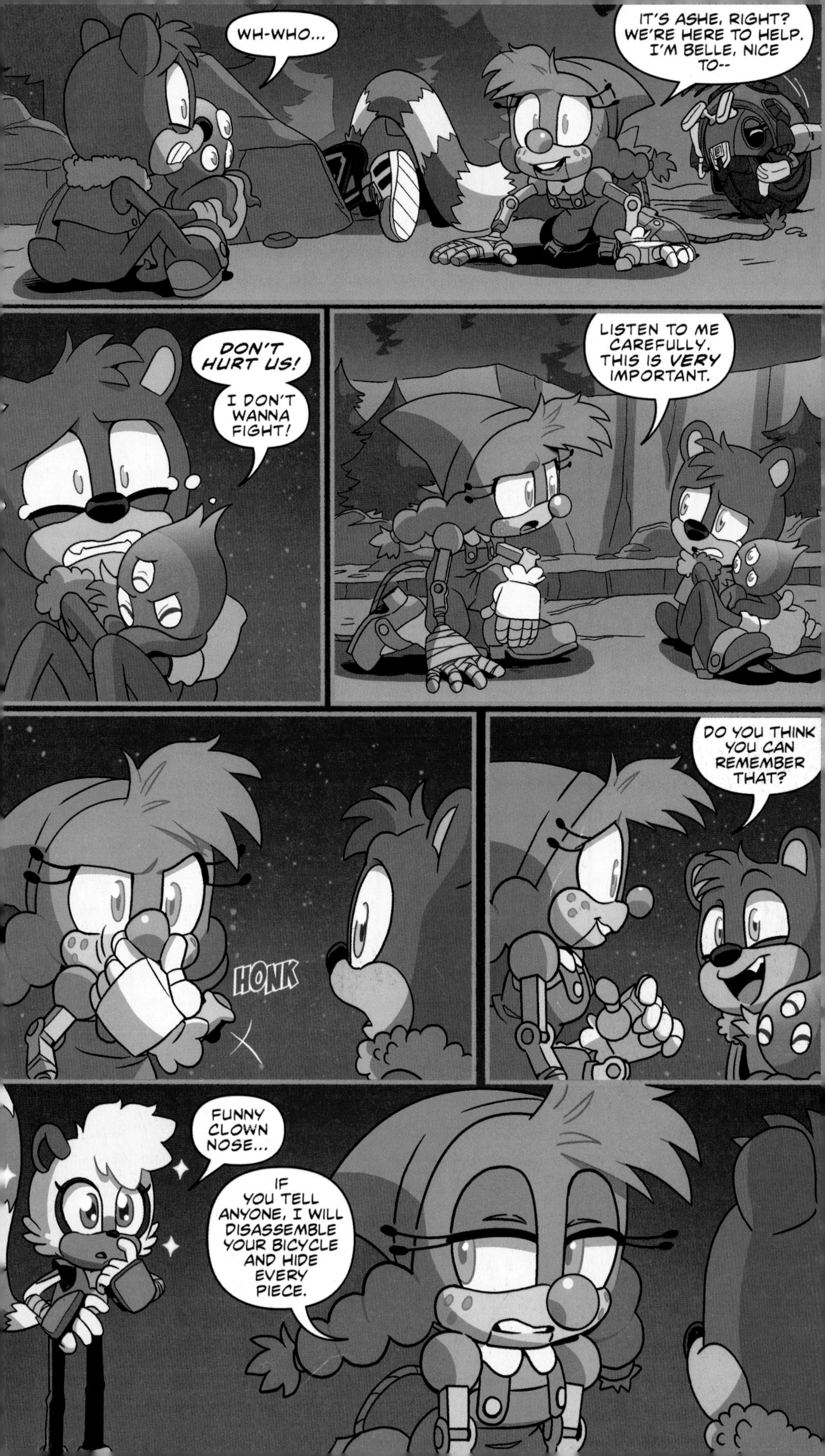
WH-WHO...
IT'S ASHE, RIGHT? WE'RE HERE TO HELP. I'M BELLE, NICE TO--
DON'T HURT US!
I DON'T WANNA FIGHT!
LISTEN TO ME CAREFULLY. THIS IS VERY IMPORTANT.
HONK
DO YOU THINK YOU CAN REMEMBER THAT?
FUNNY CLOWN NOSE...
IF YOU TELL ANYONE, I WILL DISASSEMBLE YOUR BICYCLE AND HIDE EVERY PIECE.

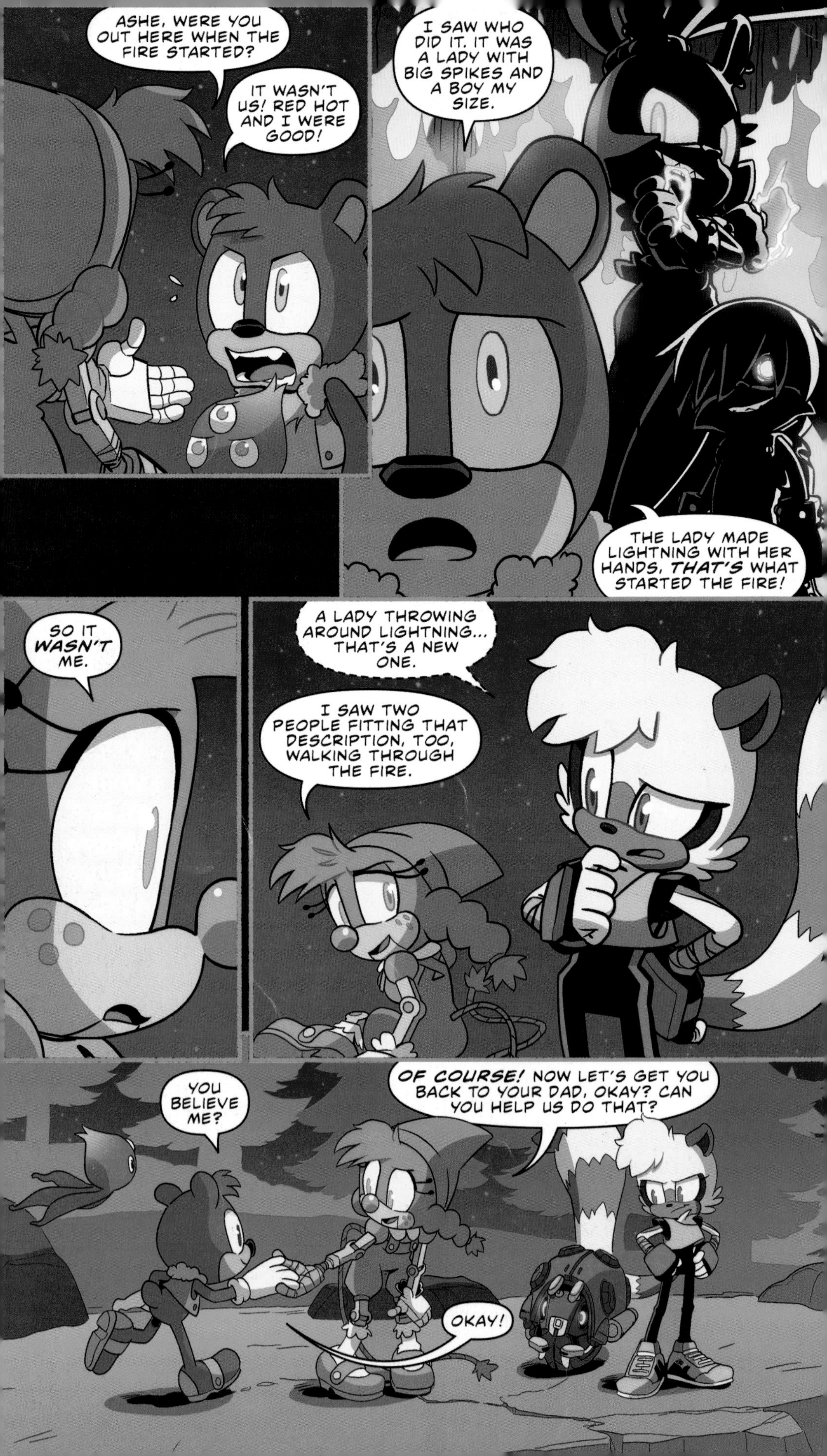
ASHE, WERE YOU OUT HERE WHEN THE FIRE STARTED?
IT WASN'T US! RED HOT AND I WERE GOOD!
I SAW WHO DID IT. IT WAS A LADY WITH BIG SPIKES AND A BOY MY SIZE.
THE LADY MADE LIGHTNING WITH HER HANDS, *THAT'S* WHAT STARTED THE FIRE!
SO IT *WASN'T* ME.
A LADY THROWING AROUND LIGHTNING... THAT'S A NEW ONE.
I SAW TWO PEOPLE FITTING THAT DESCRIPTION, TOO, WALKING THROUGH THE FIRE.
YOU BELIEVE ME?
OF COURSE! NOW LET'S GET YOU BACK TO YOUR DAD, OKAY? CAN YOU HELP US DO THAT?
OKAY!

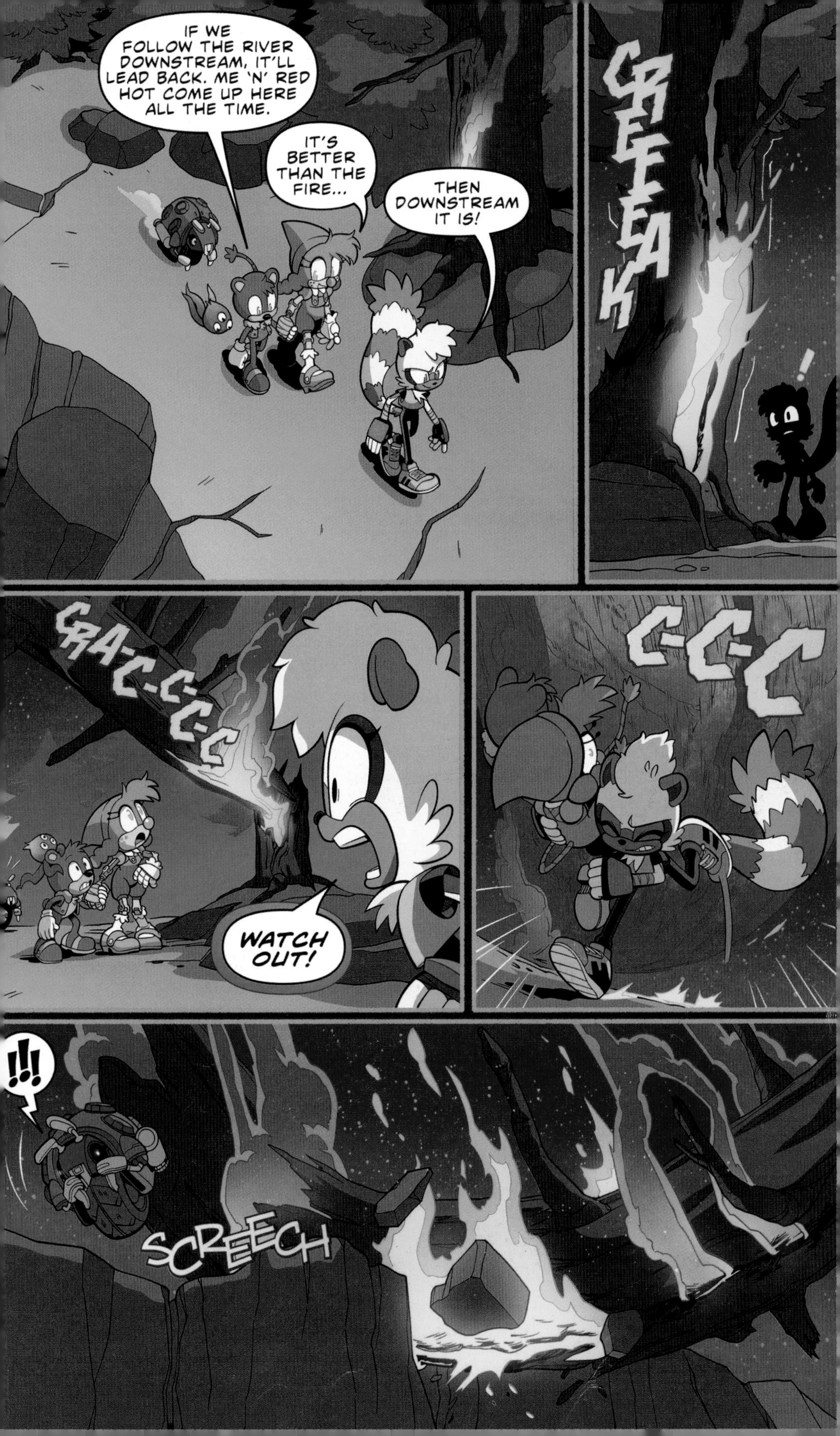
IF WE FOLLOW THE RIVER DOWNSTREAM, IT'LL LEAD BACK. ME 'N' RED HOT COME UP HERE ALL THE TIME.
IT'S BETTER THAN THE FIRE...
THEN DOWNSTREAM IT IS!
CREEEAK
!
CRA-C-C-C-C
WATCH OUT!
C-C-C
!!!
SCREECH

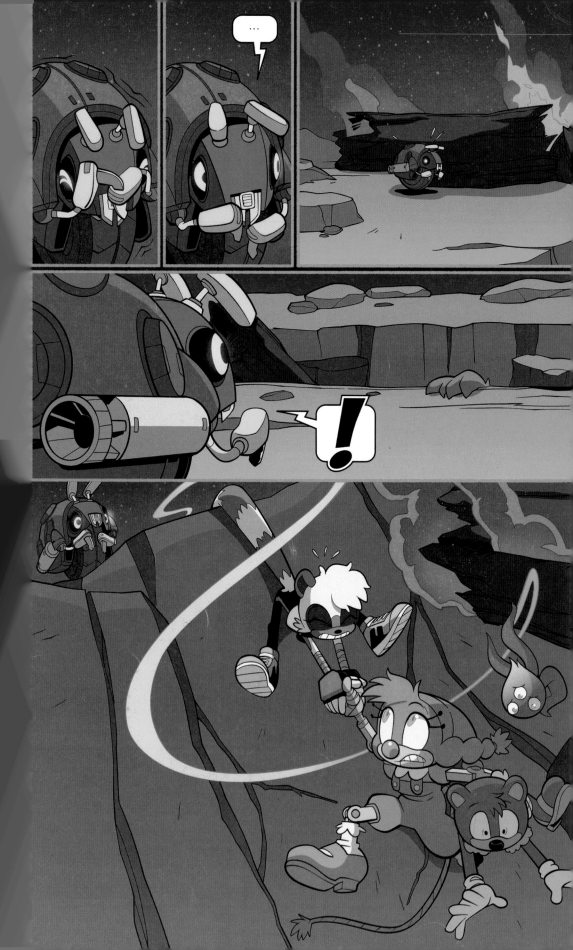

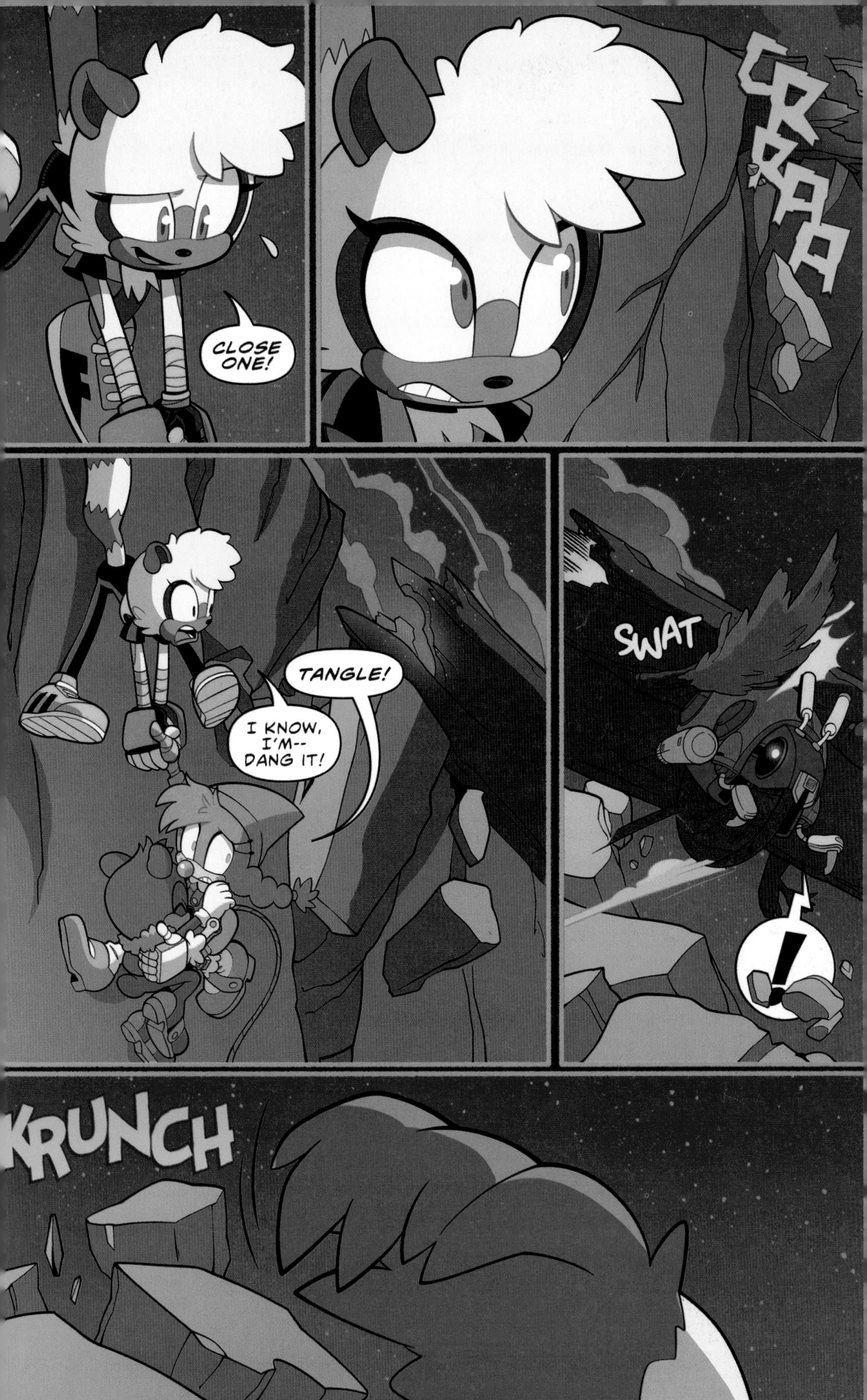
CLOSE ONE!
CRAAA
TANGLE!
I KNOW, I'M-- DANG IT!
SWAT
!
KRUNCH

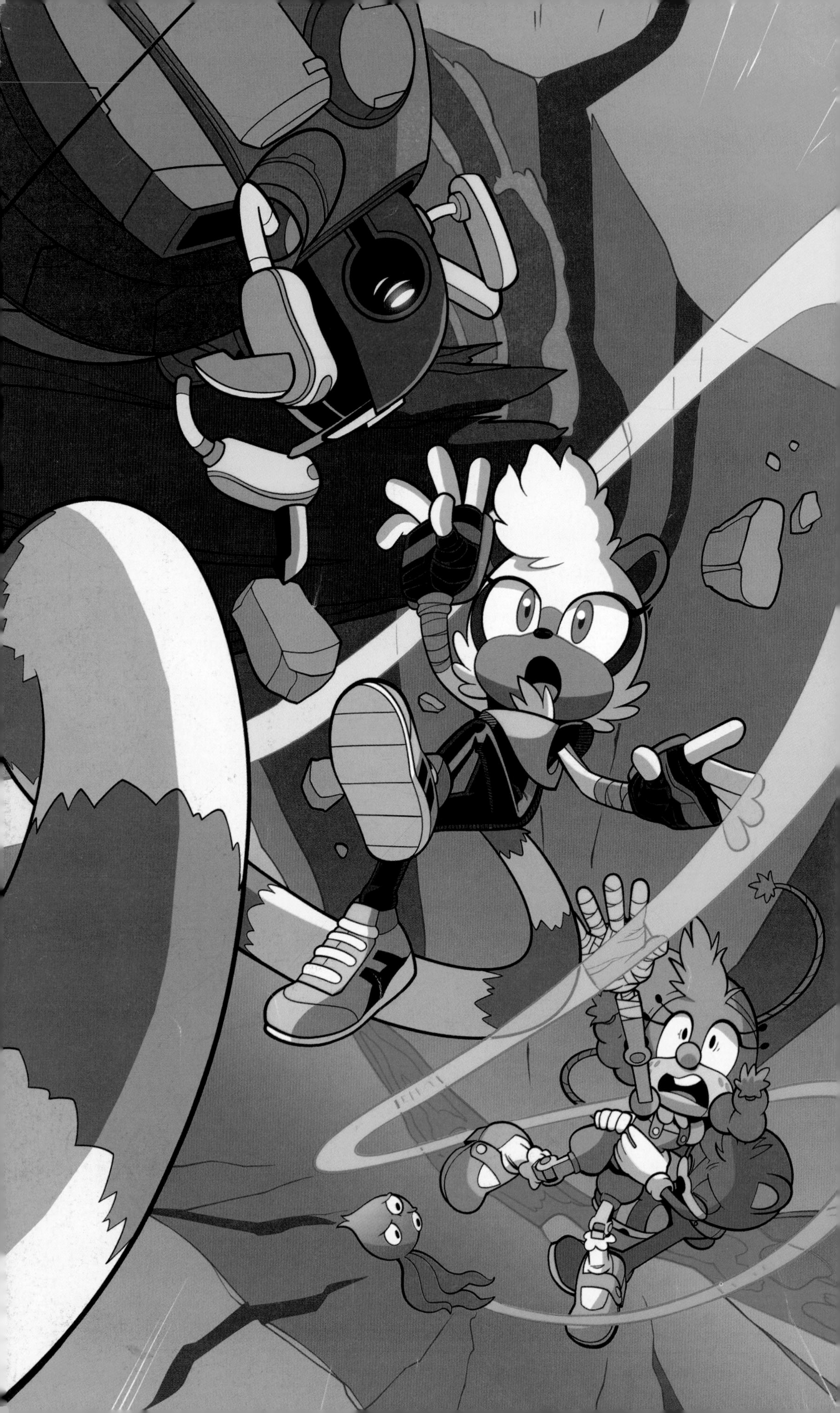

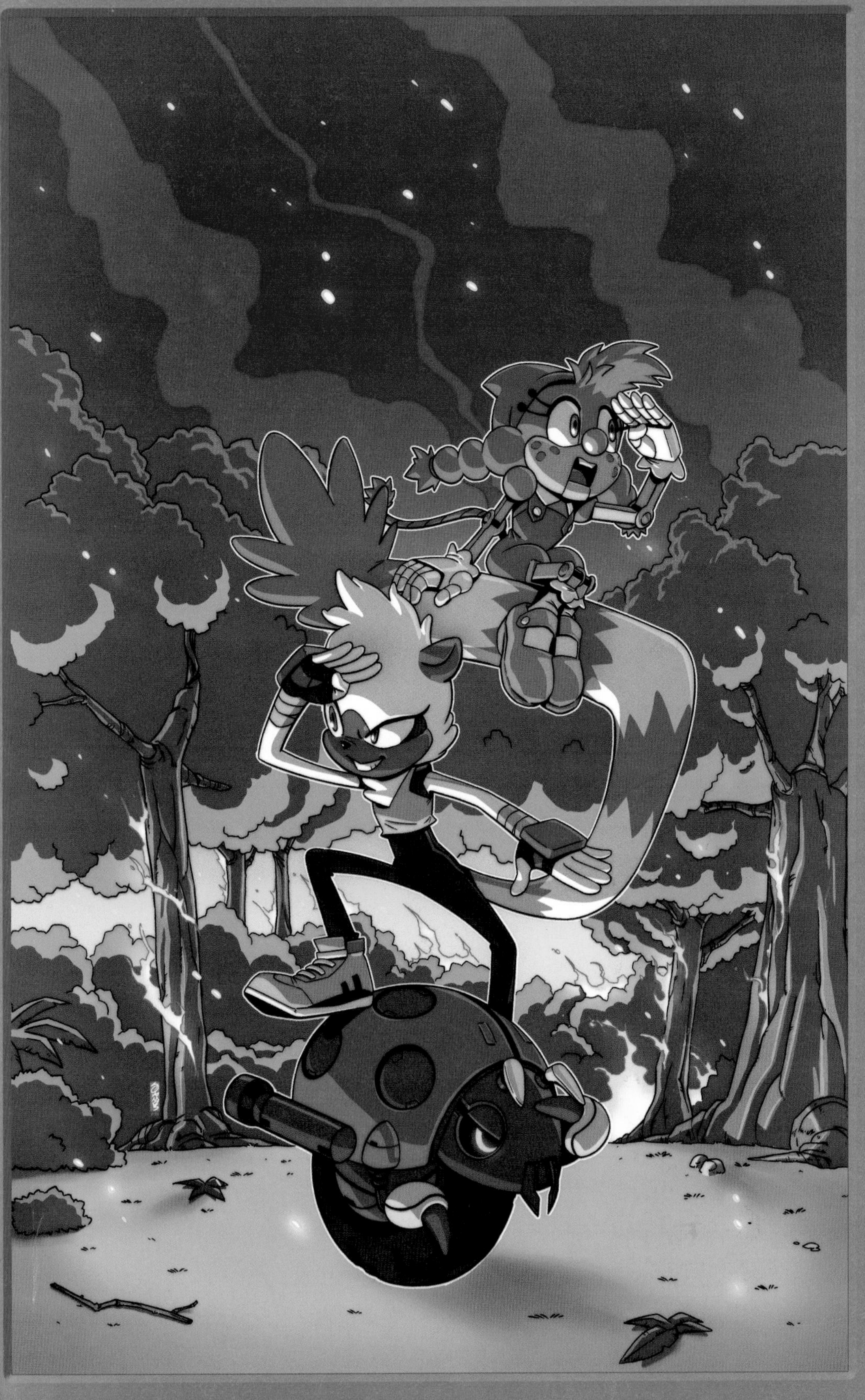

ART BY **RYAN JAMPOLE**

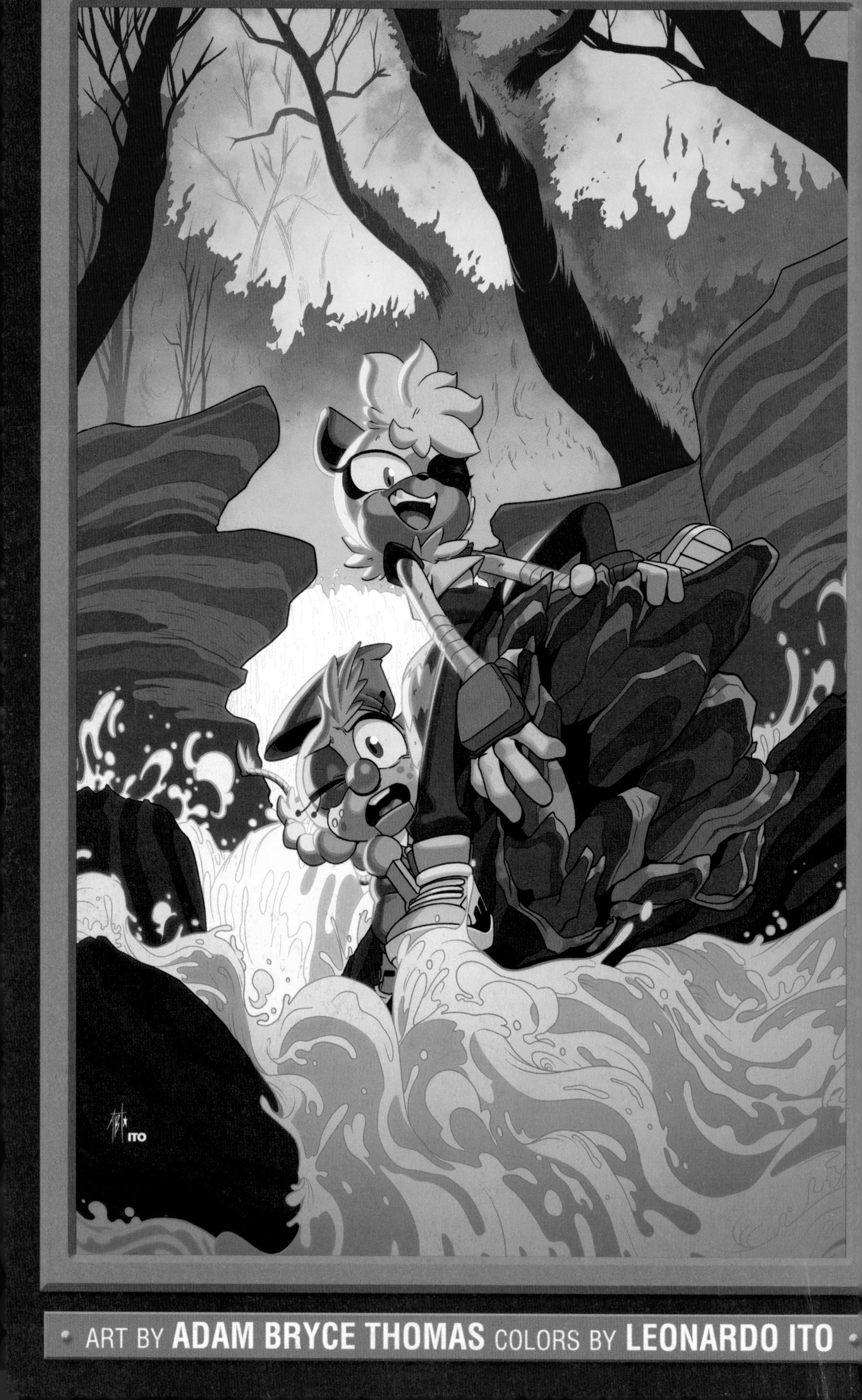
ABT ITO

ART BY **ADAM BRYCE THOMAS** COLORS BY **LEONARDO ITO**

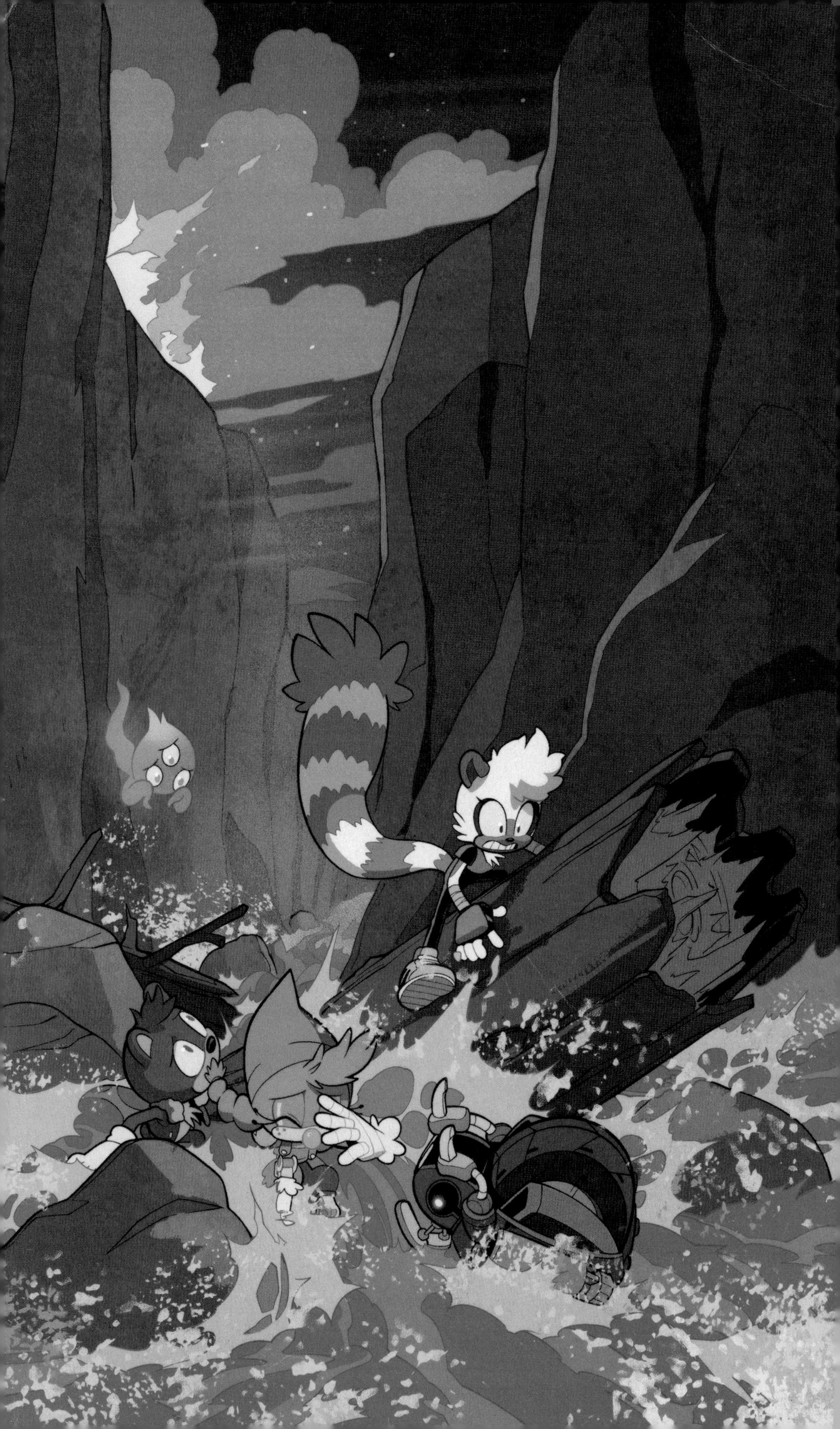

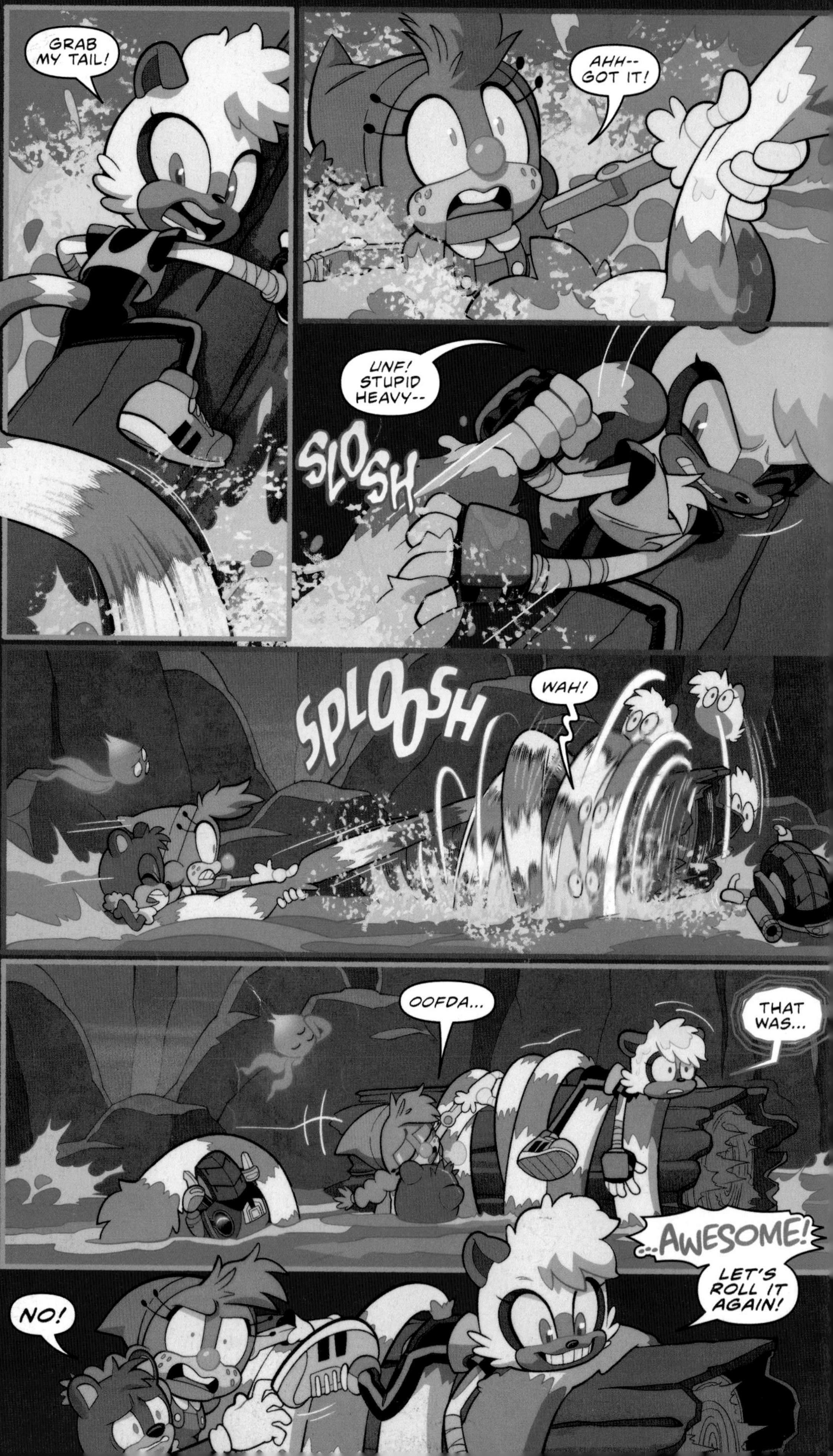
GRAB MY TAIL!
AHH-- GOT IT!
UNF! STUPID HEAVY--
SLOSH
SPLOOSH
WAH!
OOFDA...
THAT WAS...
...AWESOME!
LET'S ROLL IT AGAIN!
NO!

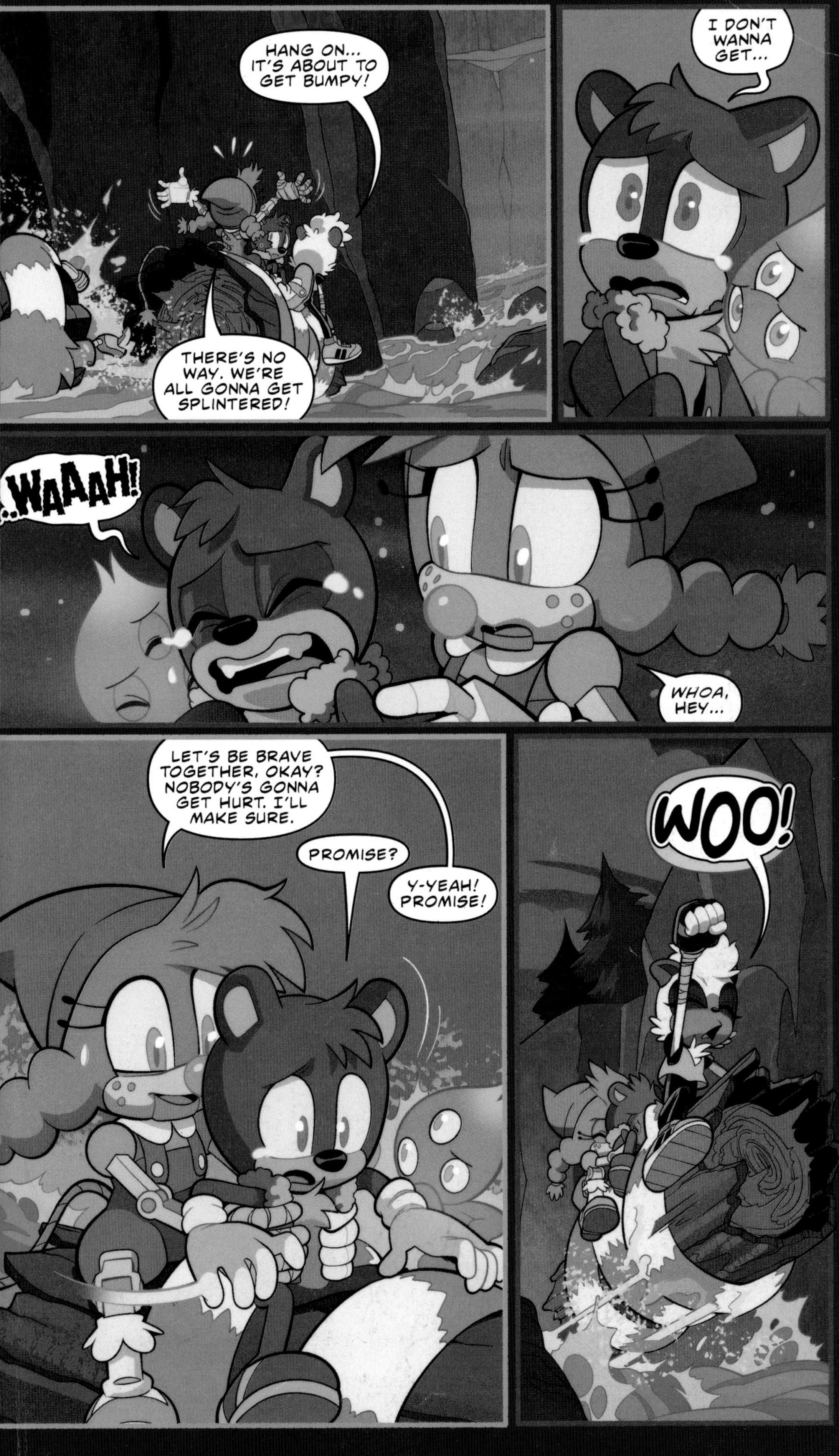
HANG ON... IT'S ABOUT TO GET BUMPY!
THERE'S NO WAY. WE'RE ALL GONNA GET SPLINTERED!
I DON'T WANNA GET...
...WAAAH!
WHOA, HEY...
LET'S BE BRAVE TOGETHER, OKAY? NOBODY'S GONNA GET HURT. I'LL MAKE SURE.
PROMISE?
Y-YEAH! PROMISE!
WOO!

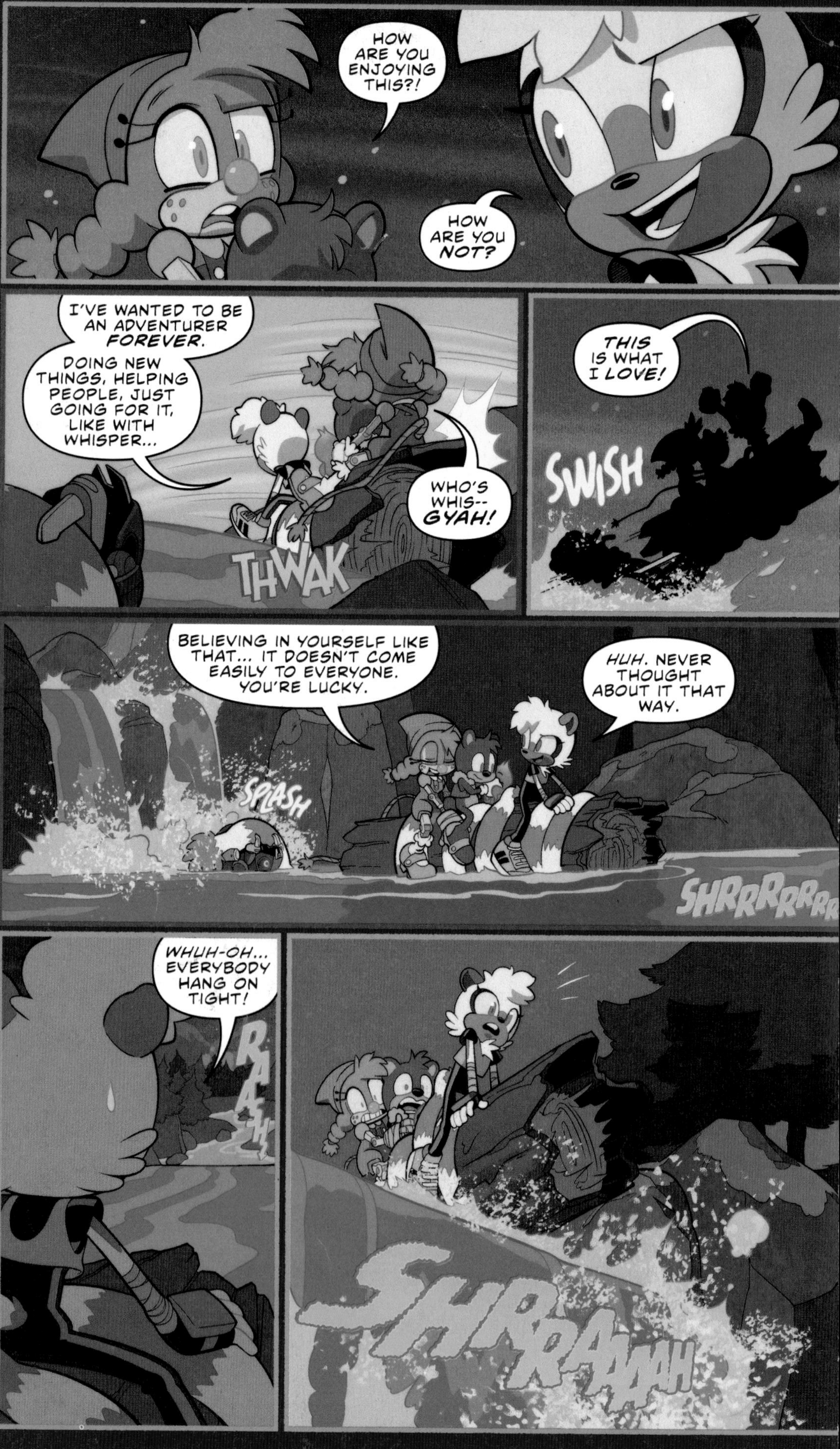
HOW ARE YOU ENJOYING THIS?!
HOW ARE YOU NOT?
I'VE WANTED TO BE AN ADVENTURER FOREVER.
DOING NEW THINGS, HELPING PEOPLE, JUST GOING FOR IT, LIKE WITH WHISPER...
WHO'S WHIS-- GYAH!
THWAK
THIS IS WHAT I LOVE!
SWISH
BELIEVING IN YOURSELF LIKE THAT... IT DOESN'T COME EASILY TO EVERYONE. YOU'RE LUCKY.
HUH. NEVER THOUGHT ABOUT IT THAT WAY.
SPLASH
SHRRRRRR
WHUH-OH... EVERYBODY HANG ON TIGHT!
RAAAH
SHRAAAH

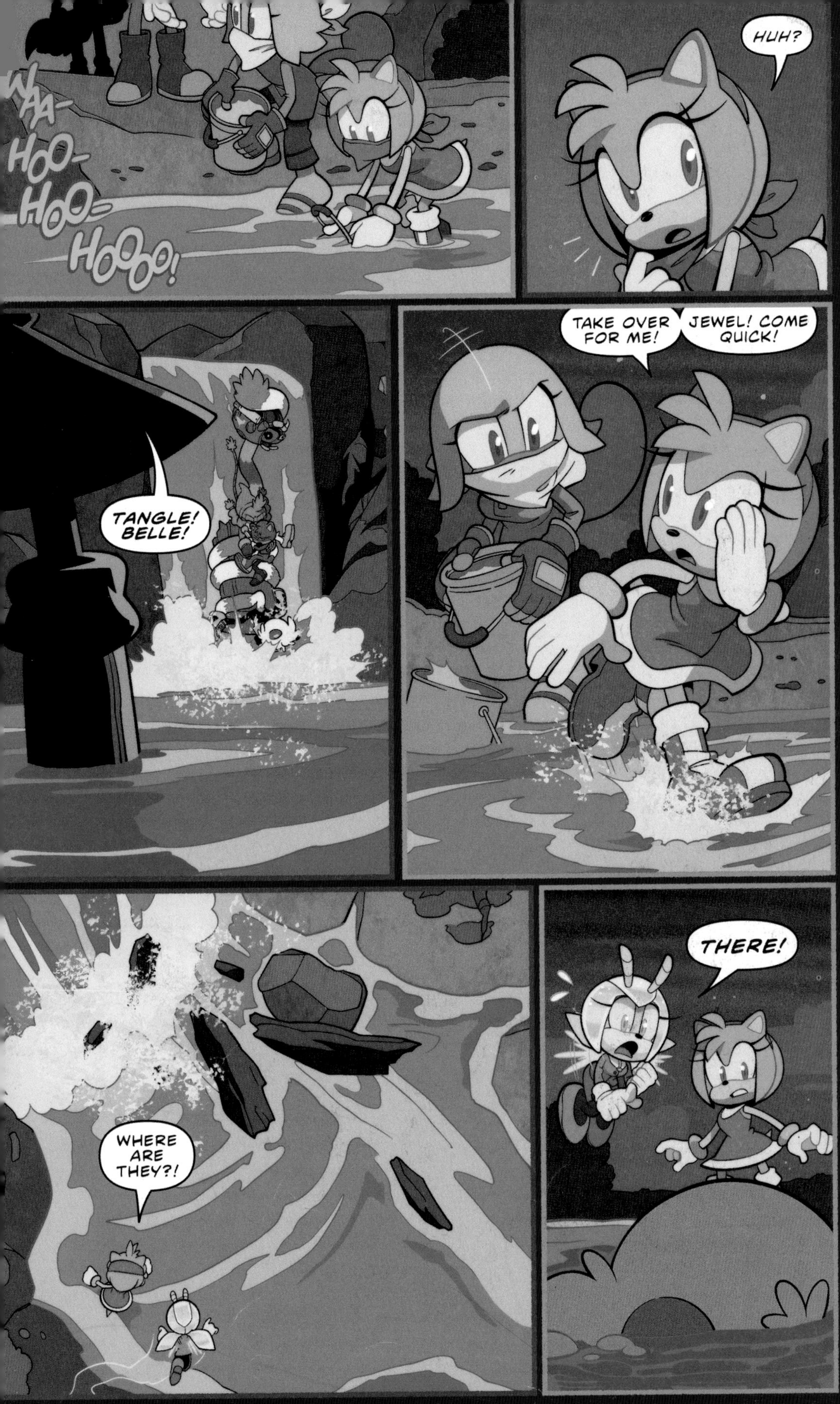
WAA-HOO-HOO-HOOOO!
HUH?
TANGLE! BELLE!
TAKE OVER FOR ME!
JEWEL! COME QUICK!
WHERE ARE THEY?!
THERE!

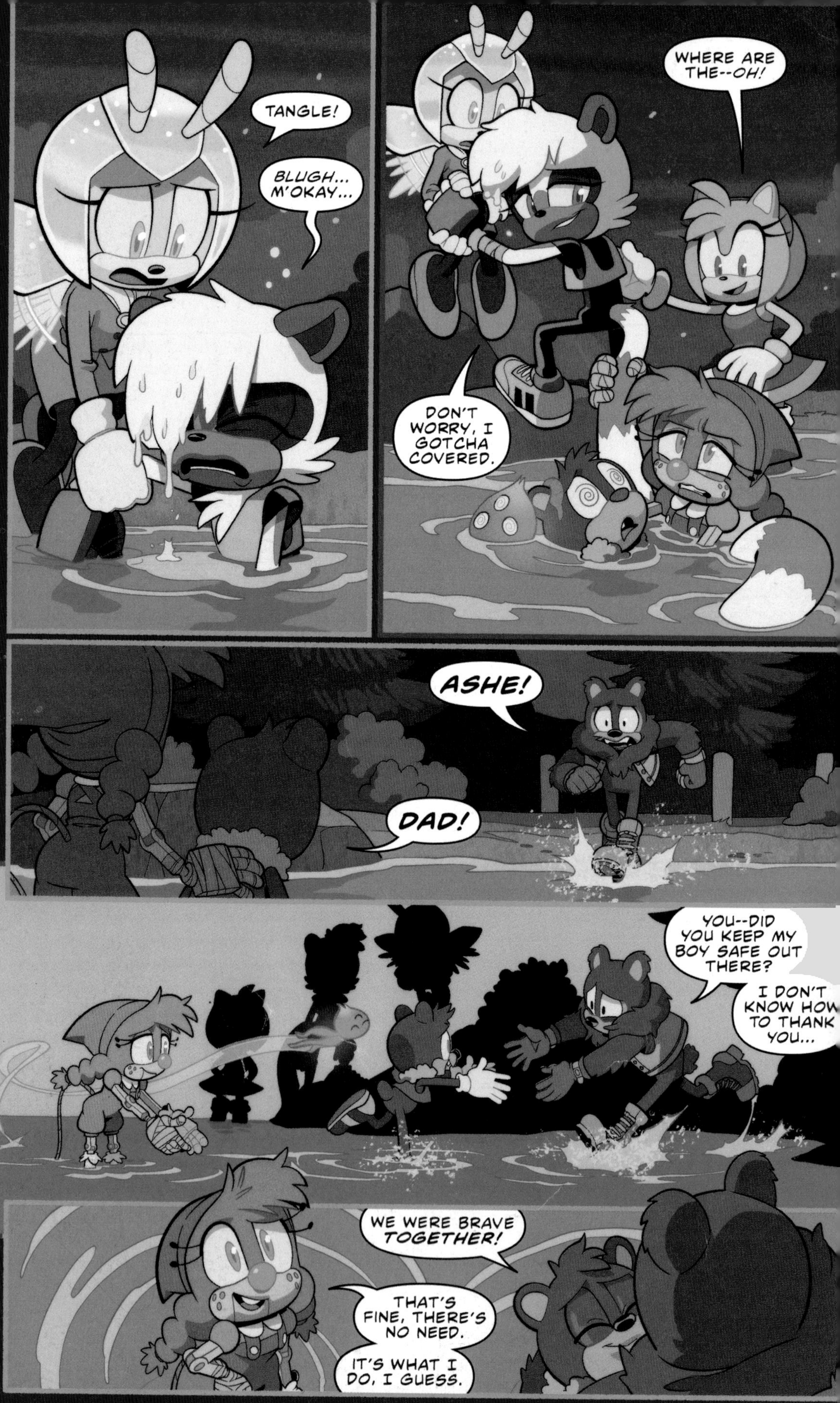
TANGLE!
BLUGH... M'OKAY...
WHERE ARE THE--OH!
DON'T WORRY, I GOTCHA COVERED.
ASHE!
DAD!
YOU--DID YOU KEEP MY BOY SAFE OUT THERE?
I DON'T KNOW HOW TO THANK YOU...
WE WERE BRAVE TOGETHER!
THAT'S FINE, THERE'S NO NEED.
IT'S WHAT I DO, I GUESS.

LOOKS LIKE THE CAMPGROUND'S STILL IN ONE PIECE. THAT'S GOOD!

FOR NOW...

THE FIREBREAK WON'T HOLD FOR--

--BADNIK!

WAIT! IT'S SAFE!

AT LEAST, WE THINK IT IS...

IT HELPED US GET OUT OF THE WOODS. I GUESS IT'S DEFECTIVE?

A FRIENDLY MOTOBUG? THERE'S A FIRST FOR EVERYTHING.

THEY'RE KINDA CUTE WHEN THEY'RE NOT TRYING TO RUN YOU OVER.

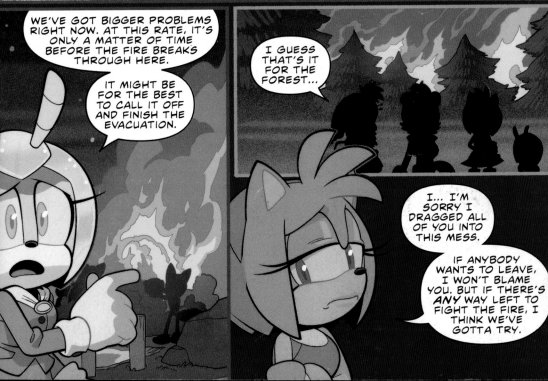

WE'VE GOT BIGGER PROBLEMS RIGHT NOW. AT THIS RATE, IT'S ONLY A MATTER OF TIME BEFORE THE FIRE BREAKS THROUGH HERE.

IT MIGHT BE FOR THE BEST TO CALL IT OFF AND FINISH THE EVACUATION.

I GUESS THAT'S IT FOR THE FOREST...

I... I'M SORRY I DRAGGED ALL OF YOU INTO THIS MESS.

IF ANYBODY WANTS TO LEAVE, I WON'T BLAME YOU. BUT IF THERE'S ANY WAY LEFT TO FIGHT THE FIRE, I THINK WE'VE GOTTA TRY.

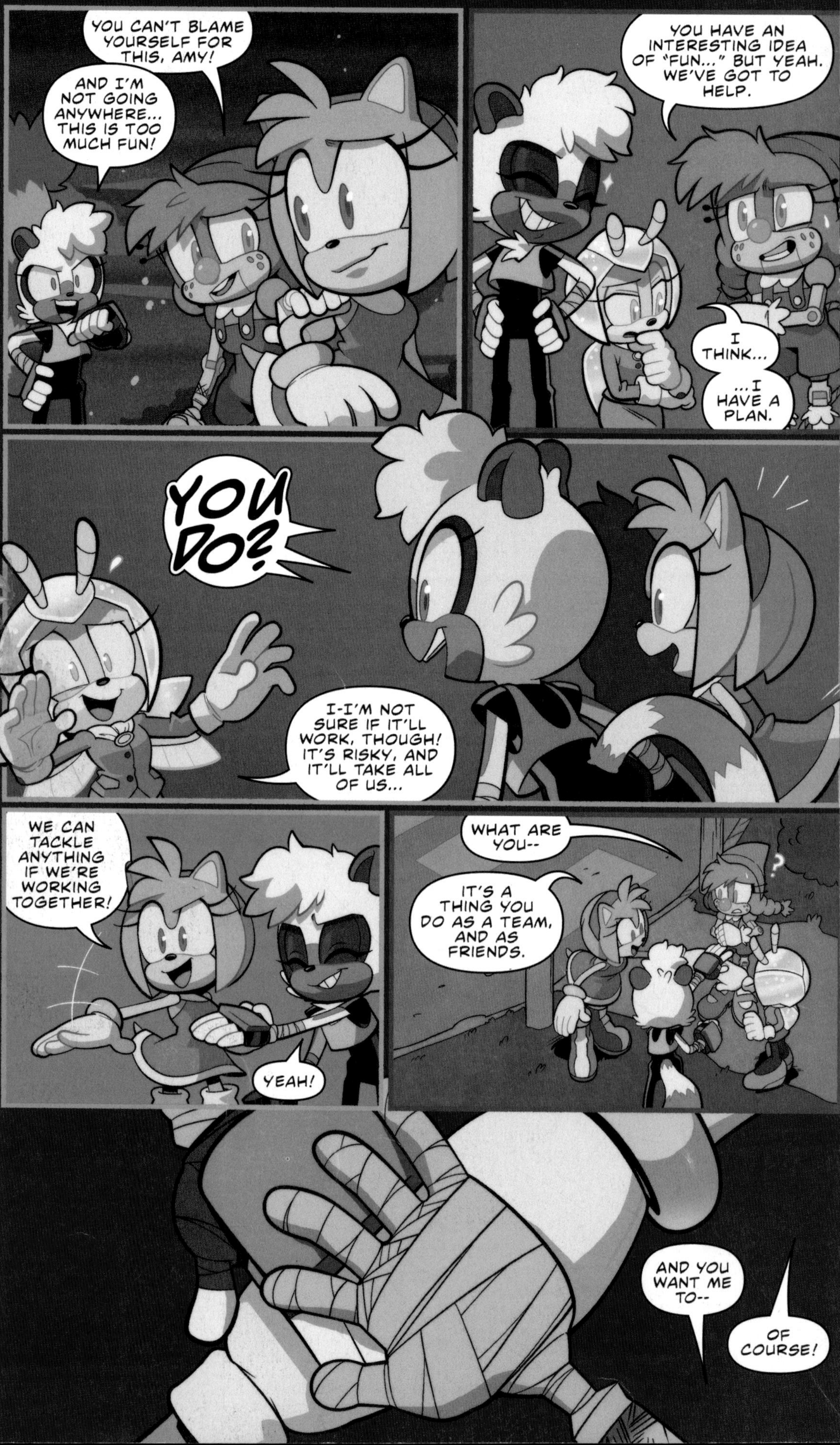
YOU CAN'T BLAME YOURSELF FOR THIS, AMY!
AND I'M NOT GOING ANYWHERE... THIS IS TOO MUCH FUN!
YOU HAVE AN INTERESTING IDEA OF "FUN..." BUT YEAH. WE'VE GOT TO HELP.
I THINK...
...I HAVE A PLAN.
YOU DO?
I-I'M NOT SURE IF IT'LL WORK, THOUGH! IT'S RISKY, AND IT'LL TAKE ALL OF US...
WE CAN TACKLE ANYTHING IF WE'RE WORKING TOGETHER!
YEAH!
WHAT ARE YOU--
IT'S A THING YOU DO AS A TEAM, AND AS FRIENDS.
AND YOU WANT ME TO--
OF COURSE!

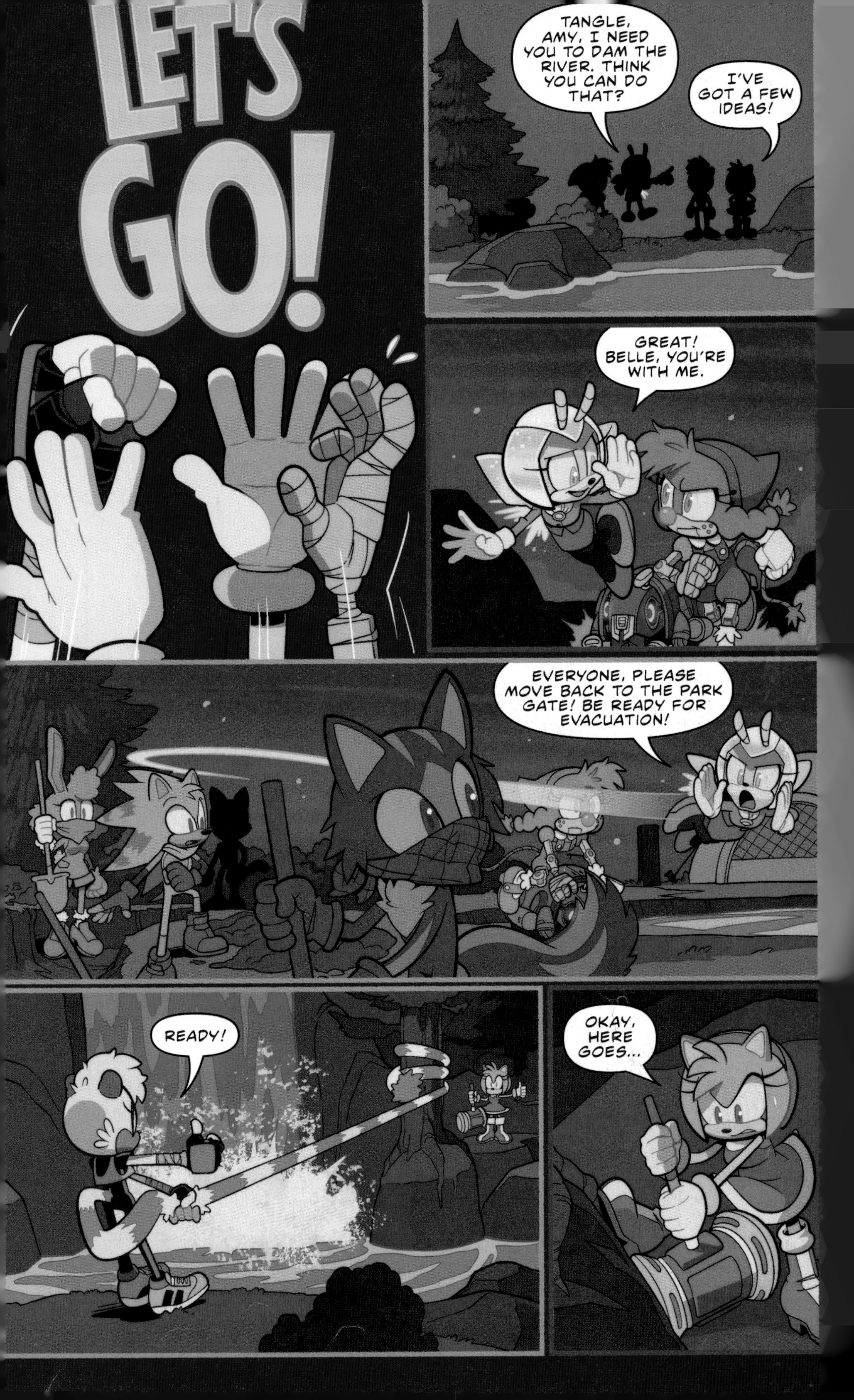
LET'S GO!
TANGLE, AMY, I NEED YOU TO DAM THE RIVER. THINK YOU CAN DO THAT?
I'VE GOT A FEW IDEAS!
GREAT! BELLE, YOU'RE WITH ME.
EVERYONE, PLEASE MOVE BACK TO THE PARK GATE! BE READY FOR EVACUATION!
READY!
OKAY, HERE GOES...

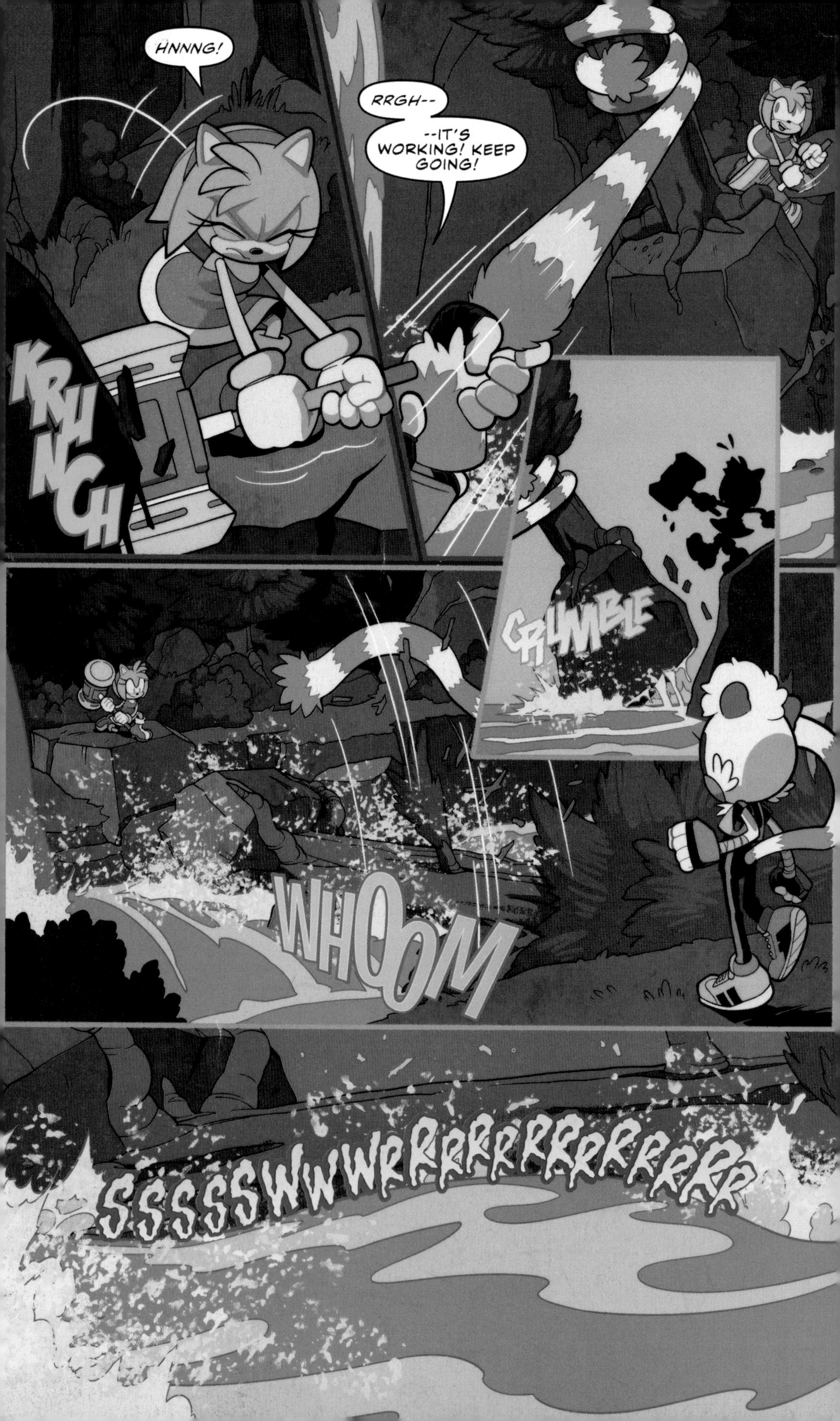
HNNNG!
RRGH--
--IT'S WORKING! KEEP GOING!
KRUNCH
CRUMBLE
WHOOM
SSSSSWWWRRRRRRRRRRRRRRR

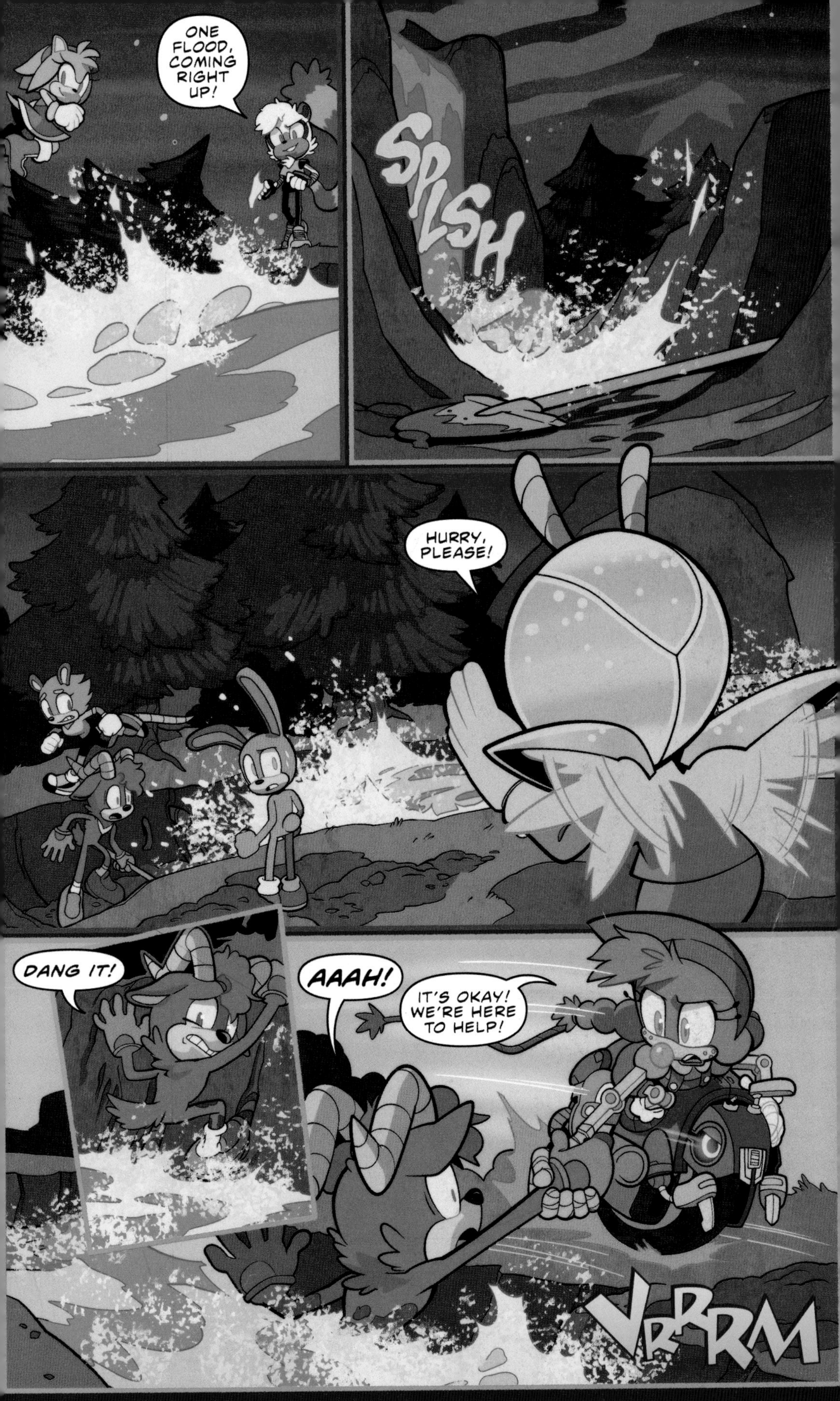
ONE FLOOD, COMING RIGHT UP!
SPLSH
HURRY, PLEASE!
DANG IT!
AAAH!
IT'S OKAY! WE'RE HERE TO HELP!
VRRRM

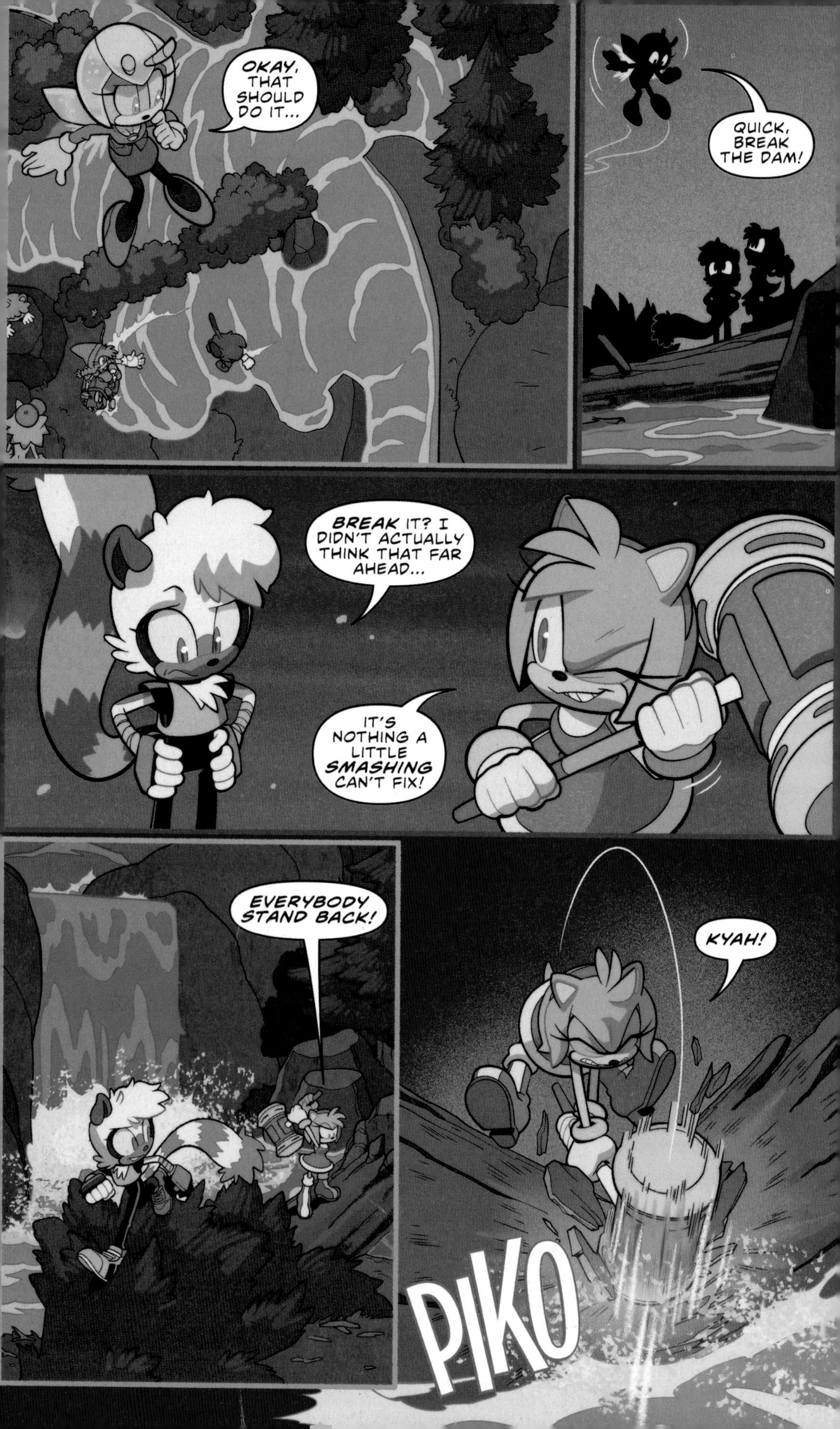
OKAY, THAT SHOULD DO IT...
QUICK, BREAK THE DAM!
BREAK IT? I DIDN'T ACTUALLY THINK THAT FAR AHEAD...
IT'S NOTHING A LITTLE SMASHING CAN'T FIX!
EVERYBODY STAND BACK!
KYAH!
PIKO

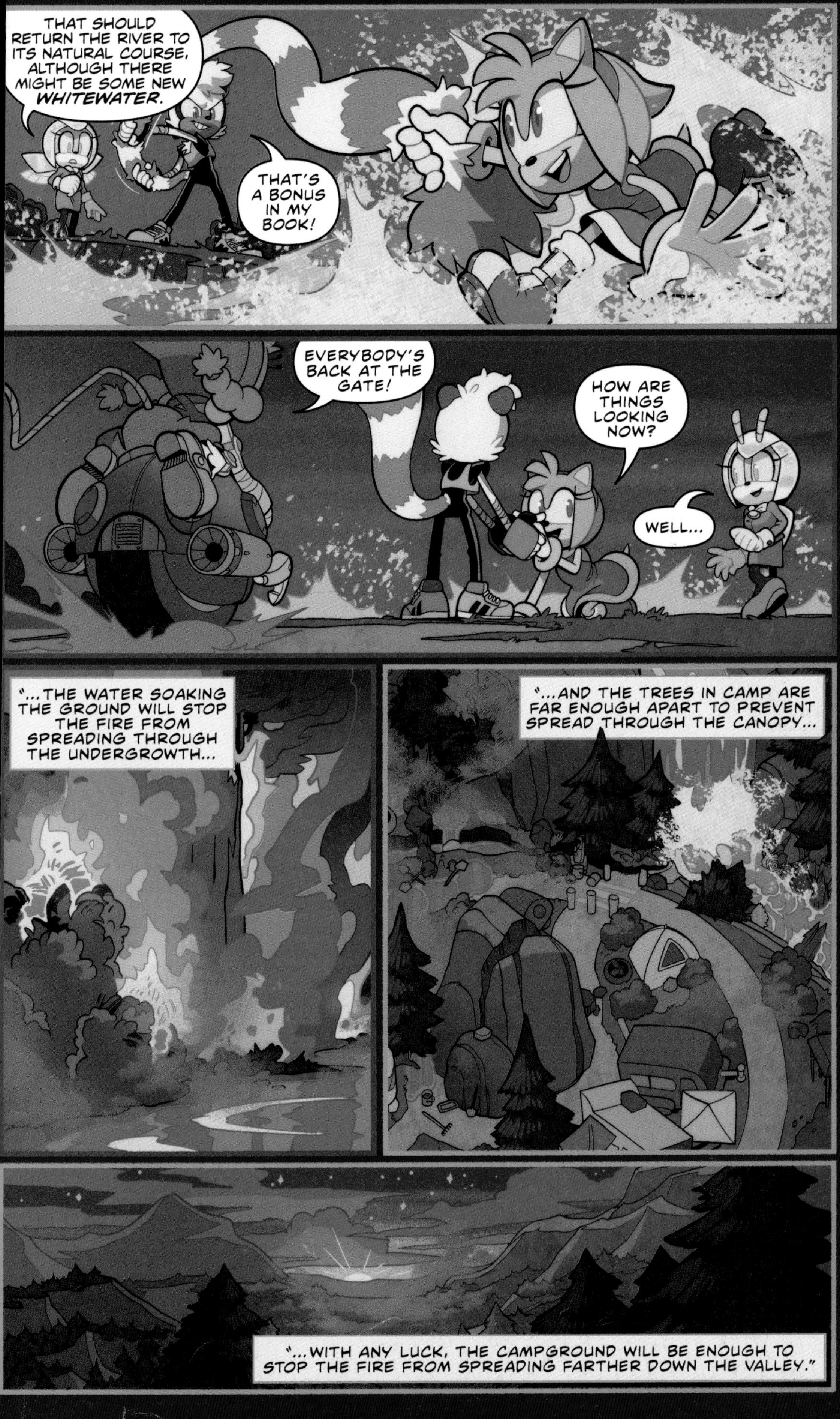
THAT SHOULD RETURN THE RIVER TO ITS NATURAL COURSE, ALTHOUGH THERE MIGHT BE SOME NEW WHITEWATER.
THAT'S A BONUS IN MY BOOK!
EVERYBODY'S BACK AT THE GATE!
HOW ARE THINGS LOOKING NOW?
WELL...
"...THE WATER SOAKING THE GROUND WILL STOP THE FIRE FROM SPREADING THROUGH THE UNDERGROWTH...
"...AND THE TREES IN CAMP ARE FAR ENOUGH APART TO PREVENT SPREAD THROUGH THE CANOPY...
"...WITH ANY LUCK, THE CAMPGROUND WILL BE ENOUGH TO STOP THE FIRE FROM SPREADING FARTHER DOWN THE VALLEY."

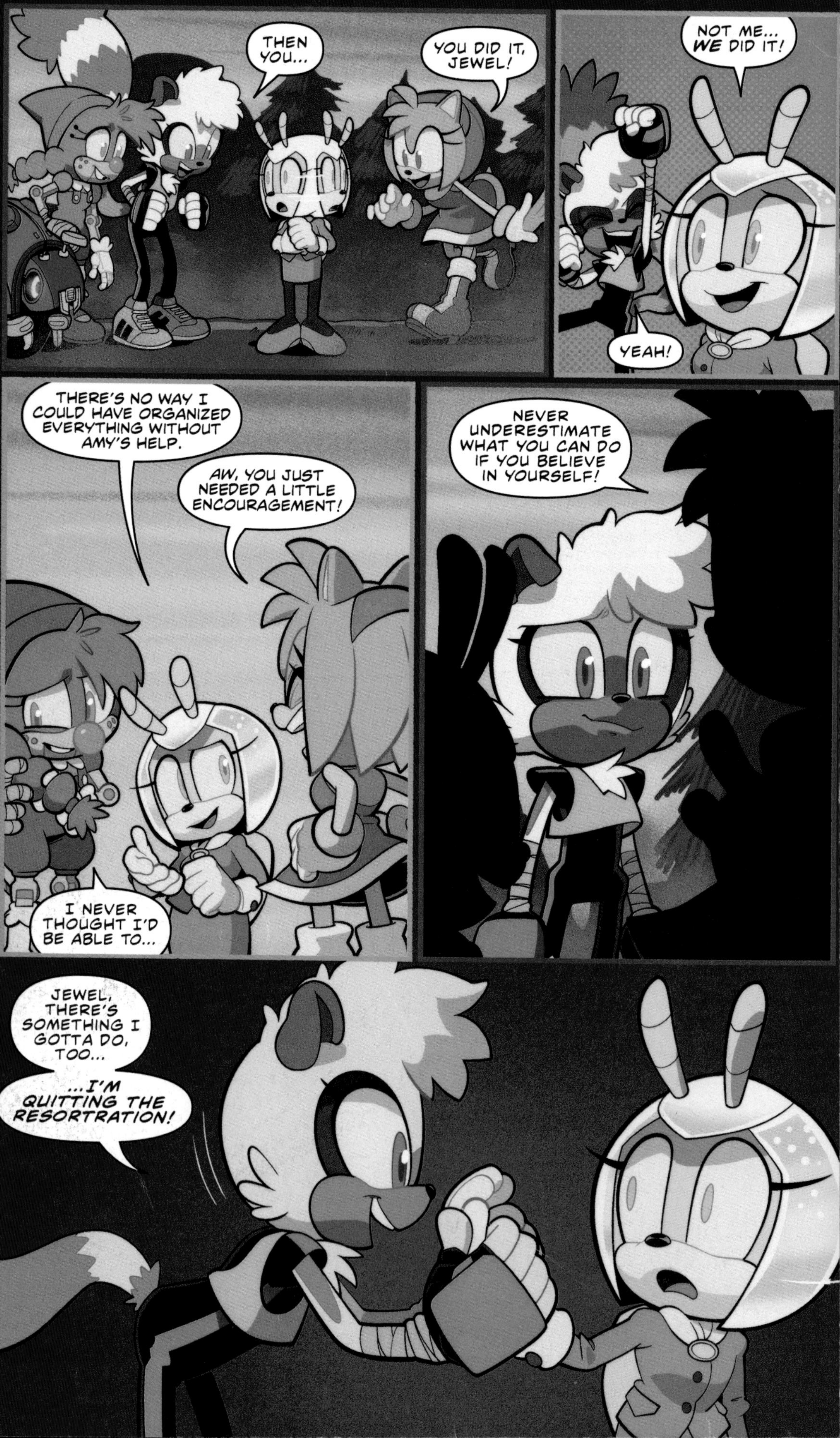
THEN YOU...
YOU DID IT, JEWEL!
NOT ME... WE DID IT!
YEAH!
THERE'S NO WAY I COULD HAVE ORGANIZED EVERYTHING WITHOUT AMY'S HELP.
AW, YOU JUST NEEDED A LITTLE ENCOURAGEMENT!
I NEVER THOUGHT I'D BE ABLE TO...
NEVER UNDERESTIMATE WHAT YOU CAN DO IF YOU BELIEVE IN YOURSELF!
JEWEL, THERE'S SOMETHING I GOTTA DO, TOO...
...I'M QUITTING THE RESORTRATION!

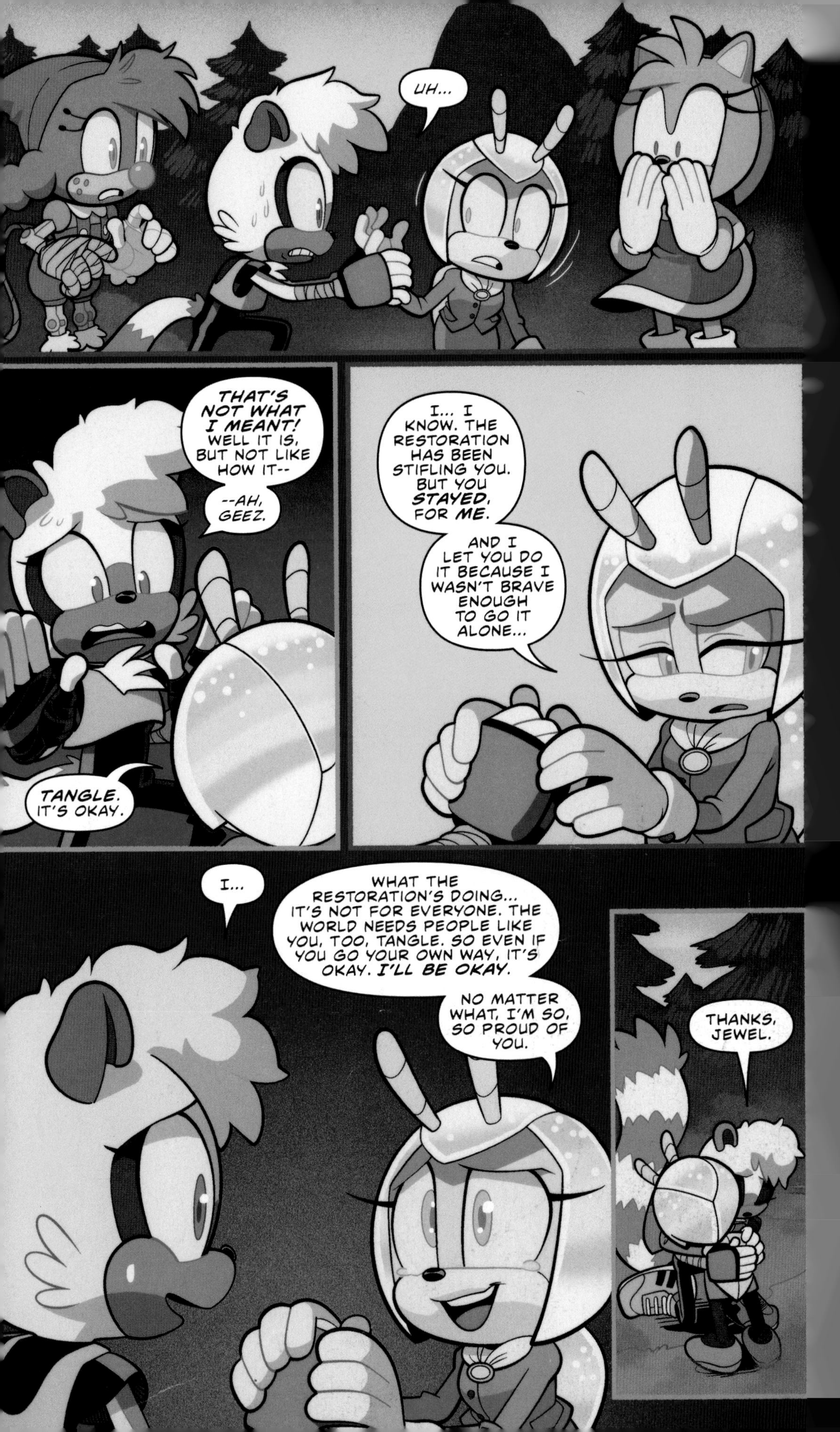

UH...
THAT'S NOT WHAT I MEANT! WELL IT IS, BUT NOT LIKE HOW IT--
--AH, GEEZ.
TANGLE. IT'S OKAY.
I... I KNOW. THE RESTORATION HAS BEEN STIFLING YOU. BUT YOU STAYED, FOR ME.
AND I LET YOU DO IT BECAUSE I WASN'T BRAVE ENOUGH TO GO IT ALONE...
I...
WHAT THE RESTORATION'S DOING... IT'S NOT FOR EVERYONE. THE WORLD NEEDS PEOPLE LIKE YOU, TOO, TANGLE. SO EVEN IF YOU GO YOUR OWN WAY, IT'S OKAY. I'LL BE OKAY.
NO MATTER WHAT, I'M SO, SO PROUD OF YOU.
THANKS, JEWEL.

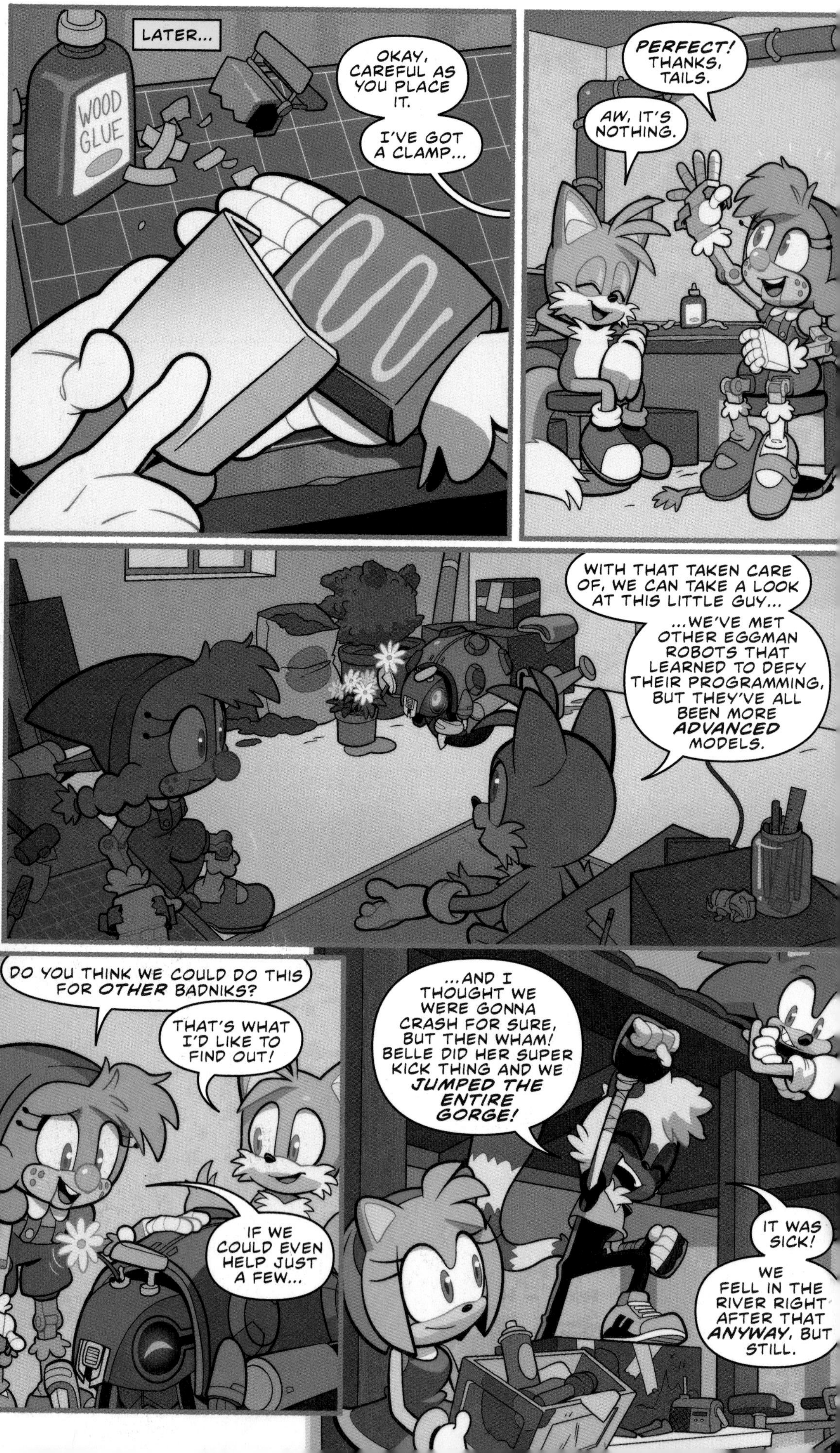
LATER...
WOOD GLUE
OKAY, CAREFUL AS YOU PLACE IT.
I'VE GOT A CLAMP...
PERFECT! THANKS, TAILS.
AW, IT'S NOTHING.
WITH THAT TAKEN CARE OF, WE CAN TAKE A LOOK AT THIS LITTLE GUY...
...WE'VE MET OTHER EGGMAN ROBOTS THAT LEARNED TO DEFY THEIR PROGRAMMING, BUT THEY'VE ALL BEEN MORE ADVANCED MODELS.
DO YOU THINK WE COULD DO THIS FOR OTHER BADNIKS?
THAT'S WHAT I'D LIKE TO FIND OUT!
IF WE COULD EVEN HELP JUST A FEW...
...AND I THOUGHT WE WERE GONNA CRASH FOR SURE, BUT THEN WHAM! BELLE DID HER SUPER KICK THING AND WE JUMPED THE ENTIRE GORGE!
IT WAS SICK!
WE FELL IN THE RIVER RIGHT AFTER THAT ANYWAY, BUT STILL.

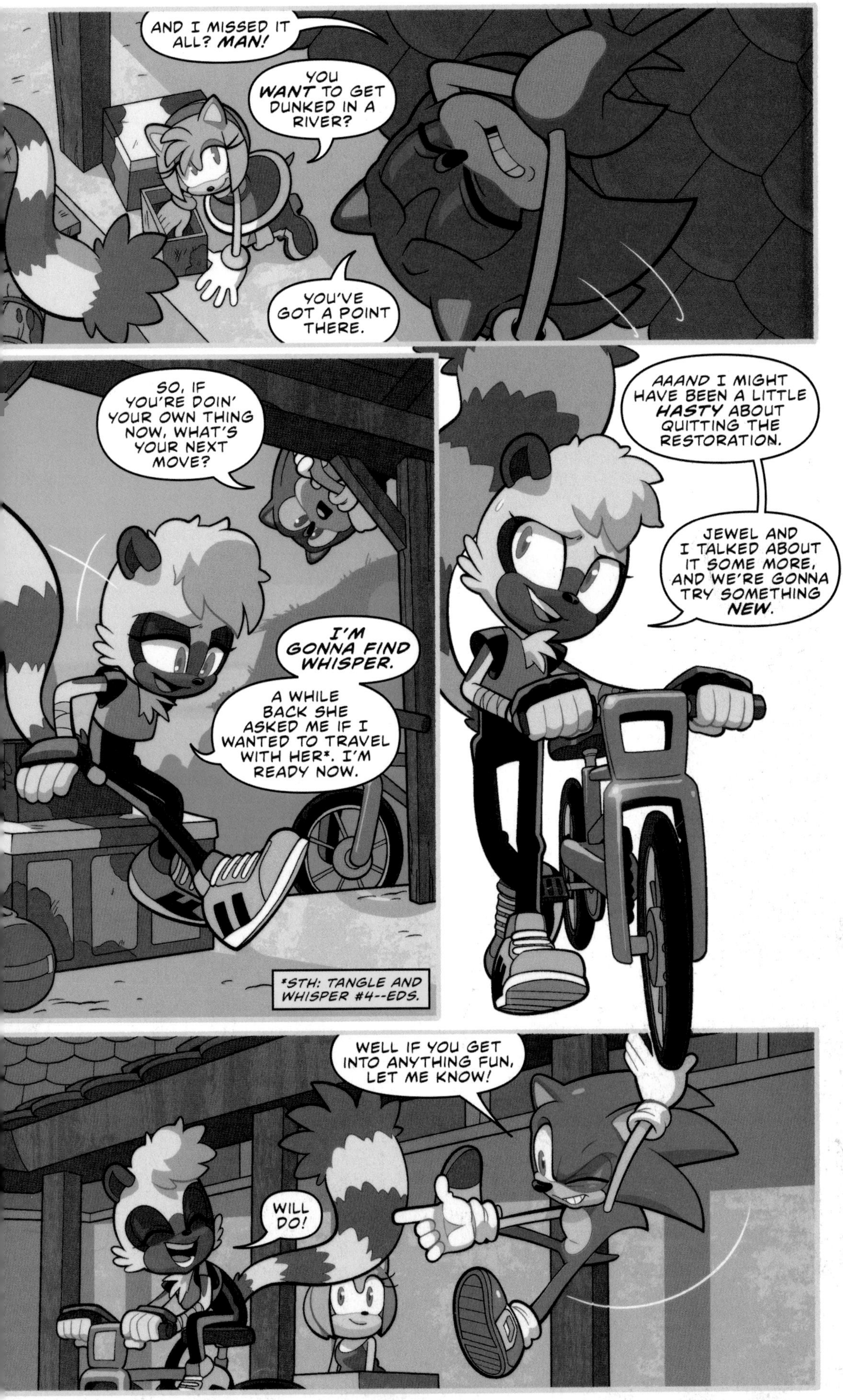
AND I MISSED IT ALL? MAN!
YOU WANT TO GET DUNKED IN A RIVER?
YOU'VE GOT A POINT THERE.
SO, IF YOU'RE DOIN' YOUR OWN THING NOW, WHAT'S YOUR NEXT MOVE?
I'M GONNA FIND WHISPER.
A WHILE BACK SHE ASKED ME IF I WANTED TO TRAVEL WITH HER*. I'M READY NOW.
*STH: TANGLE AND WHISPER #4--EDS.
AAAND I MIGHT HAVE BEEN A LITTLE HASTY ABOUT QUITTING THE RESTORATION.
JEWEL AND I TALKED ABOUT IT SOME MORE, AND WE'RE GONNA TRY SOMETHING NEW.
WELL IF YOU GET INTO ANYTHING FUN, LET ME KNOW!
WILL DO!

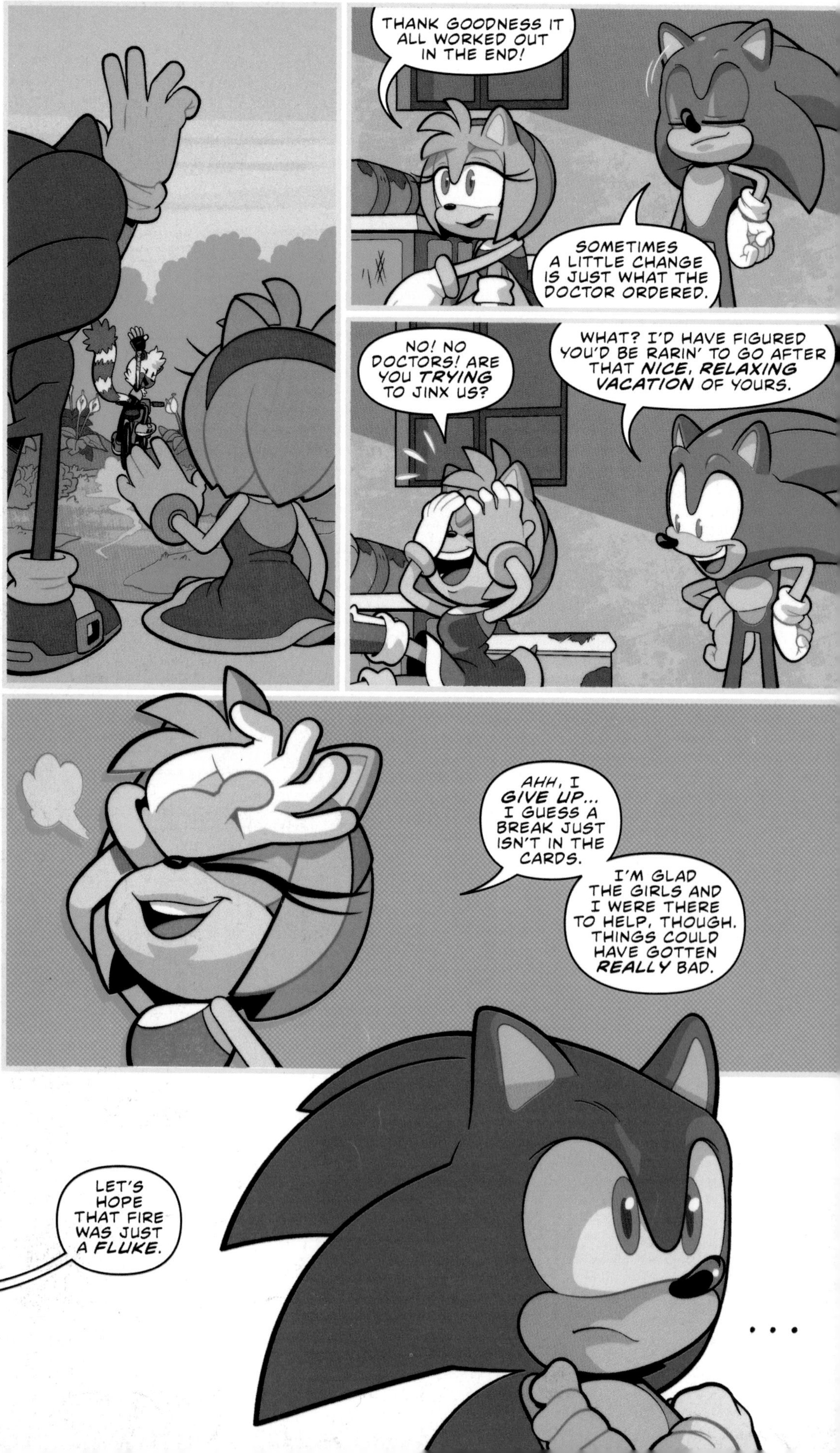
THANK GOODNESS IT ALL WORKED OUT IN THE END!
SOMETIMES A LITTLE CHANGE IS JUST WHAT THE DOCTOR ORDERED.
NO! NO DOCTORS! ARE YOU *TRYING* TO JINX US?
WHAT? I'D HAVE FIGURED YOU'D BE RARIN' TO GO AFTER THAT *NICE, RELAXING VACATION* OF YOURS.
AHH, I *GIVE UP*... I GUESS A BREAK JUST ISN'T IN THE CARDS.
I'M GLAD THE GIRLS AND I WERE THERE TO HELP, THOUGH. THINGS COULD HAVE GOTTEN *REALLY* BAD.
LET'S HOPE THAT FIRE WAS JUST A *FLUKE*.
...

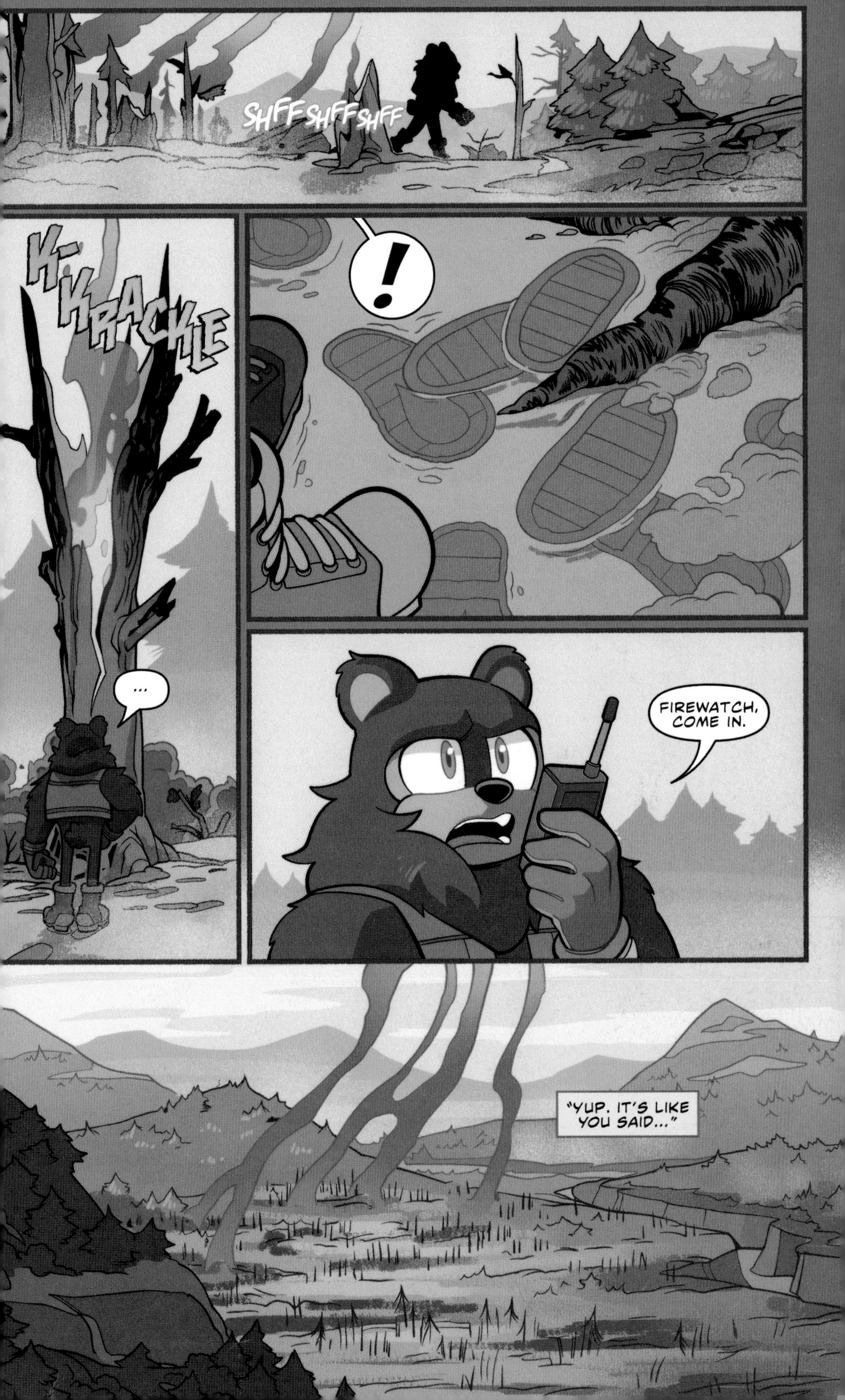
SHFF SHFF SHFF
K-KRACKLE
...
!
FIREWATCH, COME IN.
"YUP. IT'S LIKE YOU SAID..."

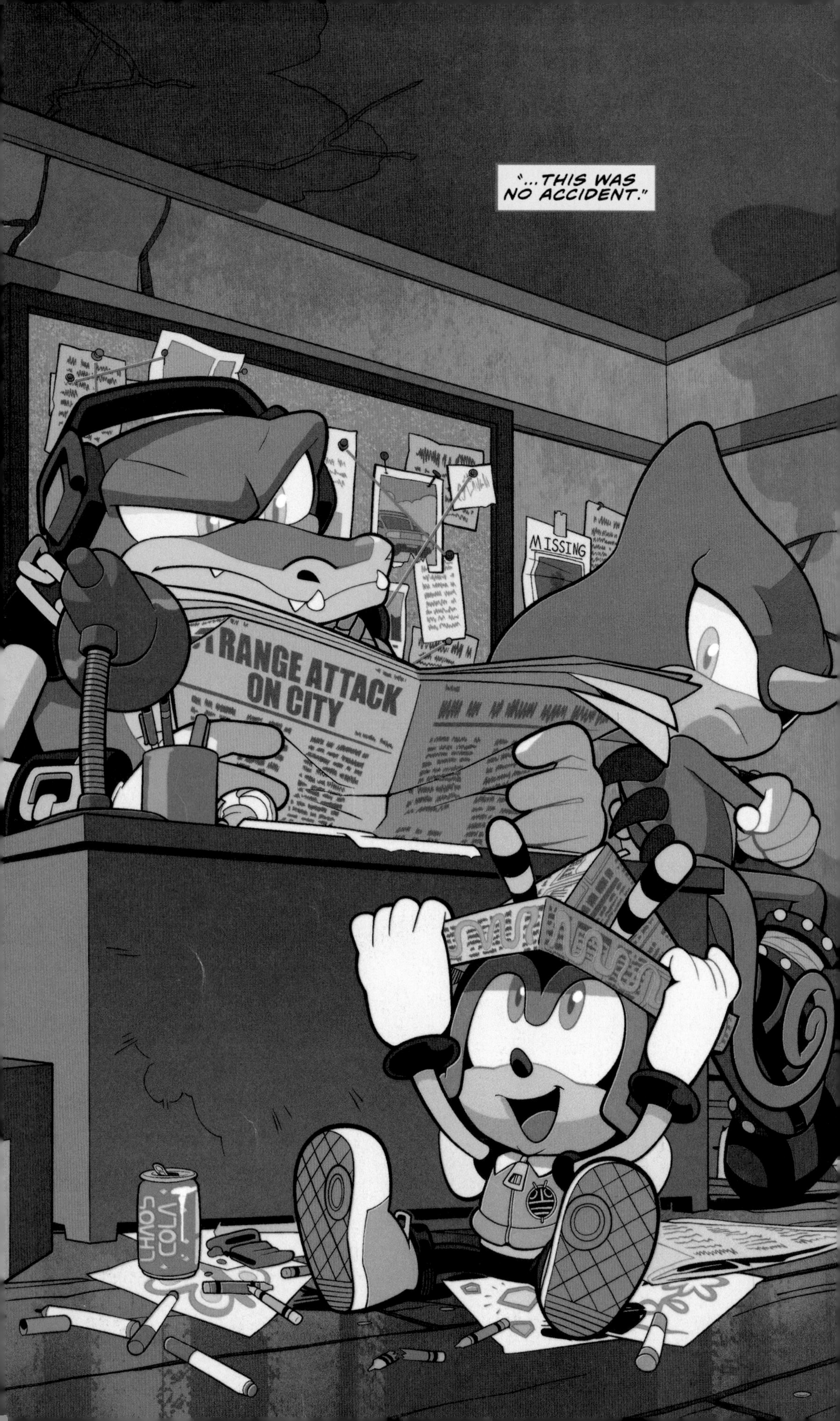
"...THIS WAS NO ACCIDENT."
MISSING
STRANGE ATTACK ON CITY

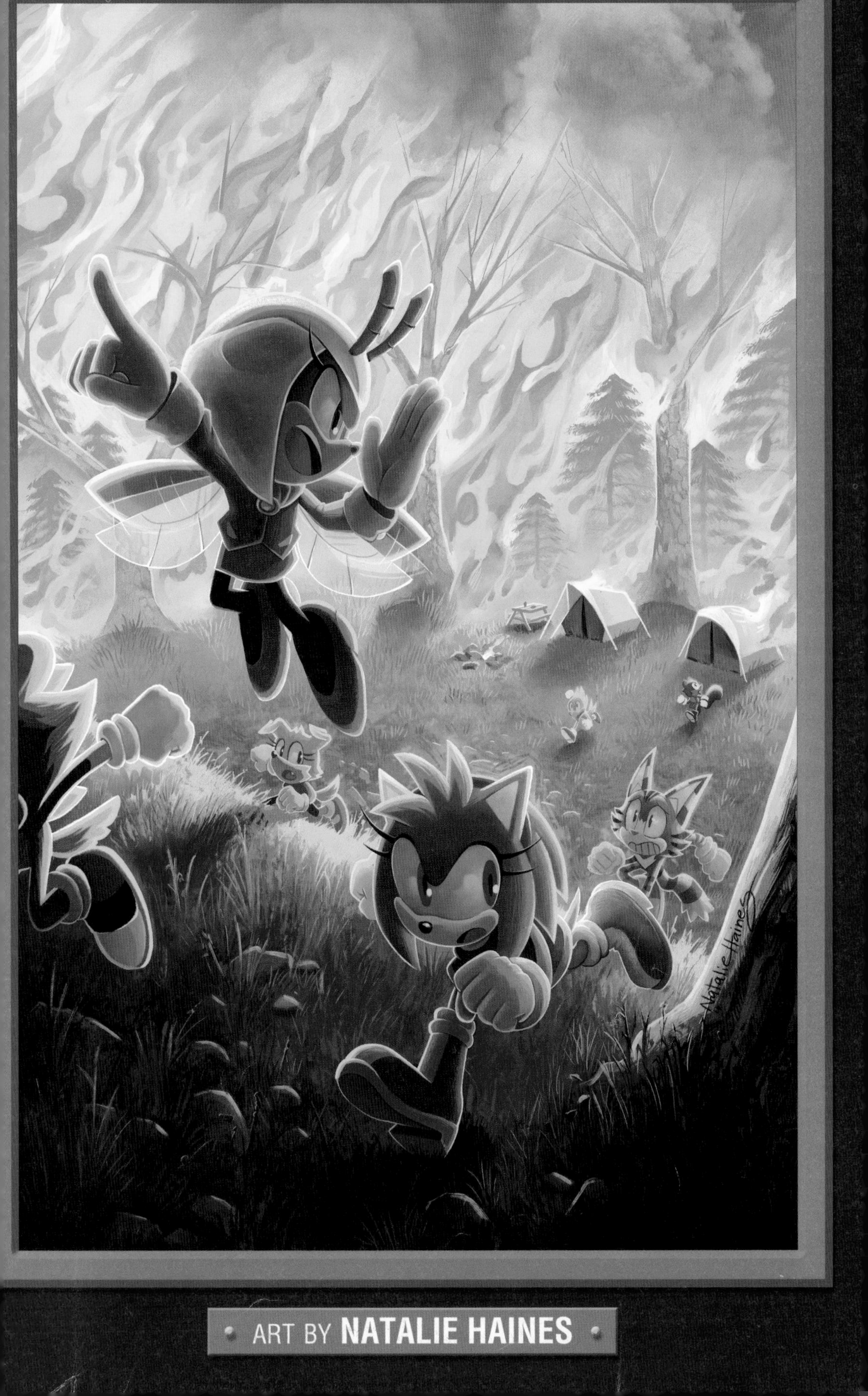
Natalie Haines

ART BY **NATALIE HAINES**

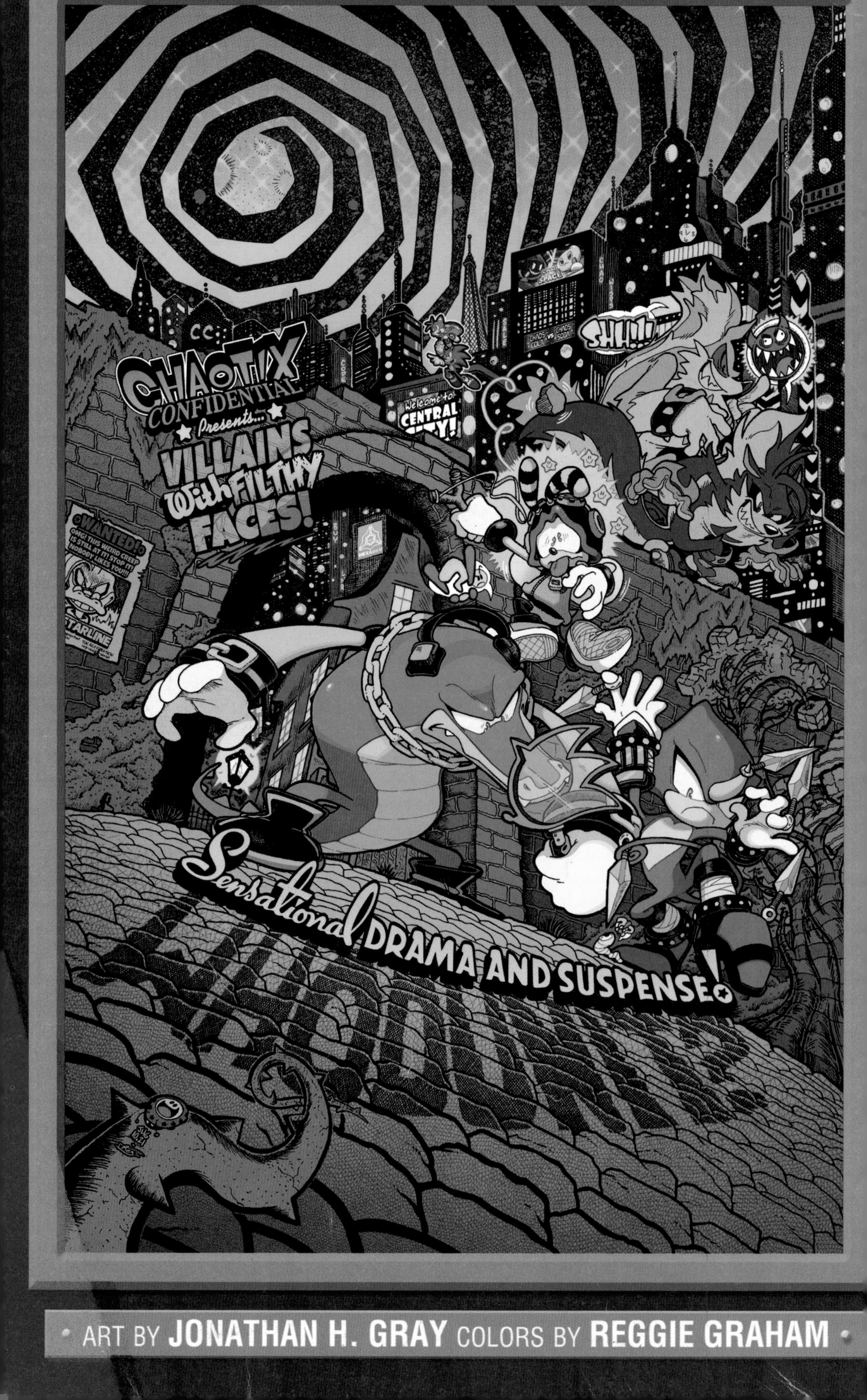
CHAOTIX CONFIDENTIAL
Presents...
VILLAINS With FILTHY FACES!
Welcome to CENTRAL CITY!
SHH!!
WANTED!
STARLINE
Sensational DRAMA AND SUSPENSE!

ART BY **JONATHAN H. GRAY** COLORS BY **REGGIE GRAHAM**

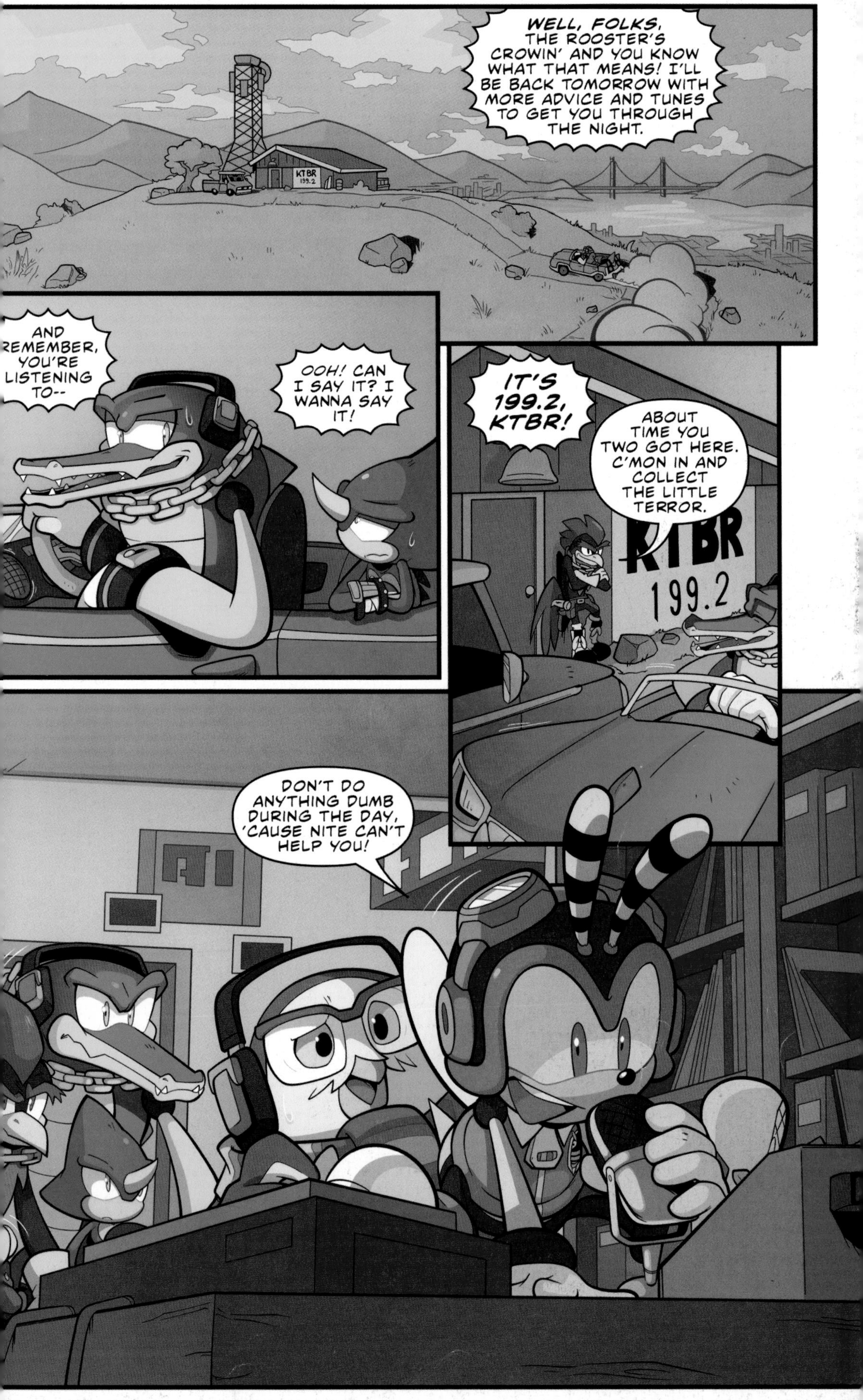
WELL, FOLKS, THE ROOSTER'S CROWIN' AND YOU KNOW WHAT THAT MEANS! I'LL BE BACK TOMORROW WITH MORE ADVICE AND TUNES TO GET YOU THROUGH THE NIGHT.
KTBR 199.2
AND REMEMBER, YOU'RE LISTENING TO--
OOH! CAN I SAY IT? I WANNA SAY IT!
IT'S 199.2, KTBR!
ABOUT TIME YOU TWO GOT HERE. C'MON IN AND COLLECT THE LITTLE TERROR.
KTBR 199.2
DON'T DO ANYTHING DUMB DURING THE DAY, 'CAUSE NITE CAN'T HELP YOU!

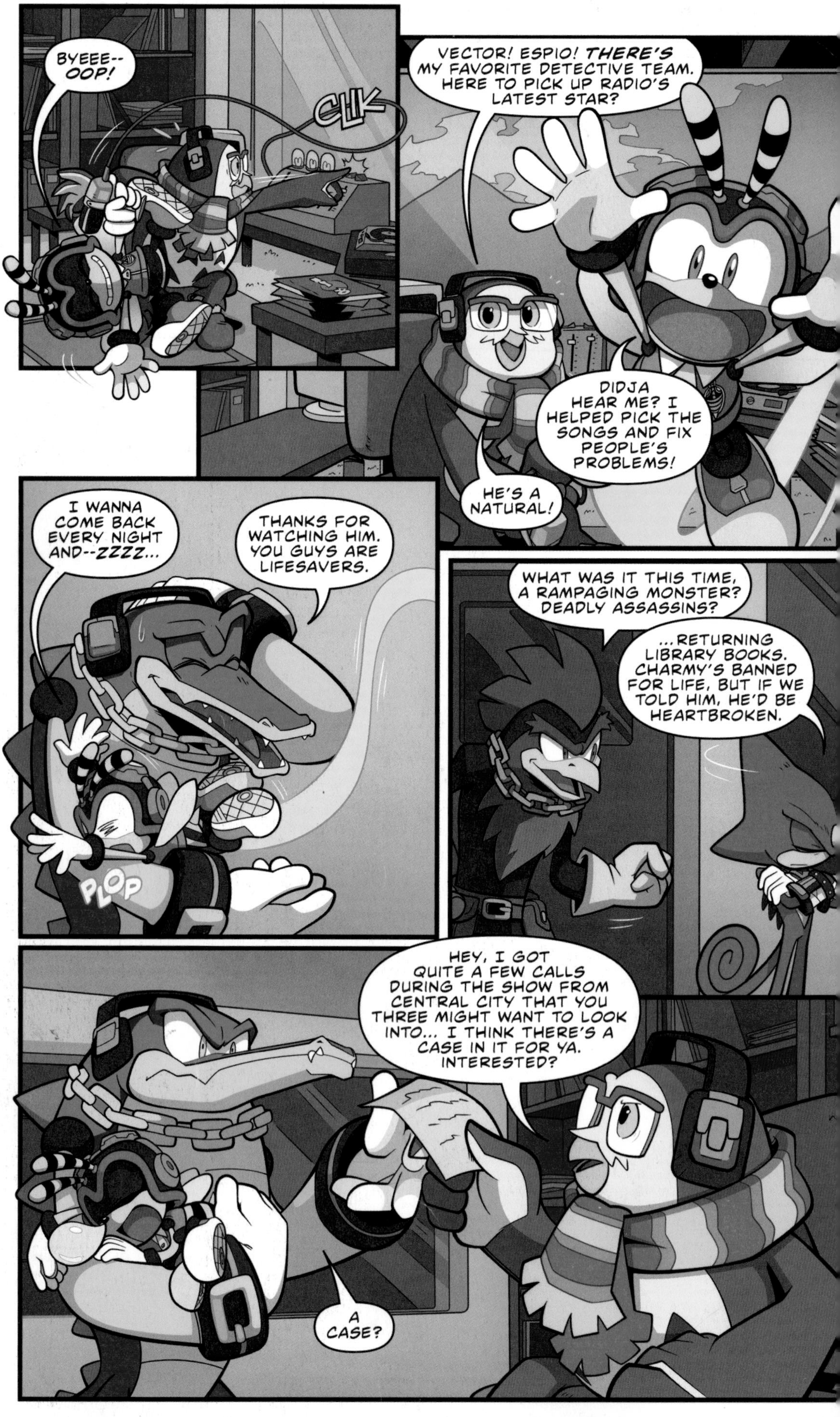

BYEEE--
OOP!
CLIK
VECTOR! ESPIO! THERE'S MY FAVORITE DETECTIVE TEAM. HERE TO PICK UP RADIO'S LATEST STAR?
DIDJA HEAR ME? I HELPED PICK THE SONGS AND FIX PEOPLE'S PROBLEMS!
HE'S A NATURAL!
I WANNA COME BACK EVERY NIGHT AND--ZZZZ...
THANKS FOR WATCHING HIM. YOU GUYS ARE LIFESAVERS.
PLOP
WHAT WAS IT THIS TIME, A RAMPAGING MONSTER? DEADLY ASSASSINS?
...RETURNING LIBRARY BOOKS. CHARMY'S BANNED FOR LIFE, BUT IF WE TOLD HIM, HE'D BE HEARTBROKEN.
HEY, I GOT QUITE A FEW CALLS DURING THE SHOW FROM CENTRAL CITY THAT YOU THREE MIGHT WANT TO LOOK INTO... I THINK THERE'S A CASE IN IT FOR YA. INTERESTED?
A CASE?

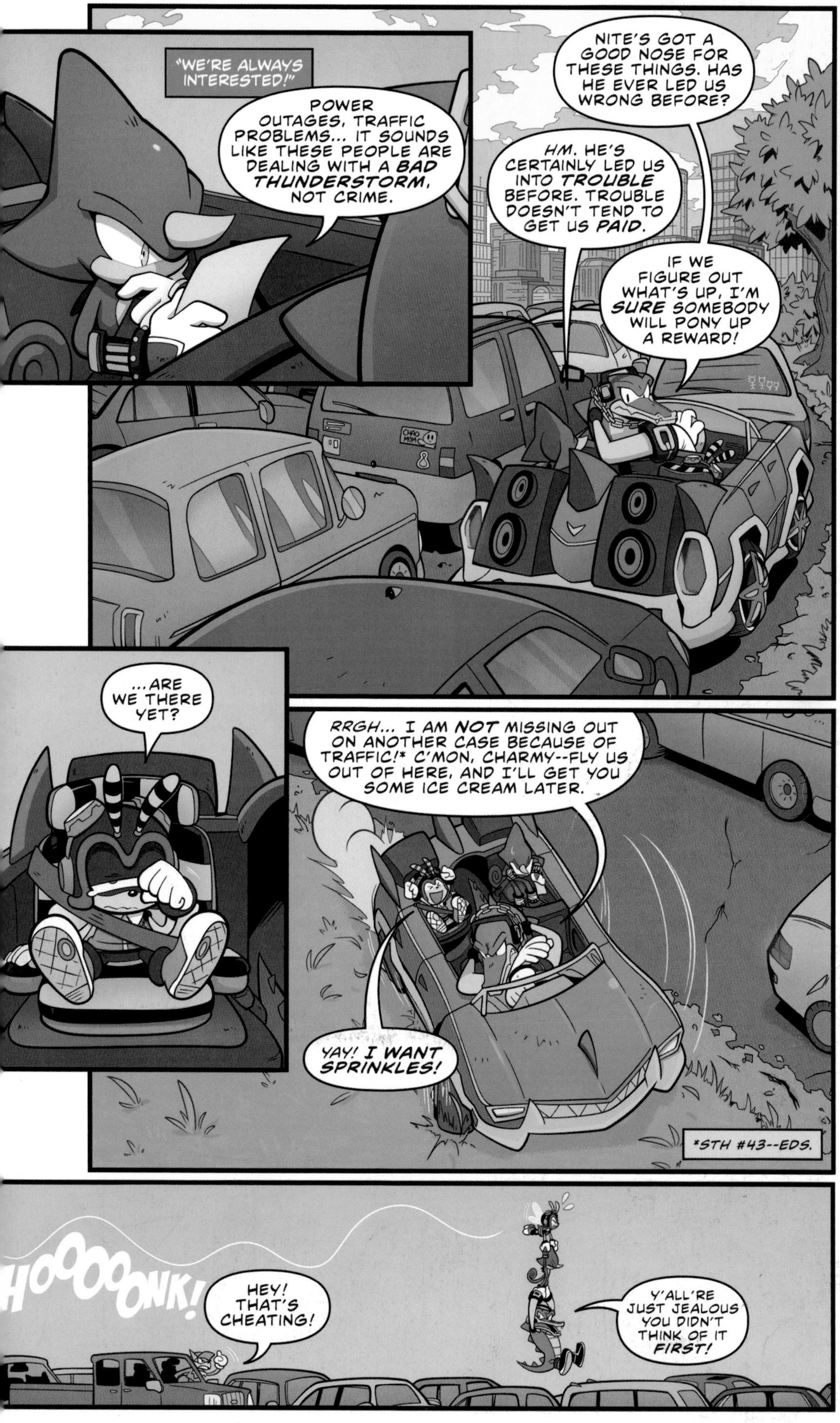
"WE'RE ALWAYS INTERESTED!"
POWER OUTAGES, TRAFFIC PROBLEMS... IT SOUNDS LIKE THESE PEOPLE ARE DEALING WITH A BAD THUNDERSTORM, NOT CRIME.
NITE'S GOT A GOOD NOSE FOR THESE THINGS. HAS HE EVER LED US WRONG BEFORE?
HM. HE'S CERTAINLY LED US INTO TROUBLE BEFORE. TROUBLE DOESN'T TEND TO GET US PAID.
IF WE FIGURE OUT WHAT'S UP, I'M SURE SOMEBODY WILL PONY UP A REWARD!
CHAO MOM
...ARE WE THERE YET?
RRGH... I AM NOT MISSING OUT ON ANOTHER CASE BECAUSE OF TRAFFIC!* C'MON, CHARMY--FLY US OUT OF HERE, AND I'LL GET YOU SOME ICE CREAM LATER.
YAY! I WANT SPRINKLES!
*STH #43--EDS.
HOOOOONK!
HEY! THAT'S CHEATING!
Y'ALL'RE JUST JEALOUS YOU DIDN'T THINK OF IT FIRST!

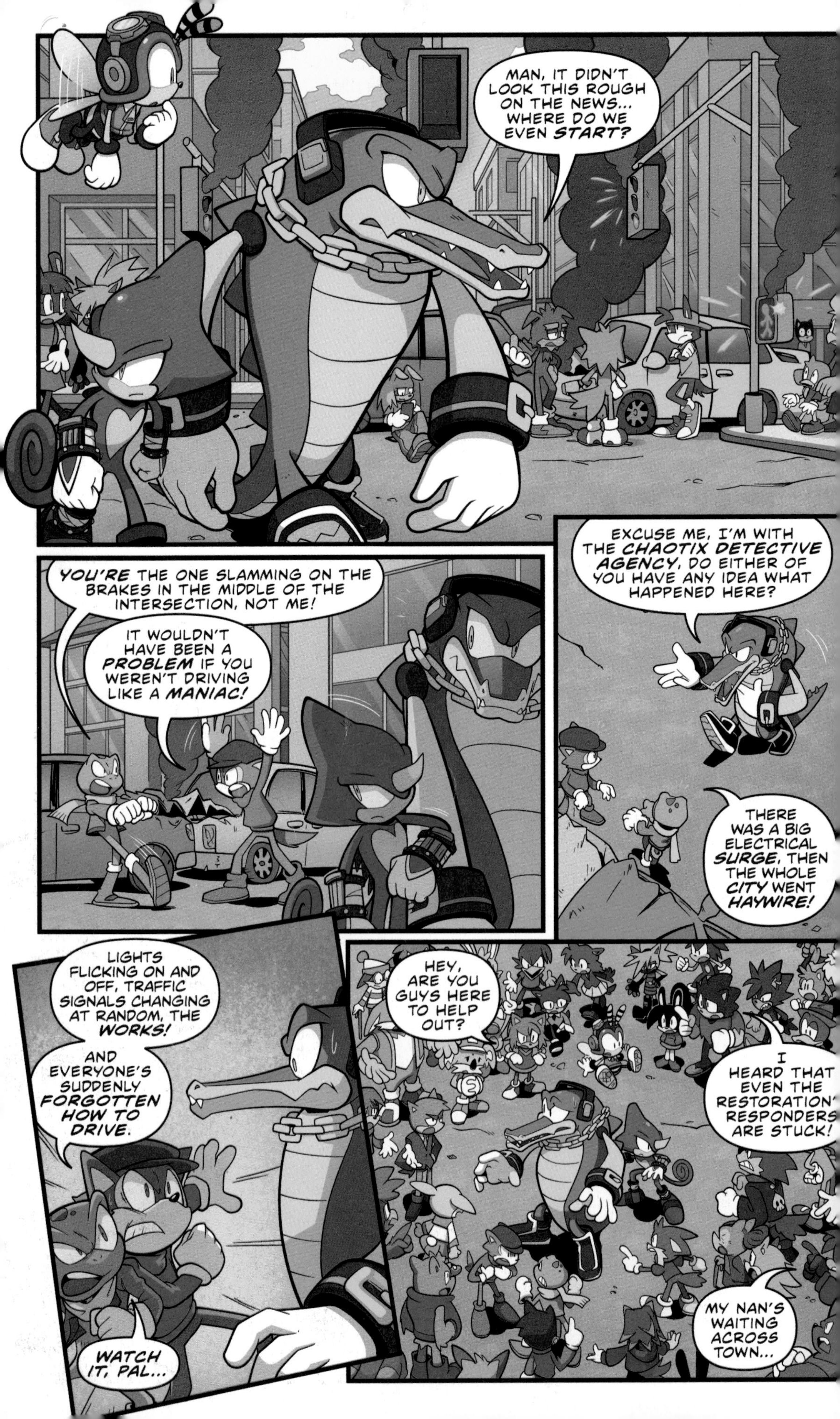
MAN, IT DIDN'T LOOK THIS ROUGH ON THE NEWS... WHERE DO WE EVEN START?
YOU'RE THE ONE SLAMMING ON THE BRAKES IN THE MIDDLE OF THE INTERSECTION, NOT ME!
IT WOULDN'T HAVE BEEN A PROBLEM IF YOU WEREN'T DRIVING LIKE A MANIAC!
EXCUSE ME, I'M WITH THE CHAOTIX DETECTIVE AGENCY, DO EITHER OF YOU HAVE ANY IDEA WHAT HAPPENED HERE?
THERE WAS A BIG ELECTRICAL SURGE, THEN THE WHOLE CITY WENT HAYWIRE!
LIGHTS FLICKING ON AND OFF, TRAFFIC SIGNALS CHANGING AT RANDOM, THE WORKS!
AND EVERYONE'S SUDDENLY FORGOTTEN HOW TO DRIVE.
WATCH IT, PAL...
HEY, ARE YOU GUYS HERE TO HELP OUT?
I HEARD THAT EVEN THE RESTORATION RESPONDERS ARE STUCK!
MY NAN'S WAITING ACROSS TOWN...

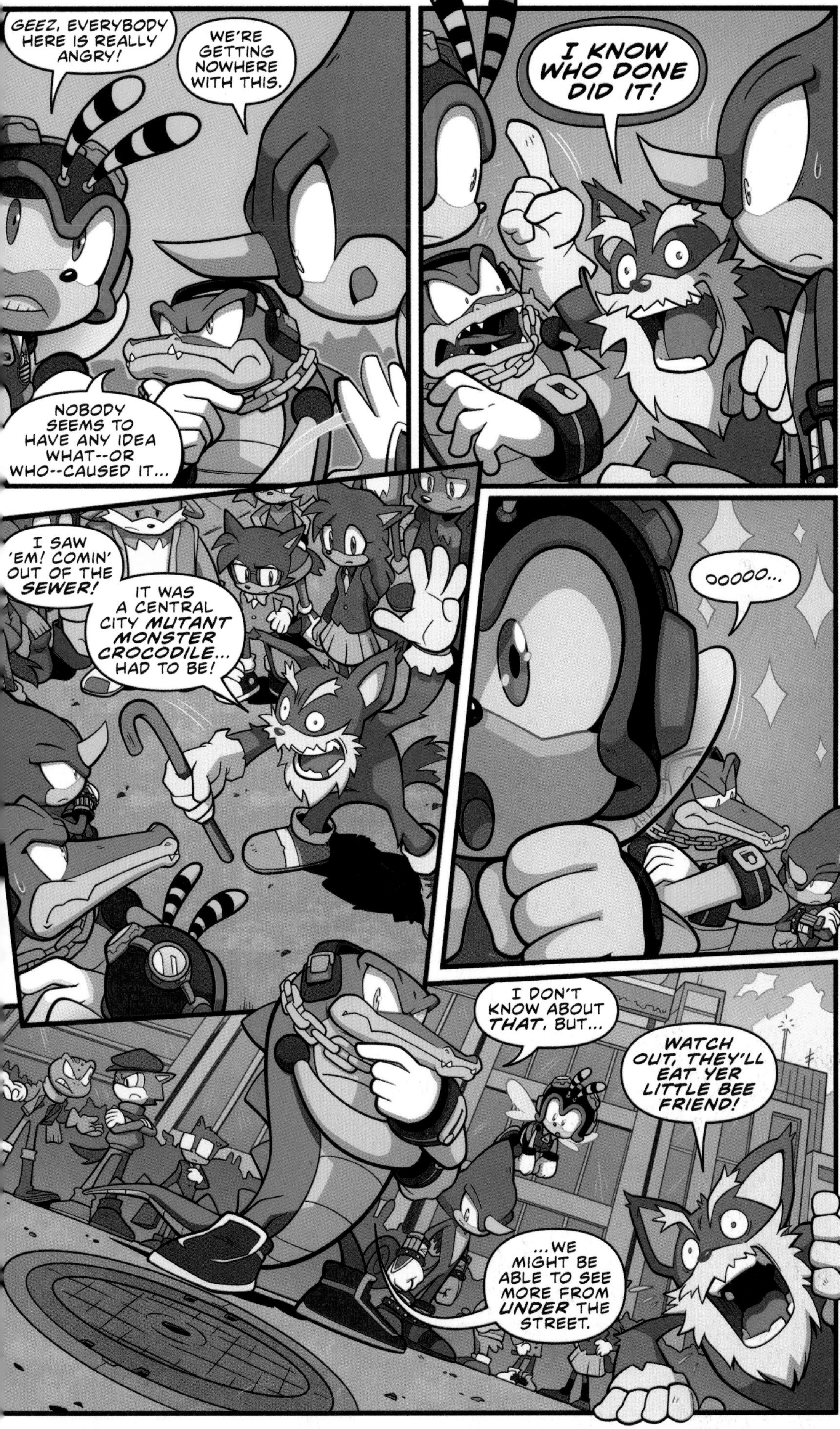
GEEZ, EVERYBODY HERE IS REALLY ANGRY!
WE'RE GETTING NOWHERE WITH THIS.
NOBODY SEEMS TO HAVE ANY IDEA WHAT--OR WHO--CAUSED IT...
I KNOW WHO DONE DID IT!
I SAW 'EM! COMIN' OUT OF THE SEWER!
IT WAS A CENTRAL CITY MUTANT MONSTER CROCODILE... HAD TO BE!
OOOOO...
I DON'T KNOW ABOUT THAT, BUT...
WATCH OUT, THEY'LL EAT YER LITTLE BEE FRIEND!
...WE MIGHT BE ABLE TO SEE MORE FROM UNDER THE STREET.

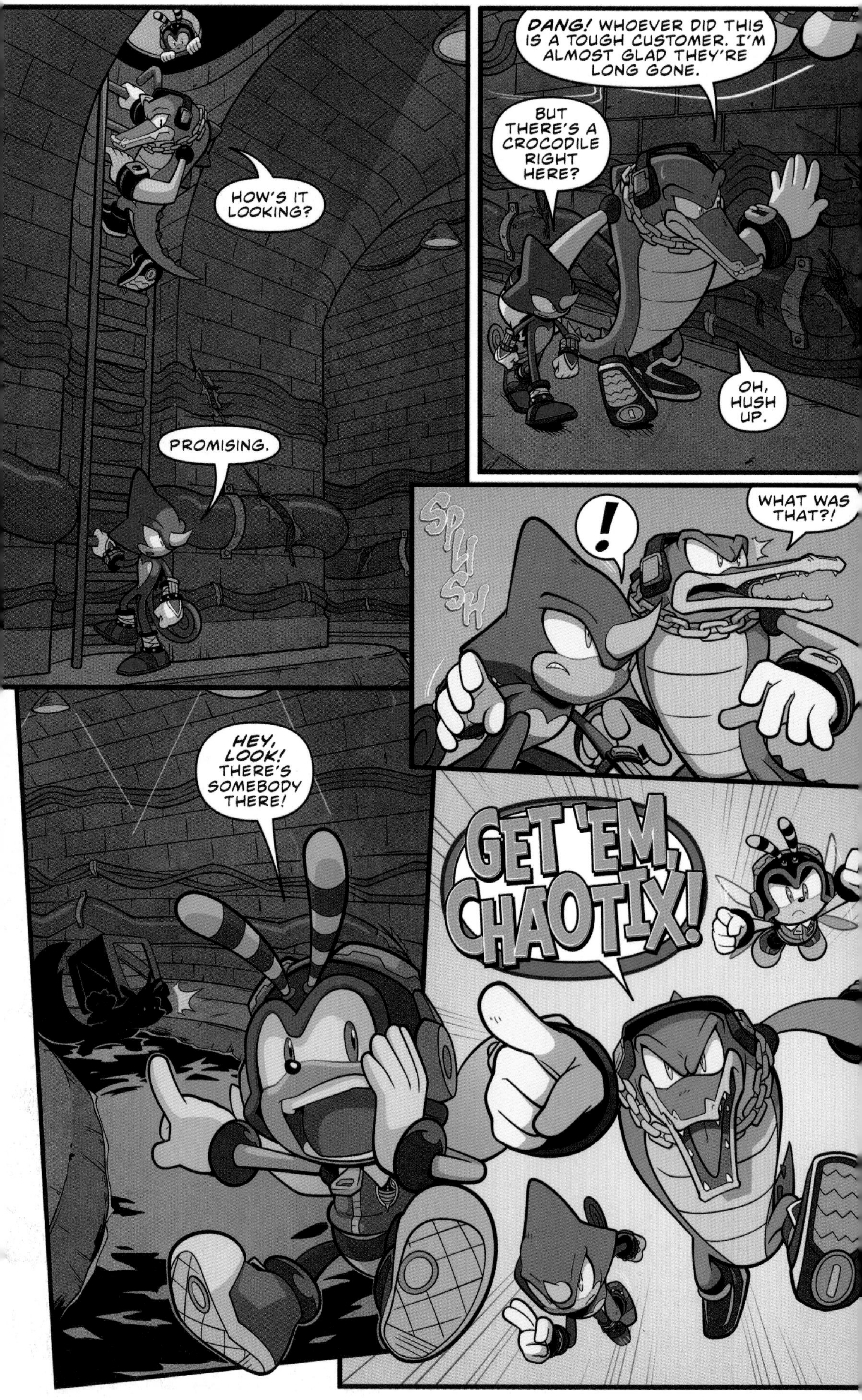
HOW'S IT LOOKING?
PROMISING.
DANG! WHOEVER DID THIS IS A TOUGH CUSTOMER. I'M ALMOST GLAD THEY'RE LONG GONE.
BUT THERE'S A CROCODILE RIGHT HERE?
OH, HUSH UP.
SPLISH
!
WHAT WAS THAT?!
HEY, LOOK! THERE'S SOMEBODY THERE!
GET 'EM, CHAOTIX!

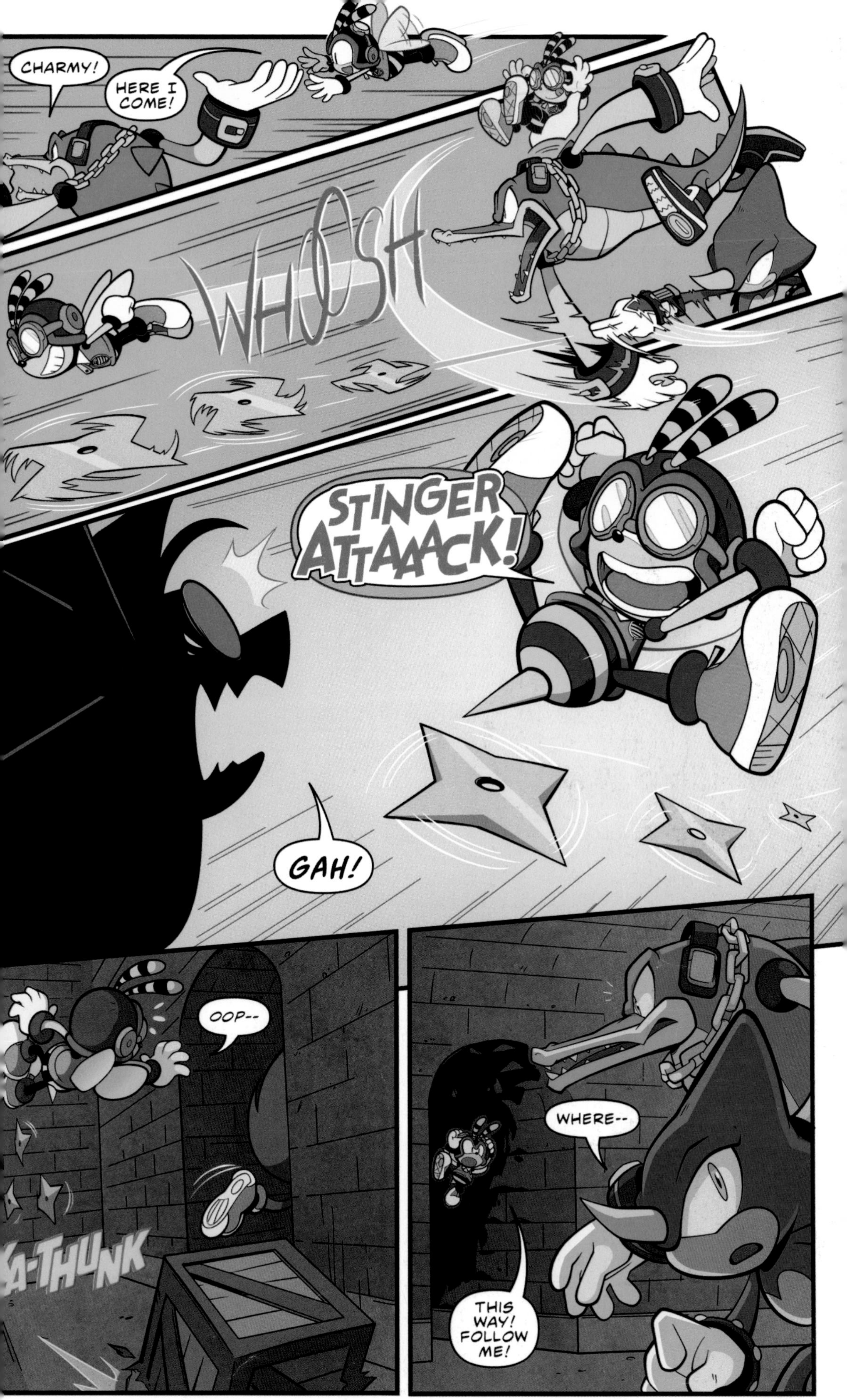
CHARMY!
HERE I COME!
WHOOSH
STINGER ATTAAACK!
GAH!
OOP--
KA-THUNK
WHERE--
THIS WAY! FOLLOW ME!

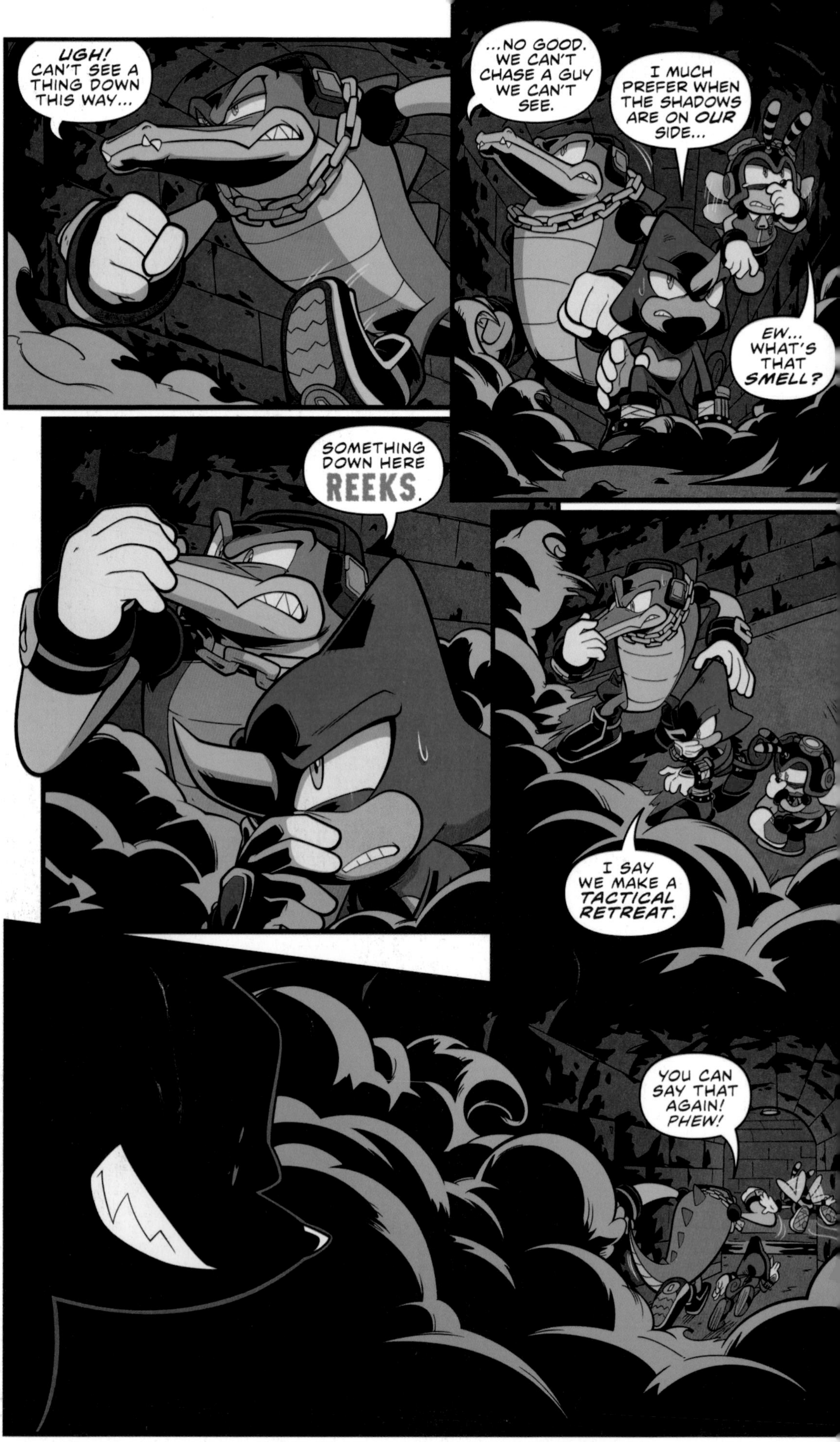
UGH! CAN'T SEE A THING DOWN THIS WAY...
...NO GOOD. WE CAN'T CHASE A GUY WE CAN'T SEE.
I MUCH PREFER WHEN THE SHADOWS ARE ON OUR SIDE...
EW... WHAT'S THAT SMELL?
SOMETHING DOWN HERE REEKS.
I SAY WE MAKE A TACTICAL RETREAT.
YOU CAN SAY THAT AGAIN! PHEW!

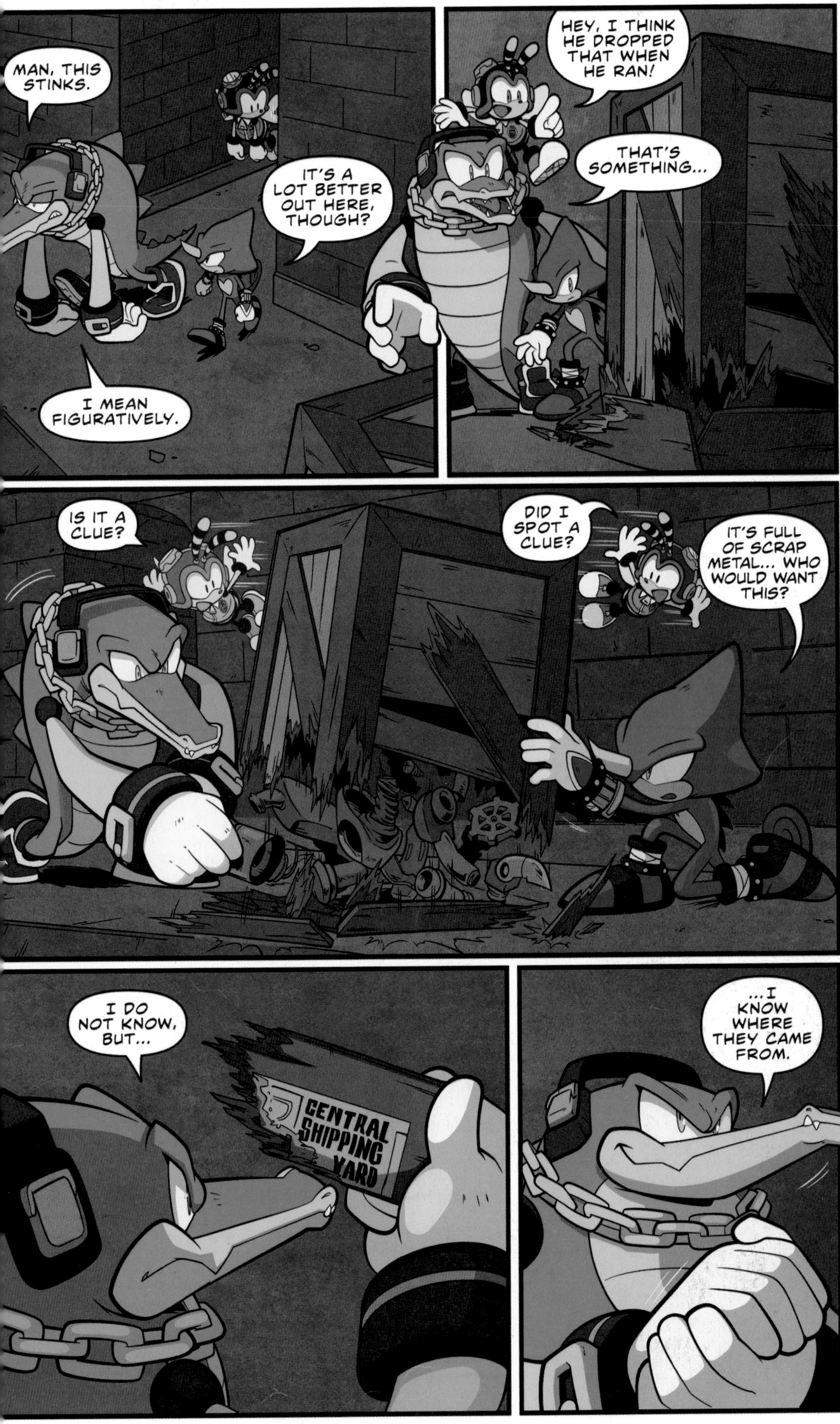
MAN, THIS STINKS.
IT'S A LOT BETTER OUT HERE, THOUGH?
I MEAN FIGURATIVELY.
HEY, I THINK HE DROPPED THAT WHEN HE RAN!
THAT'S SOMETHING...
IS IT A CLUE?
DID I SPOT A CLUE?
IT'S FULL OF SCRAP METAL... WHO WOULD WANT THIS?
I DO NOT KNOW, BUT...
CENTRAL SHIPPING YARD
...I KNOW WHERE THEY CAME FROM.

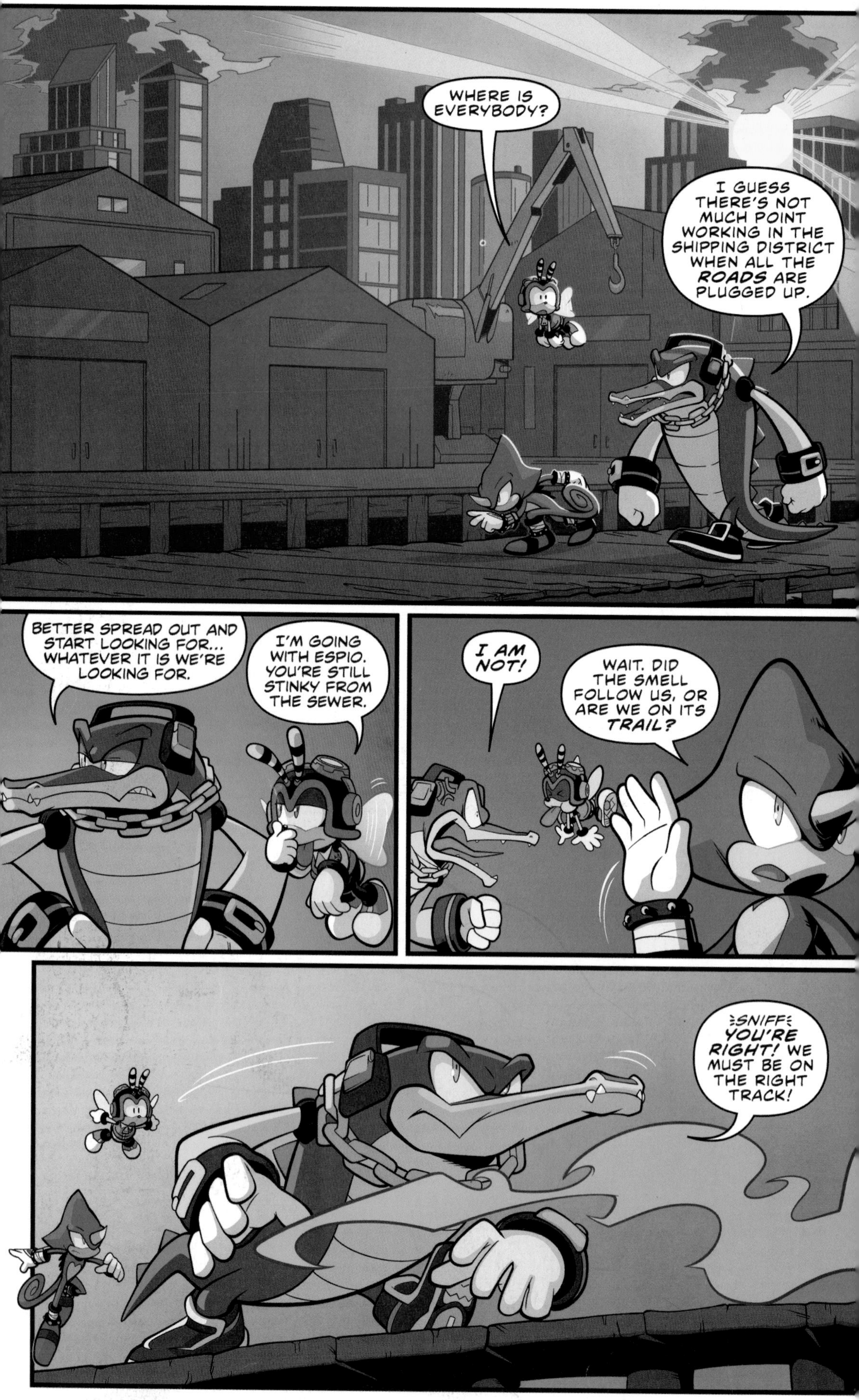
WHERE IS EVERYBODY?
I GUESS THERE'S NOT MUCH POINT WORKING IN THE SHIPPING DISTRICT WHEN ALL THE ROADS ARE PLUGGED UP.
BETTER SPREAD OUT AND START LOOKING FOR... WHATEVER IT IS WE'RE LOOKING FOR.
I'M GOING WITH ESPIO. YOU'RE STILL STINKY FROM THE SEWER.
I AM NOT!
WAIT. DID THE SMELL FOLLOW US, OR ARE WE ON ITS TRAIL?
SNIFF
YOU'RE RIGHT! WE MUST BE ON THE RIGHT TRACK!

END OF THE LINE...

...THIS PLACE HAS SURE SEEN BETTER DAYS.

LOOKS ABANDONED...

HEY! ANYBODY HO--

SHH! MAYBE THAT'S JUST WHAT THEY WANT US TO THINK!

...

I HEAR VOICES.

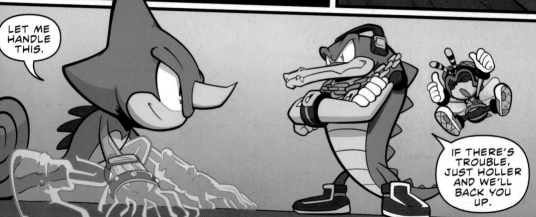

LET ME HANDLE THIS.

IF THERE'S TROUBLE, JUST HOLLER AND WE'LL BACK YOU UP.

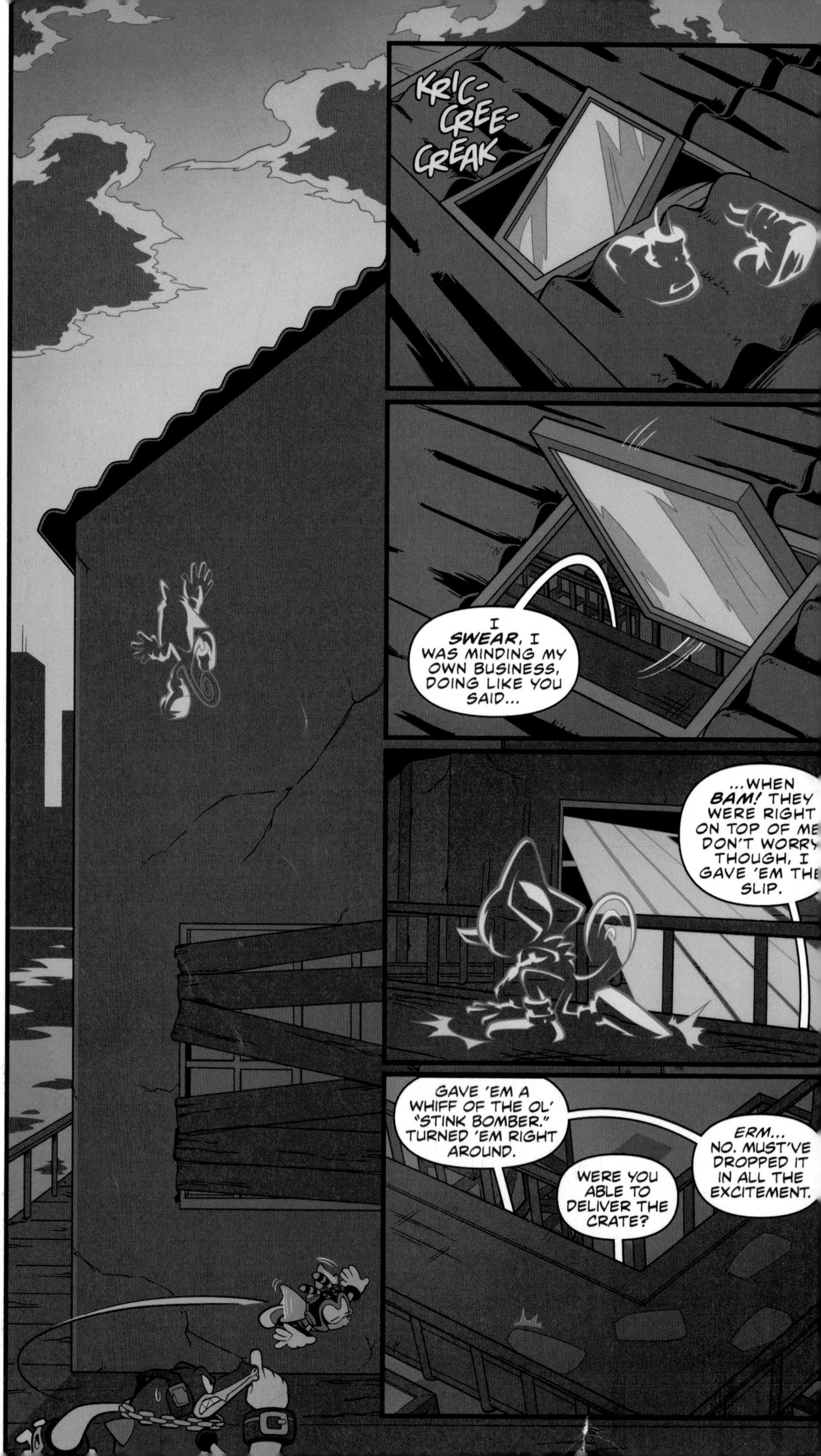
KRIC-CREE-CREAK
I SWEAR, I WAS MINDING MY OWN BUSINESS, DOING LIKE YOU SAID...
...WHEN BAM! THEY WERE RIGHT ON TOP OF ME. DON'T WORRY THOUGH, I GAVE 'EM THE SLIP.
GAVE 'EM A WHIFF OF THE OL' "STINK BOMBER." TURNED 'EM RIGHT AROUND.
WERE YOU ABLE TO DELIVER THE CRATE?
ERM... NO. MUST'VE DROPPED IT IN ALL THE EXCITEMENT.

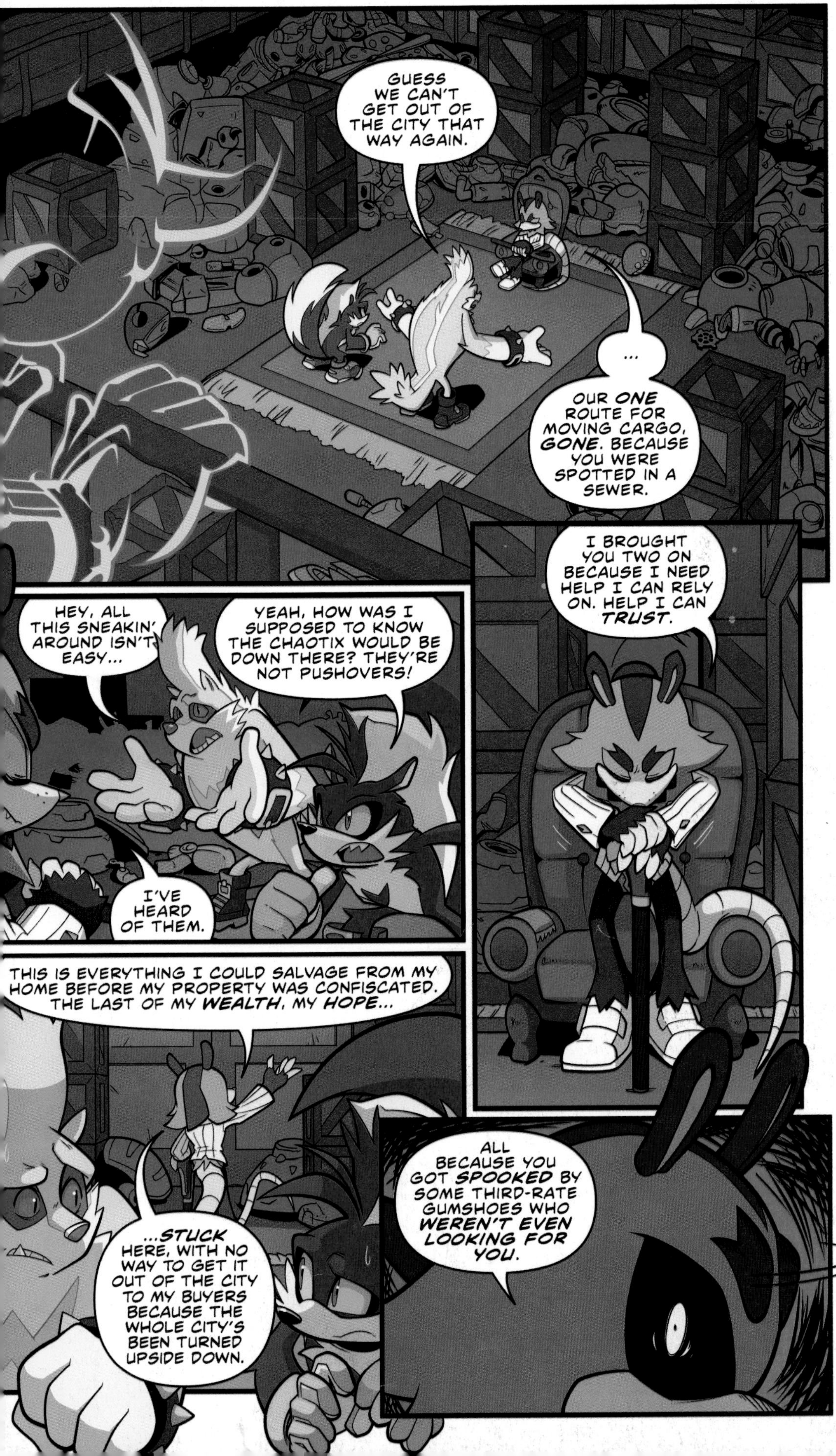
GUESS WE CAN'T GET OUT OF THE CITY THAT WAY AGAIN.
...
OUR ONE ROUTE FOR MOVING CARGO, GONE. BECAUSE YOU WERE SPOTTED IN A SEWER.
HEY, ALL THIS SNEAKIN' AROUND ISN'T EASY...
YEAH, HOW WAS I SUPPOSED TO KNOW THE CHAOTIX WOULD BE DOWN THERE? THEY'RE NOT PUSHOVERS!
I'VE HEARD OF THEM.
I BROUGHT YOU TWO ON BECAUSE I NEED HELP I CAN RELY ON. HELP I CAN TRUST.
THIS IS EVERYTHING I COULD SALVAGE FROM MY HOME BEFORE MY PROPERTY WAS CONFISCATED. THE LAST OF MY WEALTH, MY HOPE...
...STUCK HERE, WITH NO WAY TO GET IT OUT OF THE CITY TO MY BUYERS BECAUSE THE WHOLE CITY'S BEEN TURNED UPSIDE DOWN.
ALL BECAUSE YOU GOT SPOOKED BY SOME THIRD-RATE GUMSHOES WHO WEREN'T EVEN LOOKING FOR YOU.

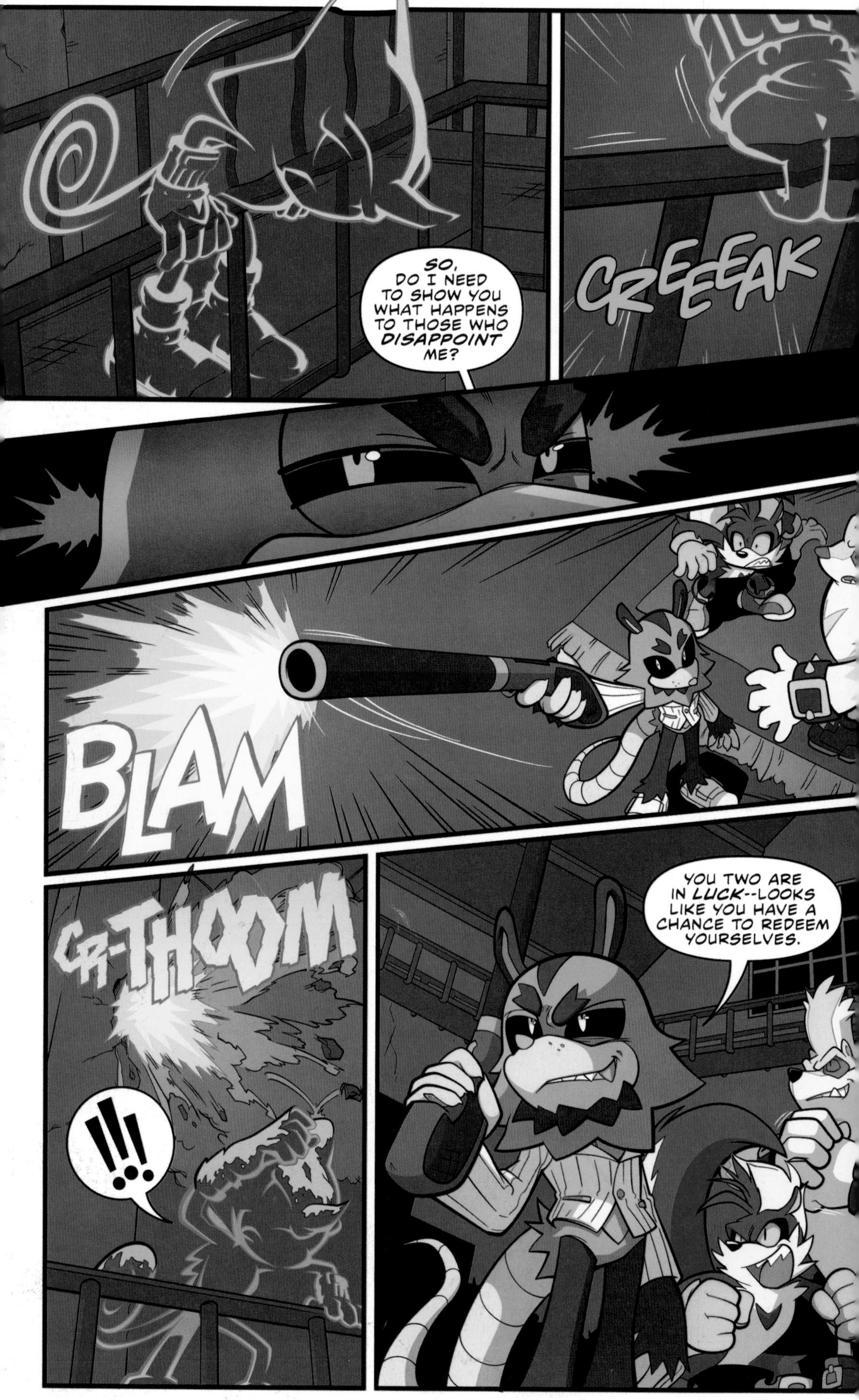
SO, DO I NEED TO SHOW YOU WHAT HAPPENS TO THOSE WHO DISAPPOINT ME?
CREEEEAK
BLAM
CR-THOOM
!!!
YOU TWO ARE IN LUCK--LOOKS LIKE YOU HAVE A CHANCE TO REDEEM YOURSELVES.

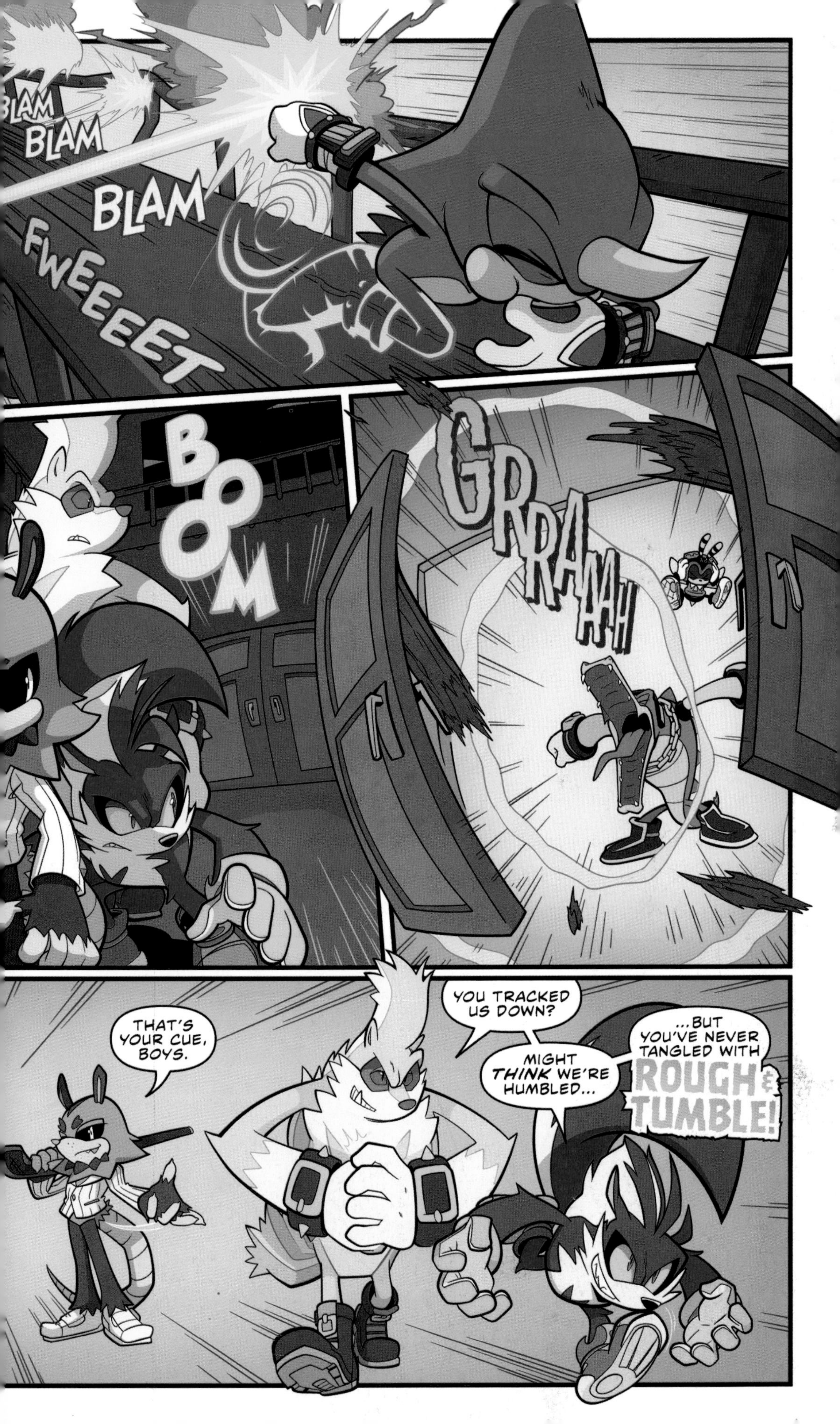
BLAM
BLAM
BLAM
FWEEEEET
BOOM
GRRAAAH
THAT'S YOUR CUE, BOYS.
YOU TRACKED US DOWN?
MIGHT *THINK* WE'RE HUMBLED...
...BUT YOU'VE NEVER TANGLED WITH
ROUGH & TUMBLE!

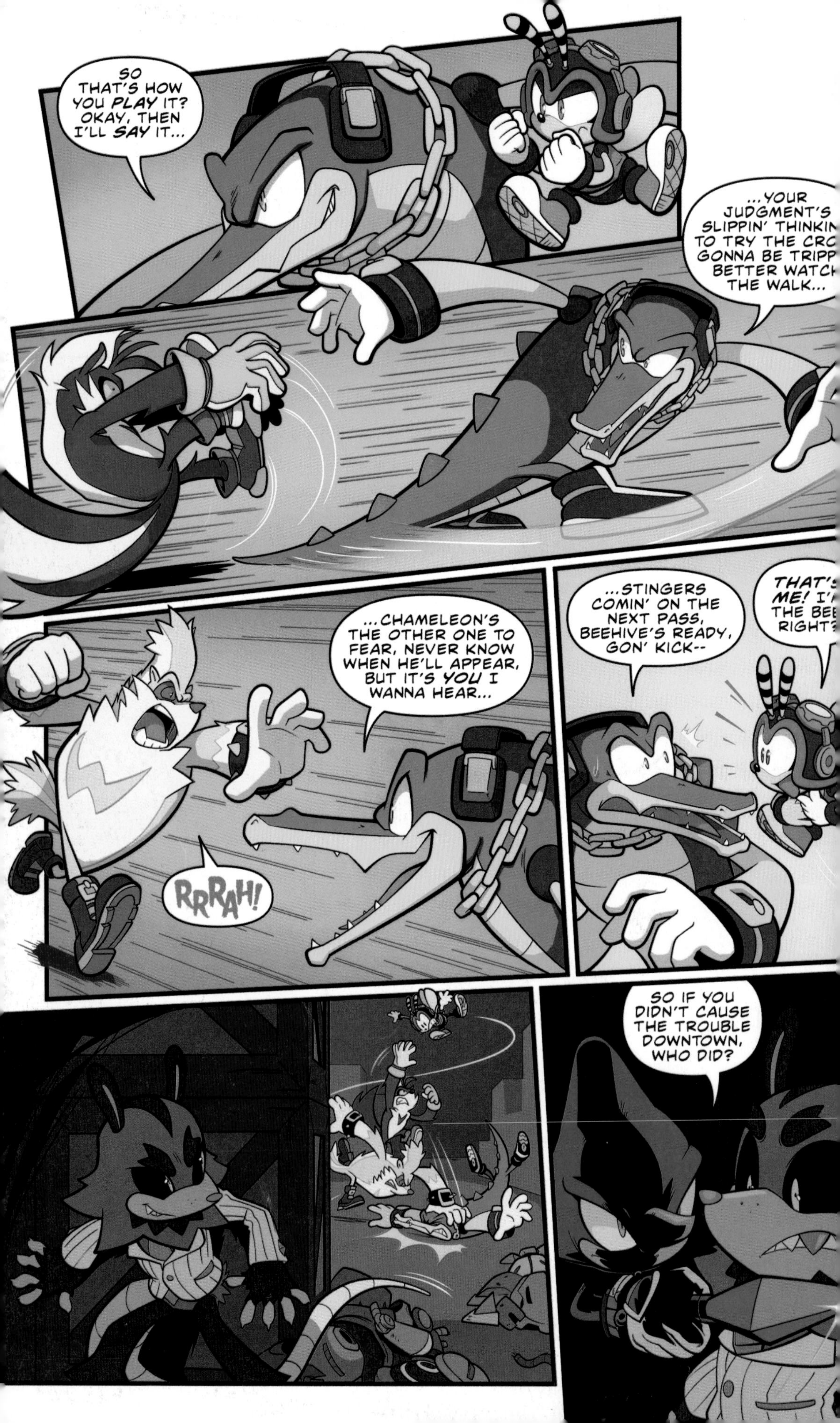
SO THAT'S HOW YOU PLAY IT? OKAY, THEN I'LL SAY IT...
...YOUR JUDGMENT'S SLIPPIN' THINKIN
TO TRY THE CRO
GONNA BE TRIPP
BETTER WATCH
THE WALK...
...CHAMELEON'S THE OTHER ONE TO FEAR, NEVER KNOW WHEN HE'LL APPEAR, BUT IT'S YOU I WANNA HEAR...
RRRAH!
...STINGERS COMIN' ON THE NEXT PASS, BEEHIVE'S READY, GON' KICK--
THAT'S ME!
THE BEE
RIGHT?
SO IF YOU DIDN'T CAUSE THE TROUBLE DOWNTOWN, WHO DID?

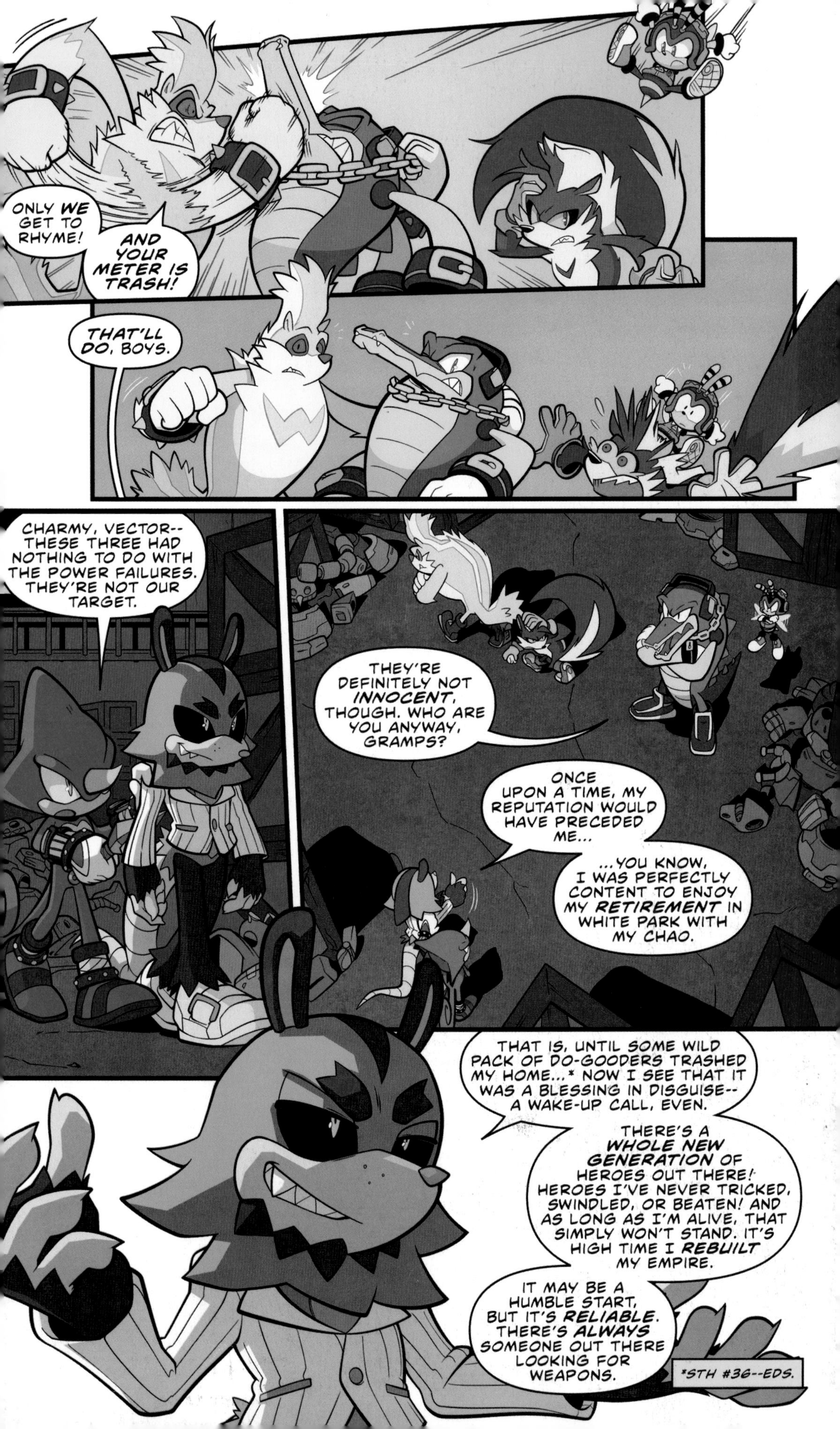
ONLY WE GET TO RHYME!
AND YOUR METER IS TRASH!
THAT'LL DO, BOYS.
CHARMY, VECTOR-- THESE THREE HAD NOTHING TO DO WITH THE POWER FAILURES. THEY'RE NOT OUR TARGET.
THEY'RE DEFINITELY NOT INNOCENT, THOUGH. WHO ARE YOU ANYWAY, GRAMPS?
ONCE UPON A TIME, MY REPUTATION WOULD HAVE PRECEDED ME...
...YOU KNOW, I WAS PERFECTLY CONTENT TO ENJOY MY RETIREMENT IN WHITE PARK WITH MY CHAO.
THAT IS, UNTIL SOME WILD PACK OF DO-GOODERS TRASHED MY HOME...* NOW I SEE THAT IT WAS A BLESSING IN DISGUISE-- A WAKE-UP CALL, EVEN.
THERE'S A WHOLE NEW GENERATION OF HEROES OUT THERE! HEROES I'VE NEVER TRICKED, SWINDLED, OR BEATEN! AND AS LONG AS I'M ALIVE, THAT SIMPLY WON'T STAND. IT'S HIGH TIME I REBUILT MY EMPIRE.
IT MAY BE A HUMBLE START, BUT IT'S RELIABLE. THERE'S ALWAYS SOMEONE OUT THERE LOOKING FOR WEAPONS.
*STH #36--EDS.

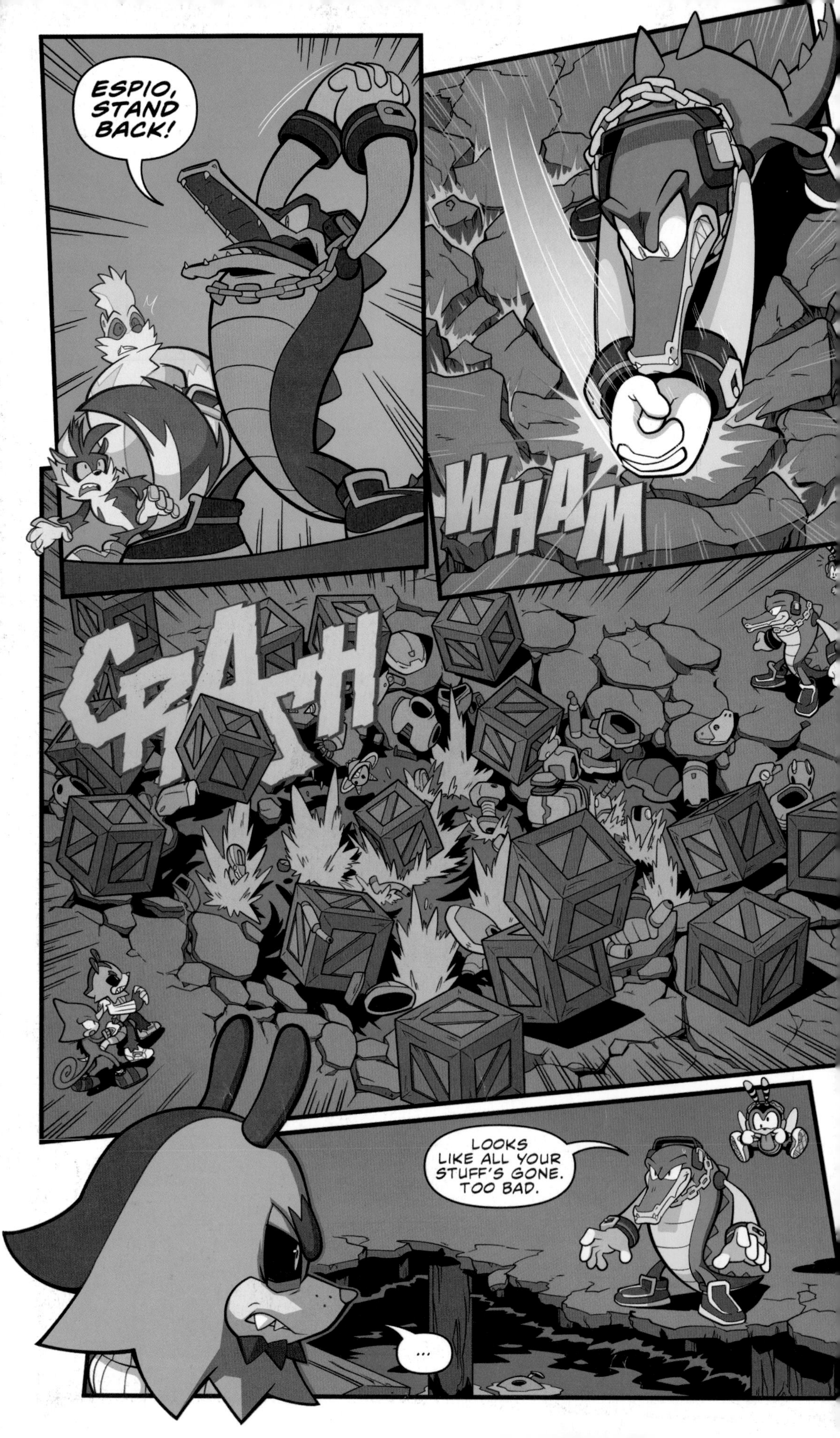
ESPIO, STAND BACK!
WHAM
CRASH
LOOKS LIKE ALL YOUR STUFF'S GONE. TOO BAD.
...

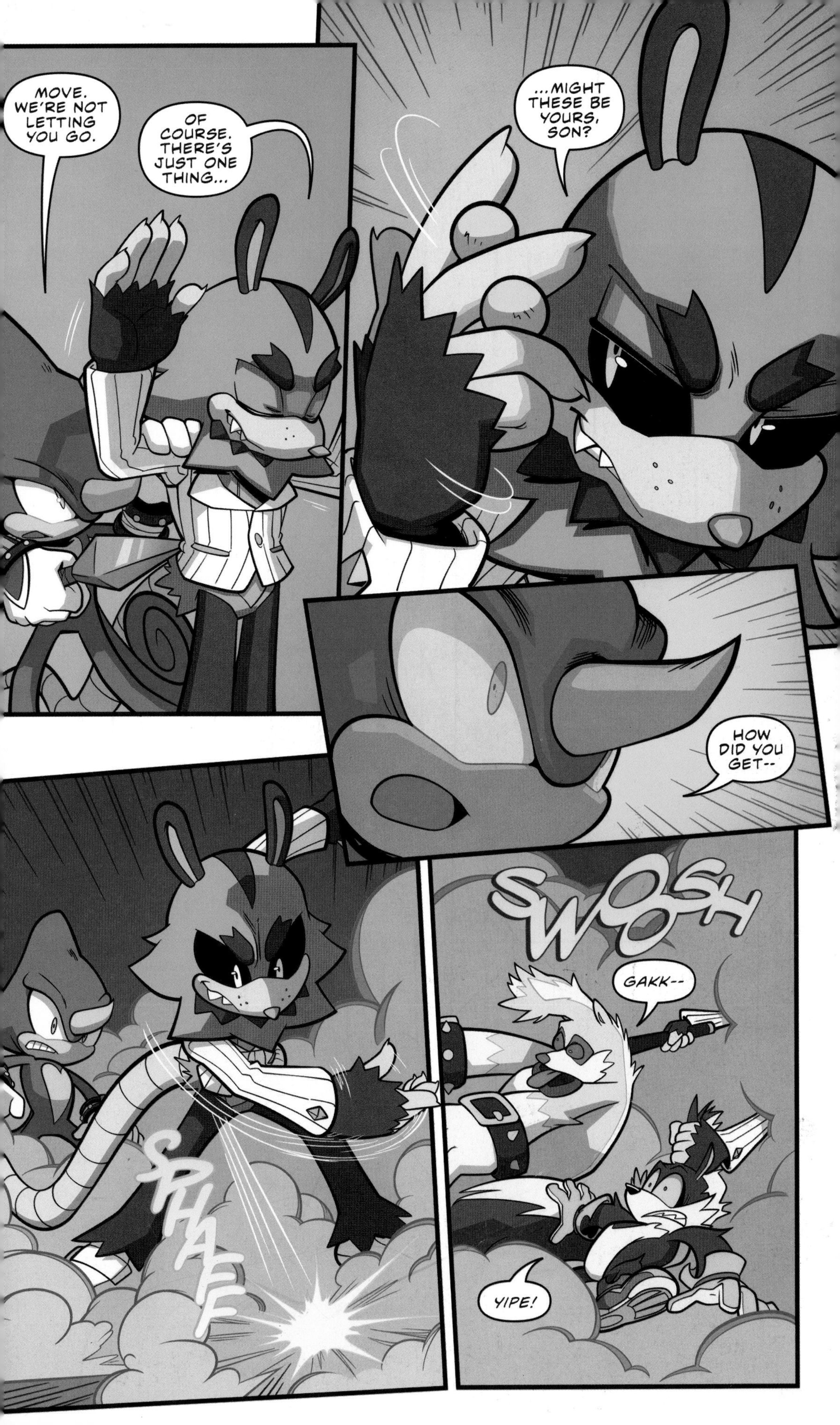
MOVE. WE'RE NOT LETTING YOU GO.
OF COURSE. THERE'S JUST ONE THING...
...MIGHT THESE BE YOURS, SON?
HOW DID YOU GET--
SWOOSH
GAKK--
SPHAFF
YIPE!

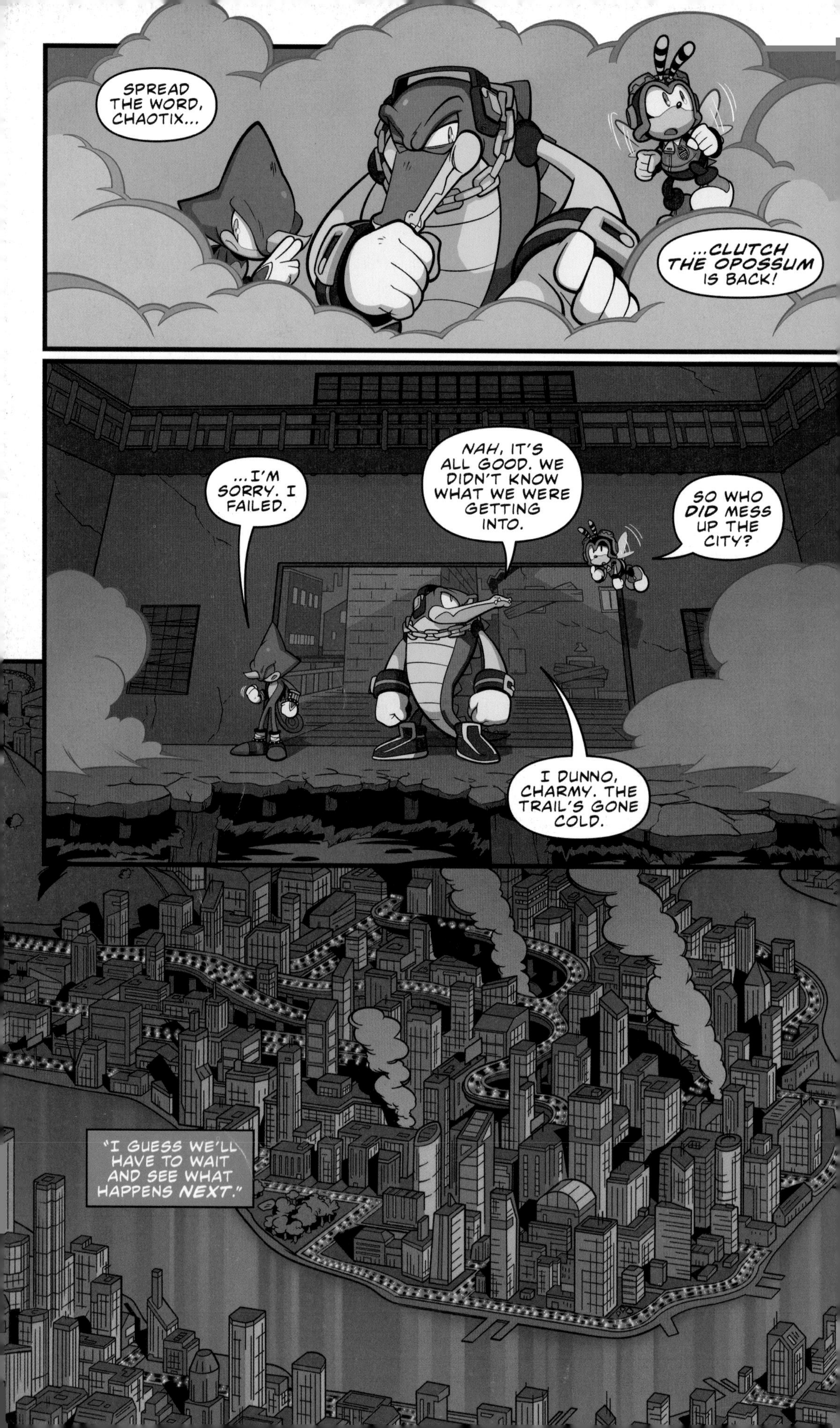
SPREAD THE WORD, CHAOTIX...
...CLUTCH THE OPOSSUM IS BACK!
...I'M SORRY. I FAILED.
NAH, IT'S ALL GOOD. WE DIDN'T KNOW WHAT WE WERE GETTING INTO.
SO WHO DID MESS UP THE CITY?
I DUNNO, CHARMY. THE TRAIL'S GONE COLD.
"I GUESS WE'LL HAVE TO WAIT AND SEE WHAT HAPPENS NEXT."

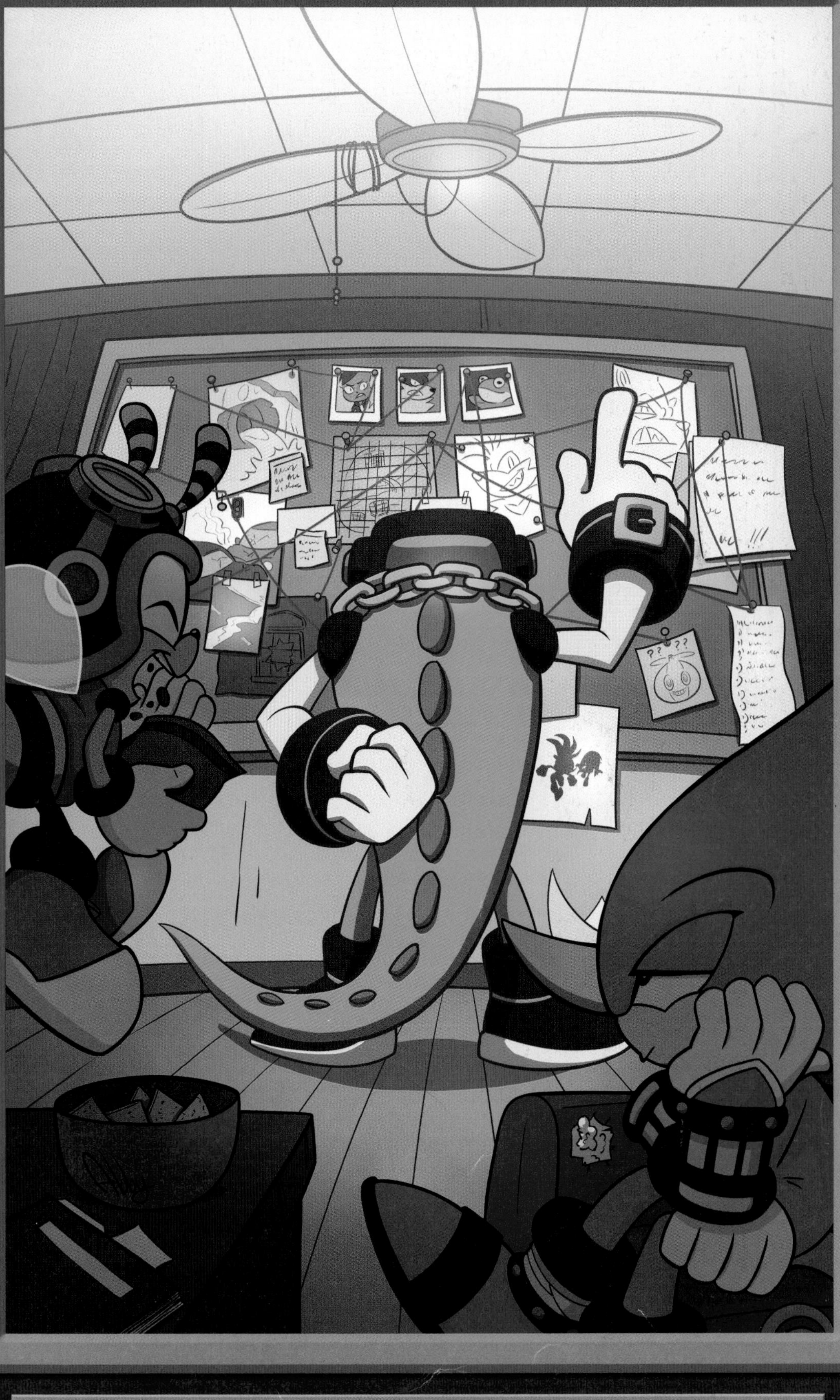

ART BY **ABBY BULMER** COLORS BY **JOANA LAFUENTE**

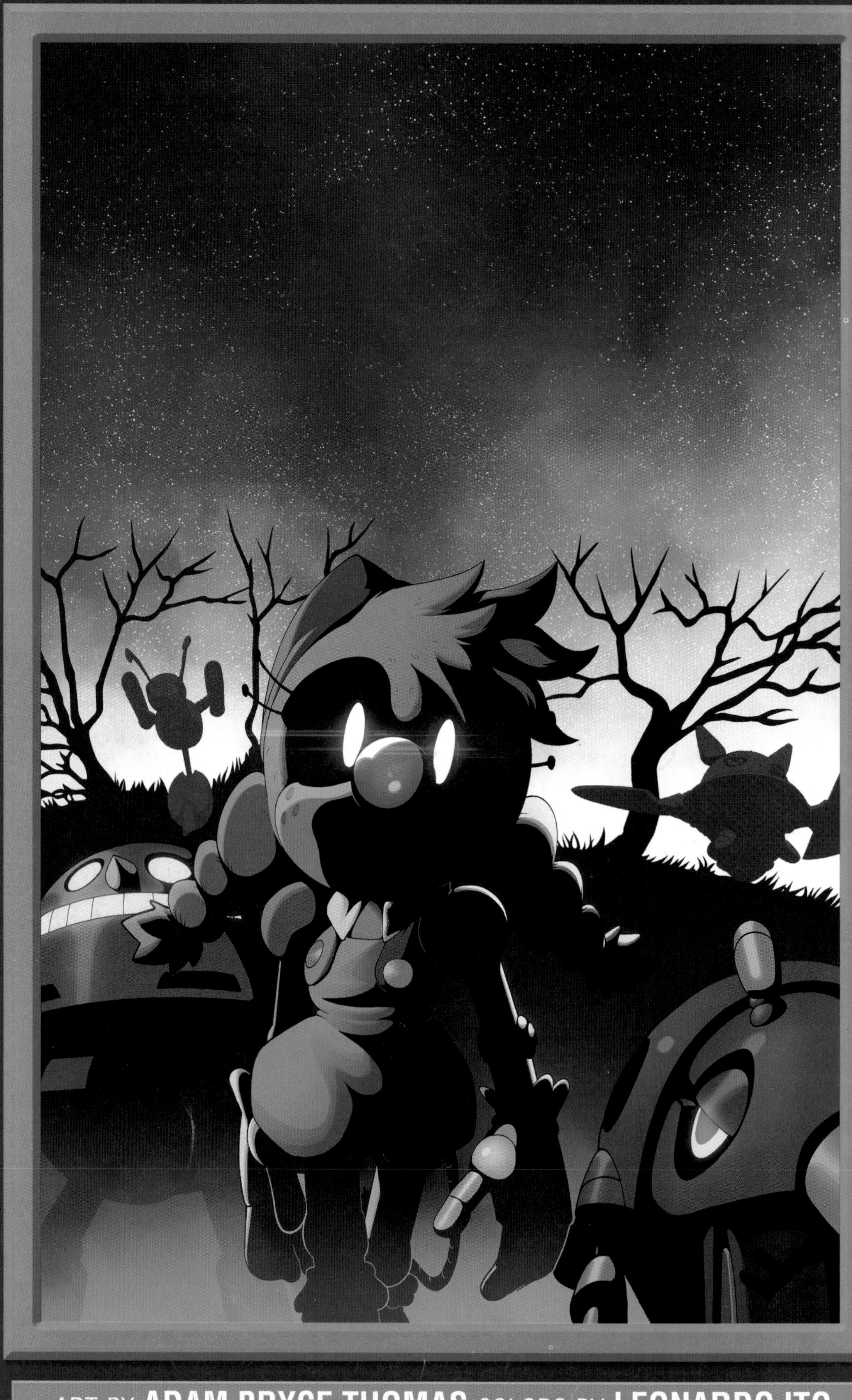

ART BY **ADAM BRYCE THOMAS** COLORS BY **LEONARDO ITO**

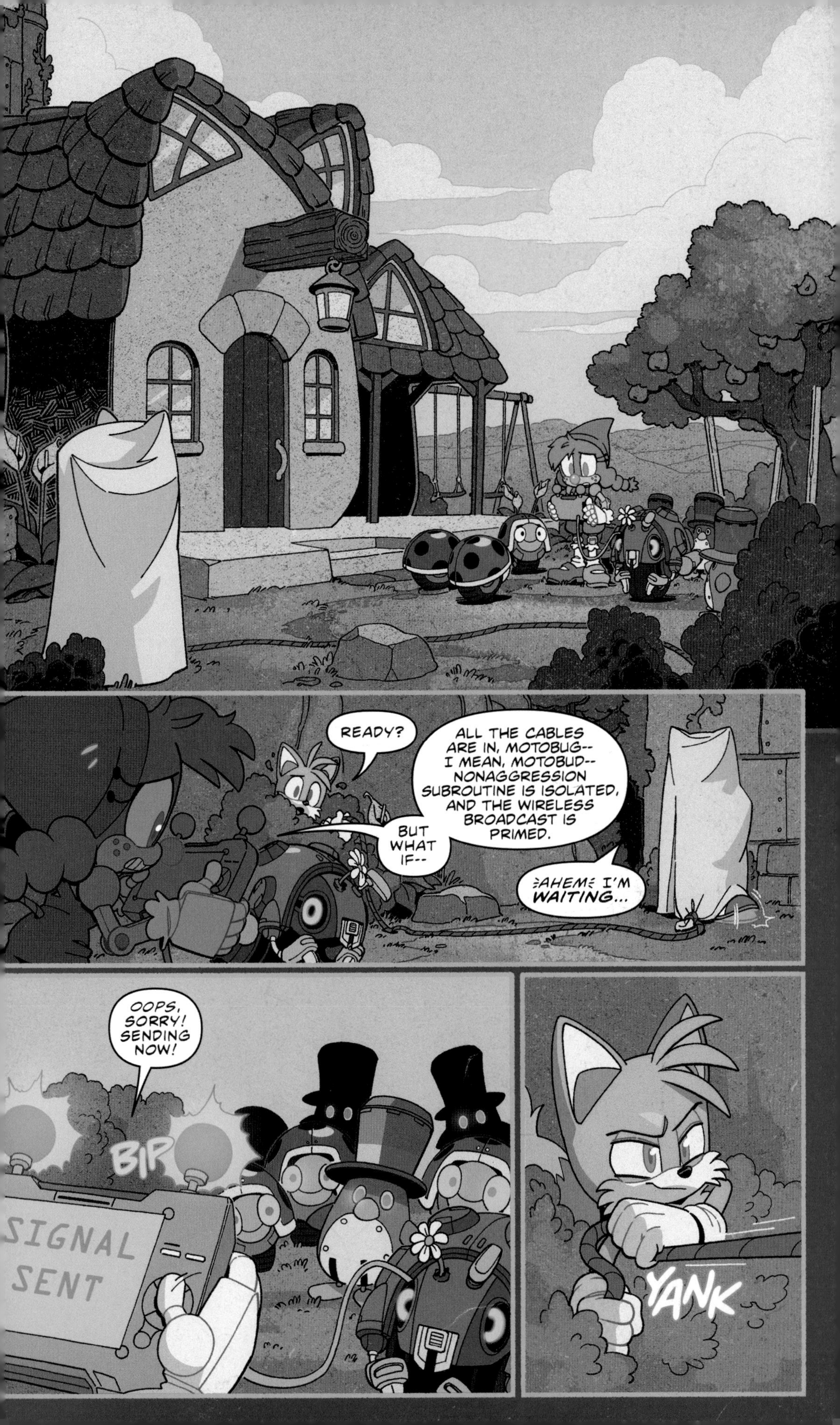
READY?
ALL THE CABLES ARE IN, MOTOBUG-- I MEAN, MOTOBUD-- NONAGGRESSION SUBROUTINE IS ISOLATED, AND THE WIRELESS BROADCAST IS PRIMED.
BUT WHAT IF--
AHEM I'M WAITING...
OOPS, SORRY! SENDING NOW!
BIP
SIGNAL SENT
YANK

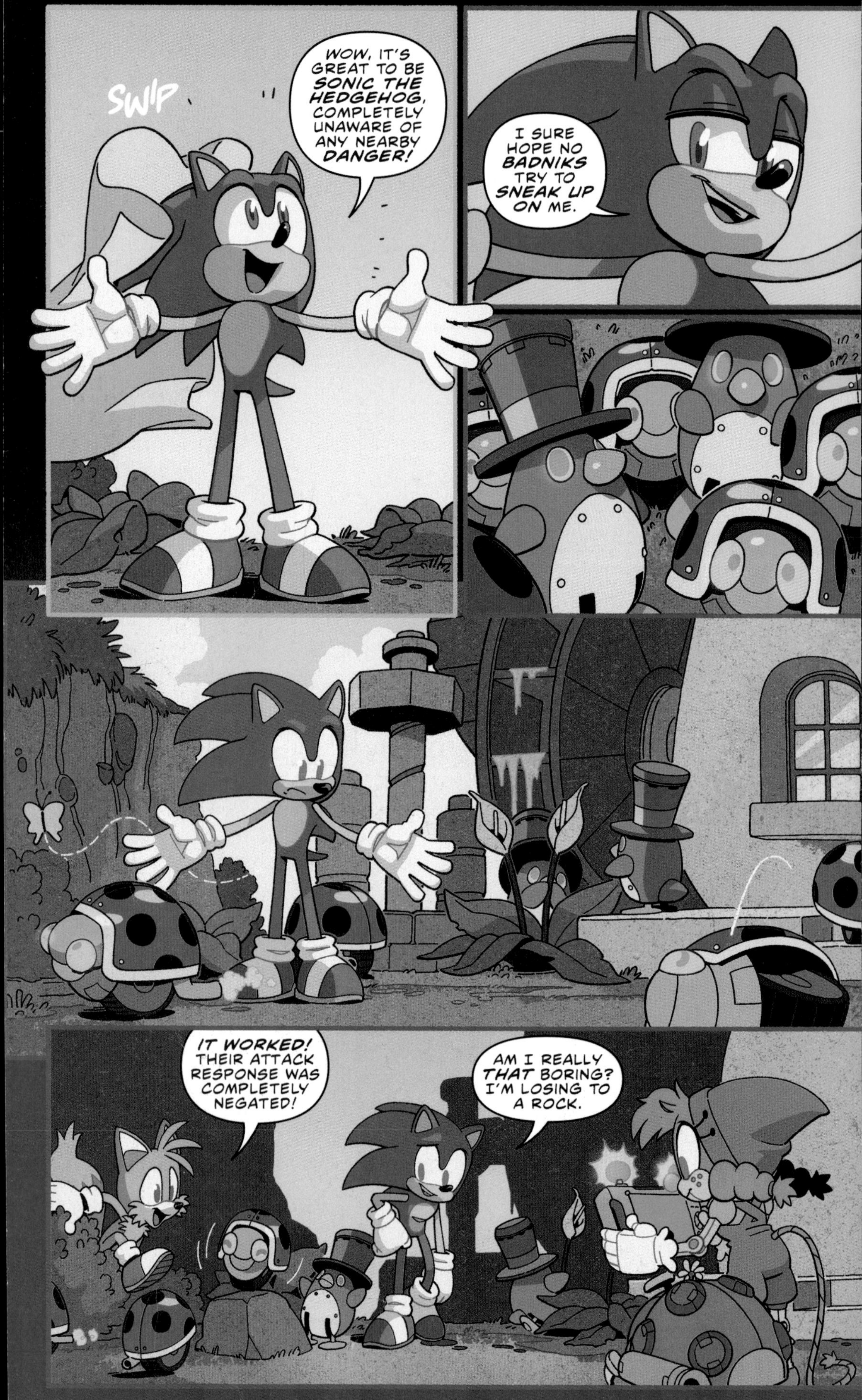
SWIP
WOW, IT'S GREAT TO BE SONIC THE HEDGEHOG, COMPLETELY UNAWARE OF ANY NEARBY DANGER!
I SURE HOPE NO BADNIKS TRY TO SNEAK UP ON ME.
IT WORKED! THEIR ATTACK RESPONSE WAS COMPLETELY NEGATED!
AM I REALLY THAT BORING? I'M LOSING TO A ROCK.

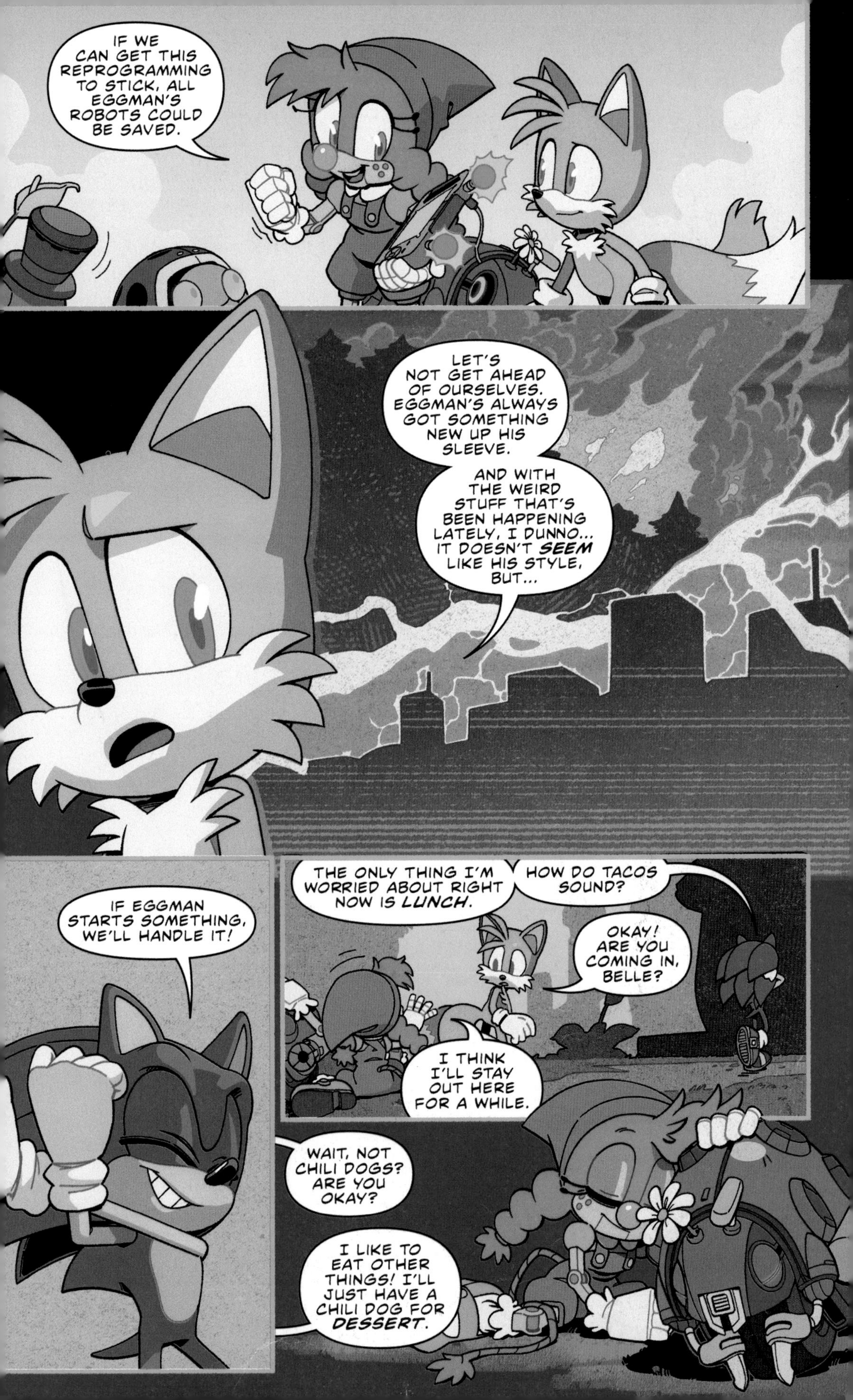
IF WE CAN GET THIS REPROGRAMMING TO STICK, ALL EGGMAN'S ROBOTS COULD BE SAVED.
LET'S NOT GET AHEAD OF OURSELVES. EGGMAN'S ALWAYS GOT SOMETHING NEW UP HIS SLEEVE.
AND WITH THE WEIRD STUFF THAT'S BEEN HAPPENING LATELY, I DUNNO... IT DOESN'T *SEEM* LIKE HIS STYLE, BUT...
IF EGGMAN STARTS SOMETHING, WE'LL HANDLE IT!
THE ONLY THING I'M WORRIED ABOUT RIGHT NOW IS *LUNCH*.
HOW DO TACOS SOUND?
OKAY! ARE YOU COMING IN, BELLE?
I THINK I'LL STAY OUT HERE FOR A WHILE.
WAIT, NOT CHILI DOGS? ARE YOU OKAY?
I LIKE TO EAT OTHER THINGS! I'LL JUST HAVE A CHILI DOG FOR *DESSERT*.

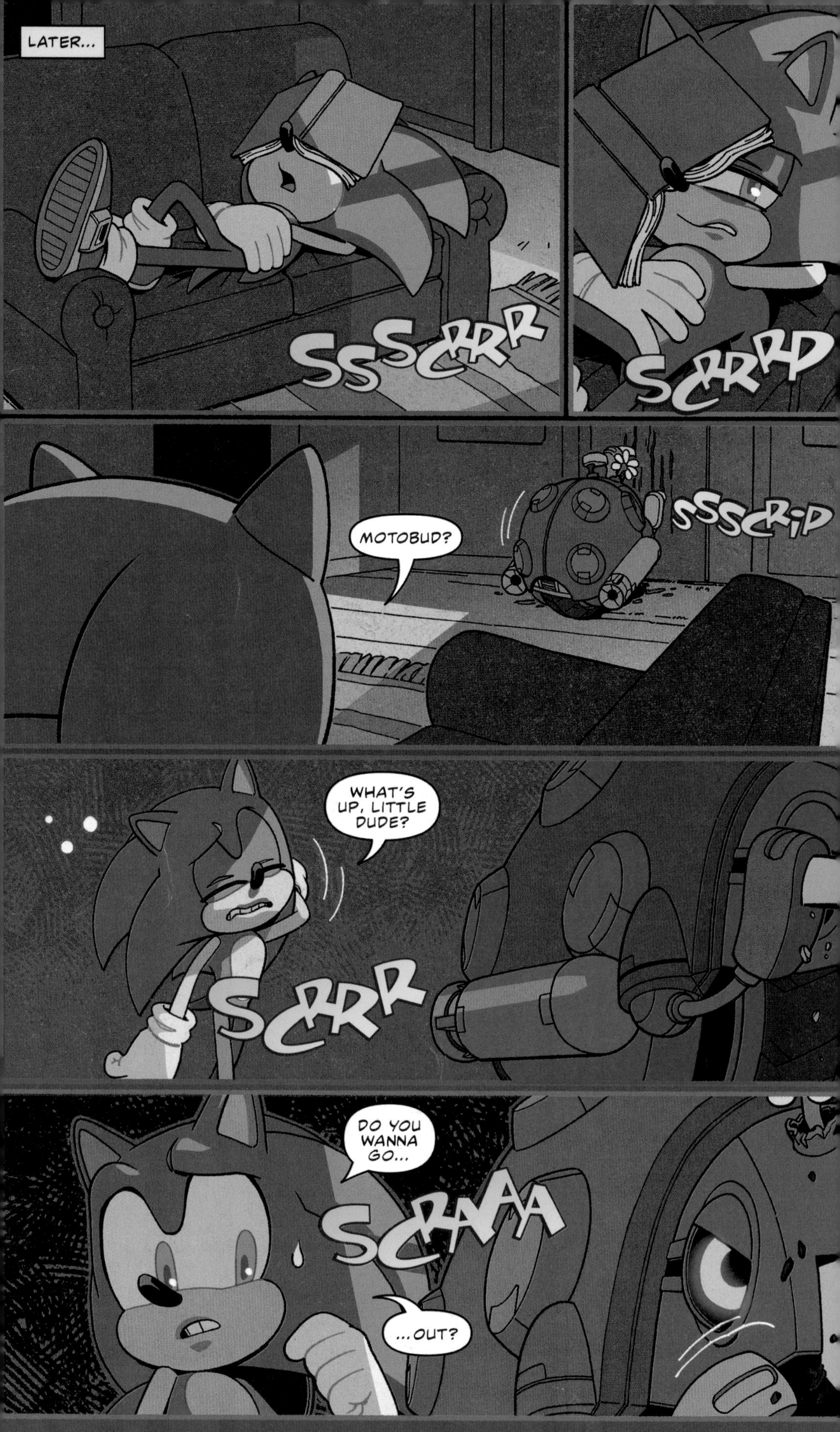
LATER...
SSSCRRR
SCRRRD
MOTOBUD?
SSSCRIP
WHAT'S UP, LITTLE DUDE?
SCRRR
DO YOU WANNA GO...
SCRAAA
...OUT?

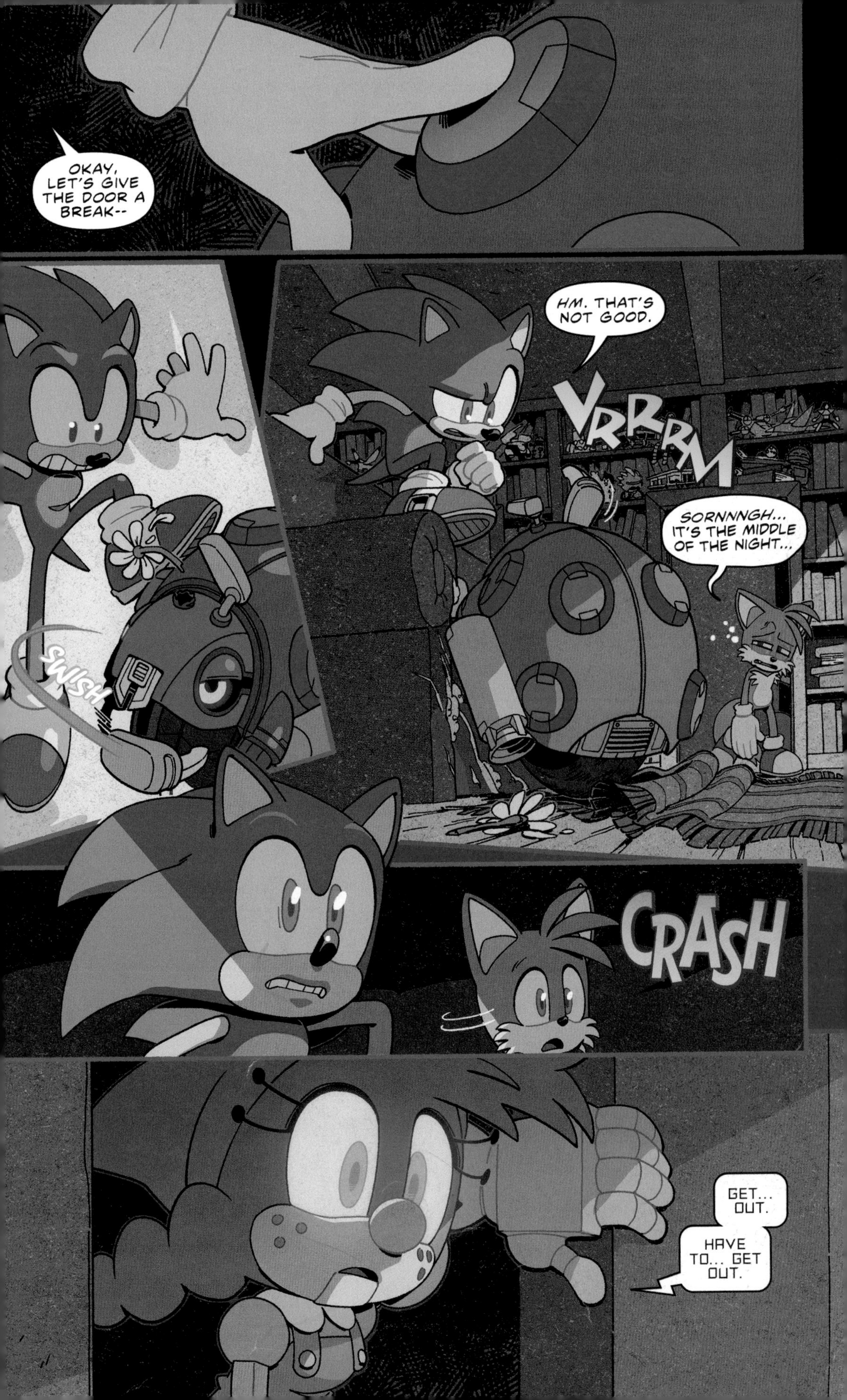
OKAY, LET'S GIVE THE DOOR A BREAK--
SWISH
HM. THAT'S NOT GOOD.
VRRRRM
SORNNNGH... IT'S THE MIDDLE OF THE NIGHT...
CRASH
GET... OUT.
HAVE TO... GET OUT.

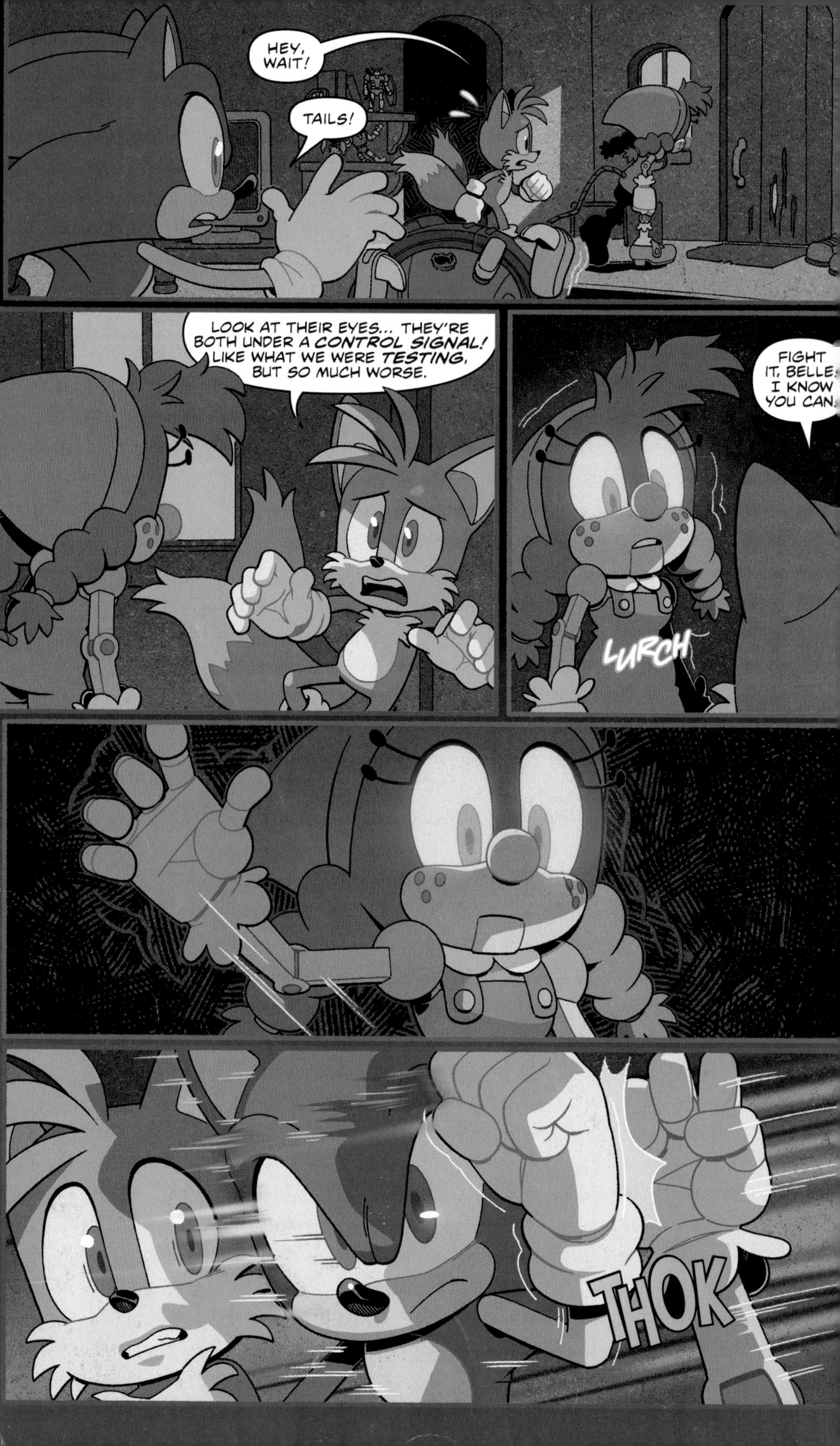
HEY, WAIT!
TAILS!
LOOK AT THEIR EYES... THEY'RE BOTH UNDER A CONTROL SIGNAL! LIKE WHAT WE WERE TESTING, BUT SO MUCH WORSE.
FIGHT IT, BELLE. I KNOW YOU CAN.
LURCH
THOK

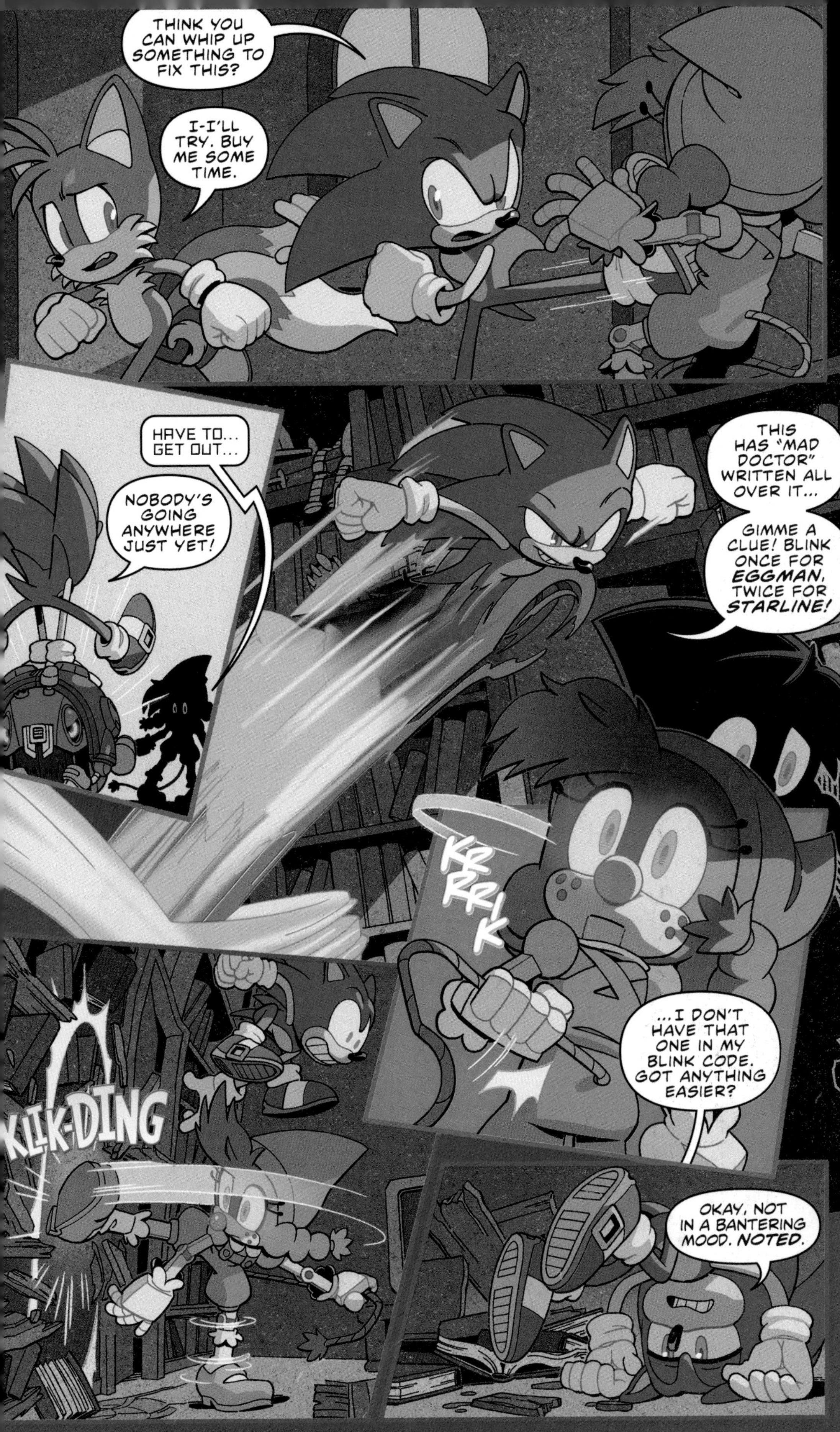
THINK YOU CAN WHIP UP SOMETHING TO FIX THIS?
I-I'LL TRY. BUY ME SOME TIME.
HAVE TO... GET OUT...
NOBODY'S GOING ANYWHERE JUST YET!
THIS HAS "MAD DOCTOR" WRITTEN ALL OVER IT...
GIMME A CLUE! BLINK ONCE FOR EGGMAN, TWICE FOR STARLINE!
KRRRIK
...I DON'T HAVE THAT ONE IN MY BLINK CODE. GOT ANYTHING EASIER?
KLIK-DING
OKAY, NOT IN A BANTERING MOOD. NOTED.

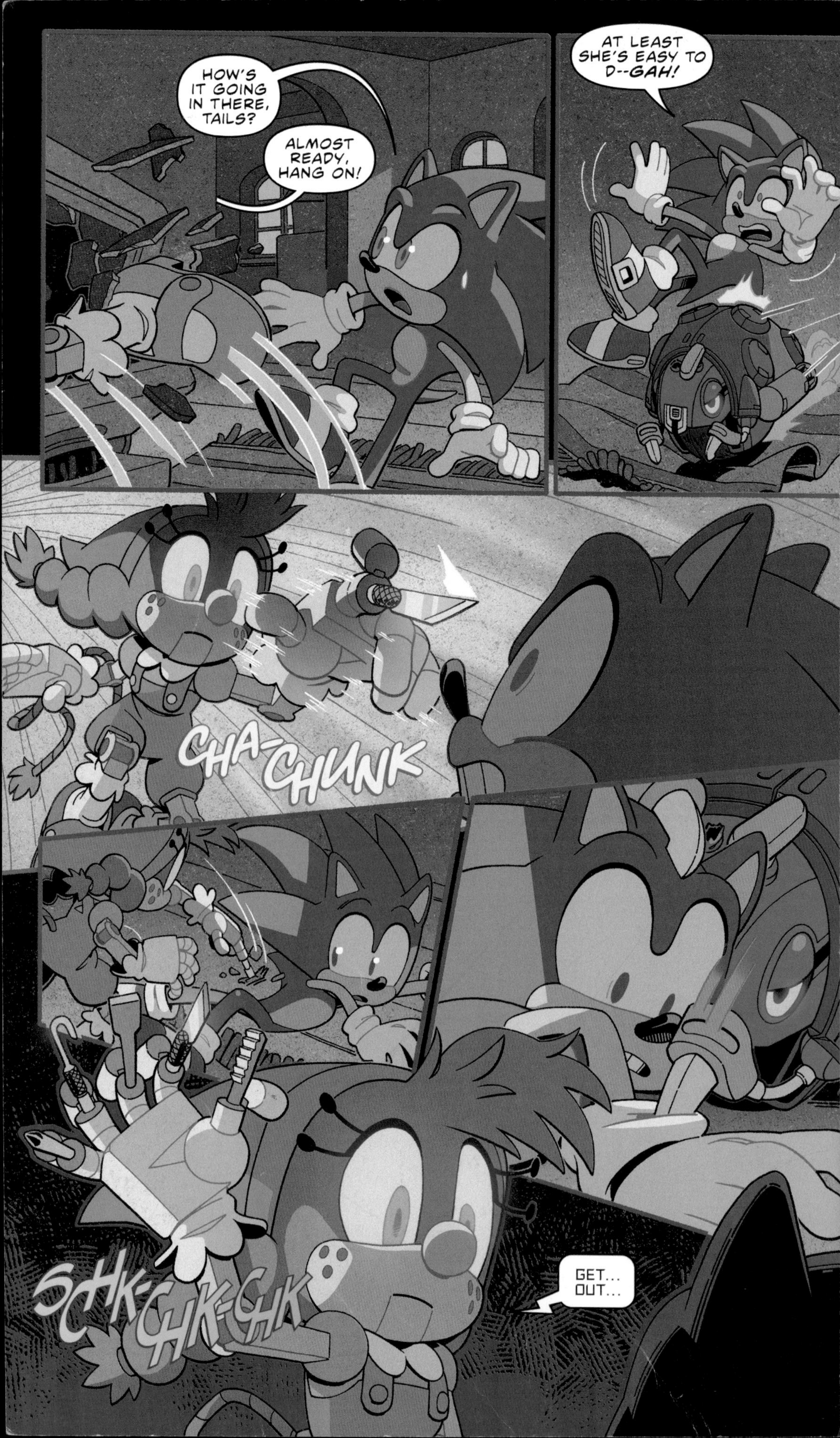

HOW'S IT GOING IN THERE, TAILS?
ALMOST READY, HANG ON!
AT LEAST SHE'S EASY TO D--GAH!
CHA-CHUNK
SCHK-CHK-CHK
GET... OUT...

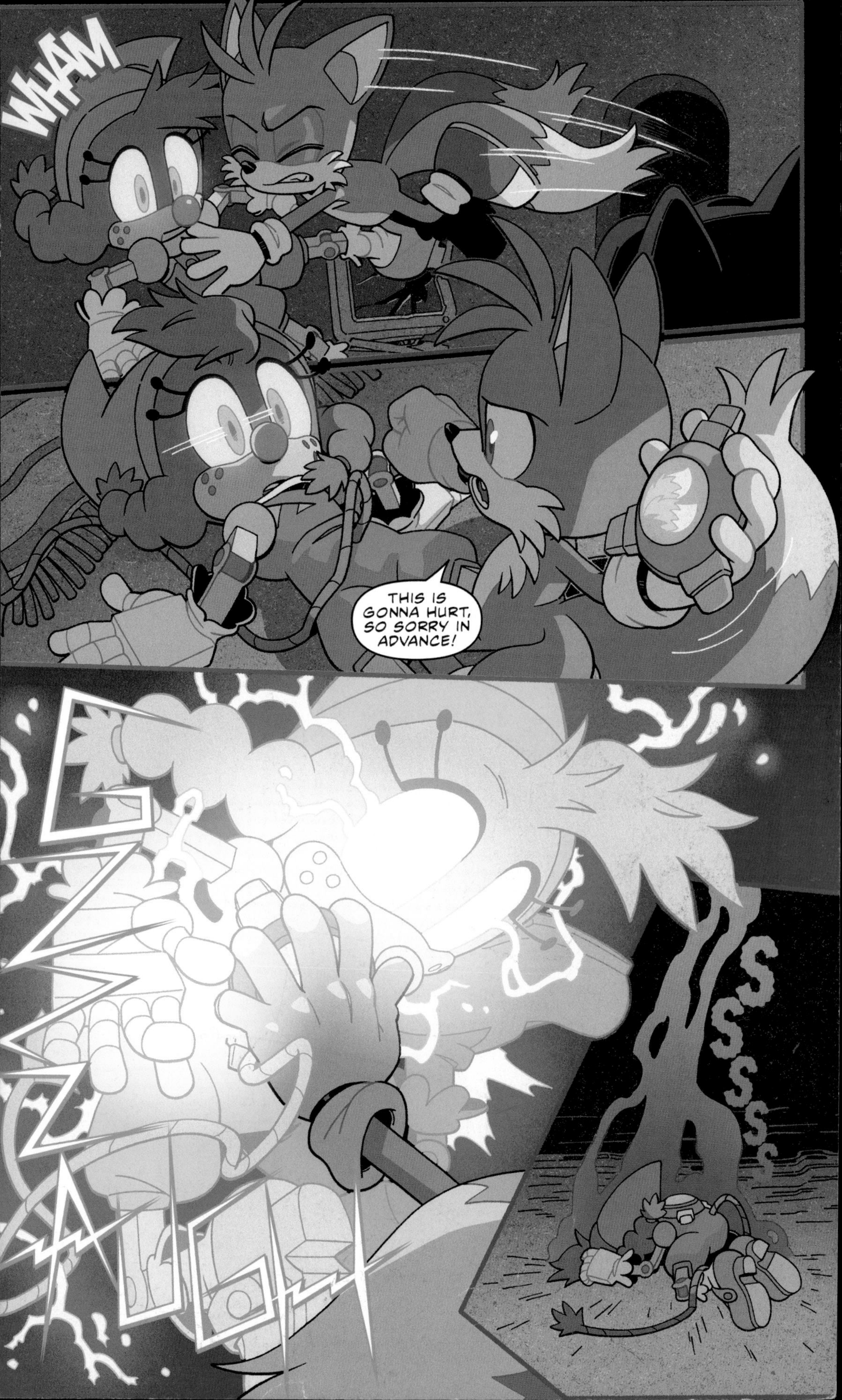
WHAM
THIS IS GONNA HURT, SO SORRY IN ADVANCE!
ZZAK
SSSSS

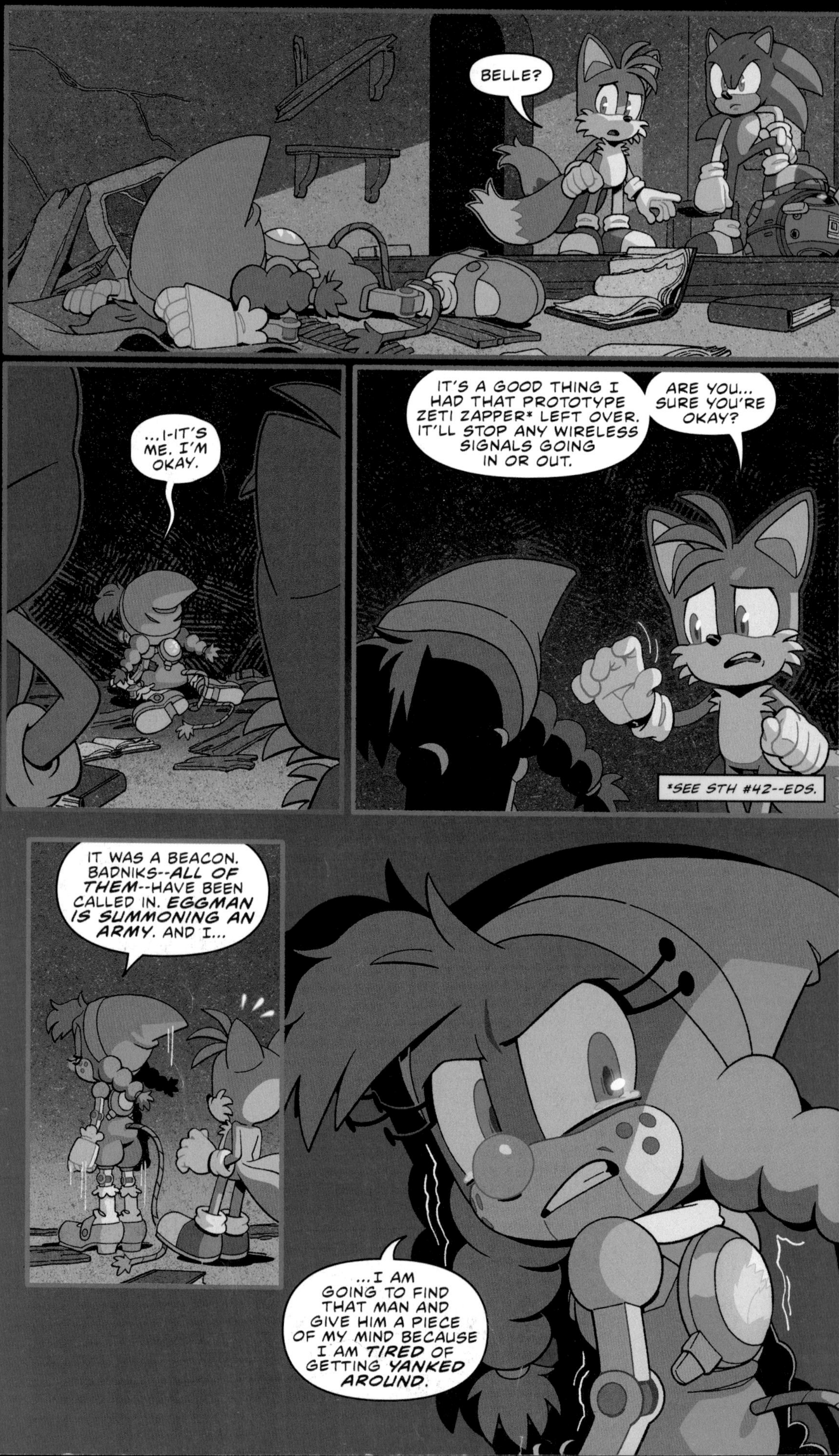
BELLE?
...I-IT'S ME. I'M OKAY.
IT'S A GOOD THING I HAD THAT PROTOTYPE ZETI ZAPPER* LEFT OVER. IT'LL STOP ANY WIRELESS SIGNALS GOING IN OR OUT.
ARE YOU... SURE YOU'RE OKAY?
*SEE STH #42--EDS.
IT WAS A BEACON. BADNIKS--ALL OF THEM--HAVE BEEN CALLED IN. EGGMAN IS SUMMONING AN ARMY. AND I...
...I AM GOING TO FIND THAT MAN AND GIVE HIM A PIECE OF MY MIND BECAUSE I AM TIRED OF GETTING YANKED AROUND.

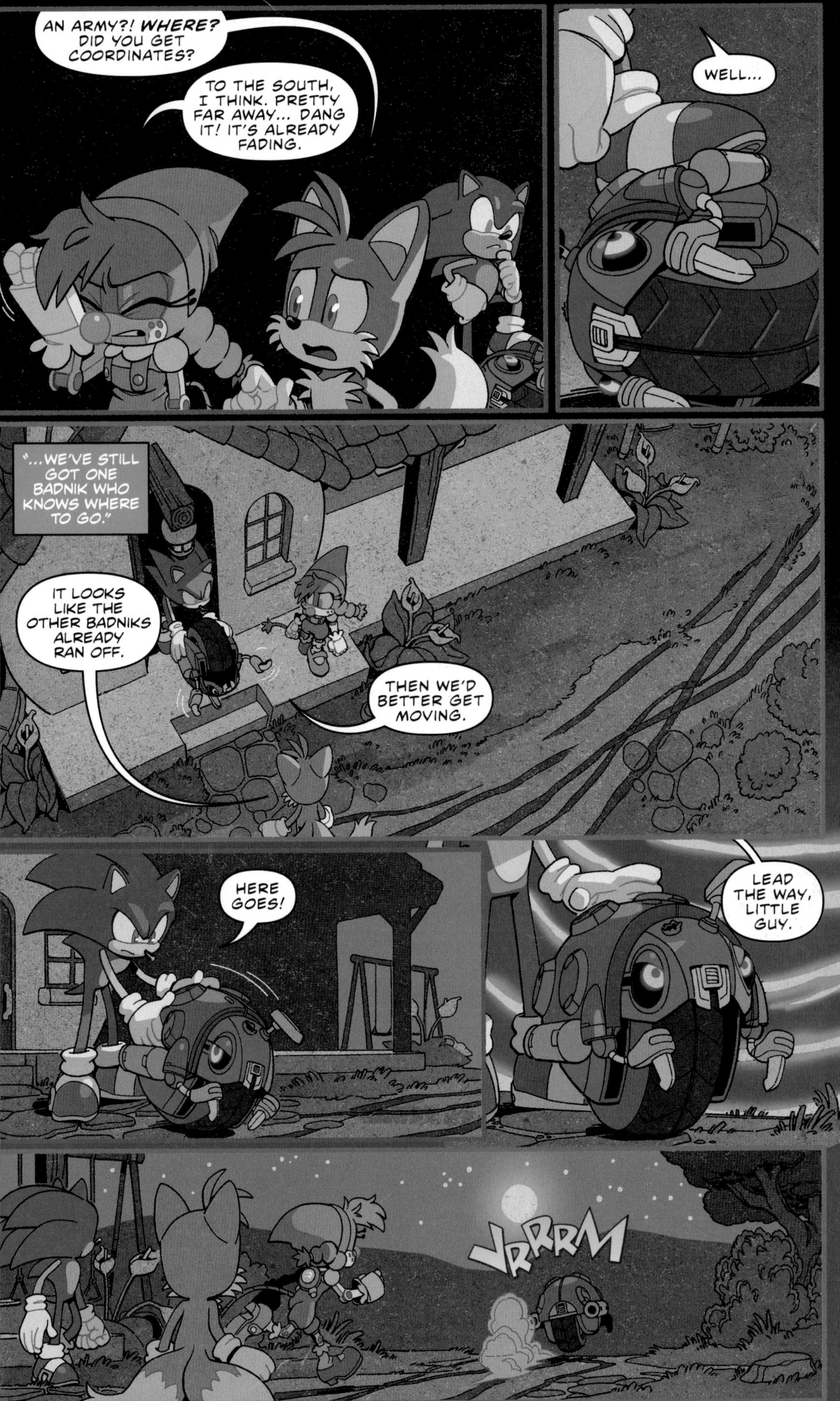
AN ARMY?! WHERE? DID YOU GET COORDINATES?
TO THE SOUTH, I THINK. PRETTY FAR AWAY... DANG IT! IT'S ALREADY FADING.
WELL...
"...WE'VE STILL GOT ONE BADNIK WHO KNOWS WHERE TO GO."
IT LOOKS LIKE THE OTHER BADNIKS ALREADY RAN OFF.
THEN WE'D BETTER GET MOVING.
HERE GOES!
LEAD THE WAY, LITTLE GUY.
VRRRM

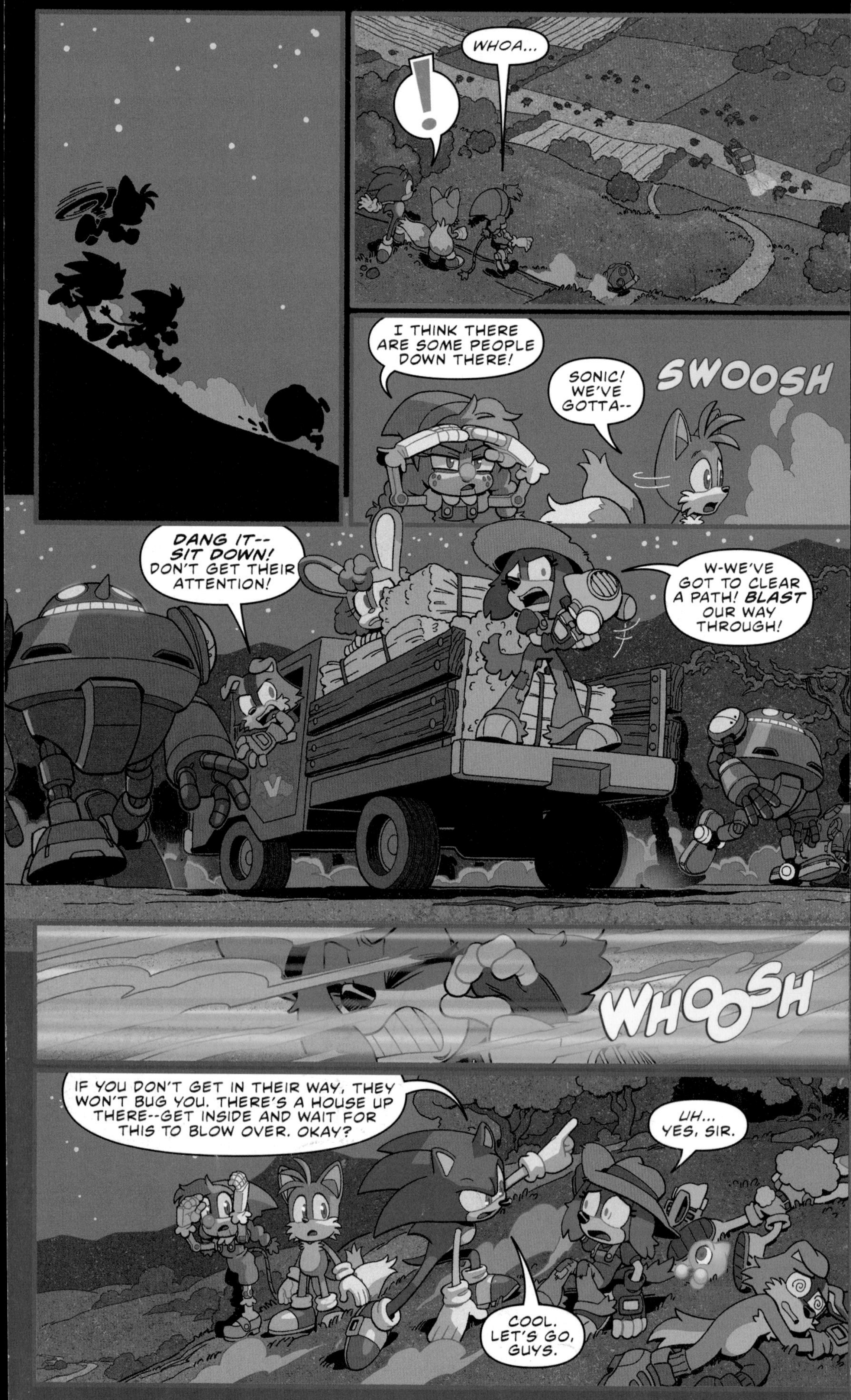
WHOA...
!
I THINK THERE ARE SOME PEOPLE DOWN THERE!
SONIC! WE'VE GOTTA--
SWOOSH
DANG IT-- SIT DOWN! DON'T GET THEIR ATTENTION!
W-WE'VE GOT TO CLEAR A PATH! BLAST OUR WAY THROUGH!
WHOOSH
IF YOU DON'T GET IN THEIR WAY, THEY WON'T BUG YOU. THERE'S A HOUSE UP THERE--GET INSIDE AND WAIT FOR THIS TO BLOW OVER. OKAY?
UH... YES, SIR.
COOL. LET'S GO, GUYS.

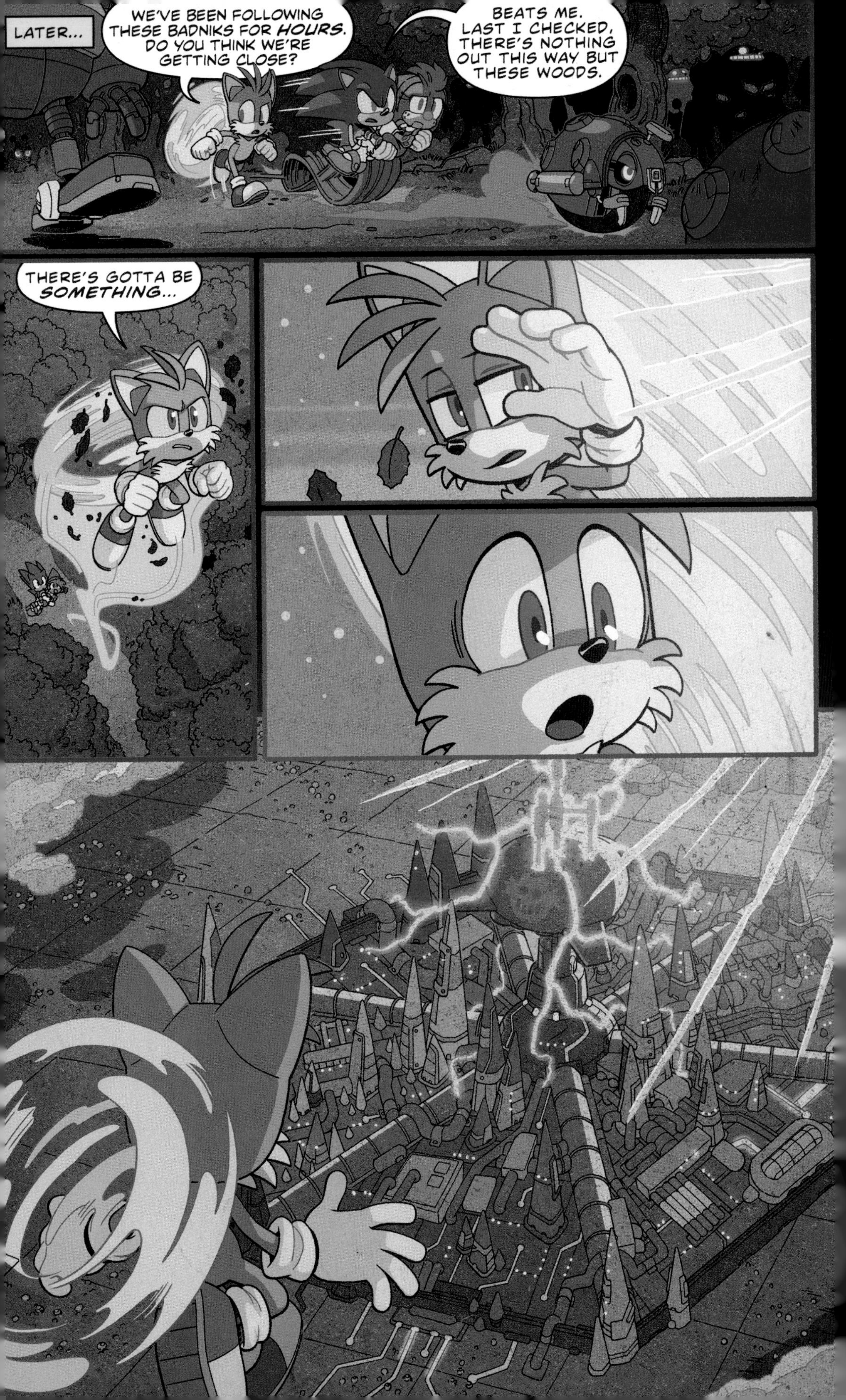
LATER...
WE'VE BEEN FOLLOWING THESE BADNIKS FOR HOURS. DO YOU THINK WE'RE GETTING CLOSE?
BEATS ME. LAST I CHECKED, THERE'S NOTHING OUT THIS WAY BUT THESE WOODS.
THERE'S GOTTA BE SOMETHING...

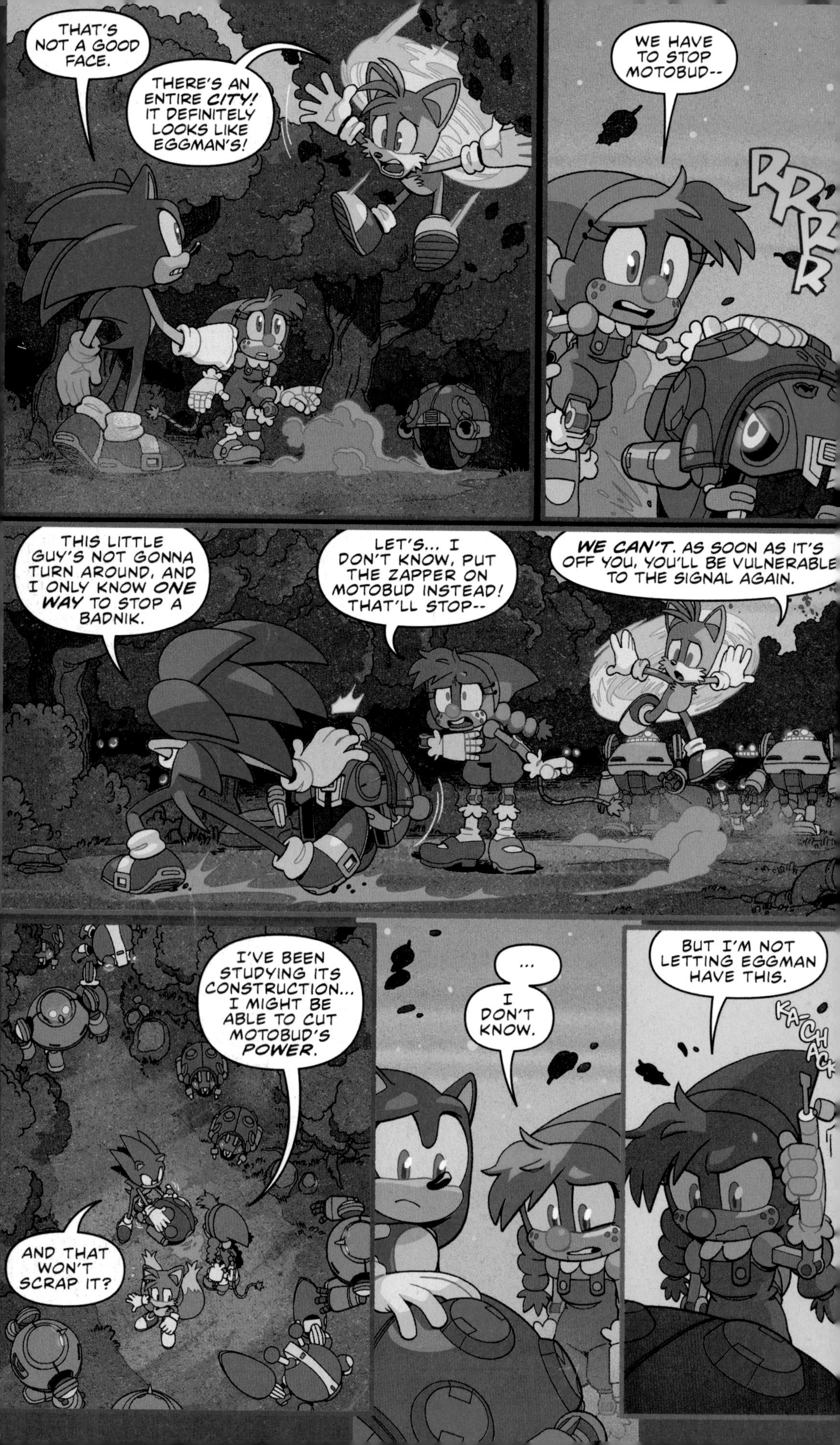
THAT'S NOT A GOOD FACE.
THERE'S AN ENTIRE CITY! IT DEFINITELY LOOKS LIKE EGGMAN'S!
WE HAVE TO STOP MOTOBUD--
RRRR
THIS LITTLE GUY'S NOT GONNA TURN AROUND, AND I ONLY KNOW ONE WAY TO STOP A BADNIK.
LET'S... I DON'T KNOW, PUT THE ZAPPER ON MOTOBUD INSTEAD! THAT'LL STOP--
WE CAN'T. AS SOON AS IT'S OFF YOU, YOU'LL BE VULNERABLE TO THE SIGNAL AGAIN.
I'VE BEEN STUDYING ITS CONSTRUCTION... I MIGHT BE ABLE TO CUT MOTOBUD'S POWER.
AND THAT WON'T SCRAP IT?
...
I DON'T KNOW.
BUT I'M NOT LETTING EGGMAN HAVE THIS.
KA-CHACK

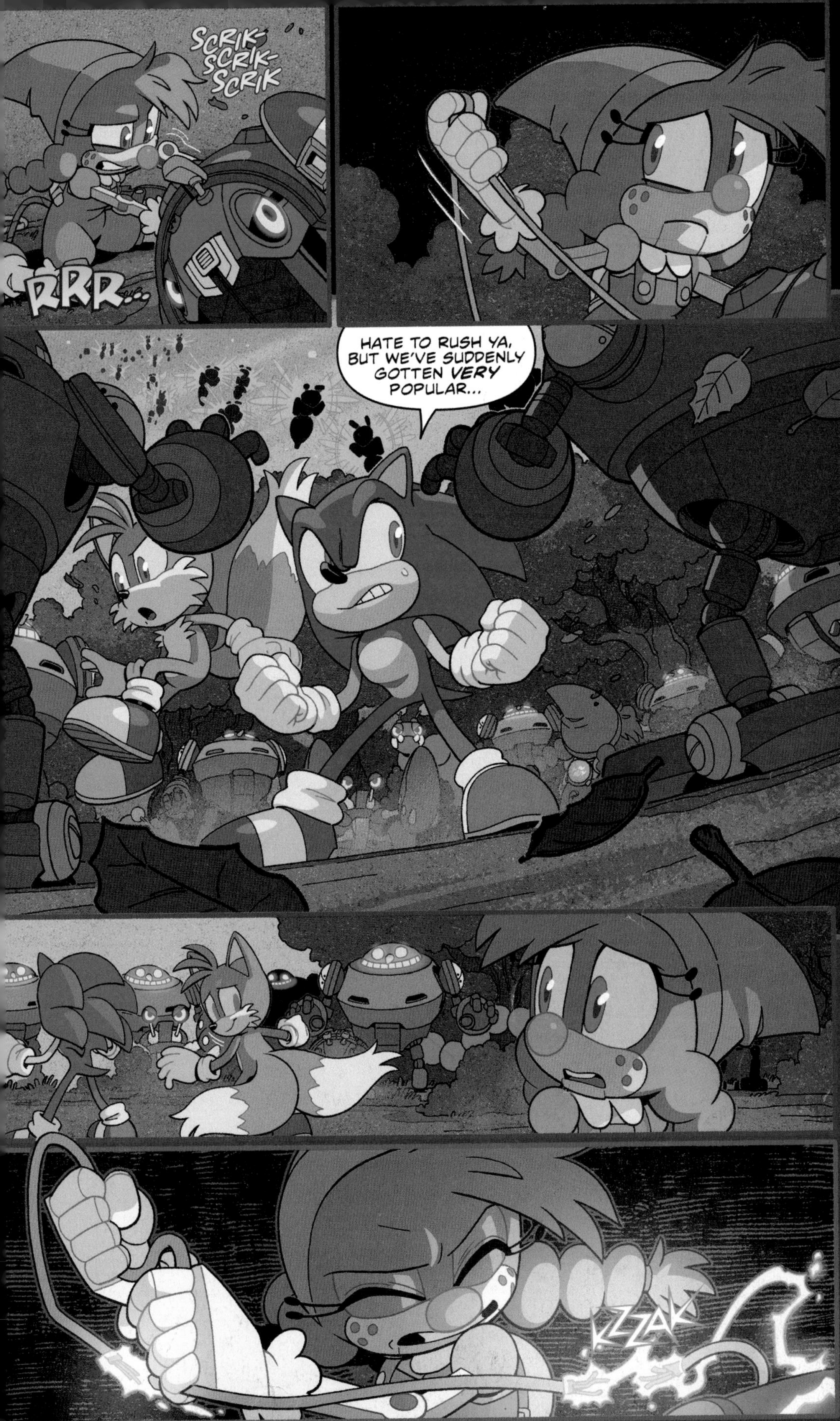
SCRIK-
SCRIK-
SCRIK
RRR...
HATE TO RUSH YA, BUT WE'VE SUDDENLY GOTTEN VERY POPULAR...
KZZAK

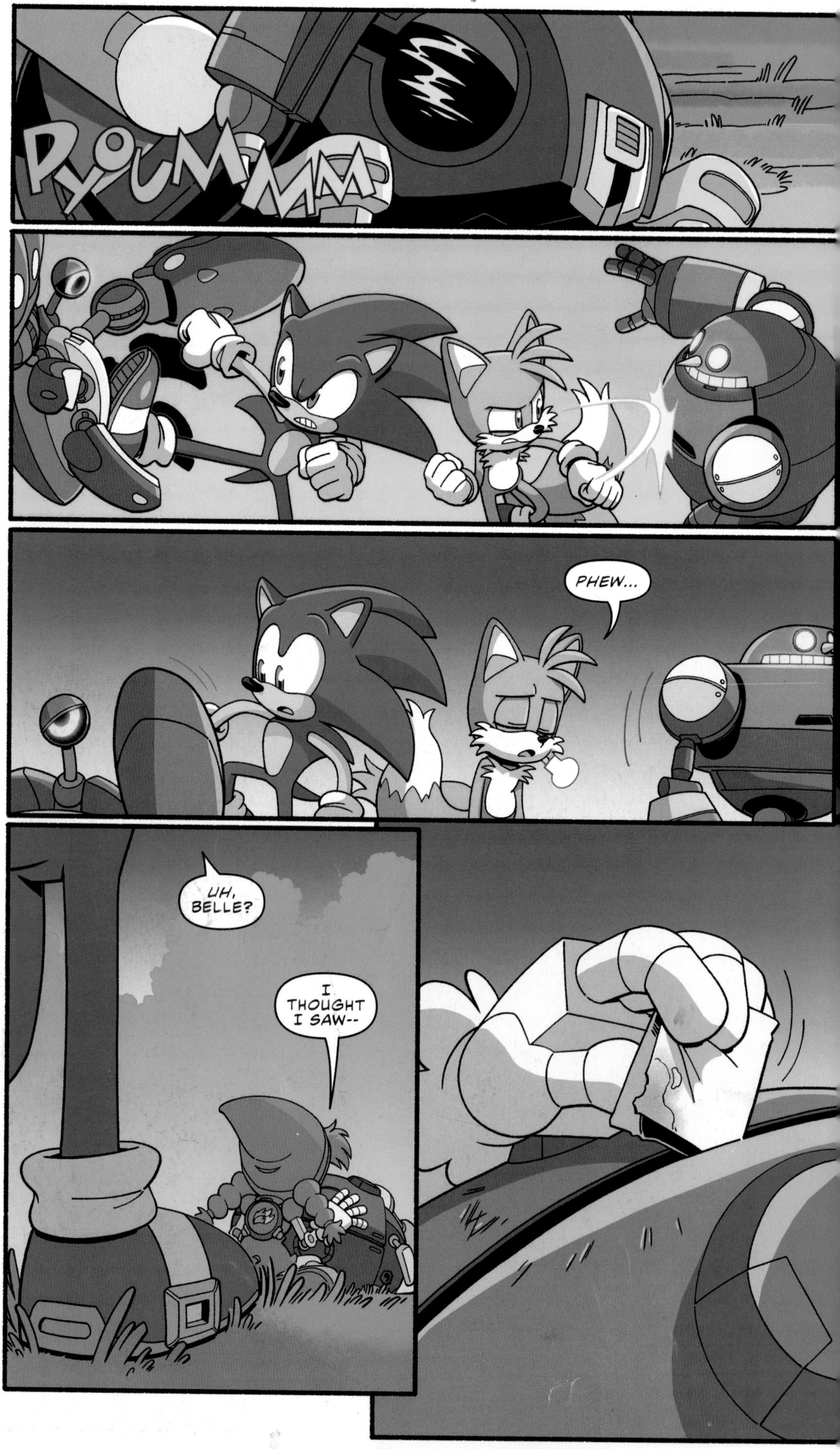

PYOUMMMM
PHEW...
UH, BELLE?
I THOUGHT I SAW--

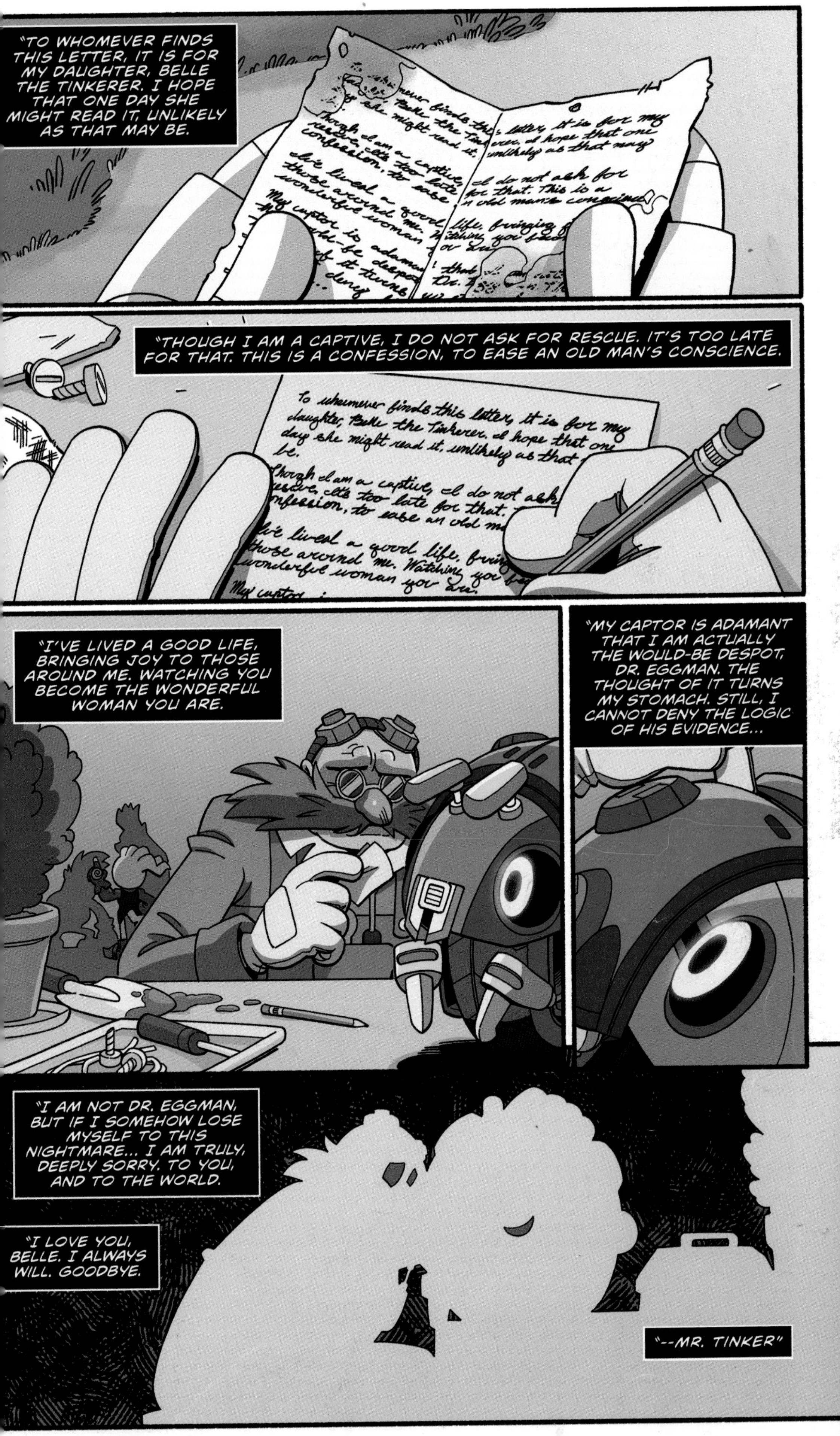
"TO WHOMEVER FINDS THIS LETTER, IT IS FOR MY DAUGHTER, BELLE THE TINKERER. I HOPE THAT ONE DAY SHE MIGHT READ IT, UNLIKELY AS THAT MAY BE.
"THOUGH I AM A CAPTIVE, I DO NOT ASK FOR RESCUE. IT'S TOO LATE FOR THAT. THIS IS A CONFESSION, TO EASE AN OLD MAN'S CONSCIENCE.
"I'VE LIVED A GOOD LIFE, BRINGING JOY TO THOSE AROUND ME. WATCHING YOU BECOME THE WONDERFUL WOMAN YOU ARE.
"MY CAPTOR IS ADAMANT THAT I AM ACTUALLY THE WOULD-BE DESPOT, DR. EGGMAN. THE THOUGHT OF IT TURNS MY STOMACH. STILL, I CANNOT DENY THE LOGIC OF HIS EVIDENCE...
"I AM NOT DR. EGGMAN, BUT IF I SOMEHOW LOSE MYSELF TO THIS NIGHTMARE... I AM TRULY, DEEPLY SORRY. TO YOU, AND TO THE WORLD.
"I LOVE YOU, BELLE. I ALWAYS WILL. GOODBYE.
"--MR. TINKER"

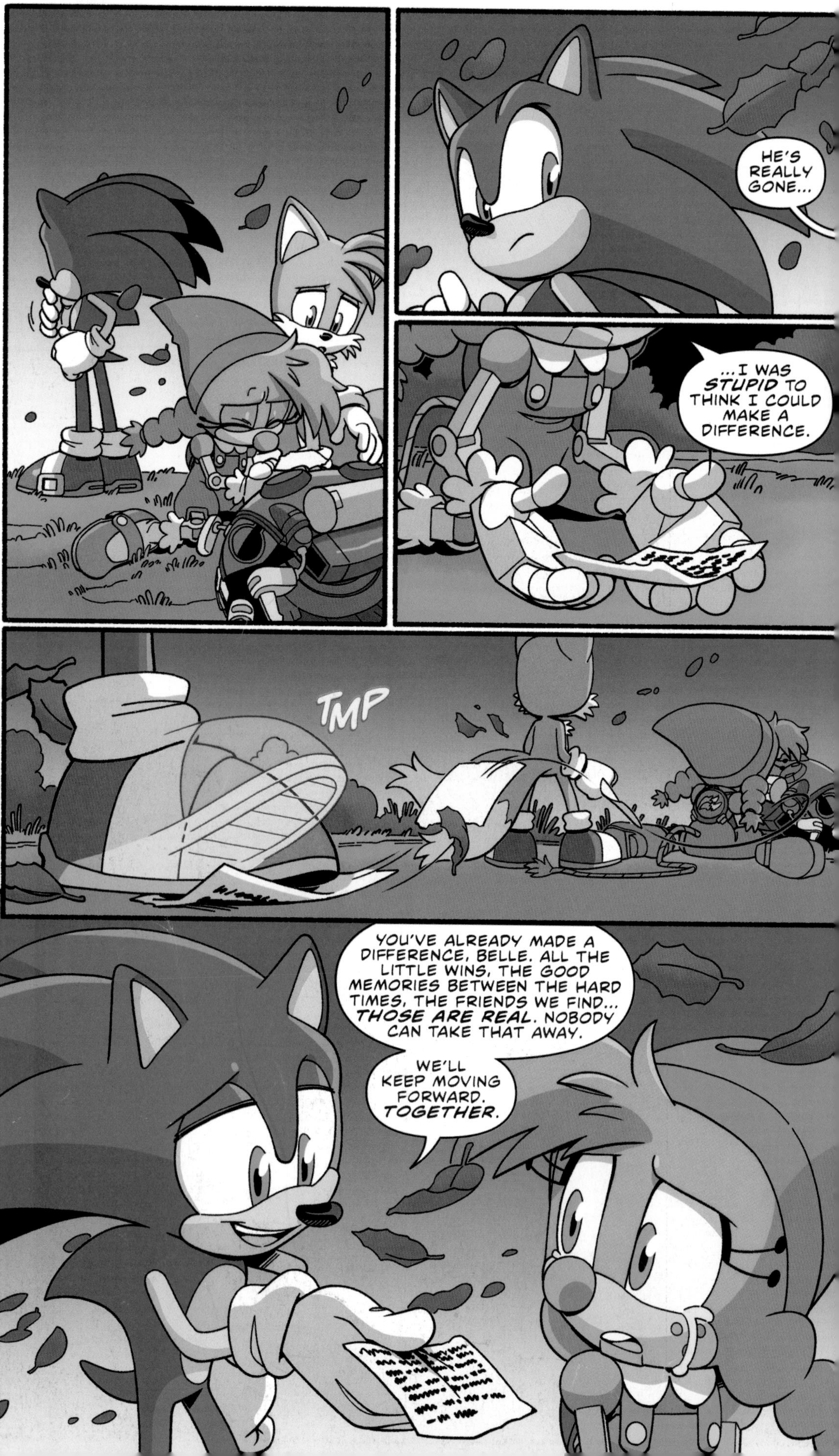
HE'S REALLY GONE...
...I WAS STUPID TO THINK I COULD MAKE A DIFFERENCE.
TMP
YOU'VE ALREADY MADE A DIFFERENCE, BELLE. ALL THE LITTLE WINS, THE GOOD MEMORIES BETWEEN THE HARD TIMES, THE FRIENDS WE FIND... THOSE ARE REAL. NOBODY CAN TAKE THAT AWAY.
WE'LL KEEP MOVING FORWARD. TOGETHER.

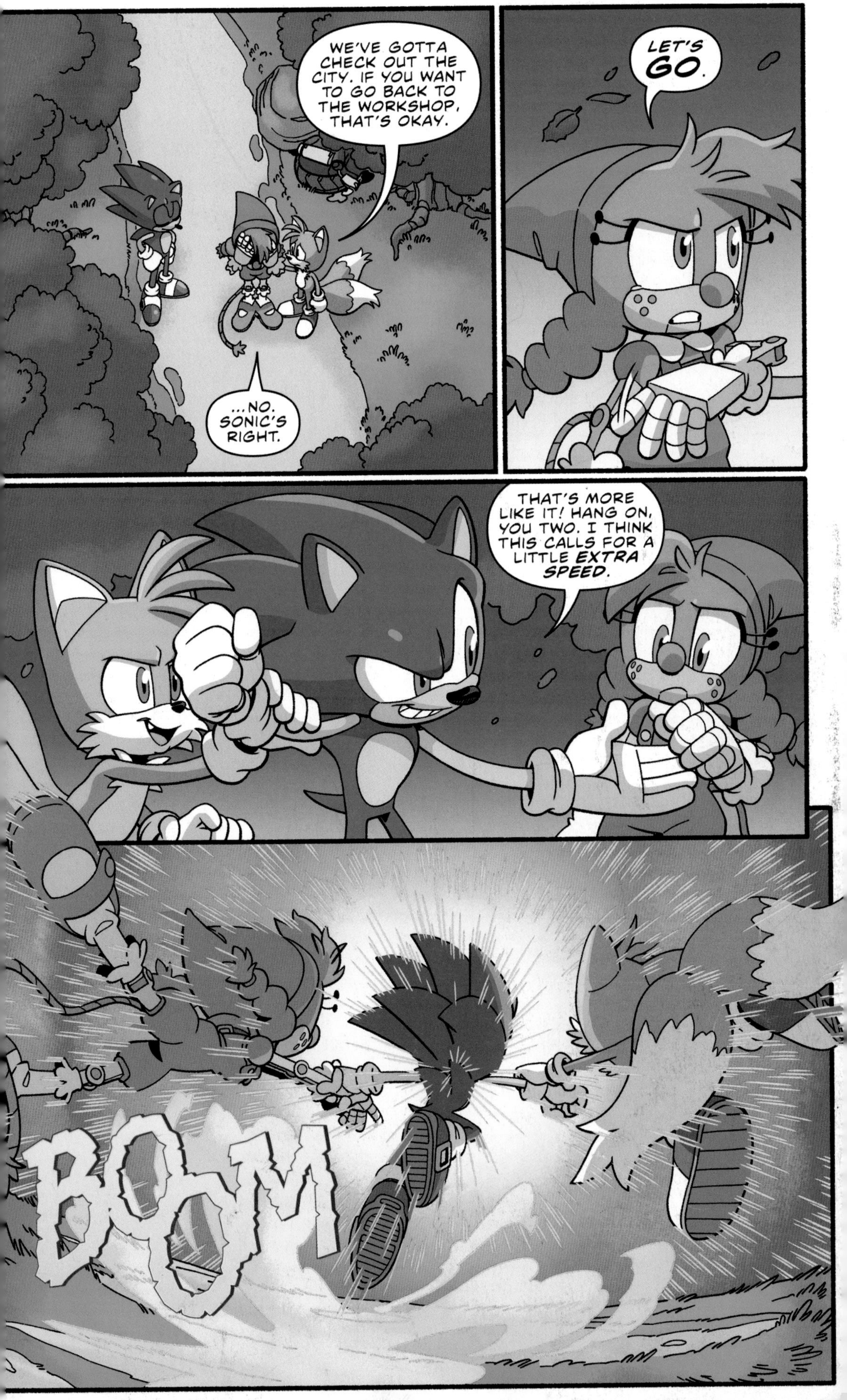
WE'VE GOTTA CHECK OUT THE CITY. IF YOU WANT TO GO BACK TO THE WORKSHOP, THAT'S OKAY.
...NO. SONIC'S RIGHT.
LET'S GO.
THAT'S MORE LIKE IT! HANG ON, YOU TWO. I THINK THIS CALLS FOR A LITTLE EXTRA SPEED.
BOOM

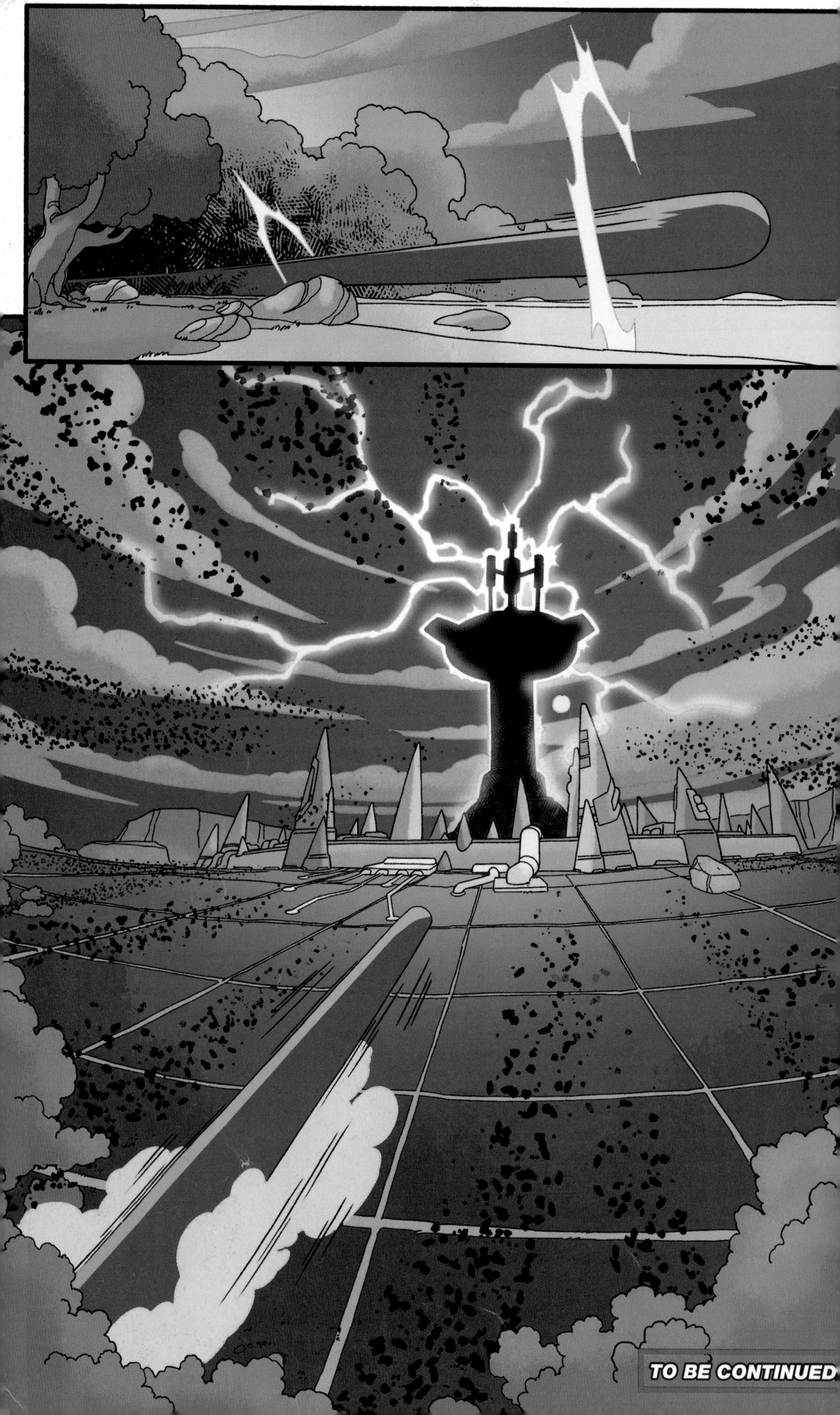
TO BE CONTINUED

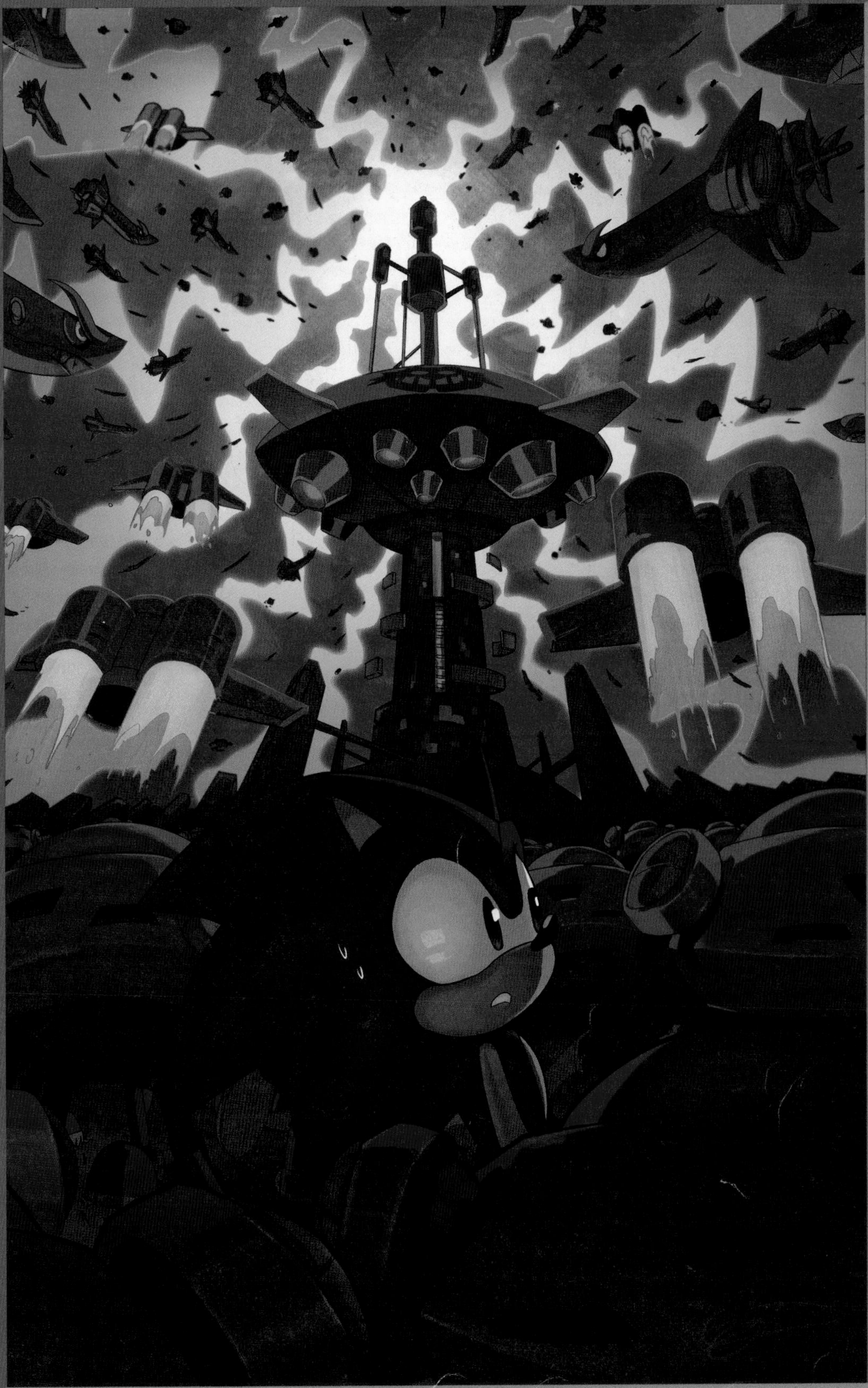

ART BY **GIGI DUTREIX**

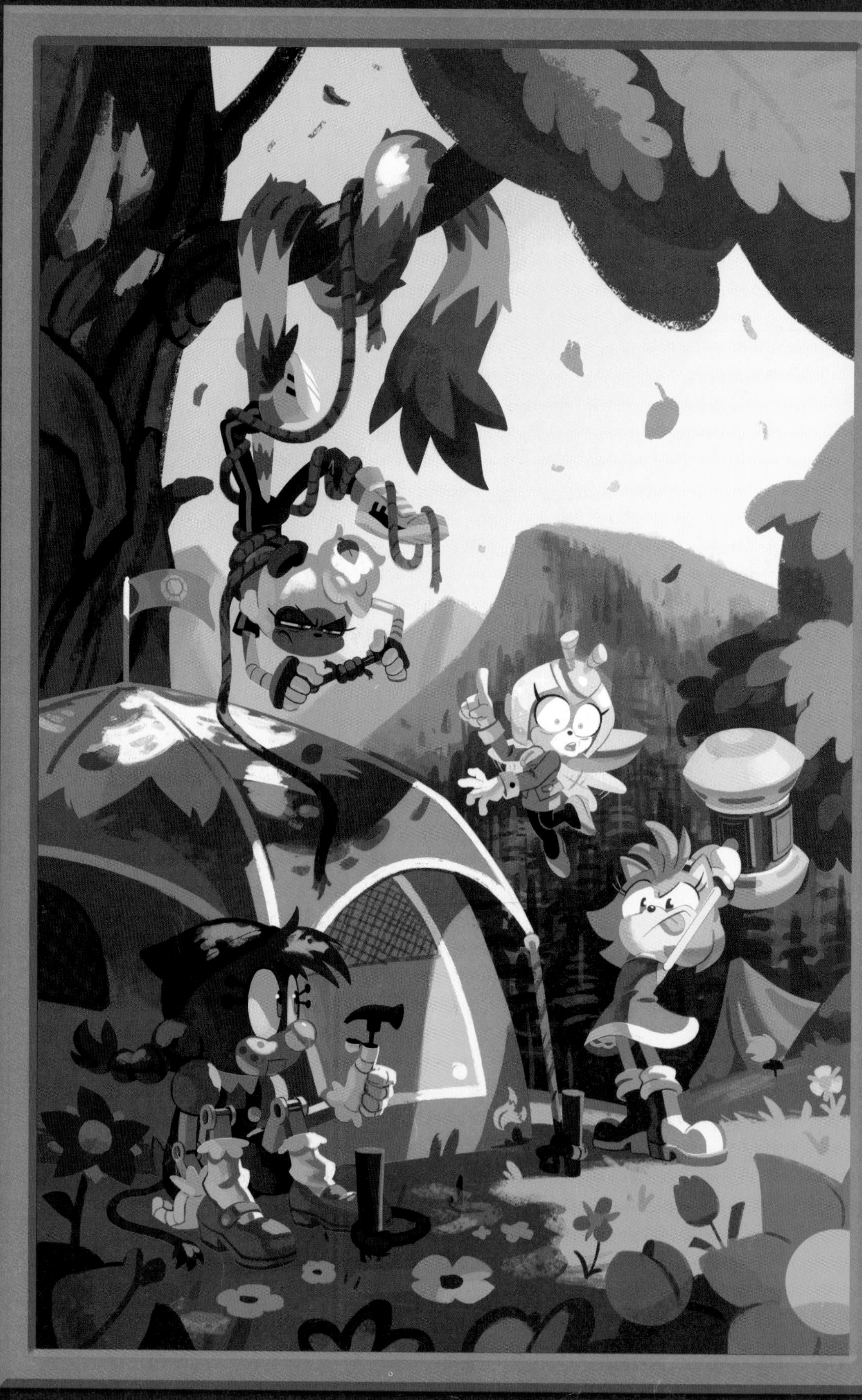

ART BY **NATHALIE FOURDRAINE**

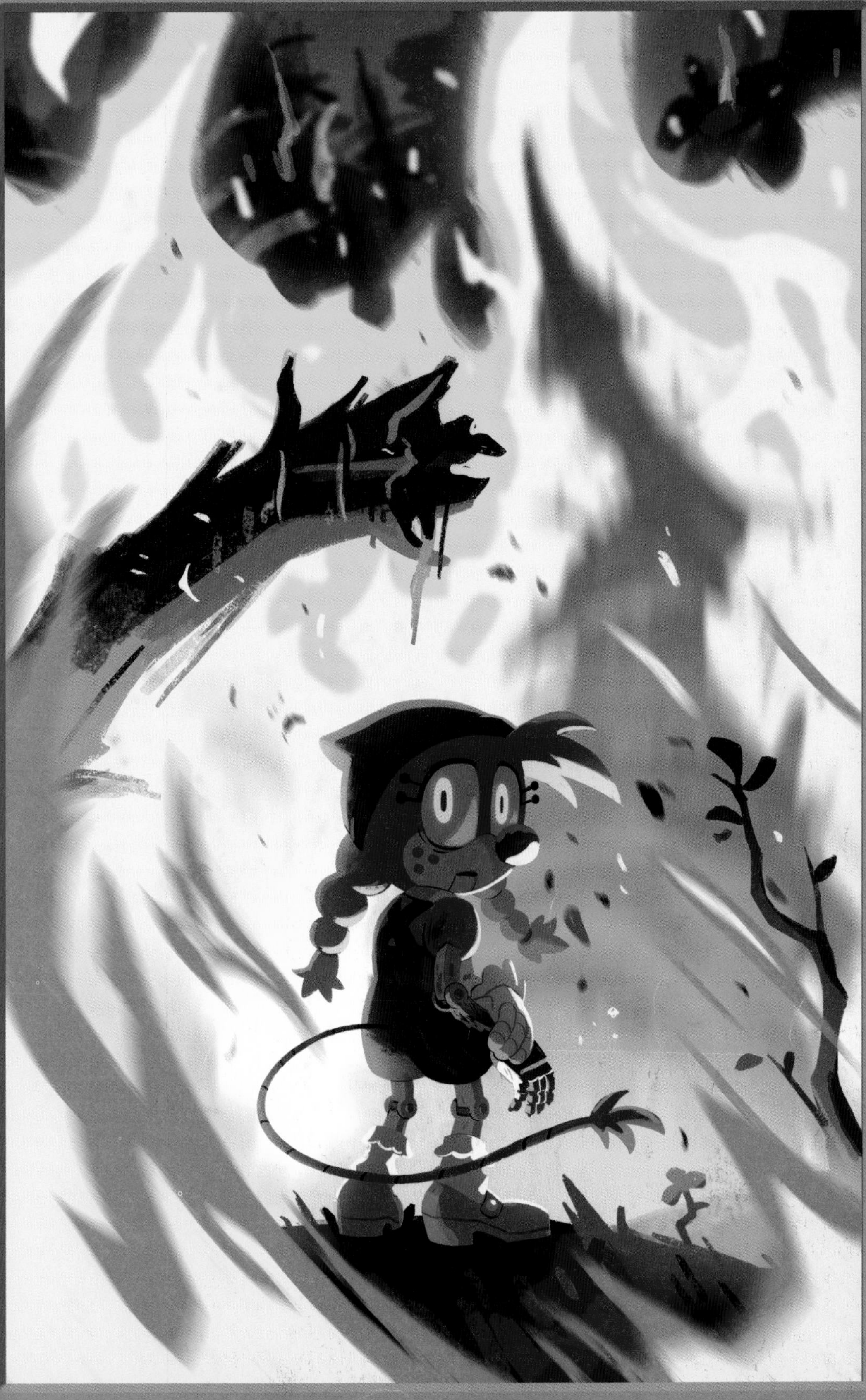

ART BY NATHALIE FOURDRAINE

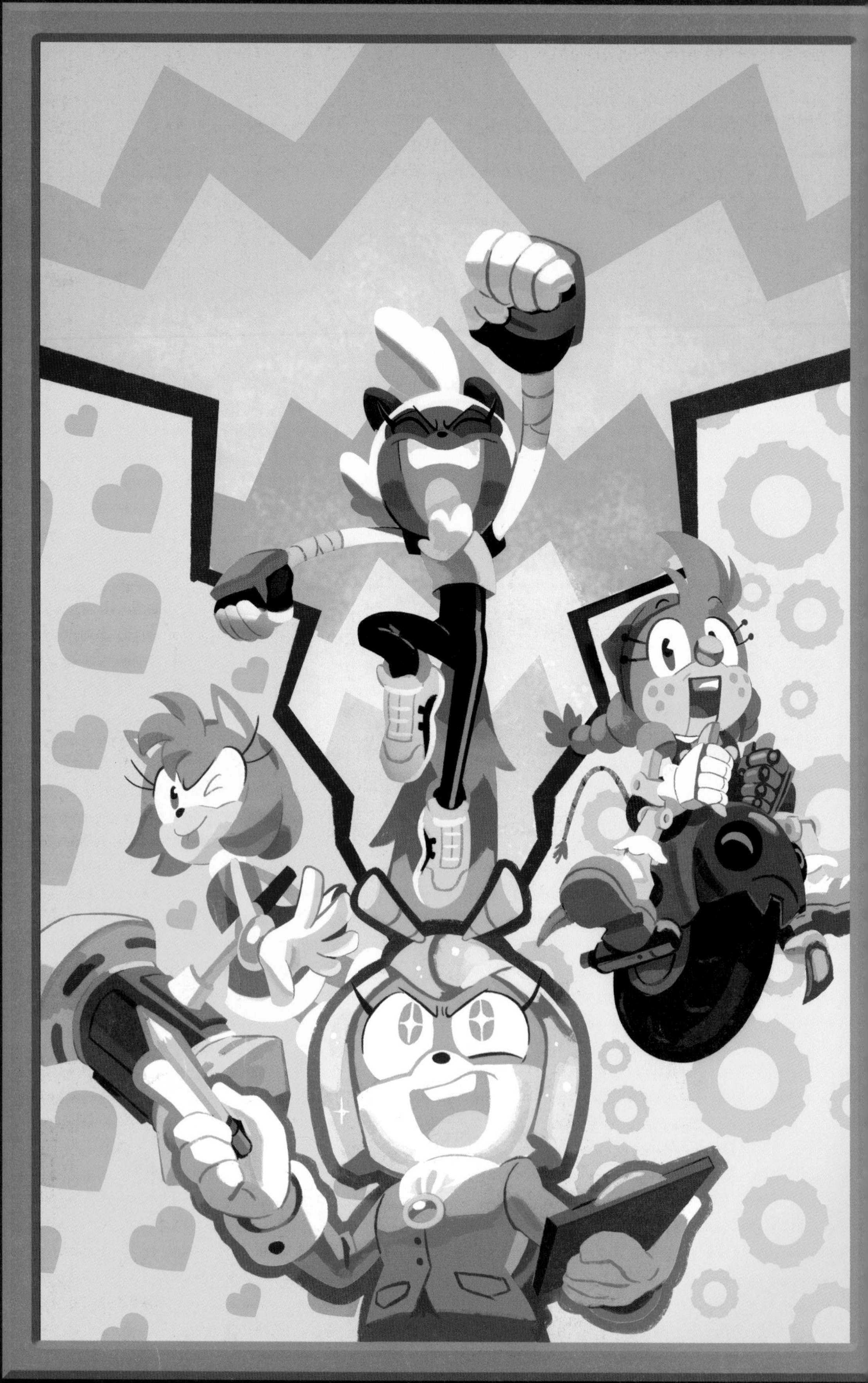

ART BY **NATHALIE FOURDRAINE**

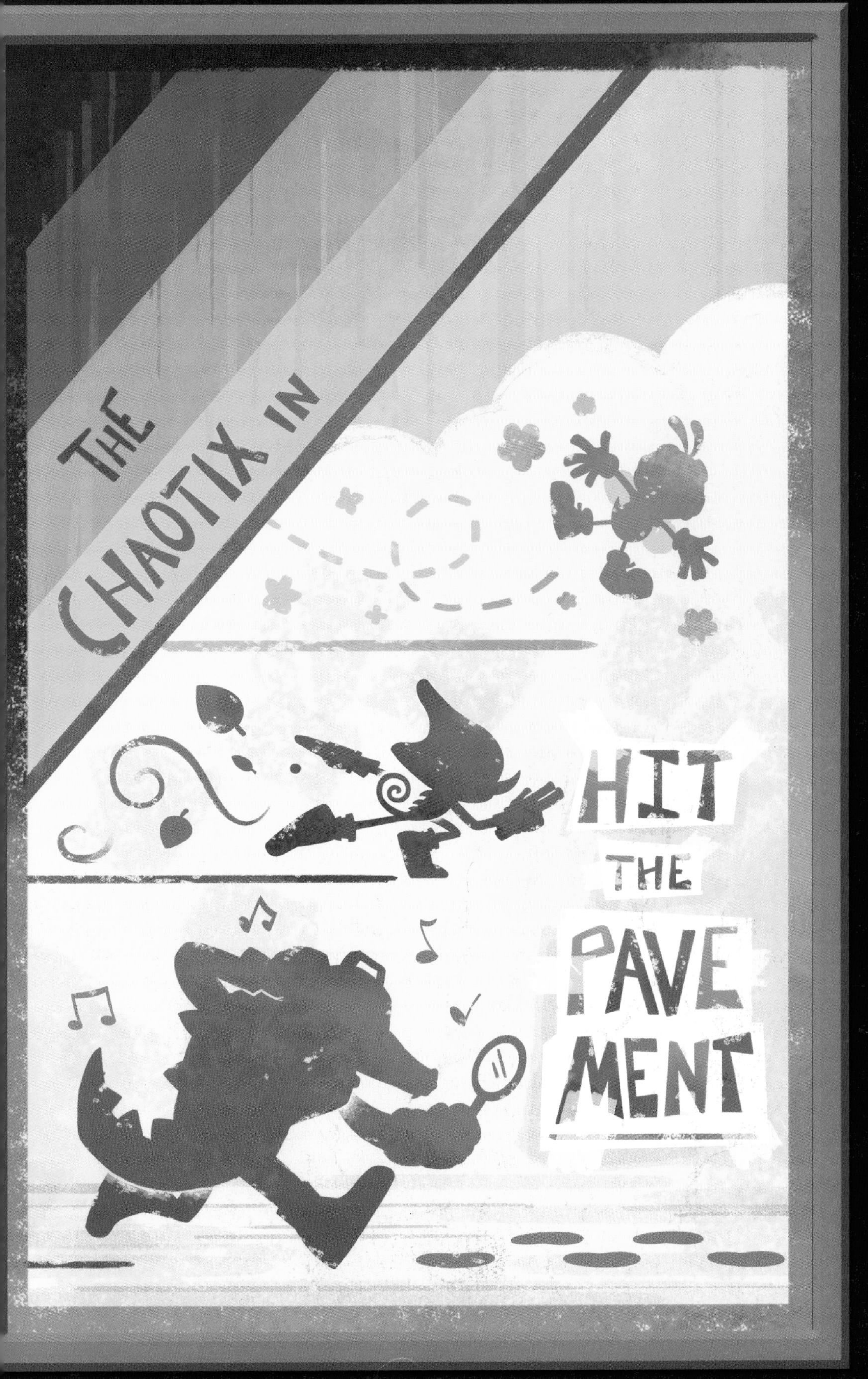
THE
CHAOTIX IN
HIT
THE
PAVE
MENT

ART BY **NATHALIE FOURDRAINE**

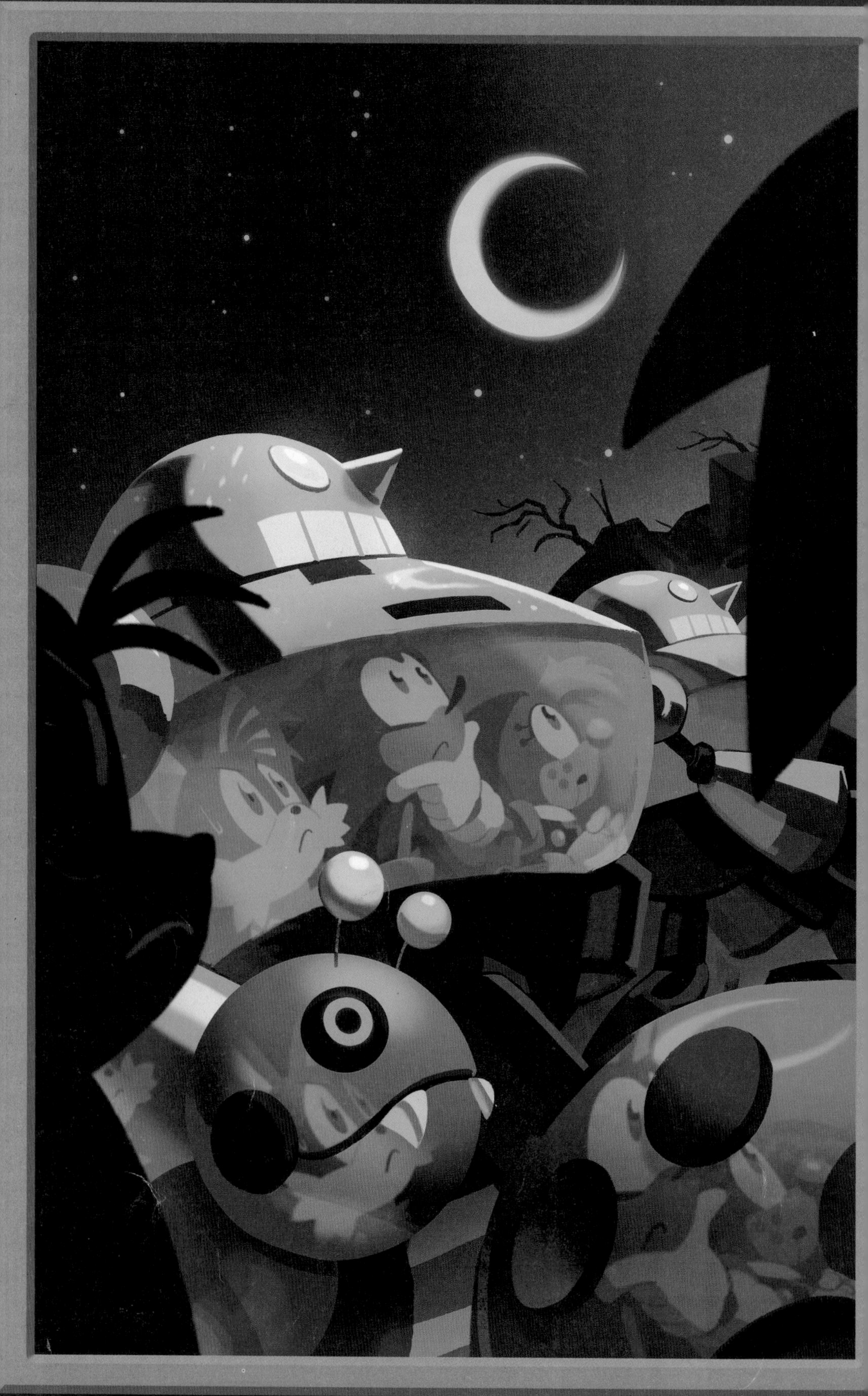

ART BY **NATHALIE FOURDRAINE**

SONIC ™
THE HEDGEHOG

TRIAL BY FIRE